ENEMY . . . SEE, HERE IS AN ENEMY COME TO KILL YOU. . . .

I felt power surging into my legs, and I swung my mighty blade.

The stabbing fangs slashed at me, whistled past my ear, hissed past my torso. I hewed a backhand blow, dancing out of danger. In the time it took, the beast changed, and now it was a Wolf, huge and black and sapphire-eyed. I thrust at it but missed. It buried its powerful muzzle in the leather of my shield and there was an explosion of spangled light. But my sword sang deep and true, a song so powerful that I could not be beaten, could not even be hurt—

Eyes, eyes all around, flickering like distant heat lightning. I fled from them, my sword silent now, and the earth yawned suddenly and swallowed me whole and I was falling, tearing my fingernails on the rocks, screaming, flailing wildly to get a grip somewhere, anywhere—

The Boy
From the Burren
The First Book of
The Painter

by
Sheila Gilluly

A ROC BOOK

ROC
Published by the Penguin Group
Penguin Books USA Inc., 375 Hudson Street,
New York, New York 10014, U.S.A.
Penguin Books Ltd, 27 Wrights Lane,
London W8 5TZ, England
Penguin Books Australia Ltd, Ringwood,
Victoria, Australia
Penguin Books Canada Ltd, 2801 John Street,
Markham, Ontario, Canada L3R 1B4
Penguin Books (N.Z.) Ltd, 182-190 Wairau Road,
Auckland 10, New Zealand

Penguin Books Ltd, Registered Offices:
Harmondsworth, Middlesex, England

First published by Roc, an imprint of New American Library, a division of Penguin Books USA Inc.

First Printing, October, 1990
10 9 8 7 6 5 4 3 2 1

 Roc is a trademark of New American Library, a division of Penguin Books USA Inc.

Printed in the United States of America

Okay, cherubs, this one's for you.
(Key questions will be required as usual.)

The Boy
From the Burren
The First Book of
The Painter

Foreword

It is a curious thing, but when I told Berren tonight, he said nothing for long moments, then all he wanted to know was why had I not told him sooner.

I had no answer that a young man, still in his first flush of kinghood, would understand. I might have said it was because I harbored resentment, and he would have believed he understood, for he knows something already of bitterness and deep hurt. Equally I might have told him it was because I didn't care, and that would have been true in part: it was so long ago that when I think of it, it is as though it happened to some other man, some poor wretch in a troubadour's tale. Nowhere else would you find such a threadbare comedy. I fancy it would be worth a copper or two to a market-day crowd. Perhaps I should get one of the Yorlandirkin to put it to the harp for me.

How would they name the song? "The Boy with the Rainbow in His Hand"? Maybe, but I did not have it: it was given to me, and at a cost that still makes me shudder. "The Fool and the Rose"? Better, but I could not bear to have the fingers of music strum that wound again. Perhaps it would be better simply to call it "The Witchman's Plaint." In fact I understand there is a song so called, but it is chanted only around the smoldering ritual fires in the skelligs of the mountain country as a curse, and of course no one here knows it. It is only among the Dinan an Lupus that I am vilified. So be it. There is no great love lost there. The priests of the Wolf chose their fate. I was only the instrument that brought it down upon them.

And yet . . .

To see the broken ranks of the purple hills rising swell on swell into the rim of the sky, to smell the gorse and heather in sweet bloom, to hear the crystal note of the lark slanting over the yellow bog iris—

Sometimes I stand here, leaning on my hoe and dreaming, and when I come to myself with a start, I sweep my eyes about this fine piece of land given to me for my own by the king, and it looks to me suddenly . . . flat. Rich, verdant, settled, and flat. And I cannot smell the sea.

I need to feel again the clean, sharp wind that comes off the ocean, broken only by weathered limestone cliffs where the gulls scream and arrow three hundred feet down into the surf. Of all the things you wouldn't think I'd miss, it would be those cliffs, but I do and that is the truth. Perhaps in my secret heart there is a youth who yearns to go back and find it was all a dream: the howling of the wolf on the wind that drove me across the wet and broken ground that wild afternoon; the awful silence of the skellig; those few heartbeats when the colored sands began to shift of their own accord, and I looked into Jorem's eyes behind his helm and realized he was terrified of me.

I have come to know that look very well. Rare is the person, in fact, who does not have it when watching me if they think I am not looking. Only Beod and the Folk and my lady were easy in my presence. Only them . . . and Bruchan, of course, who was not afraid of me and probably should have been.

Even my wife, poor girl, is afraid, though because it is the king's will, she tries not to show it. The children, too. It cannot be easy for them to have a gargoyle for a father. I hear the things their little friends say.

All but the youngest boy. His eyes are the same blue as mine, and I have seen him pause in his chores and strain toward the goldfinches with a frown between his brows, as though he heard something no one else could, a twittered word perhaps, or a distant, muted Song. He is nearly ready to ask me about it, I judge.

When he does, I shall lie and say there is nothing to hear anymore. Maybe he will be satisfied and go on about his work. I hope so, because I would not wish that my power should rest on the head of any child of mine. It is too great a curse to pass on to posterity. Let him be deaf to the Song, and human.

But in the event that things go awry and my bitter gift lives on in my sons' sons, there should be some guidance for the unfortunates. Therefore I have taken thought upon the matter, and it seems to me wise to write down as much as I can now recall of how it all came about. The Meld will have its version, no doubt, but they do not know all, contrary to their proud belief. A moment's thought will prove this: they would have everyone forget there was anything before the time you Ilyrians conquered my Burrener people, that dating begins with the Great War just past. How then to explain the multitude of stone monuments which dot every district of the highlands and crown even some of your higher hills? Plainly, those who come after us will know we were not the first to walk Earth-Above. It is only pride to think so. Pride, and the desire to forget the people we warred against, to blot out the conquered. But I tell you, if Bruchan were the only honorable man of the Burren who had ever lived, he would in himself give lie to the calumny that all Burreners are ignorant, evil savages. There was ignorance, indeed, and savagery, too, but as you will see it did not lie all on one side. The evil? Ah, yes, the evil belonged to them, and they were justly punished for it, though perhaps the followers of the gentle Three might have learned something of mercy from the Powers they profess to believe in.

This is the true story. Remember that.

I, Aengus, give thee greeting, stranger, and bid thee welcome.

PART ONE
Inishbuffin

Chapter 1

It was at the fair of Bhaile ap Boreen one year that my father sold me into slavery.

Or at any rate into indentured service, which for seven years of a boy's life amounts to the same thing. It came as no great shock; he had been in the alehouse all the day, and the click and rattle of the gaming tiles came clearly through the leather flap of the door. I knew he would ·lose. He always did. In our own village this was no great matter, because with rough kindliness the men would play against him not for money, but rather for so many hours or days of work. It was coin he could pay, and when he was sober, there was no man better to mend nets, or patch a tear in the hide covering of a boat, or cut and haul turf if the road to the cutting did not lead past a tavern. It was said once in my hearing that he'd been a fine figure of a man before my mother's death and the drink between them made off with his soul. I think there probably was not a man in the entire village to whom my father did not owe some kind of work, and be sure they got their full payment, long hours in the wind and cold and enduring the winks and the half-hidden grins next morning. I suppose it was a form of cruelty, but the truth was that a day worker got his meal out of the family's kettle at night, and there was always something put out for the drunkard's son, too. We could not have eaten for long any other way.

But here in Bhaile ap Boreen there were no neighbors, and a man fool enough to bet his life away would be let do so. I knew there was no hope of going home with even a few coppers left of the money he had gotten from selling the glass net floats we combed the beaches for. The filthydwarfs (that is how they were referred to in my village: it was years before I realized filthy dwarf was not all one word) made glass floats and used them far out at sea, but sometimes after rough weather we could find them washed ashore. Since no other folk made glass, these floats were worth money. I always loved the colors of them, the way the sun shone through them when it shone at all, and would have preferred to keep them to admire on the particularly cold days, but that was a foolish thought, and of course I never opened my mouth to voice it to my father. He had small patience when the thirst was on him.

So I had done the prudent thing and lifted a few purses—just enough to give us bread for the month. There were rich takings to be had, and if I had been in the mood, I could have stolen a tidy amount. But a town's officer was already watching me, so I was wise and quit. I waited for my father, and in between my waiting, I explored the fair, perfectly innocently. Bhaile ap Boreen was the largest town in our district of the Burren, and accordingly had the largest fair. It was held at the end of summer, in the long days when the clear golden air holds just a hint of cooler times coming, and the sellers of animals want to be rid of them so they won't have to feed them through the long stretch of ice and cold that is winter in the highlands. This was the third day of the fair, by tradition the day when all the serious deals have been struck and folk are ready to partake of the amusements which will be the last ease many will have until the roads clear in the spring. It is the day when families with young people look over marriage prospects, when old folks nod civil greetings to their peers and talk of fairs nigh a lifetime ago, when children make mischief in any way they can so long as it is out of sight of their parents. As I walked the narrow maze of streets, I was surrounded by jugglers and acrobats, fortune-tellers and fellow pickpockets, slaves wrestling to the whistles and cheers of the crowd, and craftsmen of every description. Somebody tied a cowbell to a goat, and the creature went careering off into the crowd, knocking over stalls as it went. I have seen other fairs bigger, but never one so lively as that day's at Bhaile ap Boreen. Or perhaps it is that I remember that one so much more clearly than the rest because of what happened late in the afternoon, when the smoke of the cooking fires threaded through the town, and people began gathering at the telling tent for the story competition.

I had at length grown tired of the crowd and made my way back to the alehouse near the center of the town. The aroma of spice buns wrenched my empty stomach into a knot, and I hovered around the bake stall, wanting to eat but not wanting to buy, until the woman showed me the back of her hand. I hissed a curse that made her blanch, stalked back to my post by the stack of peat at the tavern door, and settled myself to wait. As luck would have it, therefore, I was in a prime location to watch the storytelling. In fact, I had to fight off a couple of other boys for the spot, but they gave it up readily enough when my knife came out, so I stood atop the stack, leaning against the tavern wall, and could see over the heads of the crowd. The day had been fine weather, but even so, those in charge of the competition had erected a large tent over the swept sand floor that had been laid down just for the event. In these mountains sun can become fog in moments and rain soon after that. And rain would ruin the storytelling.

Along one side of the square sand floor sat the storytellers, each with his painter behind and a little to his right. When they had all composed themselves, the town's headman went round with the pot containing the pebbles, and each storyteller drew until the white pebble came up. This one would begin.

The lot fell to a thin, pale man. He stood up, gestured to his painter, and nodded to the headman. There was an excited buzz amongst the crowd, and then we quieted to hear. The headman sat down, and the storyteller bowed to the people while his painter knelt and unstrapped his satchel to arrange his color pots. When the crowd was thoroughly hushed, the story began. I found I could not hear well: the man had a guttural voice that did not carry far. I got enough of what he was saying to know the story was the old one about the seven sons of Tarry Ketchum, but the stories never interested me much anyway. I was much more fascinated by the painters.

This painter was fair. As his teller led the audience deeper into the tragic tale, the colored sands flowed surely from the painter's hands, here a broad swath of blue lake, there a thin black line, deftly drawn, that was the knife edge in the darkness. By the time the teller let the last word sigh away into the hush, the picture stood plain on the sand floor: the painter had drawn for us the moment of the betrayal, and you could see the terrible knowledge in the tilt of the old father's head. As I say, this painter was fair.

Amid applause that was only lukewarm because of the storyteller's rather flat delivery, the pair bowed to the four sides of the square and resumed their seats. The headman gave us a few moments more to study the picture and then signaled the sweepers. Under their brooms the painting dissolved, bright colors mixing in with the coarse sand, and the lots went around again. The second pair took their places, the crowd grew quiet, and the teller began.

At once, this one was different and we knew it. The fellow had a rich, full voice and he knew how to use it so that it was a pleasure to hear. The tale he had chosen was well suited to the day, the story of Grainne and her lover, and of the jealous hag who turned him to a swan, so that he can but trumpet his love once, as he is dying in the fowler's snare. It is an old story, and a good one, and that day he made us see it as though we had been there. Which was just as well, because his painter hardly did him justice, throwing down blurry lines and shapes that in no wise represented the broken wing feather, the glazing black eye, or the little jeweled dagger that found its rest in Grainne's bosom. I was so disgusted I thumped the plaster wall of the tavern and slid down to sit upon the mound of peat, all the sweetness of watching the competition dissolved. By the Flame himself, I could do better than that! I thought to myself. There should have been this, and that, and so. . . .

As often happened when I thought no one was watching, I absently crushed some of the peat between my hands, gathered the shaggy powder, and hopped down to the street. I crouched and quickly painted the curve of a feather, the proud arch of the graceful neck going limp, and the cross-hatching of the net that was his doom. The story still held me in its spell, and I was oblivious to my audience until his shadow fell over me.

"It must be difficult to paint with peat," he remarked as I looked up. Old man, good enough cloak, wide leather belt with a buckle done in some design I did not recognize, thick stick to support him, worn boots.

I felt heat in my face and rose, casting away the remaining bit of turf and drawing my foot across the picture I had made to erase the evidence of my foolishness, all the while wishing furiously he would just pass by and get himself into the tavern.

"I have never seen Grainne's lover done quite that way," he continued. "Who taught thee?"

It was on the tip of my tongue to tell the old pisspot what he could do with a willing sheep when I raised my eyes to his. He had mismatched ones, one blue, one brown, a certain sign of mystery and usually of danger. "Nobody," I managed to say.

"Ah, nobody, is it?" he mused in the same quiet voice, and looked down once more at the scrubbed-out sketch. He seemed to be weighing some heavy decision, for his brow furrowed. I took the moment to look him over again, this time more carefully. His long white hair was caught back in a tooled-leather braid, and he was neatly bearded, mostly silver with some black still showing. His tunic was woven with the Running Brook design, so I knew he was Corie Highlander, but I had never seen the peculiar pattern that formed the border, so I could not even guess at his clan. The amulets woven into the fabric included a bit of green polished stone and what looked like an osprey's feather, but that could have meant anything, either that he was born in sight of the sea, or that his clan were feather hunters. He used the old speech of an elderly country man, and his accent I couldn't place.

"Do I pass inspection?"

Those eyes again, this time with a touch of wry amusement. Emboldened, I nodded once. "Nobody's seen me paint before, is all," I explained shortly.

"No, I thought not. How old are thee, boy?"

"Don't know. The old man—my father—doesn't remember."

"Let's say fourteen, then. That seems about right. And thy name?"

"I'm Corie, born of the Spotted Sheep People, born for the Gill Fishers," I replied, giving him my mother and father's lineage. It is the way we Burreners place ourselves.

But the old man fixed me with a look. "I did

not ask thy clans. I can read them in the weave of thy tunic." He paused. "I asked thy name."

We do not tell names to a stranger. Who knows what mischief may be made of it? I stared back at him, and for a reason I could not explain, answered, "Aengus." The silence stretched between us. "What's yours, then?"

A smile flickered through the silver and black beard. "I owe thee that, I suppose. Fair enough: I am Bruchan, and not too many people know it. Thee'll do well to keep it to thyself, if thee please. I go by the name Cru." This is a word that means dog or hound, and is often given as a nickname to someone unfortunate enough to be unlovely of face. In this case, the name must have come about because of his eyes. I could not restrain a grin, and his eyes crinkled with humor that did not quite reach his mouth. "Now, young painter, I take it thy father is inside this establishment? Good. Come in with me and point him out."

I brushed some peat from my sleeve. "Why?"

Cru shifted his stick to the other hand and reached for the door flap. "I have business with him."

Another debt owed, I thought. This old man didn't look the type to be gambling away the day in an alehouse with the likes of my father, but you can never tell. Silently I stepped past him into the malt-smelling darkness and stood for a moment just inside the door, letting my eyes adjust. This house was large by the standards of my home village, but in other respects it was all the same. Smoke from the fire and the pipes, small window holes that let in a frugal light even on this summer day, rushes on the floor, thatch above, noise of gaming tiles, of shouts for drink or pie, discussions six or seven men at a time, through it all the sharper tone of arguments here and there. I scanned the crowd. "Over there, by the hearth." I pointed.

The old man nodded beside me. "Fellow in the dark green hood?"

"That's himself." I turned to go back outside.

The stick lifted slightly in front of me, barring the way, and I looked up quickly, my hand already dropping to my dagger, but Cru never looked at me. "Wait, boy. Thee'll come with me. There is a thing I want thee to know. And don't pull that dagger, or I'll have to lay thy skull open, and that would be no pleasure to either of us, I think." The stick went back to the floor. "Come," he repeated, and led the way past some men who were rolling dice on the nearest bench.

Now, usually when you threaten someone with a stick, you do not in the next instant turn your back on him. If I was conscious of anything beyond surprise, it must have been curiosity. I have always been as curious as a cat, and that day it led me to follow the odd stranger across the crowded alehouse. There was threat in this old one, and he had said he'd business with my father, who might be naught but a drunkard, but my father still. Keeping my hand at my hilt, I drew up behind Cru when he stopped by the long table near the unlit hearth where my father and some men were involved in a furious game. The tiles slapped against the table, and the players and bystanders continually shouted new bets or challenges. My father, very red in the face, had a small pile of coppers in front of him, but had taken a chance on finding three more Hawks in the dwindling pile and the odds were not good. There was a pot of drink to one side of him, and as we stood there he picked it up and emptied half of it at one pull.

Cru tapped his shoulder. "Master Gill Fisher."

Father glanced up and back at us. His eyes, wide in the dim light, had the look they always had when he was like that. Finding nothing of interest, including me, he went back to the game, slamming down a Butterfly and scooping up a Thistle. "Four!" he shouted into the cacophony. A man standing in the crowd whistled low, and another shook his head.

The old man beside me pulled abruptly at the folds of his tunic, stuck a thumb in his belt, gave me a glance, and leaned on the stick. Then he went quiet, apparently studying the game. A peculiar smile came and went across his face, and he waited.

Not long. Six plays later, the man across the table from Father slammed down his final tile. "Eight!" he bellowed in triumph, and slapped both hands on the table. "Pay up, pay up, whoresons!" he exulted. "I caught you fairly that time!"

There were rude comments upon his parentage, his children, and his sexual member, but coins began to change hands, all funneling down the table to him. My father sat still. The winner good-naturedly scooped up the small pile in front of him and added it to his take. "Now then, where's the rest of it? Dig deep, friend! Your wife'll have the skin off you for this!" He guffawed.

My father stared at the pile of coppers and said faintly, "Two Hawks. Just two more, and I'd have had it." He had gone pale now, and passed a hand over the stubble on his chin.

"Aye, well, that's how they fall sometimes, isn't it?" the winner replied brightly, beginning to arrange his coins into stacks. He did the right thing and signaled the potboy over to serve drinks all round. That would take some of the sting out of it for the other men. Then he looked at my father, a frown beginning to draw down his wiry red brows. "I make it a silver and four that you still need to put down here, friend." Other men paused in raising their horns or pots of drink to listen.

My father's head went down. "I'll have to owe it to you in work." You could barely hear him. My face wanted to twist with shame for him, and I buried my eyes on the floor.

The winner stood, pushing back his bench roughly so that it scraped loudly on the stone floor. "Nay, I want no work. What do I have slaves for but to work?" A thick finger jabbed the smoky air. "It's money I want from you, whoreson, and I want it now." There was an angry murmur of approval from the watching men. No one wanted to play against a man who went into the game knowing he could not back his bets. The atmosphere was so heavy you'd have thought a thunderstorm was boiling up over the ragged peaks.

I took hold of my father's shoulder to pull him clear and had my knife half out of its sheath to cover us with when something heavy thudded to the tabletop between my father and the man who had won at tiles, and there was a clink of coin. Eyes took in the small leather purse, then lifted to the old man beside me. Cru stood at his ease. "That should cover it, I think."

The winner pulled the drawstring to open the sack and tipped it out on the table. There were gasps of surprise. Amid the puddle of copper and bronze, a quarter sovereign of gold gleamed.

The man who had won cast a quick glance over his shoulder at the friends who backed him, then cleared his throat and said gruffly, "It's only the silver and four that he owes me."

"Yes, I heard," Cru replied, and reached to separate out the equivalent in bronze and pennies. Then he pushed the gold a little toward the man, and when the other's eyes came up, he added quietly, "The rest is to pay for the pleasure thee'll not have of beating the dung out of him."

The fellow wiped the back of his hand across his mouth, sniffed, and the tension suddenly went out of him. Throwing a glance around at his mates, he said wryly, "Truth, if it's to pay for that, you be welcome to buy my good temper at the same rate every night, sir." There were shouts of laughter.

Cru smiled and put an arm down to lift my father to his feet. The potboy was handing around the drinks when we made it to the door. My one hand shook on my dagger while I tried vainly to keep Father from walking into the lintel. As the stranger lifted the door flap, the winner at tiles called across the alehouse, "Old one, if he's a friend of yours, try to keep him in his house of nights. He's got no head for drink."

Cru looked over my father's bent head. "He

is no friend of mine," he said quietly, and led us into the street.

The air smelled sweet after the close and heavy atmosphere inside, and I was surprised to find the sun still golden and the afternoon not much progressed since the story competition. Somehow it seemed as though enough had happened that it should have been night and the stars bright in the sky. I guided my father to sit on the stack of turf and spat the copper taste of fear from my mouth, then stuck out a hand to Cru. "I'm beholden to you. They'd ha' carved him, sure."

He ignored my outstretched hand. "I told thee, I have business with him." He tapped my father's knee with his stick. "Thee. Pay attention, now. Can hear me?"

Father tilted his head up sideways, gingerly looking up at the tall man. "Aye. Who the hell are you?"

"That is unimportant. By tomorrow thee won't remember anyway. What is important is what I just did in there."

My father drew himself as straight as he could and nodded with overcareful dignity. " 'Preciate it, friend. I'll owe you. Name the work and the place, I'll be there, you'll see. Swear it." He nodded for emphasis and nearly pitched on his face in the street. I steadied him.

Cru shook his head slowly. "No. Thee owes me no work, Gill Fisher. I was not buying thy debt and thy freedom from that mob in there; I am not such a fool as to pay for a drunkard's folly. Hear me now: that was a business transaction between thee and me, a fair trade."

I was getting the drift, but, befuddled, my father squinted. "Hah?"

"I just bought thy son's service."

Father leaped to his feet, weaving. "Damn all, you did!"

Cru gestured back at the alehouse door with his stick. "Fine. I'll go back in and reclaim my gold then, and thee can explain to them all about the mistake."

My father passed one unsteady hand through his rough mane of hair and sat down hard. He peered up and said quietly and nearly soberly, "I never offered the boy for service, old one." A quick look to me. "But if I did, I'd want more for him than a quarter of gold."

"Thee wouldn't get more, Gill Fisher. An untried boy, young, no growth on him yet to speak of, good for nothing but fetching and carrying. A gold quarter is ample. Take it, or take the beating that awaits thee if I go back inside."

Father hesitated. When he finally sighed and nodded, I did not know whether to feel fear or relief, but I resolved that if things got too bad, I could always strike out on my own. Surely an old man couldn't chase me far, after all, and it was a chance to see new things. Too, I had the feeling that however Bruchan Cru lived, it wouldn't be in a tumbledown hut where the snow sifted down and buried you of a winter's night. I kept my face from showing anything to either of them, but my heart began to race.

Solemnly both men spat on their palms and then shook hands in the customary way to seal the deal. "Excellent," Cru murmured. "Come here, boy." I stepped past my father, and the old man drew from his belt pouch a small enameled brooch, which he pinned to my tunic. "There. Do not remove it." He raised his voice to penetrate my father's fog. "How is the boy called?" Over my father's head, the old man winked at me.

Father scowled. "Call him Corie dun Gill. It'll do," he told my new master sourly. Highlander son of Gill. So he would keep my real name safe for me, at least. I felt a pang at that.

Before it could turn into full-fledged hurt, Cru nodded, touched his breast in the sign of farewell, and bowed slightly. "Good fortune to thee, Master Gill Fisher. If thee would take a warning from a stranger, stay out of yon doorway. I could not answer for thy safety twice." Then he put a hand between my shoulder blades and steered me away with him. "Come, Corie. My lodging is down the street."

As we turned the corner, I looked back. My father sat hunched with his head in his hands, and I carried away with me the memory of what I like to think were teardrops spattering the cobbles of the street under his feet. But more likely it was rheum, and more likely still he was back inside that tavern by the time Cru drew me to a halt a few paces down the side lane.

Practical concerns took over my attention and I turned to face the old man squarely. "Look, let's set one thing straight right away: if you're thinking to bugger me, forget it. You'd not wake from your sleep in the morning." I meant it, too.

The white braid swung as Cru's head snapped to me. He looked shocked, then snorted what sounded to be a rueful laugh, which he quenched till it was a snarl in his throat. "I give thee my word I've no such intention, but in all other respects I will use thee

as I may, Aengus. That is what it means to be
a servant, which seems to be thy lot for the
present. Be content with the protection such
status affords. Give me no trouble, and I'll give
thee none, and thee may find being in my service much to thy liking." From under narrowed brows he scanned a group of noisy
revelers reeling toward us, passed them over,
and cast a glance up at the windows of the
houses which backed onto this lane.

"Why did you really buy me? If it's hauling
and carrying you want, a donkey would have
done you better."

"Ah, but a donkey is a singularly stubborn
creature with little imagination except to bray.
Not unlike some people, I suppose, but I suspect thee's not one of them." While I tried to
piece this out, he casually turned to regard the
street behind us. "Very good," he said to himself as much as to me. "We'll go on." He
nudged me to a walk again. "Stay well in toward the building."

"Why? What trouble are you expecting?" My
neck was prickling.

"I am expecting none. I am prepared for it,
that is all."

"All right. You've bought my dagger, so I
suppose I ought to know who to aim it at." It
didn't sound absurd to me then. One of the nice
things about being only fourteen is that you
don't realize how young that is. Again that peculiar stifled laugh behind me, and he did not
answer. "You've changed your voice, too," I
said to let him know I was no fool. "You don't
speak to me now as you did to my father, or
even to the men in the alehouse."

"Thee has a good ear, boy." We trudged on.

The revelers passed us by. The lane ahead was deserted, shadowed by the buildings to either side. The handle of the stick hooked my shoulder gently, indicating that I should stop. I looked back at him with a question forming on my lips.

Shrill and clear through the sound of tin pots clanging in the houses around us and the cheerful singing of someone stabling his horse nearby came a single-note whistle from up the alley. Cru raised his head and froze, listening. Almost immediately an answering note came from behind us. He pivoted to look quickly, but there was nothing to be seen. "Damn!" He thrust the stick through his belt, scanning the narrow lane. There were no doors standing open, and only one window, a second-story casement above my head. I had known immediately, of course; a couple of footpads had cornered us, probably following us from the tavern where the old man had foolishly thrown down that gold. Such thieves would stick at nothing, and old Cru would be an easy mark for them. It was a wonder we'd been allowed to get as far as we did.

I moved to draw my knife, but before I had it out of its sheath, the first of the dark figures was racing down the alley toward us, deadly silent, his face muffled except for the eyes, dagger a long killing sheen in the semidark. Cru bent, grasped the back of my tunic, and fairly hurled my slightly built frame upward with much more strength than I was expecting. "Go!" he yelled.

I belly-flopped across the wide sill, eeled myself over, and desperately sucked for air even as I rolled to my feet and scrambled back to

the window, intending, I think, to go back to
his side. When I got my head out the window,
there was a slithering clash of weapons below,
and I saw to my amazement that he now held
a sword. He parried a blow, disengaged, and
drove in under the thief's clumsy recovery. The
dark swathed figure fell at his foot. He whirled
to meet the racing footsteps that sounded
clearly coming up the alley. "Stay up there,
Aengus," he ordered quite calmly.

That was all right with me.

A second figure, similarly dressed to the first,
skidded to a halt when he saw what had become of his mate, but then his sword came up
and he charged. Cru was driven back against
the wall by the momentum, but the killer's
sword clanged uselessly off the stones below
my vantage point. My master took two quick
steps away and knocked the fellow's sword
sideways when it snaked toward his ribs. The
thief recovered quickly and both of them went
to guard, circling warily, looking for an opening.

By now there was noise in the house, and I
could hear a questioning voice call something
from the room below. Suddenly the thief attacked, a backhanded blow aimed at Cru's
head. The old man caught it on his blade, mus-
cled the fellow a step off balance, and thrust
him away, trying to give himself room enough
to get his own point an advantage. The thief
crashed into the wall below me, shaking his
head. Cru came in for the kill, drawing back
his arm.

He slipped on the cobbles.

At once the attacker sprang toward him,

sword already less than a foot from my master's throat.

I grabbed the only thing there was, a terracotta pot of marigolds, and with all my strength hurled it down on the swathed head. There was a solid thunk as of a melon dropping on a floor, a crash of crockery, and then silence, broken by a footstep on the stair outside the door to this chamber.

"Jump!" Bruchan commanded, and I did not wait to be told twice. His shoulder broke my fall, he pulled me to my feet, and we ran for the main street. I looked back once and saw him sheathing the sword back in his walking stick, and then his hand seized my shoulder and pulled me into the shelter of the wall while he himself took a quick look up and down the street. "Now, let's walk—slowly, boy, slowly, as if we've just come from the storytelling and are going for our supper. Don't look back. If I tell thee to run, do it."

"Aye, sir."

He seemed to know the town well, for we followed a wandering course through street and lane and once through a blacksmith's shop where the forge fire glowed dully under the embers, banked for the night. At length we reached an inn. I recollected passing it the night before with my father. It stood just inside the town wall and was a huge establishment, house on two sides of the courtyard, stabling on the other two, and travelers in the yard itself who paid for the privilege of sleeping there, surrounded by four stout walls. Cru seemed to be known here, for a potboy made him a half bow as we came through the door. "Pie and ale for two, and a kettle of hot water," the old man ordered quietly. The boy nodded, stared briefly at me, and then we passed up the stairs.

At a chamber on the second floor, Cru listened, then thrust the door open and stepped quickly inside, the stick lifted in his hand.

"Are you thinking to be attacked again?" I asked when he nodded me inside.

He reached over my head to swing the door closed without answering. "Sit with thy back against that until the boy gets here with our supper." He walked slowly to the bed and threw the stick down upon it, then continued to the small window. Standing well to the side of it, he took a look down into the courtyard. Apparently nothing he saw worried him, for he crossed the ample chamber and did the same at the window facing directly out upon the town wall. Beyond his head I could just glimpse the fair flag pulling at its pole, signaling folk in the countryside roundabout that the fair of Baille ap Boreen was still on with all its amusements and wares.

I studied the white hair caught back in the tooled braid, noticing only then that the design in the leather was the same as the one at his belt, flowing lines interlocked in a pattern of four spirals. I glanced down at the pin he had twisted into my cloak back at the alehouse, and the spirals stared up at me. When I looked up again, he was regarding me with a look of deep concentration. He saw me aware of it, and his face smoothed. "Thee's pretty handy with a pot of marigolds."

I said what I had been thinking: "It wasn't the smartest thing to have paid for me with gold. They'll all be after you now."

His eyes flicked again to the window. "Likely, but I couldn't take the chance of going back to that alehouse tomorrow and finding thee gone."

"Why not?"

Cru swung his gaze back to me. "Because, young painter . . ." He walked across the floor and stood looking down at me. "Thee's my fortune."

It came together then—the different voices, the arrested look on his face when he had seen my peat sketch, even the gold. Relief washed through me and I sprang to my feet, heedless of the door or any other danger. "You're a storyteller!" I breathed, and he laughed and made a bow grand as a lord's.

Chapter 2

Between the aftermath of the attack in the alley—it was, no matter how tough I tried to seem to Cru, the first death by violence that I had seen—and excitement over my new future, I could not sleep that night. I lay across the door on the straw pallet the old man had ordered up for me and watched the stars' slow movement across the window, and the more I thought the more uneasy I became. By the time the sky was lightening to dawn and the birds rustling in the thatched roof outside whistled and cawed any but the deadest sleeper awake, I had questions aplenty, but I judged it better to hold my tongue. If I got the wrong answer to any of them, I did not care to be on the inside of a locked door.

Cru began a snore that ended in a snort and woke suddenly. I saw him look out the window to gauge the time, then he sighed, put his forearm over his eyes, and lay like that for a moment before heaving himself upright, absently rubbing his knees and glancing over to me. Too late I feigned sleep, closing my eyes to slits and even trying to snore a little. His amused grunt told me I had not acted the part very well, so I rose up on an elbow and pretended to wipe the sleep from my eyes. "Good morning, Master Storyteller."

"Um-hmm. Get thyself downstairs and rouse Kerrig, the potboy from last night. Thee remembers him well enough? Good. I'll want breakfast here in the room and my horse saddled by the time I'm looking for it, or there'll be the deuce to pay. Thee'll fetch the breakfast up here, then see to my baggage." I got to my feet, but I must have looked confused, for he asked abruptly, "Yes, well?"

I held up a hand. "You needn't get snappish. It's just that I've never been in service before, and I don't know what you want done with your pack. I got the part about breakfast, though."

He rolled his eyes briefly to the ceiling. "Just take it out to the stable, and the groom will show thee. After breakfast. Food for me first and anything else I may require, then horse, then thine own breakfast. Got it?"

"I'm not simple," I mumbled with my hand on the latch.

"I trust not. Thee'd be no use to me if thee were. Thee's got pluck, and talent, and rather too much mouth for thine own good. Discipline is the key to art, lad: begin learning it."

"Aye, master," I told him, and escaped out the door, cursing under my breath.

I found Kerrig blearily stirring up the charcoal in his grill in the kitchen shed. "Master Cru wants breakfast quick."

He nodded irritably and yawned, saying through it, "Master Cru can shit in his shoe if he's not content to wait a bit." But he moved to the rack of loaves and lifted one down. He broke it into farls and slid one toward me on the wooden chopping block, then took up a small drinking horn from the pile of them lying next to the tipped-up washtub. He poured from an earthenware pitcher. "Ale for you, too?"

"I'd rather water, thanks."

"Get yourself a cup, then." He jerked his head at the tin mugs hanging on hooks from a shelf. The fresh water bucket stood puddling on the bench below the window. It was good water and cool, and I drank thirstily. "What's your name?" he asked. He broke off a corner of the bread and handed it to me.

"Dun Gill. He needs the horse, too," I added hurriedly. I'd almost forgotten.

"Does he now? Leaving, are you?" He buttered Cru's farl thickly.

"Don't know—guess so," I answered through a mouthful of the oat bread. "I thought he might live here."

Kerrig shook his head and wiped his hands on his apron. "Never saw him before two days ago."

"Oh. You seemed to know him well, so I thought—"

He grinned. "Paid me a farthing to look after him personally. Supper, the horse, the pot of hot water he wants every night."

"Well, he's a storyteller, you know," I told him importantly. "I guess such as he lack for nothing."

He shot me a look. "A storyteller? Is that what he told you?"

A chill spread in the pit of my stomach. "Why? Isn't he?"

Kerrig shrugged and pushed down the pewter cap on the horn of ale. "Couldn't say, but it don't seem likely, does it? Here's Bhaile ap Boreen fair with one of the richest purses in the telling competition of any town in the land, and I never heard him say he was entering it. If he's a storyteller, where's his painter, eh?"

That detail had been one of the things that kept me awake all night. No storyteller with gold to spare to buy a boy servant earned it without a painter. And why buy me at all? Why not merely offer my father an apprenticeship for me with his own painter? In such instance, my father would have had to have paid him.

Kerrig pushed the ale and the bread into my hands and advised, "Better get back with these. Your master's a right testy one in the morning." He stopped, perhaps reading the disappointment in my face. "Oh, come on now. It's all right. Wearing the servant's collar isn't so bad when you get used to it, kid." His own gleamed dully in the rising dawn light through the unglazed window. "Besides, look at it this way: he's an old man; before you've served your years of service, he'll die off anyway, and you'll have your freedom and a fine life of traveling to boast to some girl about. And who knows? Maybe he really is a teller."

"Maybe," I murmured, busy with my thoughts.

"Get upstairs, and then come out to the stables. I'll wake up Dary, and we'll get the horse ready."

"There's a pack."

"Don't I know it! Nigh broke a ball carrying it up to your room! He expect you to take care of it by yourself?"

"He told me to, yes."

"Well, drag it out as far as the stair, and I'll

meet you on the landing to give you a hand with it. The two of us should be able to get it down without waking up the whole house. My master don't like the guests disturbed early in the morning.''

I took Cru's breakfast and carried it up to the chamber. He was standing at the window facing on the town wall when I came in, eyes narrowed as he watched the sentries winching up the huge iron gate. He glanced over his shoulder at my step and came across as I set the farl and the horn down on the small bedside table. "The horse?" he asked.

"Kerrig's waking the stableboy up. They'll show me what to do."

He nodded and sipped his breakfast ale, and reached past me for the bread. I sidled away, toward the door. "Aengus."

I looked up.

"What is it?"

I figured the stairs would be too much for him so early in the morning, moving as stiffly as he was, so my chances of springing out the door and getting away from him were good. "If you're a storyteller, where's your painter?"

He set down the cup and closed his eyes a moment before squaring his shoulders and taking up the farl of bread. "He died," he said flatly. Biting off a healthy chunk, he eyed me, wiping butter from his silver mustache.

"Oh. Sorry. I was wondering, you know . . . I'll get the pack now."

"Boy." He tilted my chin to meet his eyes. "He was not a servant; he was my friend. Someday thee will know about him, but not now, not today. Today we ride out of this flea sack of a town, and both of us leave pieces of

our lives here. Ask no more questions until a
better time. Understand?"

He'd kept his fist under my chin, and against
the pressure of it I said carefully, "I have a
hard time not asking questions."

Cru nodded. "I know. And that trait is not
altogether bad under certain circumstances,
but it will not do now. Until we are home, the
less said, the better."

"Where's home?"

He dropped his hand and picked up the
sword stick from the bed, thrusting it through
his belt. "Thee won't have heard of it. It's a
place called Inishbuffin." He was right; the
name meant nothing to me. "Now, will my servant consider the possibility of getting a move
on so that we may get out of here?"

I dragged the pack to the door and tugged it
outside. Before I shut the door, I stood a moment. "Bruchan?" He turned with the ale horn
in his hand. "I'm sorry about your friend."

A look of pain passed across his face. "Thank
thee, Aengus."

I shut the door softly. So that much was explained.

Kerrig was waiting for me, and we eased the
heavy leather pack down the stairs and across
the yard among the stirring campers to the stable. There, Dary, a lanky youth with a wild
shock of sandy blond hair, stood shifting from
one foot to the other at the bit of a huge black
stallion, already saddled. The trappings were
of bronze, good quality, and the stallion looked
to be blooded. He must be one hell of a storyteller and this painter of his must have been
first-rate, I thought. You don't get a rig like
this for nothing.

"What the hell's he got in here, anyway?" Kerrig grunted as we slung the bag across the horse's flanks.

"I don't know," I answered. "He never opened it last night."

"Feels like a bloody ingot of iron."

Dary looked back at us past the stallion's neck. "Bought sum'at at the fair, belike. A pot, maybe."

Busily tying thongs and directing me to do likewise, Kerrig snorted. "You've got shit between your ears, you know that? Why would a toff like him be lugging around an iron pot? He could take his supper at an inn any night he pleased. Tie that one down to the ring there, kid."

Wounded, Dary knuckled his eyes and elbowed the horse when it tried to sidle past him. "Well, I don't know. What's your guess, then, piss-ass?"

Kerrig straightened from testing the girth. "I'll bet it's a whoring old bound-up-with-brass, padlocked-with-a-lock-as-wide-as-your-ear treasure chest, just full of gold and jools." He winked and leaned on the saddle. "What's your guess, kid?"

I fingered the worn leather pack and thought of the dead painter. "Color pots."

Dary snorted and Kerrig shook his head, smiling. "I'll take my guess over yours any day. Hie, you, get out of it!" he suddenly yelled, and aimed a kick at the dog that had bounded nearly under the stallion's hooves. The black tried to rear, but Dary pulled its head down and soothed it while it circled, trampling angrily. Kerrig jumped out of the way, and I was bumped back into one of the campers, who was shaking out his cloak after having slept in it.

"Sorry!" I told him.

"It's naught," he answered, and bent to pick up the cloak he had dropped, blue Corie pattern with brown Shepherd knots woven in.

Dary had the stallion quieted now, and Kerrig tapped my arm. "Your old man must have been watching us from the window."

I looked back in the direction of the inn. Cru was coming across the courtyard, threading a way amongst the rousing people, leaning on his stick. He ran an eye over the horse and nodded. When he came up to us, he patted the proud neck, and the black snorted and flicked an ear to him. "None the worse for a rest, eh, Shadow?" The stallion tossed his head, champing at the bit, and the old man smiled. Kerrig gave him a leg up, and Dary handed up the reins. I fell in at his left stirrup, as I had seen other servants do, and we left the yard at a walk.

He reined in for a moment just beyond the gate, leaning as if to check the stallion's near forefoot, which brought his head close to mine. "Keep a watch behind us: there may be more of those thieves from last night about. They wouldn't attack us in a crowded inn, of course, but they could have watched for us to leave." That made me feel comfortable, I can tell you. He straightened and nudged the stallion with his heel.

We turned left around the corner of the stables, and the gates of Bhaile ap Boreen were right before us, about thirty paces off. The fair flag snapped in the rising morning breeze, and beyond the opening the countryside lay bathed

in the apricot light of early dawn with the sea
a narrow edge of blue in the distance. The sentries had left after the night watch, as the land
was at peace and the fair guaranteed free passage to all, so we rode under the wall with no
one to challenge us. I own I breathed easier
when we had the rough stone barrier behind
us and the dirt road between its hedgerows
ahead.

Shadow tossed his head, wanting to stretch
his legs, but Cru held him to a walk down the
slight incline that led away from the town. At
length the mile marker fell behind us, and the
road took a bend around a copse and dipped
into a hollow. The old man halted under the
first branches and reached down a hand to me.
"Come up."

With his help, I scrambled into the saddle
before him. "Can thee ride?" he asked.

"Don't know. Never tried."

"Fairly answered. Just sit still, then. Hold on
to the front of the saddle, but don't touch the
reins or the horse's head. I'll steady thee, if
necessary. Loosen up with this leg." He tapped
my right knee where I was squeezing Shadow's
withers. The old man shook the reins a little.
"Now then, Shadow." The black stallion
started off at a brisk trot.

Clutching hard at the saddle bow, I gasped a
curse. "Is it supposed to hurt this much?"

He laughed. "Thee'll be taught by a master
when we get home. By snowfall, he'll have
made a rider out of thee."

"He'll have a job of it!" I yelled over the tattoo of hoofbeats. Cru laughed again and leaned
to say something else. Something whizzed past
my nose with a noise like a hiss in the dark.

An arrow, a small cold voice said in the back of my mind, we're being shot at. But I had no time to listen to it, because the old man's hand forced me down on the horse's neck, I felt his leg slap, and the stallion broke to a gallop. I strained to look ahead and managed to get one blurred impression of flying tree branches, gravel spattering, and a blue-cloaked figure that leaped suddenly into the road ahead, the bow at his shoulder.

Cru dropped the reins on Shadow's neck, shouted a word of command, and we wheeled to put his own back to the arrow. The next I knew I was being plucked from the saddle bows and thrown to the ground behind a huge oak. "Run!" my master bellowed in a voice surprising for such an old man. Somehow I got my feet under me and sprinted like a fox for the deeper woods, all notion of taking one of the bowmen on with my dagger knocked out of my head with the wind that had been knocked out of my lungs. I heard the sword sing out of its wooden scabbard in his walking stick, and then I was burrowing through thicket, looking by instinct for a place to hide. I dove under the overarching trunk of a fallen tree and froze there because there was sudden light on the other side. I'd be in a small clearing if I went farther. Like a wounded animal, I pressed to the earth and tried to hold back the gulping breaths that might give away my hiding place. Warmth trickled down my chin, and I discovered that my lower lip was split. I watched the blood drip into the leaf mulch, but dared not reach to wipe it away lest I rustle the brush above me. My ribs suddenly woke to a fiery pain that stabbed with every breath, and my head momentarily swam, but I forced myself to keep my head up. If death was out there for me, I wanted to see it coming.

Not too far off—not nearly far enough for my liking—I could hear the clang of metal on metal. So at least one of the bowmen had also carried a sword, or perhaps poor Cru had met with a third attacker. I wanted to help him, but could not make my limbs move. Blood filled my mouth, and I spat silently, listening for a twig to crack, looking for a blue-cloaked figure's legs to cross that clearing beyond the dead branches.

It seemed long to me, but I am sure now that it was no more than a few moments. A great crashing filled the woods, coming from behind me. I knew it was the horse, but it might not be Cru who rode it. I lay silently, my breath stopped. He was right behind me, and I could not turn to look without rustling.

I heard a chirrup to the horse, and Shadow jumped the fallen trunk to land lightly in the clearing, standing quietly while the rider swung down. I forced myself to look, inching my hand down toward the dagger trapped beneath me, dizzy with the pain as my ribs creaked when I shifted.

In the gap between the branches there were two worn boots. My head seemed much too heavy suddenly, and I let my forehead rest in the leaf mold.

"Aengus?" he called in a low voice. "Boy?"

"Here," I answered in a voice even I could barely hear.

I must have moved the brush, for the next moment he had gone to both knees at the entrance to my little cave and was reaching to grasp the shoulders of my tunic and haul me out. I believe I may have yelled, but then a thick, dark mist swirled between us, and I could only see his worried face at the end of a long tunnel. His lips moved, but he must have been a long way off, because it took a moment more for the sound to reach me. "Where ... hurt?"

I could not answer, but lifted a hand to the place. He felt to be sure, then set my head down carefully, and I heard him thudding quickly to the horse. He returned in a moment with something which he held to my lips. "Sip." It burned my cut mouth, and I felt my face draw up in a grimace, but the mist cleared somewhat. My head was supported on his knee, and he was searching my head with the hand that did not hold the flask.

"Did you ... get them?" I asked on the least breath I could take.

"Yes, the vermin. Here, can thee manage another sip?"

This time I kept the brandy carefully away from the cut and felt the warmth all the way down to my stomach. I pushed the flask away and squinted up at him. "Why are all these people ... trying to kill you?"

He ignored the question, corking the leather bottle. "Are thee hurt anywhere else, does thee think?"

I tried to sit up, but that was a very bad mistake. When I could see again, I realized he was winding something around me, pulling it tight at each turn. "I can't ... breathe!" I protested, panic at the stifling sensation making the blood beat in my temples.

He put a hand gently on my chest, holding

me still. "It will brace the ribs. I think they are badly bruised and perhaps cracked. Lie easy—I'll be done in a moment. Think on keeping thy breath as shallow as possible, but even."

I tried to obey, and little by little it grew easier, but the pain was still as fierce as though I had a gnawing badger hugged to my side. When he was done, he fed me another sip from the flask. "There's some unpleasantness coming, I'm afraid," he warned.

Fear shot through me. "Why? Are there more bowmen?"

He smiled slightly and shook his head. "No, I think not. But we have to get thee onto Shadow, and then there is a bit of a ride. We could stop at a farm," he added in a lower voice, as though thinking aloud, "but I think that would not be wise. We'll be safer aboard ship." He looked down at me. "Does thee feel up to moving?"

With his arm bracing me, I made it to my knees and then to my feet. Cru looked from the horse to the downed tree and gave a peculiar whistle. Shadow pricked his ears. I saw the old man's hand flicker in some sort of signal, and the horse gathered himself and leaped easily back to the other side of the tree, where he stood waiting patiently for us.

Cru jumped upon the trunk, gave a spring, and vaulted into the saddle as neatly as a swallow coming home to roost. "Thy turn."

I set my teeth, crawled up on the tree trunk, and stood. Cru reached down and lifted me into place, and in spite of myself I bit my lip again and moaned. He patted my shoulder. "I know," he murmured. "It's as bad as the Trial of Colin the Mariner."

"What?"

"Ah, thee does not know that one? I am surprised, for it has much of thy own courage in it, and like thee, there's a young man on a long journey to a new life."

I spat some blood. "Tell me."

He shook the reins, and Shadow moved into a smooth walk. I know the tale began well, all about a young nobleman on an adventure far from home. He is gathering seabird eggs one day when he slips and falls from the high cliffs into the water. He's carried out by the tide and found floating by a boatful of fishermen, who take him aboard, dry him out, and feed him the fruit of a wond'rous plant, the calan-calan.

Shadow stumbled on a root, and Cru pulled his head up. The jolt made the woods swing around me. "Calan-calan?" I asked faintly.

"Indeed," the old storyteller assured me. "Sweet as almond cake, smooth as custard, cool as well water in the autumn. The juice of the calan-calan grants peace to the lucky traveler who is fortunate enough to taste of it."

"Sounds nice . . ." The green leaves passed slowly overhead.

Sometime later the leaves again, and his arms holding me secure against him, my head lolling on his shoulder. "Now brave Colin knew not what to do, for she was a king's daughter and he but a newcomer in that place, but she looked upon him, and in her fair green eyes was that which made him think perhaps she did not find him displeasing to her sight. So he gathered his courage and . . ."

Now stars and his white hair glowing faintly in the moonlight. His voice, still the low, mellow sound in the twilight of my sleep. "And at the last, Colin the Mariner, seeing how grave was their plight, bethought him of the ring and resolved that they should have it."

I licked my lips. "What ring?"

His voice changed. "Thee's awake. How very timely of thee, my boy. If thee looks ahead there, thee will observe that we are expected."

I lifted my head and focused where his finger pointed. While I had slept, we had made it all the way to the sea. Ahead of us a stone pier jutted, and at the end of it a boat rocked at her moorings, gangway down and a lantern shining from the deck. I looked around. We were riding down the narrow path that passed for a road in a small fishing village, silent at this hour. "Where are we?"

"Voss a Miel," he answered. It is a name that means simply "on the sea," and told me nothing.

When we rode out onto the pier, someone called out in a low voice from the boat, "Master?"

"Of course," he answered in the same low tone. "Who else?"

Figures appeared, dark against the lamplight, hooded men who reached for the stallion's bridle and led him across the wooden plank onto the boat. One of them reached up, and Cru set me carefully into his hands. I would have fallen when my feet hit the deck if not for the sailor's steadying hand. I winced and looked around, but could see no faces within the dark blue hoods. The man supporting me craned for a look back onto the pier. "Palomar?" he questioned.

I caught the look on Cru's face and the silence among the crew. There was no need for him to answer. Palomar must have been the painter's name.

"Let's begone, Thyr," the old man urged quietly. "See to Shadow well, brothers. He is very tired."

Two of them reached to help him down. "Not as tired as you, I think, master," said Thyr, the man who held me.

"Hush, now, hush. I am well enough." Bruchan's hand came down on my shoulder. "This is Corie dun Gill Fisher. He has had a rough time of it today and wants to sleep."

They all seemed to be looking at me, and I tried to straighten my back. Thyr made a half bow. "And so he shall." He signaled one of the others, and I was led into the small cabin and helped into a bunk that had not one, but two blankets, both clean, and a pillow. I do not remember even hearing the man leave.

Sometime later there was a gentle rocking and a dim light swinging above me. Thyr's voice: "And this is the boy?"

A long silence, then Cru answered, "This is the one."

Chapter 3

Next morning I woke to a fresh salt breeze blowing on my face from the open porthole above my bunk. I lay for a moment collecting myself, then moved gingerly to see if I could. The pain was definitely still there, but I found that while I had slept somebody had replaced the scarf with which Cru had bound my ribs back at the clearing with strips of what I guessed to be linen, though I had never seen the material before, only heard about it in song and story. It was blessedly soft and very white against my tanned body. The old man and his friends went up another notch in my opinion: this was quite good treatment for a servant boy.

I inched to the side of the bunk and through some grotesque contortions to try to save my ribs managed to sit up. My own clothes were nowhere to be seen, but on a peg in the framing of the bunk hung a tunic which should just fit and under it the short length of a light summer cloak of blue. I left them hanging for a moment, a heavy fist seeming to knot in my chest. You Ilyrians cannot understand what it means for a Burrener to be without his amulets. It is a loss of oneself as great as if you had woken from an illness and could not remember your own name. My hands whitened on my knees: if the old man thought he could get away with this, he was much mistaken. The Wolf help him if he'd ordered my stuff destroyed! I flicked the new tunic on its peg and then began to piece it together: all the sailors, from what I'd been able to see the night before, had worn identical clothes to these. Obviously it was a uniform of sorts, and Thyr had called Cru "master." I let out a soft whistle of surprise. Some storyteller, to have a whole retinue of servants, a horse like Shadow, and a boat like this! My life, you'd think he was a king! Pretty good luck I had, to fall in with such a lot! But he'd give my amulets back, or I'd raise stinking hell.

I got into the tunic with some effort, for I could not raise my arms, and held my paining ribs with one hand while I reached for the cloak with the other. My hand froze. Now that the cloak hung by itself, I could see the pattern of it: blue Corie with the brown knots of Shepherd.

I hooked it off the peg and examined it closely to be sure, but I had made no mistake. Frowning, I clasped the pin Cru had given me, which had been left in the material when they had taken my old clothes.

I pulled open the door to the cabin and found myself in a narrow passage, which I followed up on deck. The wind here was brisk, and I hugged the cloak around me while I held to the frame of the hatch and looked around for the old man. The day was gray, but there was no fog and no rain, and the sail billowed from its mast. It was not a large boat, being about the size of one of the fishing boats worked by several men in a family, but there the resemblance to anything I had known ended. For one thing, this boat was clean. The deck was scrubbed, the lines neatly coiled, and there was even paint on the rails and cabin walls.

"So you are awake!" a voice said beside me. I shut my mouth and turned. A young sailor, blue-eyed and just getting his first beard, smiled at me. "The master left orders that you were to be given what you desired for breakfast. I am to fetch it for you. My name is Heggin."

Awkwardly I stuck out a hand. "I'm Dun Gill Fisher."

He laughed oddly. "Oh, I know! We are all very glad to have you with us."

"Are you?" I said cautiously. Did he know yet I was the old man's servant? "About breakfast—I'm supposed to serve the master, then see to Shadow, then I can have my own."

Another sailor passed us and nodded in a friendly way. He and Heggin exchanged some word I did not catch. My young host smiled again. "That will no doubt be part of your normal duty, but Master said this once you might be excused from it. He himself has broken his fast already, and the stallion is in good hands. So what shall I bring you?"

"A little bread and a cup of water would do."

He cocked an eyebrow. "Is the seasickness bothering you?"

"No. I just—I mean, that's what I usually . . ."

His face cleared. "Ah. Your practice is to fast. I understand now. Forgive me, I did not mean to tempt you."

"No, it's all right! I mean, no harm. I suppose I could break my, uh, fast this once, seeing Cru has given me a holiday of sorts."

"Cru? 'The Hound'?"

"The old man, you know, the master."

His face darkened, and out of nowhere his fist shot out to catch me a solid shot in the mouth. I was surprised, but I'd been in enough fights to know how to take care of it, though my mouth was bleeding again and at every move I thought my rib bones would shoot right through my skin. I caught his nose going up with the heel of my hand, and he fell away, hands rising to shield himself. I went after him.

"Hold! Hold, I say, for shame!" Two brawny arms encircled me and lifted me off my feet. I kicked back angrily. If the whole bloody lot of them wanted to pile on, I'd give them a taste of my best, by Beldis! My captor grunted and let me fall to the deck. I crouched, sweat breaking on me from pain and anger, and prepared to spring.

"Aengus, stop." It was a quiet command, and I turned my head. Cru stood there, walking stick planted not far from my hands splayed on the deck.

"Call off your men, then," I panted.

"Heggin, explain," the old man ordered.

My assailant got to his feet, blood trickling from one nostril. "I am sorry you were disturbed, master."

"I know. Explain."

The boy clasped his hands behind him. "He called you something, master. In your name, I answered the insult."

I began an angry retort, but the old man stayed me with a gesture while he told Heggin mildly, "I am quite capable of answering insults for myself, little brother, and it is not meet to have fighting aboard this ship, as thee knows well. Now, what was this terrible thing he said?"

The blue eyes flicked to mine. "He called you . . . Cru the Hound, master."

"Ah. Well, for thy information, Heggin, that is the name by which I am known in the world, and so I told the boy to call me that." He leveled a look on the youth. "Besides, names are no matter. Thee knows that."

Heggin flushed. "Aye, master." He turned to face me and bowed. "Your pardon, Aengus. I have erred through my ignorance."

I was dumbfounded. "That's all right," I mumbled. "Anybody with a left hook like you've got doesn't have to apologize for much of anything."

Cru leaned on his stick. "Thee may go now, Heggin. Have Padraig take a look at thy nose." The boy bowed himself away, and the old man glanced at the man who had caught me up, a burly sailor with bushy black eyebrows. "Thee's well enough, Symon?"

The fellow scowled at me. "I'll live, master."

"He was taken by surprise, Symon, and acquitted himself well." Cru's tongue was in his cheek. The man grunted a rueful laugh, touched his hand to his breast, and left us to go forward. The old man looked down at me. The damp wind tugged at his cloak. "Aengus, Aengus, what am I to do with thee? Thee must learn that we do not fight among ourselves except in practice."

I nursed my hurt mouth. "Is that a fact? Tell that to the bowman who was wearing your colors yesterday, then."

The stick thumped loudly on the deck, and he took a step closer, eyes narrowing. "What's this?"

I squinted up at him. "Yesterday morning in the courtyard of the inn there was a fellow shaking out a cloak that looked to be identical to the ones your people here are wearing. Then the bowman was dressed in blue from what I could see, and I'd bet his cloak had Shepherd knots in it, didn't it? You must have seen it when you fought him."

Of course he had seen it. Without moving his head, he glanced fore and aft before saying, "Do not under any circumstance tell that to anyone besides the men on this ship. I do not jest, boy. This is in deadly earnest, and it could mean thy life."

"You're a dangerous master to serve."

He smiled grimly and the cold wind suddenly seemed colder. "I am," he confirmed, "and thee does not know the half of it yet, young painter."

"That's what happened to Palomar, isn't it?"

Again, that flinching around the eyes. "Yes. Let it be a warning to thee."

I shook back the hair from my eyes. "Look, I know you've bought me and all, but I'm fair sick of riddles. I've been nearly knifed to death, shot at with arrows, had my ribs stove in and my teeth half knocked out, and I don't even know why. One minute I think the fortunes are smiling on me landing such a position, the next I wonder if I'll last till harvest time. Now, what the bloody hell is going on?"

"Aengus, it is not possible to tell thee all."

"Well, tell me *something!* And that's another thing. I'm not too damned happy about everybody knowing my real name, Bruchan. You may know these people, but I surely don't, and I'm not sure I want to very much."

He looked up at the sail and sighed. "Thee tries my patience as I have let few other boys do." Wisely I held my tongue, for I could well believe that this man suffered very little disagreement from his servants. He closed his eyes and tapped the stick on the deck, thinking, and when he looked down again at me, he cocked his head. "Very well. I will tell thee some of what thee wishes to know if thee will in thy turn answer some of my questions."

"If they're questions about me, there won't be much to tell. Naught to interest someone like you, anyway."

He gave an odd smile. "Everyone has something in his life that would make a story, thee knows."

"As you like. Can I have some breakfast? Heggin was asking me about it when—" I broke off, not wanting to remind him of the punishment that was probably going to be due me.

His eyes had a way of sparkling sometimes, and I got an inkling it might have something to do with why he tolerated a cheeky servant. "I assumed thy mouth would be much too sore to eat anything. There is water, of course."

No breakfast for the unruly.

I spat over the rail. "Water will be fine, master."

He laughed openly, and out of the corner of my eye I saw two sailors stitching on a sail stare. He beckoned me to follow.

They had made a place for him aft on the small raised steering deck with a chair lashed to the rail. Thyr was manning the steering oar, and he nodded as I preceded Cru up the short ladder. "Warmth of the Fire, Aengus," he bade me.

That was a new one to me. " 'Morning," I answered, and turned to help the old man up, but he needed none, so I crowded back against the planking to give him room. He sat down, leaning the sword stick by his side and nudging a tall, brass-and-enamel contraption with his foot to hook it closer to him.

"Hand me the flint and iron, there, would thee?" He pointed to a niche built into the side of the boat, for a cup for the steersman, likely, but now it held the familiar shapes of an iron dog and a chip of flint. I handed them over and watched in fascination while he struck a spark into the shallow brass bowl at the top of the elongated urn shape. The brown powder in it began to smoke, a thin amber stream that flattened in the salt wind. Cru unclipped a tube from the side of the thing, put it in his mouth, and drew.

"It's a pipe!" I blurted.

Two jets of smoke trailed from his nostrils, giving him all at once the look of a t'ing who has decided you will make a nice pasty for his teatime. I mentioned the resemblance, and he rasped a laugh and said, "Draw it." There was a bit of chalk and a slate hanging handy to reach by Thyr—for figuring course, I guessed— and I took the soft lump and crouched on the scrubbed deck, reaching in my mind for the image. Swiftly it flowed from my hand: the long, serpentine neck with its hackles of horn, the malevolent but witty eye, the curl of smoke from the flaring nostrils, the delicate teacup awkwardly hooked in one sharp claw.

My old man puffed his odd pipe and smiled broadly. Thyr was leaning on his oar looking a little incredulous; I doubt he had believed till then that I could do much beyond provoke fights before breakfast. I caught the satisfied glance Cru gave him, and Thyr's slight nod of acceptance. The master blew a smoke ring that broke up and got lost in the snapping sail. "How did thee know what a t'ing looks like, Aengus?"

I dusted chalk from my hands and eased myself to sit cross-legged. "Well, I don't, of course, but the way I imagine them from stories"—I gestured at my sketch—"this comes close."

The two men exchanged another glance. "Then thee's never actually seen one?"

I snorted. "Where would I ever? People go adventuring to see t'ings way down south somewhere."

"East," Cru murmured. Through the pipe smoke he regarded me. "Perhaps at a fair once, in a menage, thee saw a very young one?"

I shook my head. "No," I said truthfully. I shrugged. "I just imagined it."

The two men exchanged another glance, and Thyr suddenly turned back to the business of steering. Cru nodded slowly. "Is that how thee 'sees' most of what thee draws? In thy mind?"

"Most times. I hear a story, usually, and it starts me off thinking, and before I know it I've drawn it in the dirt with a stone, or on the hearth with a bit of burnt stick." I fiddled with the chalk. "My father hates—hated—it when I did that, said it was just notions and we couldn't afford notions."

The smoke had a rich tang to it, reminding

me of something I had smelled at a fair once, something from a spice vendor's stall. The old man puffed another cloud of it. "Strange," he remarked quietly. "I would have thought he would have valued such talent."

I drew the edge of a hand lifted in anger against the peat glow. "He didn't value much beyond his jug," I replied in the same tone. Then I straightened. "Besides, even if he had, what could he have done with it? He'd have had to pay money to have me 'prenticed to a storyteller, and we had none."

"I understand." He shifted in the chair, drawing his cloak further around him. "So thee's had no training at all? Not even for a day or two with some storyteller and his painter who wandered through and had a bit of time to spare for a lad who hung about, hungry to get into the color pots?"

I stared. "How did you know?" He smiled, but waved off my question and signed me to continue. "There was an old fellow once," I told him, then recollected myself. "Much older than you, master. Anyway, he came through our village once, he and his painter, the both of them half-blind and near frozen with sleet. It was the pit of winter, no weather for traveling if you have a hearth to hug. But neither of them did, of course, making their living on the road like that. Well, it was coming on for night as they were passing our place, and the painter put his foot wrong between two rocks and went down on it. It wasn't broken, but it wasn't whole, either, so they begged hospitality at our fire, such as it was.

"My father was out for the night, I will not need to tell you. In fact, that time he was out for near four nights. So the storyteller and his painter shared what I had and waited for the storm to stop and the swelling to go down, and paid for it with tales." I nodded at the memory. "The painter—his name was Dun Loghaire—did show me a bit about how to use the colors, but I didn't want to waste much of his sand, so mostly we sketched with the charred sticks. 'Twas he showed me how to make it look like near things are near and the farther things behind them."

Again, Cru's soft voice, which had a way of not interrupting my thoughts at all. "And the pictures thee draws now—are they like this Dun Loghaire's?"

"Oh, no. He ... well ..."

"Wasn't as good as thee are."

I felt the heat in my cheeks. "I don't say that."

"Thee need not." He surveyed me. "I suppose thy father beat thee when he got home for wasting food on them."

I grinned. "I didn't care."

He smiled back, a slow lighting of those eyes of his. "No, I don't expect thee did." Something in the back of his eyes changed ever so slightly, a flicker like the eyelid of a hawk. "Did anyone in thy village know of thy talent?"

The breeze was strengthening; I hugged my elbows to me under the cloak. "Sometimes I used to draw for the other kids—to pass the time when we were watching the flocks or mending nets, you know."

"But of the adults?"

I tried to make him understand. "Look, it wasn't a useful thing. It couldn't catch more fish, or help plow a field, or get the peat in.

Lots of people are good at things, but no one makes a huge noise about them. There's a man two farms over who can whistle like any bird you can name, and they say in her day Gran Macgwyer could dance fit for a king's hall." I spread my hands. "That's just the way it is. When there's time to enjoy such things, we do, but there isn't much time."

His pipe had gone out. He held the mouth-piece still as though he did not realize it. "Who was thy mother, Aengus?"

"Her name was Breide, and she was of the Spotted Sheep clan."

It might have been my imagination, but I thought Thyr stiffened. Cru mused, "Spotted Sheep people. So she was not from thy village, then."

"Oh, no. She was from Ard-na-mere."

Even over the wind, I heard the steersman's indrawn breath, though he faced carefully away from me. My eyes were drawn to him momentarily, and when I looked back up at the old man sitting is his chair, I caught him wiping the corner of the cloak across his face. He looked pale.

"What's the matter? What did I say?" I asked.

Cru drew a breath and took a moment to smooth his beard and touch the brooch with its four-spiral design like mine. "Nothing wrong, certainly. However, henceforth when thee's asked that question, thee will say that she was Breide ni Slian, from Terns Bay. Does understand?"

"No," I replied flatly. "Why should I lie about it?" In spite of me, my voice thickened. "Her name is all I've got to remember of her. Why should I disown it?"

I was angry and hurt, and I flinched when Cru leaned to grasp my shoulder. "Gently, boy. I do not say forget it in thy inmost heart; never that. But do not reveal it to others. It is a thing some people should not know."

I ducked from under his arm and slammed the chalk down on the deck. "It's about time to get to some of my questions, don't you think? You said I would get some answers if I gave some. I've met my part of the bargain; now you meet yours."

Thyr turned to stare, but Cru flicked a hand signal to him, and the man clenched his fists on the oar and held his tongue. Bruchan looked down at me. "Very well. As to questions, thee has three only. I have not the entire morning to spend in conversation with thee, however beneficial that might prove to us both. Ask away. If I deem it meet, I will answer." He pulled the collar of his cloak up, resetting the round brooch.

That gave me my first question. I flicked the pin with its identical design that he had ordered me to wear. "What is this?"

He stroked an eyebrow. "It is the symbol of an idea to which I and all of these men"—he waved a hand to include the entire ship's complement—"have pledged our lives."

My brain had done some slow revolutions over the night. "You are Brothers of the Wolf, aren't you?" No master addresses his servants as "little brother."

He hesitated, then wordlessly nodded.

That explained much—the fine horse, the ship at his disposal, the skill at weapons, the steady sense of authority. The Brothers of the Wolf—or Dinan an Lupus as they are known in the tongue of the Burren—form a powerful class outside the control of the nobles, though some of their members are indeed drawn from younger sons of ancient families. They are everywhere revered as the servants of the Flame himself, the mouthpieces through which the Power's will becomes known. And it is not all posture and strut: I myself had already heard that our province was saved a heavier tithe because the Brothers told the royal overseer how poor we were and paid part of the tax themselves; and also, I personally knew a family from the neighboring village—my father had worked for them once—who had a little girl blinded by being kicked in the head by a horse. They took her to the Brothers and she was healed, how I do not know, but I saw her afterward, and she could see. We folk of the Burren had much to thank the Dinan for.

But they were objects of fear, too, let it be said. They kept to themselves in the communities, or skelligs, on hilltops that were protected behind thick walls of stone, and into which I had heard no outsider was ever allowed, except for rituals, and then pity the poor wretch, because he was never seen again. The whisper was that the Wolf drank his blood, and the Brothers drank the blood of the Wolf.

Add to this their legendary prowess in weapons, both the open, clean sword and bow, and the lesser, more hidden knife, wire, and poison, and the way they had of ferreting out the least hint of disloyalty to the Flame, and you will understand why another of their names was Cruin an Lupus, the Hounds of the Wolf or Wolfhounds, from which my master had apparently adopted his traveling name. They could tear a man apart as easily as one of those great beasts and swallow his holdings like a dog that's been too long without feeding.

And now here I was aboard one of their ships, an outsider. I tried not to let the old man see my hard swallow and glanced down at the pin once more. "This is not the Lord of Fire." The Brothers had their own device, a background gules, the color of blood, and against it a wolf's head sable, eyes flaming. Everybody in the Burren knew that sign.

Bruchan's brooch pin moved slightly with his breath, and the four spirals seemed to swirl suddenly, like a whirlpool of water. "No," he agreed quietly. "It is not."

When he said no more, I took my courage in both hands and looked him in the eye. "Am I to become a member of your order, then?"

"Only freemen may do so; it is prohibited for servants, who may not do their own will, but must follow their master's wishes." As if he had read the sudden fear that shot through me about being a victim, he added, "A community such as ours has much work, and we cannot do all of it ourselves. From time to time, therefore, we bring in helpers."

Slaves, he meant, to sow and reap and thresh and grow thin working someone else's land. Disappointment welled up in me so thick I could have choked on it. I uttered the hard reality in a murmur: "I'm not to be a painter, then."

"Certainly thee's to be a painter. It is what thee were born for," he said quickly. "I do not lie, boy. Thee will not spend thy life cooking

pottage or laboring in the fields." He rearranged a fold of his cloak over his arm. "We
have many ways of serving the Flame, Aengus.
It is as meet to tell a tale well or paint it well
as to acquire skill at broadsword and spear.
Not all our work is ... martial. Much of it is
thought, and learning, and pondering the ways
of men. It is in that realm that thee will be
most useful, I think." The blue eye was a
smoky lake at dawn. The brown was merely
watchful.

Security, enough to eat, a comfortable place
to live, and the chance to be a painter. This is
what he had bought for me with that quarter
gold sovereign. I leaned an elbow on my knee
and cupped my chin in my hand. "You said
yesterday I'd be taught how to ride. Will I have
to learn weapons as well?"

"Thee wants to?"

I considered. "Only if the time spent practic-
ing doesn't take me away from my lessons with
the painting master—I am going to have a
painting master, am I not?"

"The best we have," he assured me. "I think
it would be well if thee applied thyself to
weaponry as well, boy. When we go out to fairs,
and other competitions, my servant should be
able to defend himself. Much travel is done in
the wild, and not all of the halls we will visit
will be as friendly as they might be. So, yes:
weapons as well as color pots."

"I didn't know the Brothers had roving storytellers and painters." In truth, I had not known
they had storytellers or painters at all, even
within their own communities.

He gave me a sharp glance. "We do, but it is
not generally known. Much can be learned

about an overlord's treatment of his people by listening to the folk at a festival. Thee understands?"

I nodded, wondering how many of the tellers I had heard over the years had actually been Wolfhounds.

At the steering oar Thyr turned slightly to say, "Passing Hen's Head now, master."

Bruchan lifted his head to look at the hook of land sliding slowly by to port, the barren limestone cliffs rising into the shape that gave the place its name. "Another turn of the glass then, and we shall be home." He stretched and rose. "I will take tea, and then I want to speak to the crew."

"Your will," Thyr acknowledged.

The old man turned to me. "Come, Aengus." I followed him down the ladder, across the small aft deck, and we ducked into the hatch. He opened the door to the cabin where I had slept, and I noticed that the bunk had been neatly made up. He stooped to the small corner table built in to the angle between the bunk and the bulkhead. "I had these saved for thee," he said, and turned with my amulets in his hand. "There is also a needle and thread so thee can sew them into thy new tunic before we land." My mind greatly relieved, I took the small periwinkle shell; the disc of filthydwarvish glass I had found caught in the rocky beach once, a fragment of some float smoothed and polished by the sea; and the small fragment of tortoiseshell I had uncovered in a chink of the hearthstones in our house one day. It looked like a fragment of a woman's comb and I thought it was something of my mother's that fate had saved for a special gift to me. I had never told my father about it. I made no move to tell Bruchan about it now, though he regarded it for a moment as he handed it over. Knowing what I know now, I cannot believe I saw no reaction to it in him, but I was to learn much in the time to come of this man's stern self-control. At the time, I remember feeling only a flare of suspicion as he held it a moment in his gnarled hand. "That's a pretty thing," he remarked after a moment, and let it drop into my outstretched hand.

"Aye, I thought so." A man is under no obligation, even servant to master, to tell what his amulets mean to him.

He gestured at his leather pack, which was jammed under the bunk. "Lift that up to the bed." I did, and he unstrapped it, saying as he did, "Thee will, of course, make thine own set of these later. But I thought these might do for now, to learn on." He pulled from the sack a small wooden box, elaborately carved, and set with what looked to be white bone or stone. Carefully, I slid back the lid. A fine powder, blue green as the curl of a wave, filled the box. A color pot. He was giving me Palomar's set.

My eyes stung and I did not dare look at him for fear he would think me a puling girl, but after a moment I was able to say gruffly, "A hundred hundred thanks, master."

His hand came down to pat my shoulder. "I have business with the crew. Thee's at leave to work on thy amulets. I know thee will want to have the sewing done in time to introduce thyself to the rest of the community." He swung to the door.

"Bruchan?"

He paused, eyebrow lifted.

I gripped the box fiercely. "I'll try hard not to shame you."

A slow smile. "Don't worry, boy. I won't let thee." And then he was gone.

I swallowed at the part threat, part reassurance, and eased my tunic off over my head, deciding where on it I should attach my amulets to say, Here am I, Aengus the Painter.

I let myself out of the cabin a little time later. I have always been handy with needle and thread, and it had not taken me long to get my tunic in order. I was feeling much better, my amulets in place, my self intact. I had my hand on the hatch, prepared to swing it open, when I picked up the murmur of voices. Ah, yes. He had said he wanted to see the crew assembled before we landed. Briefly I debated returning to the cabin, since I was not sure whether or not a servant should count himself part of the crew, but I reasoned that the old man would not have said it in front of me if he hadn't wanted me to know. Some instinct left over from listening for my father to stumble home made me pop the hatch just a crack, though, to eavesdrop a little first before I judged it wise to go on deck.

"—questioning your authority, master, but how do we know this is the one?" It was the voice of Symon, the man I had kicked.

Bruchan's quiet answer: "The sign has been given to me, brothers. I assure thee, this is the one."

The wind snapping the sail. Thyr: "And it will come about now, master? We are to see it?" There was a note to his voice that was hard to place, excitement perhaps, or fear.

The old man again: "I can tell thee only what

was written long ago, Thyr." His voice deepened and grew stronger, the storyteller who had told me the tale of Colin the Mariner while we rode through danger to the sea. " 'He shall come from the east with the rainbow in his hand, and in that day the Powers shall walk the earth. Then shall we see again the valley of the river, the place of our beginning, and it shall know us once more, Willowsrill the Mother of Waters, Willowsrill the Fair.' " His voice hung in the salt breeze.

Then the murmur of voices: "Be it so; yea, be it so."

A fine way to begin, was my first thought, I've landed right in the middle of a ritual. My second thought was that I had better stay where I was. This did not sound at all like servant business. If I were caught listening, I'd not care to wager that the old man wouldn't feed me to the fish, for all his talk of a fine future. I shrank back against the companionway, but my toe just would not let the hatch quite close.

Symon's voice again: "Does Jorem know the prophecy?"

"He does," Bruchan replied, and there was a murmur, not this time a ritual phrase. I thought they sounded scared, and a shiver ran over me. What would frighten men like these?

A voice I did not recognize, one of the other sailors: "Then there is trouble ahead."

Thyr: "We knew that when we sailed on this mission, Padraig. Most surely we knew it when Heggin saw one of them at Ard-na-mere. They must have guessed what we were about."

Bruchan joined in. "They know," he said flatly. "Jorem has not set spies on us for a year and half to have it avail him nothing in the end. They know we are close. How close, they cannot guess. I have taken every precaution I know to prevent it, and with vigilance our secret may go unremarked for some time yet, until he is ready."

Heggin asked, "Does he know?"

In the hatchway, heart thumping, I answered silently, He's beginning to.

There was a little silence before Bruchan replied, "I think he does not. I believe he accepts the story I have given him, that I bought him for a servant."

"But he knows he's a painter?" Symon prodded.

"Oh, yes," the old man said positively. "He knows that. But it is no great matter, and in any case could not be hidden, either from the boy himself or from Jorem's spies in our community, curse their eyes. We shall train him like any other, and when the time comes, he will be ready and so will we. Until then, hold him close, brothers, guard him with thy very lives if need be. We must not fail."

"Your will," they chorused.

"I know I may rely upon thee," he told them, "my ever-faithful ones. Now to business as usual. We must make our landing at the pier with false faces, downcast that we have again returned home empty, with naught but some indentured boys and a little tin to show for our journey to the fair of Bhaile ap Boreen, and one less of our number. When any others ask how Palomar died, we will say that he was set upon by ruffians, thieves who preyed upon the people coming to the fair. Be clear on that point: none of us saw his murderers."

"It goes hard, master," Symon's voice, with a smoldering in it that I could hear even in the hatchway. "He a martyr, and none of us can say so."

"Aye, my friend. I hear," Bruchan's voice, softer now, answered. "But Palomar himself would have been the first to understand why there can be no honoring ceremony other than a simple funeral for one who has gone to the Hag." So we referred to Ritnym, whom we called Vanu, the Crone or the Hag, who comes to collect the shades of the dead for her under-earth realm.

"Truly, master. I think only of myself," Symon said lowly.

"No. Thee's right to want to accord him the honor that is due him. I rage that we cannot," Bruchan said tightly. "I swear it to thee and to him: there will come an accounting."

I wondered at the enemy who would deliberately provoke this man.

They were shuffling on the deck now, and surely someone would come down and find me. I let the hatch swing closed, having heard already more than I cared to, and moved quickly into the cabin. The sea tossed outside the port-hole, and my thoughts tossed with it. Absently I fingered the linen strapping around my ribs. There was a hard lump under the bandage far down on my left-hand side.

My head jerked up as my fingers explored it. "What the hell?" I breathed aloud. This wasn't padding; it was nowhere near the aching place in my right side. I undid the brooch of my cloak and slung it on the bunk, and was gingerly working my way out of my tunic once more when I heard a step in the companionway and the door swung open.

Heggin stuck his head in. "Master will want you on deck presently. We are coming into the landing." He left the door open behind him when he headed back up.

I straightened the tunic and slung the cloak around me. While I was pinning the brooch, I examined the design closely. It was clear to me that Bruchan had split off from some other faction of the Brotherhood, hence his own insignia on his loyal followers. But what power did he serve? The Wolf, certainly. But what else? And how did I fit into his prophecies?

My mind boiling with mysteries, I went on deck. Sailors were busy uncoiling lines, reefing the sail, manning the oars to row us gently toward the stout jetty of rock where a similar ship was already tied up. Thyr was at the big steering oar, shouting commands, and Symon stood in the bow with a boat hook to pull us into the landing. I threaded through the activity and found Bruchan. "Well, I'm done—just in time, too." I think I did it convincingly.

The old man flicked his eyes to me. "Stand with the other boys, and do not approach me again until I beckon thee. Say as little as possible until we are safely alone."

I went to where a gentle-faced man was herding the dozen or so boys of my age out of the hold. They looked half-frightened to death. I tried to adopt their attitude. The brother in charge gave me a sharp look, but said nothing, and I took a place behind a tall boy with haunted eyes. The brother, I guessed he might be Padraig, left us for a moment to swing shut the hold doors. I heard Shadow nicker as he scented home. The tall boy pulled at his ear and looked down. "I wanted to get away from my old man, sure enough, but I own I never bargained for this. I figured to be bought by some rich farmer and work somewheres closer to home. That way I could kind of keep an eye on Mum and the little fellers, you know?"

I nodded and there were red blotches around his eyes suddenly. He turned abruptly away.

Whatever I might have said to him was forestalled by the gentle-faced man. "Well, boys, we're home." He stepped around in front of us and put his hands through his belt. "As ye can see, it's not the kind of place ye can run from and hope to get far before ye're found."

As one, we looked up to the encircling wall on the heights above the jetty. A sheer fall of cliff, that massive wall, a round tower jutting into the cloudy sky. I imagined the other side facing landward would be just as bleak. Anyone leaving the gates would be as exposed as a snail is to a sea gull. The boat touched the quay, the lines were slung to waiting hands, and we had landed at Skellig Inishbuffin. Someone choked down a sob.

Chapter 4

I happened to be looking at Bruchan as the wide gangway went down, and I saw his face change, the expression hardening. I glanced where he was looking. At the farthest end of the jetty on the small ledge that served as a landing stood a man in a calf-length robe and cloak, both of black. At this small distance I could clearly see the supple boots of best-quality leather and the wide belt, richly tooled. His brooch showed the Wolf's Head, and his black hair was as neatly cropped as a pasture where the sheep have been at work. A chain which looked to be of solid gold lay about his shoulders, and he absently straightened it while he watched our ship. I saw, I am not sure how, that his eyes and Bruchan's were locked. Beside me I heard Master Padraig curse under his breath.

The old man stepped across the railing and walked purposefully down the gangway and onto the jetty. He paused, half turned to the steering deck, and called clearly, "Thank thee, Thyr. An excellent voyage, as usual."

"Thank you, master," the captain acknowledged.

Bruchan walked on the few steps. "My lord Jorem," he said. "What an unexpected pleasure." He touched his chest. The other offered his hand, and the old man bent to kiss it. A ring, I thought.

"Welcome home, Master Bruchan. I am glad to see you safely come to port." This Jorem had the kind of voice that puts you on your guard without knowing why. If a fox could talk, he'd sound like Jorem.

Under his breath, Padraig muttered, " 'Welcome home,' he says. Think it was his bloody skellig to do the welcoming, poxy son of a . . ." His voice trailed off into an unintelligible rumble. It sounded comical, coming from a Dina, but I could see his point. Bruchan was the master of this community and Jorem his guest, not the other way around.

My master drove the point home. "Had I known thee were coming, I should certainly have been here to greet thee myself, but I trust that in my absence Brother Cathir, here, has seen to Thy Grace's comfort?" He nodded to the short, pudgy man with the worried face standing at Jorem's elbow. This Cathir would be the second in command, or the brother in charge of hospitality, I couldn't tell which yet.

The black-robed figure smiled. He shouldn't have done that; up to that moment, I had been willing to grant that maybe I had taken an instant dislike to him because of what I'd overheard and Padraig's reaction, but when I saw his pointed teeth, my dislike set in stone. Some men have pointed dog teeth and it means nothing. On Jorem, it fit. I suppressed a shudder and hoped I never had the misfortune to run into him on the night of a ritual.

Jorem was answering, "Indeed. Your Eminence's men set a fine table, though I confess

to a certain bias where the wine is concerned:
I am used to the variety we have in Dun
Aghadoe."

Bruchan smiled back, and he did it well.
"Well, of course, here in the boundary provinces, we haven't the quality of goods thee has
at court, Thy Grace, but we make do. In fact,
we like to think that our plain fare is most suit-
able for men who are the guardians of the
poor." Bruchan gave him no chance to make
an answer, turning back to the ship. "All right,
brothers, there is rain coming, so let us get the
goods unloaded and safely brought up before
it breaks over our heads, eh? Cathir, I'll leave
it in thy charge."

I could almost hear the pudgy man's inward
sigh of relief. "Aye, master. Welcome home."
He touched his hand to his breast and bustled
down the jetty toward us.

Jorem refused to be so easily taken in tow.
He stood still where he was, surveying us. I
felt his eye touch me and had to steel myself
not to look down suddenly. "A sorry-looking
lot, Bruchan. I am surprised you bothered."

My master replied loudly enough for the
boys around me to hear him, "Oh, I think they
will work out well enough, given a few feed-
ings and work that befits them. Judge them not
too hastily, my lord: any man may fear what
he does not know."

The tall boy wiped his nose and tried to
straighten his shoulders. Padraig began whistling under his breath.

Jorem flicked a bit of dust or something off
his cloak. "Your ship rides low, Eminence, so
I assume you were able to procure the tin that
Cathir tells me you were seeking."

"Aye. It was a fair enough trading voyage as these things go." Jorem swung his head to look at Bruchan, and the old man met it for a moment. "And how was thy voyage, Thy Grace? The waters betwixt here and Dun Aghadoe can be rough this time of year, I know." To me it sounded like an incantation to me for "His Grace's" trip home.

The canines showed again. "Uneventful, one may say." They weren't talking about the actual voyage, I could guess, but about this little fishing expedition of Lord Jorem's. "Enough so, in fact, that I find myself hoping the trip home will have something remarkable to report when I reach the hall of my lord the king. Which reminds me ... I have made the trip here at His Majesty's express order to request a few of your boys for service at court."

Padraig stopped whistling. Bruchan went still. The old man said, "Surely there must be boys aplenty in the city. I am at a loss to know why thee's come so far to obtain this commodity, my lord."

Jorem waved airily. "Oh, yes, we have plenty of boys, as you say, but city boys are so forgetful of their station these days. Take a well-grown youth from the country, give him the proper training, put him in livery, and he is the perfect servant. And you, Eminence, have a reputation for the best-trained boys in the kingdom. So I have come to you. I ask your permission to take two of your trained boys back with me, and to bespeak two more from these, your latest acquisitions, to be sent on to court in a year or so, when they have learned what is needful."

It may have been my imagination, but I

thought Bruchan had paled slightly. He
touched his hand to his breast. "They will."
Jorem nodded, and Bruchan turned to us.
"Padraig, bring them up."

"All right, lads, look lively," the gentle-faced
man told us quietly. Double file, we marched
across the planking and down the stone pier. I
had managed to put myself about in the middle
of the pack. We drew up before the man in the
black cloak. Jorem walked a few paces to and
fro in front of us, then slowly made his way
down the line, his eyes searching, looking, I
knew, for a boy with the rainbow in his hand.
Involuntarily I clenched my hands into fists. I
avoided looking at him, but then I realized my
mistake. All the other boys were trying to catch
his eye: who wouldn't want to go to court, even
as a servant? I forced myself to try to look interested.

The lord chief inspector, or whatever the hell
rank he held, jerked a finger at three boys and
separated them out of the herd. His finger
raised to me also, and my heart got itself up
into my throat in a hurry. I moved slowly and
stood with the others. I didn't dare glance to
my master or to Padraig.

Jorem folded his arms. "You," he said to a
freckle-faced youth some two years older than
myself. "Have you any special skill that might
make you suited for a king's court?"

The boy flushed the deepest red I had ever
seen. "I 'prenticed to a carpenter, sir, my lord."

Jorem nodded and pursed his lips. "And
you?" This to my tall friend. The flaxen-haired
boy lifted his chin. "I'm strong, my lord, and
good for a long day's work. I put my shoulder

to a haywagon oncet and got her moving 'thout
the horse."

This was stretching it a bit. The Hound
smiled and moved to me. "You?"

At first I was going to play mute or deaf, but
then I realized that a mute or deaf servant
might be much in demand in some quarters. I
looked down, thinking furiously. He stepped
up, grasped my chin, and lifted my head. "It is
not good manners to cast your eyes down when
someone is speaking to you, boy. I asked you
what you can do."

There was only one way out. I held up his
purse before his startled eyes. "I can pick your
pocket slicker than snot on a doorknob."

Martial arts, yes. I had momentarily forgotten that. He knocked me flat quicker than I had
ever seen anybody move. For the third time
since I had entered Bruchan's service, my lip
was split open and my ribs were raging. I lay
there, face to the cold rock, and wished him
heartiest hell. Above me Jorem's voice slithered. "You have a recalcitrant one here,
training-master."

Padraig answered, "We'll get him straightened out, my lord." I took it for reassurance,
but still held my breath.

"You."

I thought the bastard meant me until I heard
the last boy quaver, "I kin cook some, sire. I
was in an inn."

"Ah, really? I think you are the boy for me,
then. And you."

I was still holding my breath. "Thank you,
my lord," I heard my tall friend say. The air
tasted sweet.

I heard him move away. "Those two will do nicely, Eminence."

Bruchan answered, "They are likely boys. I am sorry to lose them."

I got my knees under me and pushed myself up till I was kneeling. The two men were beginning to climb the flight of steps carved out of the cliff. Jorem laughed. "No doubt, brother. No doubt."

Padraig reached down a hand to me and pulled me to my feet. He cuffed my ear—no force behind it, just for show—then said, "Off you go, boys. See the door opening at the base, there?" Some sort of cargo door suddenly yawned. "We'll get you settled, then there'll be some work to do before supper. Mind you're careful on the steps, they're slick with the damp." He mother-henned us toward the cargo bay, his hand between my shoulder blades all the way, as warm as a patch of sunlight.

I rubbed my sore ribs, then checked to be sure whatever he had wound into the linen strips hadn't broken when I'd fallen on it.

Padraig noted my tentative touch. "How are the ribs?" he asked in an undertone.

I glanced at him. "They're still there."

He smiled.

The skellig at Inishbuffin was the biggest structure I had ever been in in my life up to that point, a confusing warren of round tower, workrooms, sleeping quarters, storerooms and kitchen, dining hall, and a hundred odd nooks and crannies, some of which I did not discover until years later. It stood braced at the top of a cliff that looked straight out to sea, in summer a beautiful place with seabirds nesting, in winter a bulwark against the savage gales. To the landward side, the skellig was surrounded by not one, but three stout walls, the last a barbican of shattered stones set on end, a barrier as effective as a row of steel teeth. Crowded against the wall was the village, where some of the masters lived with their wives and families, initially a great shock to us boys, for we had never known any Dinan who were married. Beyond the last house lay the open burren, a stark plain of cracked natural limestone paving, some of it worn by countless rainstorms and fogs into thin soil where the grass clung tenaciously. It was a world of rock, some peat, and the blessed green grass. A bleak world, you would have said, but it could be beautiful enough in unexpected ways, the pink gentian rooted in the crannies, the dark blue of harebells sometimes, the pattern of clouds scudding over the stone, the patchwork of rock walls the community had built to create arable ground with seaweed and sand.

Of course I did not know all of this that first day—all I knew then was that the mutton stew was blessedly hot, the watered wine not nearly as plain as Bruchan had let it on to be, and the room we boys were to share was large and removed from the men. It even had a hearth in it, and a large table which we could set up on trestles at mealtime and take down again to use the floor space for sleeping. We congratulated ourselves on our lucky lot, ate the stew, and worked with a will all afternoon trucking sacks of ore up from the pier into the cave at the bottom of the cliff that had been widened as a warehouse.

Later, when we were done and back in our dormitory, lounging on the benches and looking askance at the pail of water one of the brothers had brought in for us to wash, I spotted Padraig just beyond the door. He beckoned, but put one finger to his lips, and I understood I was to say nothing to any of the others. We had been shown a place outside which we were to use for the calls of nature, so I merely got up as though I were going out there.

Outside, the training-master told me, "Himself wants to see you. Come with me." I gathered Bruchan must have gotten some time free from Jorem.

For as quiet seeming as he was, Padraig could move with surprising speed, and I was reminded again not to underestimate any of these masters. Just because I was feeling a certain loyalty to them over someone like Jorem, and just because I was intrigued by the prophecy in which I seemed to have become embroiled, it would not do to forget that these Wolfhounds were dangerous men, chancy to cross, and I was, when all was said and done, merely a servant.

Padraig said nothing further, and I did not venture to speak to him, as he was listening hard for any sign that someone might meet up with us. We went through a narrow corridor, beamed and thatched, which I thought might be near or part of the stables or barns, then crossed a small courtyard and entered a plain wooden door set into a stone wall. There was a torch bracket outside it, but no light, though I could smell pitch. The light had been extinguished, then. Bruchan was taking no chances.

"In here." Padraig stood aside, making sure no one was following us, then closed and barred the door behind me. "Up the stairs. Feel your way."

I dropped my left hand to the steps of stone and kept my right on the inside wall. The stair spiraled up, winding in a narrow band. I had no training at weapons then, but I can tell you now that it wound so that a man coming down would have room to use a sword, and anyone going up could not. At the time, stumbling in the dark, I thought it was a damned nuisance. "How high is this?" I demanded irritably. My ribs were throbbing.

"Twenty more steps," came the steady voice behind me.

I counted and there was an opening to my right sharply. Padraig reached past me and knocked in a pattern. Bruchan opened it. The candle flame behind him momentarily blinded me, and he drew me in.

"All clear, master," Padraig reported.

"Very good. Pour the tea, would thee?"

My eyes were clearing. The room was small-ish, square, stone walls of course, but they had been given a lime wash and there was a magnificent tapestry hanging showing a pastoral scene of some country that could not be anywhere I knew: it was lush, trees, green grass, a river, and beyond it hills the color of blackberry. Surely not the Burren. Something from a favorite tale of Bruchan's, I guessed, as this room seemed it might be fitted out for him. His odd pipe stood on the floor.

My master resumed the chair where he had evidently been awaiting us, fluttering the thick candle on its stand. "Thee did well in that encounter with Jorem. I am sorry it cost thee another blow, however."

I shrugged it off. "Would you have let him take me?"

Padraig handed the old man a steaming bowl of tea and then to my surprise held one out to me. Bruchan considered. "It would have been extremely difficult to refuse such a request. He is very high in our order, and in addition has the king's ear." He lay his head to one side, regarding me while he sipped. "But I fancy I would have found some way of making him change his mind. It is just as well I didn't have to try. Thy bit of quick thinking has saved us both from the close interest of Master Jorem, at least for the present." He set the bowl down on the candle table. "The whole incident gave me pause, though, and made me think. Surely it will not do to have it become known that we are training a painter here; that would alert him immediately. So I think it would be wise to keep thy painting instruction a secret, and set thee openly to learning medicinal craft with our brother herbalist. That way, thee will have an excuse to be out of the skellig many days for the purpose of learning herbcraft, but in actual fact thee and thy painting master will be hard at work in a special hidden place we will prepare for thy training."

I am sure I looked doubtful. "I'll be learning weapons, medicine, *and* painting? That's a lot to put your mind to all at once, master. I'm not sure I can do it!"

Bruchan smiled slightly. "Padraig, how many specialties have thee been trained in?"

The other master cradled his bowl in both hands, glanced to the ceiling, and sniffed thoughtfully. "Well, let's see. Weaponcraft, of course. Then I had the fortune to study gold-smithing with old Master Lucan before he died. I gave Brother Felix a hand in the forge for a few years, and was assigned to look after the honeybees for a few more." He winked at me. "I believe that's all, master."

I got the message and nursed some tea past my swollen lip. "I suppose you want whatever it is that was wound into these bandages."

His blue eyes lightened with amusement. "I suppose."

I stood and undid my cloak, drew up the new tunic, and let Padraig undo the linen enough to get at the bulge. He extracted a ring, a man's heavy silver signet set with a single gem. I got a glimpse as he handed it to Bruchan. "A chalcedon!" I exclaimed. This was a rare gem even in the Burren, and you do not have it at all in Ilyria. I had seen only one other, on the hand of a mountebank who came to fair once, and of course that one was probably not real. This one was. My eyes flew to Bruchan's face. "By the Wolf, no wonder you took pains to hide it! So you were expecting Jorem, weren't you?"

The candle suddenly let loose with a little flood of wax, which pooled in the brass holder. The old man's eyes had turned to it. Now he looked back at me, and there was no amusement in that face. "Yes," he admitted flatly.

"Doesn't his lordship know about this room?"

"No."

Padraig was rebandaging me, and now he pulled the winding tight as if to rebuke me. I winced and caught my breath.

"It is another of the things thee will tell no one," Bruchan ordered.

"Your will," I replied absently, thinking.

"Aengus?" I looked up. The blue eye and the brown were fixed on me. "Thee asked me the other day what happened to Palomar. Let it be enough to say that he died trying to bring me that ring."

I nodded. "Was it Jorem's men who killed him, master?"

This was too near the mark. He looked away. "We think so. They wore no uniform, but their methods are . . . known to us."

"A regular sodding bastard, isn't he?"

Padraig gave me a look that said plainly servants should mind their tongues where superiors were concerned, but I already knew his opinion of the man in the black robe. In his chair Bruchan stirred. "He is grasping and ambitious, and he has the ear of a king. I can imagine no worse combination, can thee?"

"No, but at least he shows you what he is. Does he file his teeth?"

The two men looked surprised, and then the master of Skellig Inishbuffin threw his head back and laughed. It was as well the place had no windows, else the entire community would have heard it, I am sure. Padraig let out one guffaw and hastily stuffed the hem of his cloak in his mouth and tried to get back his decorum. I personally did not see what was so funny.

Bruchan patted his beard and sighed, "Ah, bless me. I wonder?" He cleared his throat. "Well, now. It grows late, and I must be where Jorem can find me if he takes a notion, so I will bid thee good night, boy." I rose as he did.

"Welcome to our skellig. I think thee will find it a good place."

"I already have, sir," I answered frankly. "I haven't eaten like that in quite a while, and I don't think I've ever bedded down in a place I didn't have to fight the rats for the space."

He looked pleased. "May it be the first of many nights of peace for thee, then. Padraig will guide thee down." I was headed for the door when he added, "Oh, I have remembered me. Thy color pots are safely in the care of thy painting master—I had them removed from the ship for thee."

That put my mind to rest. "Good night, master. I hope I'll be allowed time from all the things I must study to have a talk with you now and again."

A twitch of the streaked beard. "I think that can be arranged."

Padraig nudged me toward the door. We made our way down the pitch-dark stairs, this time keeping to the outside of the spiral, the right-hand side, then back across the courtyard and the corridor to the boys' dormitory. Just before I went in, Padraig gave me a significant look. "I've taken you to Brother Herbalist to have your ribs looked at."

"Got it," I answered. He nodded and left. I made my way toward the hearth, where someone had lit a bit of fire to take the summer damp out. The rest of the boys were mostly exchanging stories of their homes, of things they had seen or done. A few were lying on their pallets at some remove from the hearth. These, I guessed, were having second thoughts about their station.

My tall friend glanced up as I approached

and obligingly made way for me on a bench. "Did you fall in?" he gibed.

"No, Brother Padraig cornered me and took me off to see their healer."

The freckled boy who had worked as a carpenter's assistant gestured at the fringe of bandage showing at the neck of my tunic. "What happened to them ribs of yours, anyway?"

"I got too close to the old man's stallion, and the bastard let fly." I hoped Shadow would forgive the quick lie.

The cook winced in sympathy. "Ow. Same thing happened to me once at the inn. Was that why they didn't have you with the rest of us aboard the boat?"

I nodded. "I couldn't keep anything down afterward, and I guess they didn't want a mess where you were."

The tall boy laughed. "Decent of them. Well, while you were gone, we've all got to know each other a bit. I'm Gwynt. The other red-top beside you is Kevyn." The carpenter nodded socially. "Cooky's name is Seamus." The innkeeper grinned. He went on to name the others, but I must confess that though I later came to know them as people who shared my community, I never got close to them. In truth, I find it hard thinking back through the years even to picture them to myself. But Seamus I would recognize instantly were I to see him today, and Gwynt and Kevyn have stayed in my mind as they were. Of course Seamus would scarcely recognize me, and if he did, it would hurt us both.

I gave them my name—my real one, for why should I fear boys who were under the same yoke as I? A little later, tired no doubt by the sea air, the physical work of hauling the ore, and the trepidation of being in a new place, we found each other yawning and agreed that the masters would probably rouse us early, so we let the little fire die out and rolled ourselves in the one blanket each had been allotted, plenty for the mild summer. I cannot answer for the others, but I myself fell instantly asleep.

I woke to the deep dark of middle night. Around me the other boys' sleeping breath was a shushing like that of the sea on a pebble beach, and the ashes were long gone cold on the hearth, so there was no sound from there, but I knew that something had woken me. I blinked and stilled my breathing, remaining absolutely motionless for a moment to listen. Had one of the boys cried out in his sleep and I heard it through mine? I turned my head slightly to get an ear free of the blanket. Something cool, faintly moist, and very narrow trailed across my hand where it lay on my breast and came to rest on the warmed stone floor in the angle of my neck and shoulder. There was a soft sibilent hiss near my ear.

How I bit off the yell that rose just behind my teeth I do not know, but if I had not, the snake would certainly have struck. As it was, my instinctive flinch away from it had set it to tasting the air with its forked tongue, weaving a little from side to side: I could feel the slight pressure against my neck, then away, then back. I did not dare even swallow the evil taste in the back of my throat and I shut my eyes tightly. Somehow, above all else in those first terrified moments, I did not want the thing to bite me in the eyes.

Sweat had sprung on me and my heart was hammering, and none of that was good; the sweat would make me a nice, warm host for the serpent, and the furious beating of my heart would tell it that potential danger was near. I tried very hard to get back some control. Rational thought began to return. It might be only a garden snake, after all, perfectly harmless, I told myself. But it is surpassing hard to convince yourself of that when you've something curled at your chin in the middle of the night. The darker voice, the one we barely listen to in the daylight hours, insisted, But it could be an adder. If it was a garden snake, it was a short one. Very, very cautiously, I swallowed.

I pleaded silently with someone, anyone, to come and rescue me, but I knew that even if Padraig did make rounds to check on us during the night—and why should he check on us? We were only servant boys—it was likely that the creature would take fright and strike before he would even see it, being affrighted of the lamp he would be carrying. Damn, damn, and damn again! My nose began to itch furiously, and then under the bandages, and then both legs wanted to twitch. Resolutely, I stayed still.

I could wait until first light in the morning and find out whether the snake was poisonous or not, if I could tolerate the hours ahead. Aye, my other voice said, and if it's a garden snake, I'll kill the damn thing anyway, and if it's an adder ... No good. By first light, someone might come to get us up for the day, or one of the other boys might have to stumble out to the privy area, and there you'll be with an earful of adder poison. You cannot wait till dawn. Do something *now*.

Wouldn't I like to, then, whoreson! Just tell me what!

By now the serpent had settled itself, apparently sensing no immediate danger and liking the warmth. My thoughts turned another cog, a wheel in a very slow mill. If you can make the damned thing less comfortable, it might move away on its own. Pulling the blanket away, even inching it away was not worth considering, as I had no way of knowing whether the snake might be curled on a portion of it. This seemed likely, and if I disturbed the blanket, I'd disturb the snake, and if I disturbed the snake ... How then to show the beast it was not welcome?

As sometimes happened with me, I began to think in images. A drowned worm in a puddle ... The water bucket was somewhere near me, on my right and a little above my head. Slowly, infinitely slowly, I moved my right hand fractionally toward it. The snake stirred and I stopped immediately, hand held just barely touching the blanket. I held it still there as long as I could, until the muscles in my arm were so tensed I thought they might cramp. That would be as bad as any other movement, so I held my breath and inched my hand off my chest. The serpent hissed its irritation. I froze.

After a while, I dared to move again. I had thought that once I got my hand away from my body and began to lift it in an arc through the air to reach up above my head, the motion would be smoother and would disturb the snake less, but it did not prove to be the case. My bruised ribs caught, and after every

slightest move I had to stop and give the thing
time to become accustomed to my new position. It took an age of the earth, it took a mountain of time, it took all my life till then, but at
last my questing fingers grazed rough wood,
and the handle of the bucket made a slight
clank.

I opened my eyes, which I had been keeping
shut to concentrate all my being upon my right
hand. I saw that my mind had not deceived me;
it really had taken hours; the first pale light of
day had crept into the dormitory through the
openings at the eaves under the thatch. I re-
sisted the impulse to turn my head, but I did
strain my eyes as far to the left as I could.
Nothing. The snake was coiled too low for me
to see. I swallowed, danced my fingers up the
bucket until I had the handle in my grasp, and
tipped it over. The icy water spread in a quick
gush under my head and neck.

In the crook of my chin there was a sudden
flurry of wriggling and the snake shot away to
the left. Simultaneously I sprang up and shot
away to the right, my hand clapping to my neck
in reflex though there was no sting there, and
the yell of terror I had kept bottled for hours
shrieking out of me.

I should have foreseen it, but I had been so
centered on my own survival that anything beyond it never occurred to me. The serpent
missed Gwynt, who had been snoring gently to
my left, and found a boy named Geri blocking
its path. Just as he raised his tousled head and
rolled over at my shout, it struck. His head
snapped back, and he made the grunt you do
when a blow finds home, his hands already flying to the place just below his eye.

I snatched up the bucket, leaped over the befuddled Gwynt, and smashed it down with all
my strength on the arrow-shaped head, again,
again, until the pail burst its bands and fell
apart. By that time, Geri had seen, and he began to scream. I tried to hush him—the worst
thing you can do, they say, is to hasten the evil
humors throughout your body—but any man
will cry out at death, and this man was not yet
ten years of age. The other boys were shouting,
question and hysterical answer, and one
grabbed my shoulder and heaved me backward, thinking in the confusion that I had
attacked the smaller boy with the bucket.

Running footsteps burst through the doorway, and then someone skidded to a halt beside me. "An adder!" I shouted at Padraig's
sickened face.

His quick eyes took in the smear and the broken pail, as they had already taken in the terrible swelling that had spread from under
Geri's frantic hands to his jawline, and a little
over it. The brother knelt to the stricken boy,
reaching to prise away his hands. "All the rest
of you, out," he ordered sternly.

Stupid with shock and revulsion, we stood
glued to the spot. Another brown robe was
suddenly among us and then several, as the
Dinan came running. They briskly set about
clearing the room. I looked back once as Symon pushed me ahead of him out the door and
saw Padraig gently prisoning the thrashing
boy's arms while one of the other men examined the two dark spots. I saw the brothers exchange glances. Already the breath was harsh
in the swelling throat. "Get along," Symon ordered gruffly, and swung the door to behind us.

But the latch must not have caught, because it was still open a hand span. I looked back, but his big frame blocked my view. I had my mouth open to protest angrily when, clear to me—though not to the others, who were milling about, cursing or weeping—there came from the dormitory a sound like a trodden branch breaking. My eyes flew to Symon's. He regarded me steadily. I found the wall, put my back to it, and let myself slide down. My hands began to shake, my knees felt like sponges, and I wrapped my arms around them to hold myself together.

I have no clear memory of how long I sat that way. I know that the masters went among the boys. There were quiet questions: Who had seen what had happened? When had Geri cried out? Who had killed the snake? Aengus, when Aengus hit him with the bucket, no, when Aengus hit *near* him with the bucket, Aengus, it was Aengus who killed the snake.

I remember seeing Padraig stoop to put a hand on my shoulder, but I jerked roughly away from him, knowing what he had done, and he went away, leaving Symon to look after me. I was in shock myself at the time and heaped all my furious reaction at what had happened on Padraig's head, but now, as a healer myself, I will say honestly that if I had such a patient as Geri in the same circumstances, I could have done nothing for him. Snake venom is a brutal way to die, and any means that can shorten the agony, so long as they are painless and quick, may in conscience be used. Knowing Padraig's hands, the end would have been quick indeed.

A pair of supple boots, best-quality leather,

stopping in my line of vision brought me out of my stupor. Jorem's voice said above me, "Why are these boys allowed to break the peace of the skellig in this fashion? By the Flame, such laxness of discipline should be punished!" His black robe swirled as he turned on his heel angrily, withering the group of boys with his scornful look. My legs coiled under me and I was on the way up when Symon's powerful hand clamped itself firmly to my shoulder, squeezed it enough to get his message through, and held me down. I slumped against the wall again, smoldering. I understood that I could not endanger Bruchan, but by the Wolf, I could all but feel my hands around the bastard's neck.

One of the masters whom I did not yet know said, "There has been an accident among the boys, Your Grace. A snake stung one of them."

"Ah, really? Some consternation is understandable then, I suppose." His voice was as unconcerned as if he were discussing a flood two provinces away. I raised my head. His glance brushed Gwynt and Seamus. "Not one of my two, I see." He pulled at the Wolf's Head brooch to settle it. "Well, you will get the mess cleaned up as soon as possible, eh?" he directed the master who had spoken.

Padraig's voice had an edge. "The boy will be buried with all due observance. Of course, since he was but a servant, there will be no need for your presence. Your Grace," he added as though the title were an afterthought. I hated Padraig that morning, but I cheered him then in spite of myself.

A quick stride came down the covered walkway, and the boys parted to let my master

through. He had obviously been briefed by the
Dina who had run to fetch him, for now he
asked merely, "Why aren't these lads somewhere warm? Take them to the refectory, for
pity's sake, and let us get some hot breakfast
into them." He nodded to Padraig, and the
training-master began herding my fellows before him.

"The refectory?" Jorem asked quickly with
a lift of the eyebrow. "Surely that is an unusual step, Eminence—to allow your servants
to take their meal among you?"

The blue eye was the color of a deep iced
lake, and the brown was nearly black. "Unusual, my lord? Not at all. Here at Skellig Inishbuffin we believe those who have raised our
food by the sweat of their brow do by their
goodwill share it with *us*. That makes the refectory theirs. Would thee not agree?"

There was a silence perhaps five heartbeats
in duration. When it was apparent that Bruchan would not break it, Jorem flicked his
hand. "It is your skellig, Eminence." His voice
was low, dangerous, the fox slinking away
from the coop.

Bruchan's eyes gleamed for a moment, then
he gestured to Padraig once more. The boys
began shuffling away. At Symon's signal I got
to my feet and fell in with them. Bruchan's
gaze brushed mine, but he did not react and
neither did I. One of the masters asked, "Will
Your Grace take your breakfast now?"

The man in the black robe replied, "No, I
think not. It is my custom to practice at arms
in the early morning."

The brother nodded and asked more quietly,
"And you, master?"

Bruchan glanced toward the partially ajar door of the dormitory. "No, thank thee, Niall. There is work I must do for this poor boy."

As we were rounding the corner past our quarters, he put a hand to the door, hesitated a moment, and went in.

At breakfast in the refectory, I managed to get close enough to Symon for a word without being remarked. When he turned his head and looked up inquiringly from his bench at my tap on his shoulder, I said, "I wanted to thank you for helping me this morning, Brother." The man across from him went back to spooning up his porridge. In the barest whisper under the cover of scraping spoons and hushed conversation, I said, "Get a message to the master, would you? Tell him that the adder was meant for me: I found it in my blanket during the night."

He stared, swallowed a mouthful of bread hastily, and gave me a terse nod. I moved away.

Chapter 5

"How does thee know?" he demanded.

He had met me by arrangement in the stable. Shadow tossed his head, and Bruchan absently sleeked his neck while he searched my face. I pulled a wisp of straw out of my hair and chewed it. There was still the sour taste of fear in my throat. "That was what woke me. I didn't realize it then, and there was too much else to think about through the night with that damned thing taking its beauty rest against my neck." He shuddered. "But I thought about it enough this afternoon while we were raking the hay, and I realized that I must have heard the latch of the door dropping."

My master was nodding. "Doubtless," he murmured. He folded his arms and studied the floor. "I'd give a deal to know who it is that knows about thee, Aengus."

"About 'the boy with the rainbow in his hand'?"

To my surprise, he smiled slightly. "Ah, thee did listen, then, back there on the ship. I had hoped thee might."

I spat out the straw in irritation. "Why the bloody hell didn't you just tell me, then?"

The smile widened. "Call it a whim. I wanted to know how sharp were thy wits."

"Are they sharp enough?" I asked sarcastically.

He lifted a quelling eyebrow. "Probably." The old man leaned against the stall. "We knew there would be danger for thee, and we needed to know in what measure thee could be trusted to look after thyself." He held up a hand as I began a hot reminder about the previous night's terrible vigil. "I know. We owe thee an apology there. We had thought thee'd be safe enough in a roomful of other boys, and Brother Timon was on watch at the other end of the portico."

"Didn't he see anything?" I demanded.

Bruchan shook his head. "He fell asleep. No, curse him not—that is not like him. In all the time I have known Tim, I have never known him to fail at a duty. On a hunch, I asked Brother Herbalist to check the remains of the bread and cheese which were carried to Tim for his supper." Our eyes met. "It was drugged."

"Who served it to him?"

He shook his head again. "Perfectly innocent. It was Brother Finian, and a better lad you couldn't find." He hesitated. "He is rather too trusting, though."

"Which makes him the perfect dupe. Who stopped him on his way and asked him just to take a look at his eye for a sty coming?"

His lips parted a little, and then he tugged at his ear. "I keep forgetting. As a professional cutpurse, thee would know all such ruses." The teasing tone died. "It was Brother Mallory."

My whole face grew stiff. "Which one is he? What does he look like?" I was already planning how I'd get him.

Bruchan looked down at me. "Paint him," he said.

"How the hell can I draw him if I've never—"

"Thee's never seen a t'ing, either." We stared at each other. Softly he directed, "Think back to that moment between sleep and waking last night, before thee discovered the snake. There was something just at the edge of thy mind, a sound, thee thinks. Paint the face that goes with that sound, Aengus." His eyes drew me in, the blue one wool, the brown a thick blanket. My mind went quiet and blank, and then the picture began to come.

He pushed a bit of chalk into my hand, swept a place clear of straw with his boot, and gestured. I crouched and my hand seemed to move of its own will: the questioning tilt of the eyebrows, the short nose, the broad face folding into its double chin, the mouth open to ask a question, the eyes (I hesitated), the eyes hard to get, but finally I finished them off with the worried crow's-feet. I took a breath and rose slowly.

We stood looking down at the picture I had made and I remember neither of us spoke for some time.

"Cathir!" I said sharply.

"Cathir." Bruchan sighed.

Jorem sailed for Dun Aghadoe the next morning, and the skellig of Inishbuffin visibly relaxed. Gwynt confided to me that he'd felt like a thunderstorm was brewing the whole time "his bastard lordship" was there. "I don't think anybody around here could stand him, you know, Aengus," he said, flipping the light hair out of his eyes as we went down the path to the hay field once more. His fair skin was burned and painful looking from the day before, but he seemed not to notice, having something far weightier on his mind. "Do you think I could get out of going to be his servant next year?" he asked worriedly.

I shrugged, shouldering my scythe. "I'd speak to Master Padraig about it. There might be something you can do—work a swap, or something."

"I'll bet I could get out of it if someone would agree to go in my place." He eyed me sidelong. "Wouldn't ye like to go to court?"

I whistled the scythe through a clump of thistle for answer.

"Right. I feel the same way about him," he agreed, but I doubted that: he could not possibly know the depth of my hatred for the man in the black robe. Gwynt stooped to pick up a stone and add it to the rock wall that bordered the path. It is a Burren belief that the traveler who does so gains himself a measure of good luck to add to his life's store. I have known people to walk the borders of their district, adding a rock to the field walls at every stride in the hope of healing a seriously ailing relative.

The rock pinched his finger as he wedged it into the wall. Gwynt popped it into his mouth and said around it, "I hope we start learning weapons pretty soon, don't you?"

"It can't come soon enough for me," I answered honestly. There were still two of Jorem's men to deal with, Mallory and Cathir, and those were only the ones we knew about. I paused, picked up a stone, and added it to the wall.

Bruchan must have been thinking along the same lines, for the very next morning we were surprised when we went along to the big barn to collect our scythes and hitch the horses to the hay wagon. Padraig came bustling down

the walk after us. "Wait, lads, wait up!" he
called. We halted obediently. He pursed his
lips and stuck his hands through his belt. "I
think we'll let the older men have a crack at
the hay field today. You boys can't have all the
fun." There were grins at that; most of us were
sick to death of haying. Gwynt rubbed his peel-
ing nose and his eyes slid to me. I raised my
brows. We held our breath.

The gentle-faced man really had a gift for
teasing us. His eyes went around the group. "I
wonder, have we any likely fighters here, do
you think?" There was a chorus of "ayes," and
he laughed. "Aye, is it? Well, we'll soon see
about that. Follow me."

He led us past the barn, past the chicken
house, through the tack shed and stable, past
the forge, and through a high wooden gate into
an open yard. The wall of the skellig formed
one border of this area, and the other bound-
aries were the wall of the keep, the low block
of the bathhouse and laundry, and a separate
building of stone which later proved to be the
armory. In the course of the time that I was at
the skellig, I spent many, many hours on that
practice field. It seemed large to me at the time
I first saw it, but probably if I could return
there today, it would have shrunk the way
places, and even people, do in adulthood. Still,
it was well equipped, having a post sunk for
the quintain in the middle, a row of straw archery
butts lined against the outer wall, soft sand un-
derfoot—what a place for painting! I thought—
and knotted ropes dangling from the keep wall.

Padraig gave a hail in the direction of the
armory. "Brother Weaponsmaster, your little
chickens are here!"

Brother Symon appeared at the open doorway of the shed, his huge biceps bulging below the sleeveless leather jerkin he wore, and a wide grin on his face. Behind me I heard Kevyn's wordless groan of dismay. I was inclined to agree.

Symon looked us over. "What's this lot here for?" he demanded gruffly, as if he didn't know.

Padraig played along. "Well, they tell me they'd like to learn a bit of your craft, if you please."

The weaponsmaster snorted, fisted his hands on his hips, and spat. "They do, hey? Shirking work in the hay field, are we?" I sneaked a peek around. Most of my fellows looked dismayed ranging to scared, but Gwynt's eyes were shining. "If you think you're going to get out of work by taking up weapons training, think again," he advised in a bark. He mopped his face with his forearm, let us consider it for a moment, then nodded to Padraig. The latter touched his breast with a twinkling in his eye and left us there.

Symon gestured a line in the sand. "Line up." When he had us all facing him, the blustery act he had put on for our benefit was put aside, and the real business began. "You lads are all indentured for the next seven years. For purposes of your training in this yard, that means one important thing: you will be taught to defend yourselves only. As you know, a slave or indentured man who raises hand or weapon to attack first forfeits his life. The law of the land is very clear, and there is no mercy in such cases." We were sober and so now was he. "If at the end of your term of indenture you choose to become one of us Dinan, you will of course get intense training at arms, the kind that will make you a Wolfhound." He smiled slightly at the startled looks we gave him. "Oh, yes, we know what the folk call us behind our backs. In other places, from other skelligs, they have reason to fear. There have been excesses," he stated flatly. His jaw firmed. "But never here, never at Skellig Inishbuffin. We here take our duty to protect Lord Fire's people very seriously."

I hardly heard his last words, because the dark voice in my mind was thundering. *You don't call a boy dead of an adder's sting an excess, whoreson?* I clamped down hard on the rage. Not Symon, I thought. He wouldn't be part of such filthy work; he's not the sort to kill in the dark. My breath was bound at the bandage on my ribs, and I tugged at it angrily while the weaponsmaster went on.

"Self-discipline, boys, that's the secret. Self-discipline and strength. It is one thing to be able to kill a man: it's quite another to be able to decide when to withhold the blow."

Withhold the blow long enough to think about it, I answered him silently, and you'll be dead a good percentage of the time.

Perhaps he read my expression or maybe he was just taking advantage of the circumstance, but Symon mopped his forehead again, beckoned me forward, and turned me to face my fellows. "Now," he said, "just to give you something to think about when you're at chores this afternoon, I'll use Aengus here as a demonstration. You all know about his bruised ribs by now, and having had some myself a time or two, I can tell you it hurts surpassing much." Even I chuckled. He made it sound like an old hero's tale. "Ordinarily I think Aengus would agree that he might not feel like doing anything too energetic till his injuries heal up." I nodded. The past two days while we were raking hay, I had been able to do only some scything and a little raking. Most of the time I had been the one to keep the tally. The weaponsmaster held up a finger. "But if your mind is trained as well as your body, you can do extraordinary things. Watch." He looked down at me. "Trust me on this, lad. I want you to let your mind go empty and listen to my voice. I'll not hurt you, I promise."

I managed a tight smile. "Just please don't make me squawk like a chicken." I had seen it once at a fair.

He reassured me with a nod. Should I trust him? *He could do something to you,* the dark voice warned. I regarded the ham-sized biceps bulging and relaxing, bulging and relaxing before my eyes as he swung a little bob on a bit of string. *He probably could kill you any damn time he chose to,* my normal voice said rationally. *Anytime ... he wanted to ...* His voice faded in my ears, and I was left with vision only, curiously bright-edged, as though I had never seen sand, or stone walls, or faces before. This was a silent world, more silent than a dream and a great deal clearer.

Something bright glinted in my eye, and I followed it to its source. There was a round wooden buckler strapped to my left wrist, one of the nail heads on the battered surface winking. I felt my right hand come up and discovered I was holding a wooden stick with a crosspiece, a dummy sword of the kind they give children to pretend with.

Symon was suddenly there, holding the same kind of stick loosely, and he had no shield. En-

emy, a distant voice seemed to say. See, here
is an enemy come to kill you. His black curly
hair became a flat arrow shape, and his eyes
went beady and bloodless. I felt power surging
into my legs, and I swung my mighty blade.

The stabbing fangs slashed at me, whistled
past my ear, hissed past my torso. I hewed a
backhanded blow, dancing out of danger. In
the time it took, the beast changed, and now it
was a Wolf, huge and black and sapphire-eyed,
and I thrust at it but missed and it buried its
powerful muzzle in the leather of my shield
and there was an explosion of spangled light,
but my sword sang deep and true, a song so
powerful that I could not be beaten, could not
even be hur—eyes, eyes all around, flickering
like distant heat lightning and I fled from them,
my sword silent now or maybe that crying was
it, and the earth yawned suddenly and swallowed me whole and I was falling, tearing my
fingernails on the rocks, screaming, flailing
wildly to get a grip somewhere, anywhere—

"Three, Aengus, three!" A man's voice,
strained and rough.

I came to myself with the sword-stick raised
high over my head, poised for a killing blow.
Opposite me was Symon, his leather jerkin
stained with sweat, sword stick halted midway
through the swing that would have knocked me
out, a cut on his temple bleeding freely. "Put
it down," he ordered steadily.

I dropped the stick and cast away the buckler. "By the Fire! Did I do that? I'm sorry, I—"

He touched a finger to the swelling knot on
his head and wiped a smear of blood off on the
jerkin, staring at me all the while with his
heavy brows nearly meeting over the bridge of

his nose. "What did you see?" he asked wonderingly, then abruptly shook a hand. "No, never mind. It doesn't matter, anyway." He took a step closer and I flinched. Drawing me around to face the other boys, he asked clearly, "You've seen what the kind of discipline I'm talking about can do for you." They had seen it all right; even Gwynt looked awed. He tapped my shoulder suddenly. "How are the ribs?"

My mouth fell open as I realized. "Fine!" I moved to test them. "It doesn't even ache!" I marveled.

"Go easy," he advised. "Just because it doesn't hurt right now doesn't mean it's healed. You're still a few weeks from being able to do without mind focusing the kind of work you've just done."

I looked up from under his arm. "Master," I told him, "I'm years from being able to do that again."

The boys laughed at my tone, but Symon didn't. In his eyes was an arrested look, like a man who hears a far-off signal for which he has been listening a long time. Under cover of the boys' movement and released tension, he said, "No, I don't think so, young painter. I don't think so at all."

We were put through some strength-building exercises, and then Symon took us into the armory. A little stir went through us. We thought he would issue us wooden swords and shields, maybe even real iron ones, though unedged, of course. Instead he took from a sack something which he tossed to Gwynt. "Catch!" The startled boy fumbled it, but hung on. In his hand was a small leather ball, soft as though it might be filled with sand. The weaponsmaster grinned at our expressions. "Disappointed, your lordships? You were expecting something rather more dramatic? Well, let me tell you—these are the most important pieces of training equipment you'll be given to work with." With that, he handed out to each of us a set of juggling balls. "When you can keep them in the air long enough to suit me, you'll go on to the next stage. While you are working with them, try to improve how well and how quickly you see things with your side vision. That's all for today. Report to Master Padraig back at your quarters."

As we passed through the gate of the practice yard Gwynt stretched his long legs to overtake me and fell into step. "He's going to have it in for you, sure, Aengus." He shook his head.

Kevyn looked back over his shoulder at us. "You fetched him a good clop on the head," he said in a tone that agreed.

"I didn't mean to," I protested. "By the Fire, he had me under a spell when I did it! I don't even remember fighting him!"

"What was you fighting, then?" Seamus asked to my other side.

A chill ran over me, and I looked away.

"It was that snake again, wasn't it?" Gwynt guessed shrewdly.

"That and other things," I mumbled. Nightmare things, things heard in a tale, perhaps. Except that I couldn't remember ever hearing the story. Maybe they were things from Symon's mind, suggested to me by a word. I glanced up at my tall friend. "Did Master Symon say anything to me while I was under?"

He peeled his nose thoughtfully. "Well, he told you there was an enemy out to kill you, and he didn't have a chance to say nothing more. The next thing we knew, you lit into him like holy old hell, and old Sy had all he could do to fight you off. He didn't make too easy a job of it, neither." He cocked an eye at me. "You been shamming on us, Fat Lip: you've had some training, haven't you?"

I grinned past the split in my lip that was just beginning to close. "No, I swear it. Today was the first time, and of course I couldn't have done that in my right mind."

"I guess to hell I wouldn't want to meet ye in your wrong mind, then," he said fervently. " 'Cause you're a regular demon when your blood's up, Aengus."

And so I acquired my reputation early, and thereafter most of the boys walked warily around me. They did not quite trust a fellow who could become a regular demon at the drop of a hat. Truth to say, I didn't quite trust him myself.

That afternoon we were assigned to the jobs at which we would work the main years of our indenture. As they had hoped, Kevyn was put to work in the skellig's carpentry workshop and Seamus in the kitchen, a vast affair which would prepare him well for duty in a royal household. The brother herbalist turned up at the door of our room to beckon me, as Bruchan had arranged. Gwynt's face was growing longer as the brothers and their helpers filed out, leaving the dormitory empty. I paused for a word to cheer him up, saying that I was certain Master Padraig would not have forgotten him, when a tall man, lean, with the kind of whipcord energy one sees sometimes in woodcutters or huntsmen, ducked under the lintel.

"Which of you is Gwynt?" His voice was easy on the ear. I judged him a singer.

"I am, master." My friend swiped his sleeve across his nose nervously, wincing as the sunburn peeled a little more.

"Ah, good, you're a strong one." He came forward extending a hand, much to our surprise. None of the other brothers had done that. "I'm Niall. My charge is the horses. Master put you with me because he thought they'd have need of a good farrier and groom at court. It'll give you a good chance of being treated well."

Gwynt turned a beaming look at me. "Well, I'm off then. Good luck, Aengus. See you tonight."

I followed them out to where the brother in charge of medicines, simples, and draughts waited for me. "Forgive me, master. I am sorry to have kept you."

He had brown hair beginning to go gray, mild hazel eyes, and the kind of quiet authority that all the best healers have. I liked him immediately, and I was not much given to quick approval of people. "I am Brother Nestor, Aengus. Come, let us to work. The day is ripe for gathering sea moss, and we do not get so many clear days here." He had two gathering baskets over his arm, one of which he offered to me.

We went out the main gate, passing through the two outer walls, then turned right to skirt the base of the skellig. As I have explained, the back of the community itself was built right on the cliff edge, but with all the outbuildings it ran some distance down the hill, and the fortification walls extended even farther. The result of this was that as I followed Nestor on the well-trodden path that led away over the burren, we were roughly paralleling the cliff edge, but we were at some distance from it and considerably lower, for the land climbed abruptly as you neared the edge. When we had gone some way, the rock gave way to springy turf in places and Nestor stooped to pick a few leaves of a plant which had rooted itself in the lee of a boulder. I saw him glance back at the walls of the skellig, now shrunken in the distance on its headland. "Excellent," he murmured. "Pick a little of this and put it in your basket, would you? I think we are unobserved, but precautions are still in order."

I did as he requested. "What is this plant, Brother? I really am interested in learning as much as I am able."

He smiled over the sleeve of his gray robe as he stooped to the plant. "Even though this is but a diversion for enemy eyes?"

I felt the heat rise in my face. He seemed as good a master as one could ask to prentice with, and if the painting had not been such a burning in my blood, I would gladly have taken this assignment and counted myself lucky.

Nestor seemed to understand, for he straightened and said, "I'm sorry. That was tactless of me. It cannot be accounted your fault that you must guard your gift like a precious jewel that every thief covets." He held up a leaf. "This is popularly called foxglove, but its medical name is digitalis. From it can be made a drug to stimulate the action of the heart. I will be showing you how to compound it, together with many other medicines, later in your training. For now, it is well to begin with the identification of our healing plants in the wild and also the ones I grow in the garden. Obviously we cannot make the medicines we need unless we can recognize and gather the plants from which they come." He seemed struck by a sudden thought. "Can you read and write?"

I shrugged. "I can make my mark, but it's not the sort of thing that comes much in handy to a pickpocket."

Nestor blinked. "I suppose not." He cleared his throat. "Well, I have bad news for you, then—you'll have to learn it. At least enough," he added hastily at my dismay, "to read the labels on the jars in the apothecary and follow the formulas for preparing the medicines."

I very nearly let loose with a string of invective that would have scorched the turf, but such words did not come so easily in front of this man. I permitted myself a heavy sigh. "Well, if I must, but by the Fire, it's a lot to ask. If you want to know the truth, I think I was better off living with Dad, for all he was a drunkard, and trying to keep bread in our mouths by lifting a purse or two."

He laughed.

"Well, could you read when you came here?" I demanded.

"Oh, yes," the healer replied modestly. He tucked the foxglove in the basket. "I was just remembering how it was at first to find myself in Skellig Inishbuffin." Inviting me by a nod to walk with him, he moved off down the path. "I was in different circumstances than you, since I had come here of my own will as a novice to study with the masters, but my father drank rather too much, too, and like you I had thought getting away from him would free me from all my worries."

I stumbled over a rock and had to take a couple of quick steps to catch up with him. "Was your father a healer?" I thought he might have picked up the trade.

"No, he was a prince, actually."

I tried not to gape. "But—but that makes you . . ."

His eyes crinkled. "The son of a prince. Mind your step, that bit of rock's slippery."

"Didn't you want to be a ruler?" I could not comprehend giving up such a life.

"No, not much. And besides, I had two older brothers who did very much want to be rulers. After some consideration, therefore, I left the field to them and came here to be a Dina."

We walked a little in silence, then I ventured, "Do you ever see your brothers or your father?"

Nestor looked down at me. "My father died of the drink soon after I came here," he related. "As for my brothers . . ." He looked away toward the horizon, and when he spoke after a moment his voice had hardened. "One killed the other, and the brother who is left I do not see."

My curiosity had gotten the better of me again, and I berated myself roundly for giving in to it.

Nestor came to himself with a start from wherever his memories had taken him. He touched the four-spiral pin in his robe and sighed. "Well, so much for ancient history. Come along, lad, with a little more haste, if you please. I fear Brother will have grown impatient waiting for us."

My spirits rose with a bound. "My painting master?"

"Aye. Master Bruchan is anxious that you should begin your lessons with him as soon as possible. I take you to a meeting place, one of many we will use to avoid those who may be watching."

While we had talked I had not paid it much attention, but I saw now that the cliff line had curved around till it lay in front of us. We toiled up the rise, a moderately steep climb, where the turf broke again into rock fragments, and finally gained the top. I was out of breath with the exertion, but I would have lost my wind anyway when I got my first glimpse of the majestic vista that lay before us. To my right was the open sea, blue and violet today under the summer sun, and sluicing around the upstanding rocks which dotted the nearer waters. Directly in front of our vantage, the ocean thrust into a narrow cove, surging between the cliff on which I stood and the one across the cove, which was somewhat lower, so that I could look down upon it and watch the wild goats scrambling with their kids to forage on the thistles. We were, I would judge, two hundred feet above the surf foaming on the pristine little beach tucked at the back of the cove.

I let out my breath. "By the Flame, that's the prettiest picture I've e'er seen."

Nestor gazed down, a look of peace on his face. "It is a bonny place. I come here ofttimes when my heart is weary."

"Thank you for showing it to me."

He smiled, took a step, and vanished over the edge.

I cried out and dove on my belly at the cliff edge, frantic. His grinning face was two feet below mine. "It's a little jump, but I think you can manage it," he told me with a twinkle in his eye.

I let go with the curses this time, be sure.

At length when I was ready, I scrambled

over, hissed at the pain in my ribs when I
landed, and followed him on the zigzagging
narrow path that led down toward the beach.
Sometimes the cliff was too sheer even for a
footpath, and there ladders had been spiked
into place to help with the footing. Nestor, I
noticed, carefully checked each rung before he
put his weight on it, and I could see why: if
one of the wooden bars let go, you'd be in the
surf before you had time to wonder what had
gone wrong. Thus forewarned, I was extra alert
and made the descent easily. I did not look
down any more than I had to do, however.

Finally there was a last bit of scramble down
a jumble of boulders higher than a man's head,
then the soft sand was beneath my heels. I spat
into one palm that had been a little scraped,
blew on it absently to cool it, and looked down
the curve of the beach to the opposite cliff tow-
ering over us. I saw no one, and cold bat's
wings seemed to brush my nape. It was a lovely
place for a trap. Nestor was standing at the
edge of the foam, hands on hips, looking out to
sea. I inched my small eating dagger into my
hand and closed on him.

Around the promontory down which we had
climbed nosed a small boat. The figure in it
gave a hail, and Nestor waved a reply, while I
sheepishly rammed my dagger deep in its
sheath and sat down on a rock to wait for him.
The boat was a coracle, a craft made of ox
hides stitched over a wooden frame, a strong
type of boat and a very maneuverable one for
coastal waters such as these. The man rowed
skillfully around the point, fended himself off
the rocks with an oar, and then let the waves
carry the boat in through the creaming surf.

He splashed ashore, and he and Nestor dragged the coracle up on the sand till it rested on one side, looking like a whale calf. I got to my feet as they turned.

"Aengus, this is Brother Ruan," the healer said.

The other cast back his blue hood. I was surprised to find him not as young as his rowing would have suggested; he was not quite of an age with Bruchan, I judged, but he was certainly older than Nestor. He might have had the same flaxen hair as Gwynt at one time, but now it was white, thinned on the crown of his head to a bare few strands and trimmed neatly short everywhere else. He had mild blue eyes the color of a rainwater-washed spring sky, and high color in his cheeks, and he looked the kind of man who is perpetually bemused about something. He put a finger alongside his nose, thinking for a moment. "And this is ... oh, yes—Aengus. How d'ye do?" He started to offer his hand, then stooped to pick up a stick, then as I was standing there with my hand out, looked up and remembered. We shook hands.

Nestor smiled affectionately. "I shall leave you two to discuss your work. Aengus, if anyone should ask, you and I spent the afternoon collecting seaweed to dry. It is sovereign for goiters of the throat. I will fill your basket as well as my own, and then we three will row back together."

"Right," I answered. "Foxglove: digitalis, used for heart ailments; and seaweed, throat goiters.

He grinned. "Tomorrow we'll begin your reading lessons." I made a sour face, and he laughed and strode off up the beach.

Master Ruan settled himself on the rock I had vacated, pulled his hood off over his head, and fanned himself. "Well, now, first let me say that I am extremely happy thee's here, and I am honored to be thy teacher, and so forth, and now I think we had better get to work." He stood up energetically. "We won't want to do too much today where we might be seen from the cliffs up there—no, lad, don't look up, if thee please, thee'll just tip the trick that way, won't thee? Innocent, that's the ticket for us— but I think it might do well to get some idea of what thee already knows. So here's a nice bit of stick, and all this sand, and now thee'll draw me a tree, please."

He spoke so quickly and ran his thoughts together so much that it was like playing leap-frog with a firefly to try to keep up with him. I took the stick, swept a patch of sand clear with my toe, and crouched. "What kind of tree, master?"

"Oh. Oh, yes, what kind. Well . . ." He waved a hand. "Let's make it, um, an oak."

I nodded, searched in my mind for a picture, and quickly sketched the solid trunk, the lift of heavy boughs, the thick canopy of heavily veined leaves, the acorns bunched and ready to drop. I looked up confidently.

"Lovely. Very nice, thank you, now a sea gull flying?"

I scraped out my oak, smoothed the sand absently with my hand while I thought, and then drew the sharp angle of the wings, the solid, rather chunky body, the large bill and tucked, webbed feet, the round, intent eye. Below him, small with the height, I added a small boat with a single sail and nets out over the side.

Ruan nodded, his thin hair wisping in the salt wind. "Yes, exactly. Now a teardrop."

"A what?"

"Teardrop, there's a good fellow."

I smoothed the sand once more. The image came to me. I drew a man seated on a stack of peat outside an inn door, his hands on his knees, head down, drops pattering into the dusty road. I sat back on my heels and looked up at Ruan quizzically.

"Poor man," he murmured. "He has lost something of great value to him."

"He has," I agreed shortly.

"But, Aengus, I didn't ask thee to sketch a portrait of a man grieving. I asked for a teardrop."

I frowned and thrust the stick into the sand. "How can you show a teardrop in a picture like this? Usually that's what painters use color for—a drop of silver shavings. I don't know how to do it otherwise."

He smiled the gentle, luminous smile I would come to know so well, the smile that said, I've got you, pupil mine. "Ah, but there must be a way, don't you think?" he suggested. "We'll find the way to draw it first, and then we'll add the color, the color is only to enhance, thee sees, what is already there." He stood up. "Our next meeting will be in the place master is preparing for us, a place perfectly safe from gulls' eyes, thee knows. Do keep working on the teardrop problem. When thee's solved it to thy satisfaction, ask Padraig to pass me a word, and then we'll meet again, now I have some traps to pull, so thee, and I, and Nestor had better get going or we shall be late for the supper bell, where has Brother Herbalist gotten himself to, does thee suppose?"

I shaded my eyes and pointed. "Up around the point, there. Shall I fetch him?"

"Much easier in the coracle, grab the bow, there, and we'll give her the old heave-ho and row like otters and we may actually get out of this cove without breaking ourselves in two on the rocks." We shoved the boat back into the water, Ruan climbed in, and I pushed off, splashing through the cold shallows and lurching awkwardly in, hissing once more at my damned ribs.

The old man fitted the oars to the locks, stood astride the midthwart, and rowed strongly against the waves coming in. Slowly we rocked out toward the figure of Nestor on the headland to our left. I put my fingers to my lips and gave him a whistle. He turned inquiringly, saw us coming for him, and dumped a last armload of seaweed into one of the baskets. The other, as I could see when we drew nearer, was already full. Ruan expertly steered between the rocks and drew up close enough that Nestor could swing the heavy baskets to me and then jump lightly aboard himself.

"Have you traps to pull, Brother Ru?" he asked.

"I have, and some fine lobsters in them if it pleases the Fire." He handed over one of the oars, the two men sat down side by side, and bent to the rowing.

When the rhythm was established, Nestor gave me a nod where I lay against the stern. "And how did the lesson go?"

"Oh, very well," Ruan answered. "I've given the poor lad a bit of a problem, a puzzle to gnaw away on, don't thee know, just for the fun of it." He winked at me.

"Poor Aengus," the healer teased. "So much to learn and—" He broke off, staring up to the cliffs beyond me.

"What is it?" I asked quickly, and turned to look.

"Someone was on the cliff. I'm sure of it, though I only glimpsed him for a moment."

Ruan had not followed our gaze. He rowed with his chin on his chest. "Well, that's no more than we expected, eh, lads, unfriendly eyes about, all that."

Neither Nestor nor I said anything, and it was silent for some moments except for the lapping of the water against the leather hull, and the squalling of the seabirds on the cliffs. My painting master suddenly looked over at me. "It might be very interesting to see who's late for the dinner bell, though, thee thinks? So stand by to pull in the traps, boy, and Nes and I will just keep rowing along, nice and smooth, till we get home and find what fish we've caught."

He wasn't talking about the lobsters in his woven wooden traps, either. Would it be Cathir, or Mallory, who would come in late, with an apology on his lips for the brothers already at their evening meal, and an eyeful of the sketch I had done of a man weeping back there on the sand of the cove? And how would he try to get word to Jorem that Skellig Inishbuffin was training a new painter?

Chapter 6

We landed at the small pier below the skellig, and handed the lobster traps up to the waiting hands of Brother Thyr, who had come down to help Ruan take care of the coracle, not knowing Nestor and I would be with him. "Yes, found these two beachcombers up the shore a ways, so I very charitably decided to save them a step," my painting master lied cheerfully, loudly enough to carry up the cliff. Then he added quietly to the ship captain, "We had company."

"Did you?" Thyr's tanned face grew worried. "Was it a serious problem?" His eyes flicked to me.

"There were no snakes, if that is what thee means," the old man answered more crisply than I had yet heard him speak. Again I had to remind myself to watch these men: Dinan were Dinan, having unsuspected depths.

Nestor, Thyr, and I hauled the coracle out of the water and carried it to the open cargo door. Because the tides could get much higher in storms, the captain told me, all of the skellig's coracles were kept inside to prevent them from being battered to pieces. There was a neat rack of the dark boats just inside the door to the left. We must have passed it that first day on the way up to our dormitory, but I had been so preoccupied by my meeting with Jorem that I had given it no notice. Now I looked about with interest as Ruan spent a few moments tipping his day's catch into a wide wooden half cask sunk into the damp stone floor. I walked over to peer into it and saw that my painting master must have been busy for some days past. The cask was thick with the crustaceans, each with its claws bound shut with durable straw rope. I looked up at Ruan. "You've quite a catch here."

He nodded and smoothed back his white hair. "Brother Cook will put them to good use, thee knows, for the feast tomorrow night. Oh, thee didn't know? My. Well, I don't think it's a secret, it's a regular event with us, and everyone enjoys it so. It seems to make the work go better if one can see some result of it now and again."

Nestor, seeing my confusion, stepped into the breach. "On the first night of every full moon, Aengus, we have a half holiday, a big supper, and then a seisun." This is a Burren word that has no Ilyrian counterpart. It is an entertainment comprised of song and sometimes dance, and usually storytelling. A seisun may be a festival for an entire province, but more often it is limited to the folk of one village, or of one family and their neighbors. Originally seisuns were spontaneous affairs, and the best of them still are, but now some are planned ahead of time, such as this one at the skellig.

I allowed that I would be glad of some fun, and both my painting master and my medicine master laughed heartily. But I wondered as I followed them up the inner stairway if a seisun in a skellig might be another word for a ritual, and if so, whether I was going to like it.

We came to the top of the stairs and opened the door into the corridor running across the back of the main building block. Off this corridor were the storerooms, a sensible arrangement that allowed for supplies brought in by boat to the pier to be loaded on a square wooden platform in the chamber below and raised by means of a pulley to this corridor. We walked across the platform of the supply elevator as Nestor led us right, toward the kitchen. I could have found it by nose alone; there was new bread and onion soup, if I was any judge of kitchen smells.

When we were a little way along the corridor from the kitchen, the customary entrance to the dining hall for men coming from the landing or work in the storerooms, Nestor held up a hand. In a low voice, he cautioned, "We went nowhere near Gull's Cove this afternoon; you and I, Aengus, went to the shore not far along the cliffs here and were met by Ruan coming back from his traps."

"Right, but where is the path down to the water, just in case I'm asked?"

"Good thought. You remember the path that branched to the right when we cleared the wall out front? That one goes down to a stair built in the cliff."

"The one Master and Lord Jorem climbed that first day?" I asked Thyr.

"That's the one," the captain replied.

I nodded, and we passed into the steam and slamming pot din of the kitchen. Seamus wiped his face on his shoulder, his hands up to the elbows in dishwater, and gave me a tired grin but ventured nothing further in the presence of all the masters around me.

We crossed through the broad open arch into the refectory. This was a large room, easily the largest in the skellig, with a flag stone floor and a hearth at both ends. The walls were lime-washed plaster and hung with tapestries de-picting the cycle of the seasons from sowing to harvest and beyond to the land's rest in winter. These embroideries were very fine, the borders rich with intertwined flower, nut, vegetable, and fruit, and the main scenes themselves filled with figures, men behind the ox as it plowed, and scything the hay and grain, and burning off the stubble. Woven into the scenes were lit-tle unexpected things, too: here a dog and boy racing each other after a ball, there village men and women watching mummers at an autumn fair. Gwynt had told me that he had even seen the depiction of someone pissing from behind a haystack, but I didn't credit that. Neverthe-less, I had looked for it at every meal since.

Not tonight, however. Tonight as I stood in the line before the serving table with my bowl and spoon, I swept the tables for the two of Jorem's agents that I knew. Mallory was sit-ting far down on the left and had been there awhile; he was leaning on his elbows over his empty bowl, listening to something another brother was saying. I continued looking for Cath-ir, but it was not until the savory onion soup had been ladled into my bowl and I was handed a hunk of cheese and dill bread to go with it that I caught sight of the portly overseer. He was next to my master Bruchan, his usual seat had I but remembered it, and he, too, was already finished with his supper.

Sweat broke on me suddenly and I spilled some of the hot soup over my hand. By the Fire, there was a third enemy in the community! I made my way down to where Kevyn beckoned and slid onto the bench next to him. "How was your master?" he asked excitedly.

I spooned soup and blew on it. "Fine, only he's going to make me learn to read, can you believe it?"

His eyes widened. "Boy, that's rough," he commiserated, then launched into an account of how his carpentry master had been so pleased with him that he was going to let Kevyn help him with the building of the new barn for the skellig's milk cows.

I congratulated my happy companion on his good fortune and tore a chunk out of my bread. "Where's Gwynt?"

He shrugged, picking wood shavings off his tunic. "Hasn't come in yet. Belike his master's kept him late to feed up the horses."

I nodded agreement. No worry there: the watcher on the cliff wouldn't have been Niall. The more I looked about, the more I realized the near impossibility of determining who it had been. Many of the seats were empty tonight; no doubt, because of the impending holiday tomorrow, the married brothers' wives would insist that their families eat at home tonight to use up whatever fresh meat or fish they might have on hand so that it would not spoil. Also, many of the brothers would be taking advantage of the long clear light of evening to work their own fields, having had to devote the main part of the day till now in the discharge of their duties to the community. I shook my head in irritation.

"Soup's hot, isn't it?" Kevyn remarked, having seen my action and thinking he knew the reason for it.

I nursed a mouthful of it and nodded for his benefit.

"Oh, say, I almost forgot to tell you! There's a half holiday tomorrow, isn't that fine? We've only been here a few days, and already we have some time off. And the best part is"—he rushed on without waiting for my reaction—"we're let to do whatever we want with our free time. So Conor, that's my master's eldest son, says to let the 'dentured boys know that the lads of the skellig—all that can come—are going swimming at someplace called the Caldron. It's got cliffs to dive from and good water, and it sounds like fun. Are you coming with us? We'll be back in time for supper," he hastened to assure me.

I grunted a laugh. "I was fair sure we would be. Aye, I'd like to come. Thanks to Conor, when you see him."

Kevyn nodded and leaned his elbows on the table. "You know, I really like this place," he said simply.

Nobody's tried to kill you, I thought, but did not have the heart to bring up Geri's death. "I do, too." And as I said it, I realized with some surprise that I had spoken the truth. Despite the danger and for all that I wasn't quite sure yet who was friend and who was foe, I did like my lessons with Nestor, Ruan, and Symon, and I liked, too, the feeling of knowing there would be food on the table for me.

The dining hall was beginning to empty, as

people were drawn outside by the lingering sunlight to resume their chores or simply to enjoy the evening. "Well," Kevyn said with an air of decision, "I'd better get along home. I've tools Master wants sharpened before the morrow."

I was startled. "You've moved into your master's house? When did this happen?"

"This afternoon," he answered a little smugly. "I wasn't the first, neither: Alec and Donal were already out by the time I came up the hill from the workshop to collect my stuff."

He might have thought my long face as he took leave of me was due to jealousy, but in fact I was thinking that the fewer boys left in the dormitory, the greater was my danger. I doubted I'd get much sleep tonight.

"Thee's troubled in spirit, lad. Come walk in the free air with me," a soft voice invited.

I looked up to find Bruchan by my shoulder and scrambled off the bench to follow him out of the refectory. We strolled past the round tower and made our way down through the cluster of stone-and-thatch buildings to the gate in the first wall, which stood open at this time of the evening to allow for coming and going to supper. The door ward, a brother I had not yet met though I remembered seeing him at meals, jumped to his feet from his stool at our approach, a piece of intricate needlework dangling from his hand. "Warmth of the Fire, master," he greeted the old man.

"Warmth," Bruchan answered. "Thee's a fine hand with a needle, Finian."

The Dina, whom I promptly and uncharitably had characterized to myself as a half-wit upon hearing how he had allowed the sentry's dinner to be drugged by Mallory on the night of the snake, blushed and handed the master of the skellig the handwork he had been laboring over while keeping watch on the gate. By the Fire, I thought as I looked over Bruchan's arm, this fellow might not be very sharp, but he's a master at tapestry. The narrow piece, which looked to be a border for some kind of ritual garment, was done in a style somehow familiar, a flowing intricacy of knots and circles within circles, all shaded with the most brilliant hues. Suddenly it clicked and I looked at Finian with new respect: the tapestries in the dining hall were his work, too. Not many wits, perhaps, but a fine eye for detail.

"It's beautiful," I murmured appreciatively.

" 'Tis but plain," he demured shyly, his ears flaming.

"Thee's too modest in this, little brother, and must learn to accept praise where 'tis due," the old man rebuked gently.

Finian bowed his head. "Aye, master. 'Tis a great failing in me."

Bruchan chuckled. "Not so great a one that we may not hope for success in correcting it soon." He handed the embroidery back to the needleworker, clapped him on the arm, and we went down through the gate into the middle strip of enclosed land that served in winter as a sheepfold. In summer, as now, this was left fallow so that the grass might grow long for winter's use. The grasshoppers sprang out of our way as we followed the cart road down the slope toward the second wall. "Thee's thinking the dormitory be not so safe with few sleepers."

His quiet voice startled me, as we had walked with silence between us since the dining hall, I occupied with trying to devise a plan to uncover Jorem's other agent, and Bruchan looking as though he was intent merely on enjoying the cool of the evening. I looked up at him. "By the Fire, are you a mind reader, too?"

A slight smile played about his lips. "Nay, I am no soothsayer. But it takes no great wit to read a man's face, or the actions of his hands. I knew many of the lads had moved to their new homes today, and thy young friend seemed to be telling thee that which made thee think deep." He looked down at me. "I had taken thought for this already. Nestor tells me thy lodging place in the apothecary will be ready on the morrow, and so for tonight we will put it about that thee's sleeping in the infirmary, the better to be dosed for thy ribs. In fact, though, Padraig will show thee up to my study."

That was as safe a place as I could ask, with a stout door and a stairway even a boy should be able to defend. I relaxed for the first time since we had seen the watcher from Ruan's boat, and took as deep a breath of the sweet, hay-smelling air as the bindings on my ribs would permit. "Will it seem odd to anyone that you are out walking with one of the indentured boys?"

Bruchan smiled briefly. "I think not. It is a well-known custom of mine to wander about a little after dinner most nights when the weather is fine, and I often pick up the stray dogs or cats of the skellig for company."

I gave him the look the remark deserved, and we walked on. Rather than heading for the second gate, as I had expected him to do, Bruchan led me to the stairway up the wall. We emerged on the narrow platform of grassed-over earth that had been put down to hold the stones and make a better footing for defending troops, if that should prove necessary. Bruchan leaned against the low parapet and looked out over the lower slope of his skellig. He said nothing for a time, and caught by his spirit of peace, I joined him at the wall, hoisting myself up until I could sit and dangle my feet over it.

In the hazy golden light—the light is almost always hazy this close to the sea—the rough beehive shapes of the mounded turf heaped to dry and store in the lower ring of the wall showed a rich brown that contrasted sharply with the same sized haystacks that the older men had spotted close together in the lower ring. These were precious stores against the winter ahead, and prudently the skellig kept at least part of its hoard protected this way. The bare outlines of what I recognized to be fish-drying racks were lined here, too, and I surmised that when the salmon ran in the spring, the field would be full of smoky fires and pink fillets curing.

Beyond the third wall with its heavily fortified gate studded with precious iron and rampart of upthrusting sharp stones, lay the oblong mud-and-wattle homes of the brothers and their families. Each dwelling had its neat bit of vegetable garden in front of it, facing the cart path which there turned into the main road of the village, and bounded by the ever-present low stone walls. Two or three small fields lay behind each house, partitioned off by still more walls, and some of these fields had been turned into orchards; I fancied I could see even from this height the apples ripening in the evening sun. Turf smoke curled from under the eaves of the houses, and a pack of dogs wrangled down the main street of the village over something they had pulled from a midden.

Bruchan stirred beside me. "Who would credit that men exist who would destroy all this?"

I whipped him a look. "Because you are sheltering me?"

He shook his head. "Nay, the matter is an old one, Aengus, not having to do exclusively with thee. Though, to be sure, the two matters will become one in the years ahead, if we are granted the time." The master might have been talking to himself.

I rubbed my hands on my knees and wet my lips. "I would not bring harm down on other folks if I could do something to prevent it."

Bruchan smiled. "And what would thee do? Could thee choose not to be a painter? We might as well ask raven to change his voice! No, boy, the problem does not lie with thee."

His attitude seemed to invite questions, and there was no one about to hear our talk. I waved away a fly and asked, "Master, what does Jorem have against you, if it isn't me?"

Bruchan absently resettled one of the unmortared rocks of the parapet while he answered, "It is not only Jorem that we of Inishbuffin must guard against; a place such as this, with stores of grain, animals, and ore, is a honey pot to attract marauders." I nodded to show I understood. Even in my own poor village, pirates were a problem, and there were outlaws prowling, soldiers whose lords had been killed or savage men who chose to live in the wilds and prey on travelers. My master sighed and continued. "As to Jorem ... It is not only ambition and the chance to destroy a rival that he sees when he turns his eyes this way." He turned his head and regarded me. "One of the first things thee asked about was this symbol." He brushed a finger over his cloak brooch. "And I told thee it represented an idea to which we of Skellig Inishbuffin are sworn. Thee remembers?"

Again I nodded. "You're a rival sect, then, of the Wolf Cult that has split off from the—"

"No!" he interrupted with surprising vehemence. "It is not we who have left the path, but them—Jorem and those he has seduced to his new way."

I had not seen this intensity from him before, and it made me vaguely nervous. "But, I mean, the Dinan aren't—"

"Aren't what?" he prodded.

"Well, I never knew that it could be like this." I swept a hand out to include everything in sight.

His white hair gleamed slightly in the lowering sun. "Peaceful, thee means?"

"That and . . ." I scratched my head and tried to explain. "When you told me on the boat that you were taking me to a skellig, I wasn't taken with the idea, because one hears all sorts of stories about what the Dinan do inside their walls." His eyes were steady and I took a chance. "About rituals, for instance."

Bruchan made a snort of disgust. "About blood sacrifices, thee means, and arcane mysteries."

"Yes."

His jaw clenched. "Indeed, that is the great change Jorem has wrought in our religion, boy. He has made it a harsh, unlovely growl in the throat, a whispered threat to the very people

we Dinan are supposed to protect from those
who would abuse the power they have over
them." He shook his head. "As if the strength
of the Fire were found only in the Wolf, he has
ignored all other observances and focused only
on the most obscure branch of our knowledge
and practices, and he has lured followers like
himself, who believe that excessive severity is
the same thing as strength." His eyes became
clouded, and his voice dropped. "I fear, though,
that false ascetics may be the least of our problem. The world itself seems to have grown ...
darker and less loving, somehow." Bruchan
sent his brooding look out over his skellig.

"Dinan have no wives, I had been told." My
tone was a question.

"There, again, Jorem has convinced people
that for the elite Wolfhounds"—his voice
dripped sarcasm—"the encumbrances of wife
and children detract from that single-minded
devotion to the commands of the head of the
order which is the foundation of Jorem's new
idea of what a skellig must be." The old man's
face twisted. "Fool. He knows nothing of life,
or of the Power himself, if he believes that the
love of a woman or the sweet cares of raising
children can take away in any wise from meditation on the mysteries." His voice had fallen
again, and I think at that moment he was arguing his case to some other ear than mine.
The master straightened, glanced at me, and
drew in a lungful of the sweet air. "Ah, well,
Aengus, thee's a good lad to bear with an old
man's ramblings."

"I'm interested," I told him honestly. "And
relieved," I added, clearing my throat. "I had

been worried about this holiday tomorrow and the seisun."

He saw what I meant immediately and his eyes crinkled with humor. "Thee fancied not to drink of the blood of the Wolf?"

Even after what he had told me, even knowing that Jorem's cult was not the only way of worshiping the Flame, I still felt the vague crawl over my skin that comes in the presence of blasphemy. "How do you worship, then?"

There was a flicker in his eyes. "As thee can imagine, we must be guarded about how we keep the major observances. In the times to come, thee shall know, I promise, and I think it will not frighten or disgust thee." He drew himself to his full height. "But it is for the future. The morrow's holiday from work is only that: a chance for our folk to rest a bit before the heavy work of the harvesting begins." His odd-colored eyes rested on me. "At the turn of the season, summer into fall, will come the next major ritual. If thee's willing, I will take thee to it."

"You don't hold it here, then?"

Again, the slight flicker. "Nay, Aengus, not just here." He gathered his cloak about him against the sea breeze that had come up with the waning of the day. "Shall we go down now and join the brothers at their game of horseshoes?"

I should like to have asked many more questions, but I had enough to think about to stagger a mage, so I nodded and followed him down the steep stone stairway and back up the hill. Then until dark the skellig rang with the clang of the horseshoes against the stake. Bruchan wasn't a bad pitch at all, for an old man with so much on his mind.

* * *

That night I slept in Bruchan's tower room, feeling so secure that I believe I never once stirred. The good weather held for the next day, incredible luck considering that the coast receives more rainfall than the rest of the Burren, and the rest of the Burren is wet enough. We boys ate with gusto our breakfast of dried oats and currants wet down with a little milk, and then went cheerfully off to work the morning away. I had a word with Gwynt as he was going out, and he could not have been happier with his new master. Apparently Niall was something of a wizard with horses, and my friend was already smitten with a full-blown case of hero worship. I gathered there was a daughter in the family, too, just a little younger than us. Gwynt went whistling off to the forge, where Brother Niall would meet him to teach him the rudiments of making iron horseshoes.

As Nestor had promised—or threatened, depending how you look at it—we spent that morning with an old roofing slate and a bit of chalk, and I tried in vain to find meaning in the sticks he drew until I finally comprehended that the sticks represented nothing you could put a hand on and say, Ha! This is A. It was confusing beyond belief, and I could not see why everyone did not merely draw what they wanted to communicate, or hire someone to take a message, if it was over a distance.

"But what if you wanted to leave this message for someone two lifetimes hence. Would you expect a picture on the sand to last so long?" my medicine master pointed out shrewdly. "Nay, 'twould not last. So—" He handed the chalk to me once more. "We write it."

I snorted. "It won't last in chalk on a piece of slate very long, either."

The man's patience was extraordinary. If I had had so dense a pupil, I'd have set him to hauling turf like the ass that was his cousin. "Which is why, when you have learned this craft well, you may be allowed to read in some of the ancient scrolls we have here. They are written on specially prepared lambskin, and are over five hundred years old. Yes, I thought that might impress you. So many glories are written there, Aengus; so much wisdom!" His eyes shone and then dulled down to normalcy. "In truth, if I were a painter, I would want to learn to paint not with sands, but with inks. Then my work should last in such scrolls."

It was a wholly unfamiliar concept to me then, and I remember that it started me thinking, wondering if it could be done. I could not get much beyond puzzling how one would drip the ink onto the lambskin so that it wouldn't puddle, though, and if that seems supremely ignorant to you who are reading this book, I think I may be pardoned for it, because to that time I had never seen handwriting, much less a manuscript. Books are not so common in fishing villages of the Burren.

The upshot of this conversation with Nestor was that I developed an intrigue with seeing what "glories" and "wisdom" were in the skellig's old scrolls. As I say, I have always been as curious as a cat, and like tabby, I sometimes did not know what was good for me. So I got on fire to learn to read and also to write. By the time the bell rang from the round tower to declare the holiday at noon, I was cramped from hunching on my stool over my slate on the stillroom worktable. With painstaking care, I had managed to trace out a few letters which resembled those Nestor had given me as a pattern. I handed him the slate, sweating and triumphant.

He nodded, pleased. "Thee's a quick study, Aengus," he murmured, eyeing the slate full of crowded letters. He tucked the shingle behind him. "Now sketch them on the table."

The entire morning's work flew out the open window of my mind. I stared at him, dismayed and disgusted with myself.

Nestor understood. "It is no great matter—it just means that though you could copy the patterns, they mean nothing to you in your mind. Try this: pick one of these letters and we will find a word which begins with that letter."

Shamefaced, I pointed to the "B" on the slate.

The medicine master said, "Let us use the simplest word: bee. You know, honeybee? Now, take the letter here"—he handed me the slate—"and make it look like a honeybee."

I added wings, stinger, and bands of solid color.

"Excellent," he said. "Now, when you see this shape of B, you'll think of the bee. So doing, you will remember the letter."

His stratagem worked, and before Kevyn appeared at the doorway to collect me to go swimming I had mastered all the letters he had shown me that morning.

So began what has been to me a great solace, to be able to record in several volumes the events which have been so crucial to me and to those I have loved or hated, according to their natures, or perhaps according to my perception of them. And to this day, I still see the shapes of chalk-drawn animals and birds in all my letters.

* * *

The swimming place to which Conor led us was well out on the peninsula of Inishbuffin, in fact not much distant from the skellig itself, though he took us by a roundabout route to make it seem farther, and the adventure seem the greater as a result. I thought we were headed for the cliffs on the other side of the jut of land from Gull's Cove, for we seemed steadily to approach them, but when we were nearly there—near enough that we could hear the booming of the surf—Conor took us up a little swell of land and the rocks suddenly opened at our feet to reveal a kind of broad well, nearly fifty feet in diameter, with sides almost as sheer as the gigantic coastal cliffs themselves. The surface of the pool must have been almost sixty feet below us, and there was a current in its depth because the water surged with a motion vaguely reminiscent of the sea, gentle swells that lapped the sides and curled over to splash back into the pool. So crystal clear was the swimming hole that you could see the sand at the bottom of the turquoise water and swear that you could count individual grains. "Isn't it grand?" Conor said proudly.

"It's beautiful," I agreed. "But it looks a little chancy for any who aren't strong swimmers."

"Oh, it's safe enough at high tide like this. There's plenty of water, and it's quiet. I've promised my father that we'll leave by the time the tide turns." He pitched a small stone down into the crystal perfection. "You wouldn't want to be here when the tide is going out!" The carpenter's son laughed a little.

Another boy, one of those thin, dark fellows who always has a drippy nose even at high summer, squeaked. "There's a whirlpool! We threw a stick down in it once, and it sucked it right under!"

"Aye," Conor verified. "It's a bad place then, for sure, and in storms, too. I've come out here after a night's gale and found a column of water shooting up, like a whale blowing."

It didn't sound such an inviting place, and Gwynt looked dubiously at me. But the day was hot out here on the rocks, the water looked wonderfully refreshing, and none of us new boys wanted to look timid before our comrades. We fell into line as Conor led us down the narrow path that had been scraped to the water's edge. Everybody cast his clothes on the boulders, held noses, and jumped in. The cold salt water felt delicious against our sunburned bodies, and soon we were having water fights and disporting ourselves like a lodge of otters. Had there been any fish in the Caldron—Conor had blown water out of his mouth to tell me that is what the place was called—we would have frightened them off or killed them with disturbing the water. The rocks were perfect for leaping off, holding your knees and sending up a geyser when you hit the surface.

After not nearly enough time, the sun no longer stood within the round horizon of the stone walls above us, and there was the beginning of a stronger current dragging at our feet as we played. "All right," Conor called. "Everybody out. Come on, Ban! The tide's on the turn, I can feel it. If we stay longer, we won't be let to come again next holiday." That was the only argument that would have coaxed any of us out, but it was one that couldn't be argued with, so we hoisted ourselves out of the pool.

We were going to wait for the sunlight to dry us, but once out of the water, we discovered an astonishing hunger, so we merely dressed wet and reckoned that the walk home would dry us and our clothes both. Again, Conor led us in the climb out of the Caldron. This time, a slave to his stomach and worried that we might be late for any of the holiday's seisun, he took us by a much more direct route.

Before we left the cliffs above the pool, though, I remember looking back down into the water, which seemed somehow bluer since the direct sunlight had left it, bluer and colder. Something black suddenly hurtled past my head, and I ducked instinctively. A raven cawed raucously and arrowed down into the Caldron, flapping heavily to sit on the high boulder from which we had been jumping. It looked up at me.

I shuddered and backed a step into Kevyn, who had grabbed my arm to steady me, as we were still quite near the edge. "By the Fire!" he exclaimed. "I never seen one of them do that before!"

The bird of death, the Hag's familiar, stared at me, beak open.

My feet moved of themselves, and I ran up the path where the rest of the boys had gone.

Kevyn caught up with me, and together we drew up where the others had stopped to look back for us. Conor frowned a little. "What's the matter, Aengus? You're as white as milk."

Kevyn explained, "A bird shot right past his head on the rim of the Caldron! I've never seen one of them do that before!" he repeated.

"It was a raven," I said tightly, my breath coming short.

Kevyn looked at me, his mouth a little open.

"No wonder you look scared, if that's what you thought you saw!" He took a confidential step forward. "But it's all right, boy-o: I saw it clear, and it was only a sea gull." His honest face was full of concern that wanted to bring me comfort. He was a generous boy.

I swallowed. "That's what you saw? A gull?"

He nodded vigorously. "And heard it, too. Really, it was a sea gull, I'm not just saying so."

I allowed him to persuade me and grinned sheepishly at Conor and the others. In any other group of boys much derision would have been heaped on me, and I was prepared to take it, but apparently the sons of the Dinan did not know that they were supposed to ride me unmercifully about the incident, and my indentured companions followed their lead and let it drop. Talk turned to the feast and the seisun, and then someone started singing, and we all made our way over the heath's scant earth and stone until the walls of the skellig rose up outlined against the sky before us.

I never said anything more to the boys about the occurrence, but I knew what I had seen was no gull. I could not get out of my mind the memory of those shiny black eyes glaring into mine. Death was about, and it was looking for me.

When we arrived back at the skellig, we found that our return had been looked for with some impatience by the adults so that the seisun could get under way. They were waiting for us in the great dining hall, younger brothers and sisters tucked firmly on father or mother's lap. The benches and tables had been taken up, and everyone save Bruchan was sitting on the floor on small cushions they had

brought for the purpose. The master of Inishbuffin was in his customary carved chair, but
even it had been pulled to one wall against a
tapestry to leave room for the open square that
had been left in the middle of the refectory.
Here a smooth leather floor had been made of
three large calfskins quilted together, and to my
excitement I saw as we came in that Master Ruan
knelt along one side of it, arranging his color pots.
So he and Bruchan were going to tell a story! I
quickly scrambled for a space on the floor.

I tried not to be disappointed when another
brother arose first with his set of pipes and
began to play for us. People grinned and urged
him on, keeping time with their hands, and to
say the truth, he was an accomplished piper.
When he finished, two or three singers started
a tune, and the whole community quickly
joined in, splitting off into harmonies that
made me marvel. I had never heard so many
good singers assembled in one place before.

Then, finally, there was an expectant hush,
and eyes turned to Bruchan. He scratched his
head. "Oh. Thee waits for me?" A general laugh
greeted this. "Well, Brother Ruan, shall we tell
these folk a story, then?"

"An' it please thee, Brother, I'd as soon get going, my knees not being what they once were."

There was an affectionate laugh, and Bru-
chan left his chair and stepped to Ruan's side.
He looked around at his assembled commu-
nity. "Taking thought last night for what tale
it should be that I would tell thee, I hit on one
I think may suit. Shall it be Auntie and Biddy
Macroom?" At the chorus of "ayes," he smiled.
I smiled myself, for I knew it well.

Bruchan started to narrate, and Ruan to paint. This is the story as they told it that day.

Once a long time ago—and if it was a short time and I told thee, thee wouldn't believe me, would thee?—aye, so a long time ago it was that there lived an old woman name of Maire Macroom, but nobody called her anything but Biddy, for that her tongue was sharp enough to clip a hedge and she not shy about using it.

Now as it happened, Biddy Macroom was not what might be called wealthy, for she had no fine, big herd of cows or many sons, but she was not poor, either, for the one cow did she have and a son to milk it. The son's name was Bryn, and he was that sort of man who might do well if he lived in the Cloud Kingdom; I mean he was a dreamer. Not that he had not a quick hand to work—he labored long on the bit of land between the bog and the fen, but never seemed to get anywhere with it, no fault to him. And all the while the patient man worked and worked, didn't his mother have something to say about what crop should have been planted here or there or anywhere but where he had it, and didn't she run on and on about him not being sharp enough concerning the cow to make some sort of profit with it?

And Bryn scratched his head, wondered how deep she'd sink in the nearest bog hole, and went on with his work, all the while hoping she'd not get onto his secret.

What was Bryn Macroom's secret, thee asks? Only this: there was in that village another widow woman having no son and no cow and hunger looking in over her half door all the time, and this woman Bryn Macroom gave what milk he and his mother did not need for her to drink a little and use the rest to make bread so she might sell it for a copper to any that passed by. The woman's name Bryn never knew. All in the village called her Auntie and had done so since he was but a bit of a boy and his father, poor man, was still with the breath of life in him. And Auntie would sometimes ask him, "Bryn Macroom, will ye not take some bread or this copper in payment?" And he would shake his head, leave the pail of milk on the table, and go his way, warm in his heart.

So things continued for some time, till one day Biddy Macroom determined to find out why their old cow was giving less and less milk, and they feeding her more and more all the time. She spied from behind the curtain of her alcove bed the next morning as across the room her son milked the cow—the season was winter, and like sensible folk they kept the cow in with them so she wouldn't freeze her udder. All was well so far. She could find no fault with the milking, and when Bryn was done, three buckets brimming stood on the rushes. Old Biddy Macroom rubbed her nose, wrapped her shawl about her, and came out of bed to make up the fire and start the kettle boiling for tay. Then back into the warm bed she went to wait for the fire to get a hold on the cold that was in the house.

In a bit the kettle sang out that it was ready and would she move herself to take it off the fire, so she did and poured herself and Bryn some tay. She liked her tay white, that's to say with cream, did Biddy, so she went to dip some out of one of the three pails. But only two pails were standing in the rushes. Biddy Macroom blinked and rubbed her nose. "Bryn, where be t'other bucket?" says she.

"Be only the two, Ma," he made her answer, drinking down his own tay scalding hot and without the benefit of milk. He got up from the stool, pulling his hood about his face. "Well, I'm off. Told a neighbor I'd give him a hand with a ewe he's got lambing."

Biddy's eyes drew together, for well she knew that a ewe does not plan to have her lambs at a particular time of day any more than a woman says, "Aye, I think I'll have my baby in time to get a good night's sleep tonight for both of us, and don't we deserve it?" She watched Bryn go out and when she was sure he must be on his way, she followed him.

And she saw the whole of it, the third pail of milk in his hand, him hurrying along so it'd not freeze, the pinched face of Auntie opening the door to him, Bryn's good-bye to her, and his turn for home without the milk. And no money exchanging hands at all.

Well, didn't she have plenty to say to him when he got back inside their own door! People from that place always said that the beams of the Macroom house smoked for a few days after, not enough to blaze, thee knows, but just a tickle of charred wood in the nostrils. Aye, it was an awful drubbing she gave him, and him not deserving a bit of it, good soul that he was to help a poor old woman in need.

By and by, Auntie came to hear of it, how I cannot tell, probably the one told another, and he told her, and she told somebody who happened to mention it to Auntie. Thee knows how such news travels. However it happened, Auntie found out that Bryn had caught his mother's temper on her behalf, and she resolved that the goodness in him should not be soured, and the only way to do that was to sweeten his mother.

'Twas one job and a half that she'd taken on, but then Auntie was no ordinary one. There was the mouse that lived in her house with whom she chatted like an old friend, for instance. Not many people can claim something like that, or if they do, they daren't say it aloud. Then, too, Auntie had a way about her of making things happen. Her bread never burned and the milk never spoiled till she wanted it to. She had a pot that stayed full of good stew all the time, even though she ate from it each evening, and if thee had looked very closely at the thread in her needle, thee might have said 'twas gold. To put it the short way, she was no old widow woman, but a witch, a very good one and no bad tricks about her, and she only played poor to see who was worthy of a little witchly help.

So now Bryn was in for a little good luck, though he did not know it.

That very night when it came time for the evening milking, the Macroom's old cow seemed to have got the making of milk firmly in her big head, for Bryn was surprised when she gave four pails. His eyebrows went up, he sniffed and scratched his head, and then he put the milk all covered in the corner where it was cool, tied up the cow in the end of the house, and went to bed. The next morning when he was done with the milking, there were five pails in the rushes, and that was all the pails he had in the house. He patted the cow's neck, shook his head, left his mother talking about making cheese, and went along with four buckets to Auntie's.

Auntie grinned a little behind her eyes, thanked him for the milk, and sent him home with a loaf that he was too rattled to deny.

That evening at milking, the cow gave six pails, and Bryn had to run out to the neighbor's to borrow a few more buckets. By the time the candles were blown out in the village houses that night, everybody knew that the Macroom's cow had developed a talent for making milk and seemed determined to flood Bryn out of house and home.

Next morning—ah, thee's ahead of me now— it was seven pails and a firkin of milk that she gave, and looking very content with herself she was as she chewed her cud, a fine cow, the best in all the district.

Bryn counted the pails for Auntie's share and started out down the path, but he hadn't gotten far when up comes a party of riders, well mounted and not feeling the cold a bit through all their fine clothes. And wasn't the leader of them the king himself, and hadn't he been wanting just such a cow as the one he'd heard the Macrooms had? "I'll give ye a bull and three milch cows for that one," says he, eyeing the cow that Bryn had led out into the yard.

Bryn thinks it over. "She's an old one," says he.

"That's no matter to me," says the king. "I'll have that cow, no matter what the price."

All that heard this whistled to themselves, but Bryn was ever the honest one and he answered, "Ye'll no get much milk out of her, King. Like as not, this is the last of it, and she do be going out with a rush before she goes dry."

Behind the door, Biddy was biting her lips to keep from screaming, but when she heard that, she could keep still no longer. Out into the yard she rushed and took hold of the king's own boot. "A bull, three milch cows, and the two good hay fields up on the hill, and we'll call the deal done!"

Well, the king was a sharp one and saw how things stood. "See here," he says. "I just happen to have an extra daughter hanging about that I don't know what to do with. Why don't ye take the daughter, Macroom, and the bull and three, and the two fields, and I'll take your mother back with me to keep my house. What d'ye say to that?"

Bryn scratched his head and up went his eyebrows. He sniffed. "I'm willing," he says, "though it goes hard to be parted from the cow."

The two of them spat on their palms and shook hands to seal the bargain, and then the king rode off with the cow and Biddy Macroom. It might have gone badly if he'd been a bad king, because, as thee has noticed, Bryn hasn't got his bull, three milch cows, land, or princess yet. But as it happens this was a good king, and he kept his word. Bryn Macroom became the wealthiest man in the district and a happy one with his new wife.

Auntie got more milk than she could use from Bryn's herd, made a lot of bread, and then took up bee keeping for amusement.

And what happened to Biddy Macroom? I'll tell thee. She was put to keeping house for the king, and didn't the queen have something to say about how she washed the clothes, and how she should have oiled the pots before she let them dry, and a host of other things petty and faultfinding? Aye, she did. No mistake, Biddy Macroom had gone from bad to worse, and she isn't the only one headed down that road, if thee take my meaning.

If Bruchan was a masterful storyteller, then Ruan was his match as a painter. By the time the tale wound to its closing moral and he had encircled the painting with the double line of traditional black and red which would seal the goodness in it, my painting master had shown us Biddy spying from behind the curtain on Bryn as he took the pail of milk to Auntie, the man's astonished expression at his old cow's sudden production, and the fine king driving his bargain. And somewhere in every scene, hidden in the lines, was the portrait of Auntie's face, smiling as if to say. See, I am behind it all.

People could not stop clapping and nodding to each other in delight, accustomed though they were to the talents of the pair. I, who had never before seen such caliber, felt as though I had stumbled into attaining my heart's wish: to learn to paint from such masters. Even the image of the raven hanging in the back of my mind could not dull my keen pleasure. I told it to shut up its cawing and take itself away for the duration of my holiday. Tonight, during sleep, would be time enough for us to meet again.

So much excitement from the storytelling had to go somewhere, and it was apparently the custom of the skellig at such affairs to repair to the courtyard outside the dining hall and dance off the good spirits, while those who wished could admire the sand painting inside until it was swept up by the old painting master and the leather quilt rolled until the next holiday. Needless to say, when the others went outside and their shouts and laughter rose above the pipe and bodhrun, I knelt close to the leather telling floor and studied the painting Ruan had made us with something like the reverence that a young goldsmith might feel if he were asked to mend the High King's crown.

Ruan was sealing his color pots, muttering the secret words of his own incantation or prayer for each one. He eyed me, then made a point of joking with some of the other people who had also stayed, Finian and Conor among them. Finally, when no one would have remarked anything beyond boyish curiosity in my presence, the old man gestured for me to help load his pots back into the scuffed leather satchel in which he stored them. Three or four of the group drifted outside.

"Did find it interesting, Aengus?" my painting master asked.

"Wonderfully." I ducked my head, leaning over the satchel with him, and added for his ears alone, "I didn't see any teardrops, though."

Ruan's washed blue eyes twinkled. "Nay, should I have made the cow cry, then? That would have quite ruined the effect, don't ye think, and made thy work much too easy!" I grinned an answer and strapped the satchel for him. He leaned on my back, pulling himself to his feet, and Brother Finian and I took two corners of the floor covering while the old painter and Conor took the other corners, and the four of us carried the ruined picture outside and emptied the colored sands into a barrel which stood outside the kitchen door to quench grease flares. Nothing at that skellig was wasted, but it was a pity to me that so noble an effort as

that painting should come to no better end than
to put out a fire under a joint of meat.

Later I helped some of the other boys set up
the tables and benches once more, and the
dancers began to drift into the hall, breathless
and pleasantly worn out, to see when the feast
might be on the boards. Poor Seamus, who already seemed to me to be losing some of his
chubbiness with all the running about he did
between kitchen and storerooms, was stationed
at the door to fend off people's questions and
assure them that Brother Cook was getting it
ready just as quickly as water could boil. The
savory aromas of steamed lobster and seafood
chowder began to waft through the refectory.

It seemed a long time, but probably it wasn't.
Finally Master Bruchan was summoned from
where he was walking in the herb garden with
a little one by each hand, the dinner bell was
rung, and the entire skellig assembled for the
special meal. Gwynt and Kevyn came to the
bench I had singled out for us, and taking our
cue from the actions of the others, we stood at
our places and waited.

Seamus, flaming scarlet with the heat of the
kitchen and embarrassment, had been given
the honor of bearing in the first large platter
of lobsters. Obviously he had been instructed
what to do by the cook, because he made his
way to the middle of the hall and set the dish
before Bruchan. Then he made an awkward
bow of the kind he would be expected to know
at court when he went there the next year.
There was hearty clapping, and our friend
withdrew with haste back into the kitchen.

Then there was a pause, everything having
gone quiet once more, even the small children

hushed. Bruchan looked up from the steaming lobsters and with a gesture I did not recognize, said, "My people, let us give thanks for this bounty of the sea. First, to the Power who provides all the folk of the ocean, the dolphin and turtle, the shark and shrimp, that we may have enough to eat and their grace to enjoy, we say 'thank thee.' "

"Thank thee," the community intoned. (I was still back at the Power providing the fish. I had not thought the Wolf had aught to do with water, though I supposed since Beldis was the provider for men, all things could therefore be said to come from him. It gave me pause, though, and it was a moment before I realized that Bruchan had gone on.)

"Then, let us be sure to thank those whose labor has given us this catch, Brother Ruan and Brother Thyr."

"Thank thee," the skellig offered. Neither man looked up from his clasped hands.

Bruchan smiled a little. "So now we have our feast, and a time to enjoy our companionship together. Since it is their first time among us, I think it fitting that our indentured boys shall be served first with the rest of us to follow. Good health, my people, and Warmth of the Fire."

"Warmth," the assembly answered. There was a scraping of benches and shuffling of feet and a baby began crying, wakened maybe by his mother's movement in sitting down. The volume of conversation quickly rose, and people waited to be served, following with their eyes the dinners that were borne to us boys. When the platters and cups were set before us, we did not take long to set to work on them, you may believe.

The cooks had done themselves proud. The lobsters were accompanied by chowder and good bread and greens fresh from the gardens. To follow, there was sweet bread and cheese, or if one preferred, blackberries, raspberries, and cream. By the end of it I was so stuffed my stomach would not hear of trying to bend enough to get up from my bench. Evidently nearly everyone else was in the same condition, for folk lingered, picking more and more slowly at sweet bread and fruit, and listening to one of the brothers' wives, who now played upon the harp very sweetly, as good a musician as the pipers had been. That was another surprise to me: I had never seen a woman play a musical instrument before, not even the spoons.

At length the feast was done in time for the evening chores to begin. Families began paying their respects to Master Bruchan and then leaving for their own homes. I helped clean up. Seamus, looking as though his feet were about to fall off, limped out from the kitchen to direct me and another boy, a master's son named Jack, in picking up what unused food there was and carrying crockery to the kitchen wash tubs. We were about to throw out all the broken lobster shells when Jack told us it was a custom to throw at least a portion of them from the cliff of the skellig for the birds. It was quite a show, he added; the gulls would catch them right out of the air if you threw them in an arc.

It was a turn of the glass or more by the time Brother Cook told Seamus he might have leave for the rest of the night and would not have to report to the kitchen for breakfast duty the next day, as he had put in yeoman service for the feast. My friend beamed at the praise, wiped the sweat from his forehead, and grabbed one rope handle of the large tub I had heaped with lobster leavings. We lugged the heavy buckets out the rear of the kitchen block, climbed the stairway of the encircling wall, and found ourselves atop the parapet. Far down below us was the boat jetty giving onto the rear of the skellig.

We pitched shells to the screaming gulls and soon had them diving around us as thick as bees around a hive. It was dizzying to stand at the top of the world—it felt like it—and have all that race of slanting wings and rushing air around us. Mindful of the raven, I stayed well away from the parapet itself, and once or twice urged my companions to be more careful, though there probably was no real danger; the wall was in good repair and came nearly breast high to us boys.

Suddenly Seamus froze in the act of throwing out a shell. His other hand grabbed my elbow. I thought instantly that he was falling somehow and reached to steady him. "Look!" he gasped.

Following his staring gaze, Jack and I both peered out to sea through the darting flock. At first I could not credit my eyes, but Jack lost no time in springing away down the stairs. I shook off Seamus's clutch, pushed him ahead of me, and we threw ourselves down the steps as the first brass clanging of the alarm bell at the top of the round tower shattered the glow of the holiday.

Pirates had come to Inishbuffin. So the raven had known what he was about, after all.

Chapter 7

By the time we skidded through the kitchen door, Brother Cook was already pushing Jack before him and untying his apron one-handed. "To the tower, lads, quickly now," he urged.

"Where's the master?" I demanded, following after them.

The Dina pitched his apron on a table in the refectory as we sped through. "Master is where he is. Get to the tower and help the families with young children up the stairs."

"But where is Master Bruchan?" I repeated urgently. The old man had bought my dagger, and I aimed to stand by him.

Cook pushed me, not roughly but firmly, after Seamus and Jack across the crowded courtyard outside the dining hall. "Master will stay with the men, boy, where else? Go to safety and it will ease his mind. You cannot help us much until you are trained to arms as we are. Go!"

It was a sensible argument, and I saw that I really couldn't do much that Dinan couldn't, so I gave the man a half salute and ran for the tower, anxiously keeping an eye out for Gynt and Kevyn, who would have to come up the hill from the village with their masters' families. The bell was still clanging and with the screaming of the little children and the air of frightened but purposeful activity of the adults, it was enough to dry the inside of my mouth and make my knees not quite right. Please, raven, stay away from my masters and my friends, and take someone I don't know, if thee must take any at all, I prayed selfishly, confusedly falling into the gentle "thee" of the skellig.

At the tower, the ladder had been let down from the only entrance, the open door which was set twenty feet above our heads as we milled in the courtyard beneath it. The smallest children were passed from hand to willing hand, two men stationed on the ladder itself, another at both ends, and some of the women already up in the tower to receive the tots. There was some confusion, but not much: it was evident that the folk of the skellig had done this many times before.

Thyr and Ruan passed by me, running from the direction of the kitchen—of course, I realized, they would have been down seeing that the cargo door was secure—and called some words of encouragement to me that I did not catch in the din. I could not see Nestor or Padraig or Bruchan. The littlest children were all in, and now the women and middle children had formed a line to climb the ladder to the sanctuary of the stout tower. "Boy! Help with this!" a deep voice roared behind me.

I turned, and Symon motioned impatiently for me to grasp one handle of a large carved chest. I did so, stifled the rasp of my ribs, and a way opened for us through the throng of mothers and their children, so that we climbed with the heavy trunk into the tower very quickly. It was dark inside after the late-afternoon sun and before my eyes had time to adjust, someone put a helpful hand under my elbow and guided me onto the planked wooden floor. "Is that the last of them?" the unknown brother asked Symon.

The weaponsmaster nodded, but added, "But there's one more trip."

"I'll be standing by with thy good pike, then, at our regular station," the brother told him.

Symon clapped him on the shoulder and turned me for the opening. "Come, Aengus, there's something you may do for the master."

I followed him without question. We climbed a few rungs down, then jumped from the side to make room for those coming up. Trotting beside the powerful man as we ran out of the courtyard and toward the workshop block, I clapped a hand to my side and asked, "Is the master somewhere safe?"

Symon gave me the look you give an exasperating idiot. "Himself is here, boy, what more is to say?" I shut up and followed as he led me past the apothecary. Nestor was there gathering a satchel of medicines. He looked up at our footsteps. "Aengus! Take this with you to the tower." He thrust the satchel into my arms, I touched my chest in the sign of respect and raced after Symon.

He had gone through a door in the angle of the workshop block and the barn. I would have recognized the steps by touch alone and darted up the winding stair. I knew now where he was going. He turned as I came through the door in Bruchan's study, a small plain box in one hand and the sword stick in the other. The box he thrust out to me. "Keep it in your tunic, next to your heart. Let none, even of our own brethren, know that you have it."

I dropped it down the front of my garment. "Shall I wrap it in the bindings?" I asked smartly, but I forgot that Symon had no way of knowing, so he merely glanced sharply at me and then passed the remark over, having too much else on his mind. "How about the pipe or the tapestry? Shouldn't they be moved to the tower?"

"Not time enough," he answered. "And anyway, Himself would never hear of his pipe taking up room that a child might have had. The tapestry is a pity, though." He jerked a thumb toward the stairs, clearly ordering me out to safety.

I lingered. "Can you, all of you . . ." I found the words thick in my throat suddenly. "Beat them back?"

The weaponsmaster ruffled among some slates and papers on Bruchan's small writing desk, found what he was looking for, and cocked an eye at me. " 'Tis not the first time these fellows have paid a visit, Aengus. We are still here. Go now."

"Warmth," I said, and his eyes lifted back to me, surprised, before I whirled and ran down the winding stair.

The place had gone curiously quiet, only a few hurrying men going purposefully to their stations, weapons in their hands. I ran past the workshops and was in the courtyard when I was hailed. Gwynt caught up with me. They had brought the horses up within the walls, he said, panting as we made our way toward the tower. "Are the pirates landed yet?" I asked him.

"Oh, aye!" he gasped. "Coming up the cliff walk as fast as their filthydwarfish legs can take them!"

"Dwarfs!"

"Aye," he said grimly. He had no need to say more; the cruelty of dwarven pirates was the subject of a hundred tales, something we of the Burren learned at the breast.

They had waited with the ladder down for us, the last two of the boys unaccounted for, and now hands fairly hurled us up the rungs. We stumbled across the threshold, lurched into more hands, women's hands, which steadied and redirected us, and found ourselves as our eyes adjusted on the crowded first floor of the tower. The ladder was swiftly drawn up after us, the thick door slammed, and the bolts driven home. Darkness, save for the thin light finding its way through chinks in the stone or down from the upper floors, where there were window slits and the belfry to let in both light and air. A child cried out somewhere above and was shushed. "I feel like an ass, cooped up here with the women and children," Gwynt whispered in my ear.

I nodded. "Makes you want to pay attention to Master Symon's lessons, for truth. Maybe next time there's trouble, we might be of some use."

I felt more than saw him scramble to his feet. "I'm going to see if I can make it to a window or the roof," he said. "I've got to know what's happening out there!"

We stepped carefully in the dimness toward the ladder we could see rising in the center of the floor. "Mind thee watch the stair going down," a woman's soft voice advised. " 'Tis just to thy right there."

I could see it now she had drawn my attention to it. This would be the ladder down to the water barrels and stores of food on the first level below us, and the privy scuppers on the lowest level, even with the ground outside.

Gwynt stepped past me and quickly climbed the ladder, and I as quickly followed. On every floor, each growing progressively smaller as the round tower narrowed toward its top, the women gathered their children around them, talking quietly, singing softly, muting the fear. We met a few adventurous little lads who wanted to run up and down the ladders but were scolded from doing so. Their eyes followed us as we went toward the roof. On the third floor there were narrow windows, but we could not get near them for the older women and half-grown boys clustered about each narrow strip of light. People were quieter here, but I could hear no clash of weapons from outside yet. "What's happening out there?" Gwynt paused on the ladder to ask of the room in general.

"Dwarfs," came back several voices. "The dwarfs are in the village."

My friend began to climb once more. At the next floor, the one immediately below the roof, we found Kevyn amongst the older boys and eeled our way through the webwork of roof timbers to him. Beside him stood an elderly brother, who, judging by the wood shavings that dusted his gray robe and canvas apron, must be the father or perhaps father-in-law of Kevyn's carpentry master. He stood peering intently out one of the four wide windows that faced in the directions of the jetty, Gull's Cove, the Caldron, and out over the village. A sword hung in the scabbard he had strapped on over his apron, and the rope of the alarm bell hung loosely from his hand. His charge must be the defense of the tower, should it come to that, or the all-clear peal if events went well. His eyes were sharp under bushy gray brows, and he and Kevyn were looking the same place. I craned for a view over their shoulders.

"Are they fighting yet?" Gwynt asked, stretching his tall frame to find a view.

The old man answered without taking his eyes from the window, "Nay. The dwarfs do not come nigh the lower wall yet. They go in and out of the houses first to see what they might find to their liking."

Kevyn turned his chin on his shoulder, his eyes somber. "They took Conor's dog: I saw a couple of them leading it back down to their ship."

The old man's gnarled hand found our friend's shoulder. "Hush now," he chided gently. "That's hard news, sure, but 'tis only the dog they got, not the boy himself. We must not make a tragedy out of one gone dog, though 'twas a pretty bitch. Likely they'll breed her for the pups she'll throw, so she'll be treated well, never fear. The dwarfs know their hounds."

I had found an angle now and could just spy out the two lower walls of the skellig and a glimpse of the main street of the village with some of its houses. As the old man had said, the dwarfs were going in and out of the homes, their arms already laden with booty: woven rugs and blankets, chickens, fine basket work, some pottery, and no doubt a quantity of personal ornaments such as combs, brooches, and finger rings. I could not restrain an oath when I saw them prodding along the road two cows that someone had left grazing in a field.

The old man glanced at me and a smile twitched his wiry gray beard. "Thee thinks some oaf should have looked after the skellig's cows better, eh? Well, do not fault ere thee know a thing: those two be our oldest cows, not good to last the winter, and Master Bruchan left them for the pirates to find. How do thee think on that?"

"Clever," I admitted, abashed.

He chortled, coughed, and spat out the window. "Aye, he's father and grandfather to a fox, is our Bruchan. 'Tisn't often that he's o'ermatched for wits, and he won't be by this paltry crew." He indicated the dwarven pirates with a jut of his beard. Then his eyes narrowed, and he said, "They'd best not think to disturb our fruit trees or the hay fields, if they know what's good for them."

Evidently, the dwarfs had enough to fill their bellies and their ships, perhaps having freshly come from raiding other settlements along the coast, because they did not advance into the fields or orchards at all. I was mildly surprised at this, but too relieved overall to give it much thought at the time. After a while, I watched as the main body of the pirate force withdrew along the path to the cliff walk. A few of the invaders were left, taking what appeared to be a last leisurely look around. I saw one of them working over something that seemed to be a bundle of straw in the street. "What's . . . ?" I began to ask.

Fire flared from the sparks he had struck into the straw, and I knew then that the pirates would leave their ugly mark. I swore unconsciously, and the old carpenter echoed it. The man who had lit the fire stuck a torch into it, got that going, and then walked deliberately toward the last house on the street, one that stood at some remove from the others, and tossed the torch up onto the thatch roof. Out of bowshot below our last gate, one of the dwarfs, probably their captain, mockingly threw an obscene gesture up at where Bruchan and our men watched, turned on his heel, and with the rest of his crew trotted off toward their waiting ships, though perhaps a sling stone had caught him, for he limped. The fire leaped hungrily behind them.

Hard as it must have been, Bruchan restrained our folk from running down to try to put out the fire until we had seen from the tower the pirates row their ships out and set sail. Then the old carpenter rang the all-clear, and people poured out of the round tower and off the walls to get the line of buckets going. By the Power's blessing, the fire did not spread far; we lost only two houses, and that was not nearly as bad as things could have been, except of course for the families involved. But there was already immediate talk of holding house raisings for them as soon as materials could be gathered, and being part of a community such as the skellig meant that they should not go hungry in the coming months, though both had lost their vegetable plots and household stores of oil, dried fruit, and grain.

After the fires were safely out, the doused embers being watched over by teams of boys alert for the slightest flare-up, people went to their own homes to see what needed mending, salvaging, or crying over. The dwarfs had carried off much good weaving, and that would hurt in the cold months; I heard many women talking about how the loss could be made up in the quickest time. Conor was miserable over his dog, though he tried for other people's sake not to grieve openly. Perhaps the most damaging thing the dwarfs had done was to carry off a quantity of iron tools—stoneworking hammers, tongs, a cask of nails. These were virtually irreplaceable over the short term because of the smelting and working of metal that would have to be done, and they were all items needed for the construction of the new barn. They would have to be gotten from somewhere, people agreed.

A long while after dark that night, candle lanterns went to and fro among the houses, neighbor visiting neighbor to see if they were missing something which could be supplied between the two households. I watched from the place on the second wall where I had sat the evening before with Bruchan and thought that I had never seen a more peaceful place. Well, the peace could be shattered at a moment's notice, as I had seen that day, but all in all we had not come out of it so badly. No children were taken for slaves, no women raped, no men murdered.

The raven had squawked himself hoarse for nothing.

I grinned to myself in the darkness and sent a pebble spinning out over the hay field below me.

* * *

The lovely weather broke during the night into the more usual fog and light rain, chilly and damp, true Burren summer. As there was special work to be done, we boys did not go to our weapons lesson or to our workshops. Instead, like nearly every able-bodied person in the skellig, we went down to the village and helped the two families who had been burned out to rebuild their houses.

The wreckage was cleared, salvaging what could be used again, the floors smoothed, and the stout posts reset. Since these pirate raids were not an infrequent event, I was told, the community kept some quantity of building material safely on hand within the skellig walls. So the wattle to weave in and out among the posts was waiting, and as soon as some of the brothers hauled it down on the flat haywagons, the house raisings began in earnest. Everyone took a hand at the weaving, making certain the twigs were secure and the wall stout enough to take the daub. As the weaving of the lower walls was completed and taller folk took up the weaving of the upper walls, we boys and others began stuffing straw into the interlacing of the wattle, making this insulation as tight as we could to cut down on the winter drafts. Finally the walls were ready to daub. This is a smelly job—to work best, the mixture of straw, mud, and cow dung should be fresh—but everyone worked with a will, no shirkers in this lot. Anyone who felt inclined to slip off for too long to answer a call of nature had the example of Masters Bruchan and Ruan before his eyes. The two brothers did not scorn to get their hands dirty; indeed, I know my own young back ached with the bending and stretching long before either of my masters could be prevailed upon to give up his place at the wall long enough to drink a cup of tea.

The day went very quickly, both because of the steady work we were doing and also because the passage of time was very difficult to judge in the fog. While those of us who had daubed swilled the remnants of the weather-tightening mixture off our hands and sponged it from our rain-beaded clothing, the thatchers went to work. The lashed rafters with the crosspieces that would form a base for the roofs of both houses were already in place. The ladders went up, the bundles of long straw were passed up, and the men began putting the roofs on. There was a continual call for green sticks, sharpened on both ends, and we boys whittled as fast as our daggers could work to keep up with them. As each bundle of straw was lapped over the row already laid down, it was secured in place by bending one of the green sticks in half till it just cracked, and jamming both ends of it down into the thatch, rather like a woman's hairpin or the staples I have seen some wandering merchants use to stake out a tent. Then the next course of straw was laid down to cover the pegging so that no rain would find its way in along the stick.

Last of all, two large nets were brought down from the storerooms—Brother Ruan claiming that they were his best two and pretending to grumble to give some sport to the day—and with a giant heave-ho these were cast over the new roofing and weighted with fist-sized stones all along the edges to keep portions of the straw from being lifted up by the fierce gales to come.

At length, when the sun was setting somewhere behind the fog, two new houses stood upon the foundations of the old ones, stout homes against the drizzling rain. I stood with my fists on my hips and nodded with satisfaction. "Well, there are two families that will sleep snug tonight," I observed to Gwynt.

Conor, standing nearby with the old master from the round tower who had indeed proved to be his grandfather, overheard my remark. "Oh, no!" he said in a shocked voice. "They can't move in until there's a Fire blessing."

"Thee forgets," his grandfather chided. "Aengus does not know our ways yet." To me, he explained, "We bless each hearth, lad, so that the family which gathers there may be kept from harm and steady in their love for each other and the Four."

"The Four?"

I had spoken in a normal tone of voice, but several people nearby suddenly interrupted their own conversations and looked first to me and then to the grandfather. One of them murmured something that sounded like, "Have care, Brother," and the old carpenter flushed and pulled at his beard.

He cleared his throat. "Conor, I mind me that I told thy father this morning we would do the milking for him tonight. Do thee go fetch the cow, please. Aengus, thee will excuse us for now?" They melted quickly off through the crowd of people into the mist.

Plainly here was a secret no outsider was to stumble upon. The folk of the skellig had no way of knowing that Bruchan had already given me hints of it, though I was still baffled. Four? Four what?

The dinner bell rang clear down the hill

through the fog, and its summons was welcome. With others, I began to walk up to supper. Gwynt had disappeared somewhere, and I was disappointed until I saw him some way ahead walking next to a shawled girl and her mother. Aha, the farrier's daughter, I thought. Flax-Hair, you rascal, here's a topic for teasing!

I was smiling wickedly to myself when I became aware of a step just behind me. I glanced back over my shoulder.

"Careful, careful!" Cathir said with concern as I stumbled. "The rocks and grass are slippery with the wet. So, Aengus, I have not had the chance to welcome you to Inishbuffin. I am Brother Cathir." He nodded in friendly fashion.

You are a murderer, the dark voice hissed at him from behind my eyes. I did my best for Bruchan's sake not to let him see anything other than an indentured boy's shyness before one in authority. "Thank you, Brother," I heard myself say. You snake . . .

"How do you find our community?"

"I am glad to be learning a trade I can use later, Brother." That was true.

Just for a moment there was something in the depths of his eyes. A whirlpool in a caldron . . . "Indeed," he agreed. "An herbalist is much in demand no matter where he goes."

"Aye, and it's the sort of training I never could have hoped for at home." Also true.

"Ah, no doubt. And where might that have been? Home, I mean?"

It seemed a casual enough question, but knowing what I did about him, I remembered Bruchan's warning. Now what the hell had my old master instructed me to answer? No, it was my mother's village I could not reveal.

We had walked several steps meantime, and Cathir was now frowning at me. I answered, "It's a little difficult to call any place home, Brother. My father drank a lot, and we . . . had to keep moving." Not true, but I did not regret the lie.

His frown clearing as he thought he understood that I was a beggar's son, the stout man nodded. "Well, you will find that we do not hold a boy's past against him here. Taking each for an individual, it is his talents that are of interest to us."

Perilous ground. I gave him what I hoped passed for an innocent look. "Brother Nestor says that he may be able to make a middling fair healer out of me."

I thought a flash of irritation came and went across that oily face, but I may have imagined it. "Does he?" the administrator of the skellig murmured. "You're fortunate to have such a patient master."

"I am," I agreed. "But I have found all the masters patient, so far."

Now there was a definite glint of amusement in the eyes and the crow's-feet deepened. "Fire grant that you find it always so. Your pardon; there's someone I must talk to."

I touched my hand to my breast, and he walked swiftly away through the straggling groups as we came up through the middle gate. I pursed my lips and whistled silently.

When I walked under the arch in the main wall, Finian, again the door ward, caught my eye and beckoned. I stepped aside with him. "Someone waits for thee in thy workshop," he whispered. "Go there before thee go in to supper."

I could feel the hairs rise on the back of my wet neck, and a chill that was not all due to the damp crawled down my back. "What's the big secret?"

He gave me a blank look. "For that no ears may hear," he explained in a puzzled voice.

I gave it up, brushed the hair out of my eyes, and, almost glad that the whoreson was finally being so open as to lure me to an ambush this way, strode across the courtyard to the work-shop block. I paused at the entrance to the por-tico, took a good look around, and edged my dagger from its sheath. Keeping the wall at my back, I slunk down the outside hall, past the armorer's shop, past the carpenter's, until I reached the window of the apothecary. I ducked under the sill so that my shadow should not cross his line of vision, straightened on the other side, and let my anger propel me around the doorjamb, knife leveled.

"Never lead with thy knife, boy, it gives thy enemy too much chance to kick it from thy hand at no great risk to himself, thus." A soft-booted foot shot out of the dark of the unlit shop, and Bruchan knocked the blade from my hand that was already beginning to drop.

Disgustedly I bent to retrieve it. "What's the proper way, then, just in case the next sum-mons to an ambush isn't from you?"

He laughed softly. "Lead with thy empty hand, reserving thy weapon near thy body. That way, when he kicks, thee has knowledge of where his groin must be."

I sheathed my dagger, wincing. "Ow."

"Aye, it is not for play, that trick. It is a kill-ing stroke if thy knife finds the large blood way. But I did not call thee here to teach thee fight-ing, having only the few moments to spare be-fore they look for me up in the dining hall. I

must go on a venture tomorrow. Would thee
like to come?"

I didn't even know where he was going; I
didn't care. "Of course!"

My master laughed again. "Thee will have to
work doubly hard at thy lessons the day after,
I warn thee!"

"That's the day after." I shrugged.

Outlined against the door as I was, he must
have seen, for his voice was amused. "At the
rising bell, then, make ready in haste and leave
through the front gates, using the pretext that
thee are carrying a message to thy young carpenter friend from Padraig."

"Kevyn?" I questioned.

"Aye; Kevyn. This will give thee reason to go
to the village in early morning. Once there, thee
will walk out the main road, thy collecting basket over thy arm. What plants has Nestor taught
thee?"

"Foxglove and seaweed. We've only had the
one lesson, don't forget," I added defensively.

"I said nothing, boy. Go collecting foxglove,
then, if any should ask thee. I will meet thee
somewhere on the road near the village, if the
fog holds as I think it will. If the weather should
clear, the road dips into a hollow about a mile
past the last house. There will I meet thee to go
on our venture. Do me the courtesy of not leading with thy knife." Even in the dimness, his
eyes twinkled.

I touched my breast, and he slipped past me
out the door, moving so silently that I could not
hear the slightest scuff of his boots against the
stone paving outside.

I went up to my supper of hot soup and left-
over bread with the tiredness of today and the

intrigue of tomorrow giving a fine edge to my appetite.

How could we have thought that the fog would lift?

As I picked my way down the cart path through the gates the next morning, the thick mist was blowing across the walls and through the thatched buildings of the skellig in visible currents that eddied and streamed across the land, carrying the smells of salt, turf fires, and wet wool. I hunched my cloak around me and wiped the moisture from my face, the osier basket bumping against my hip at every step.

The gates were already open for the day, and I had no difficulty in passing through. One of the brothers on his way into the cow barn gave me a smile. "Nestor has thee at it early, eh?"

"Aye," I told him with a wry face, and he laughed.

Down in the village was here and there the squall of an infant or the complaining of a young child made to wash in cold water, with over all the aromas of porridge and oat cakes. I patted a dog that came gamboling to sniff at the hem of my robe, faced down a goose that wanted right-of-way in the road, and scattered a flock of hens pecking about in the trail of hay leading to the two new houses which stood silent and empty for now.

The road led between its bordering stone walls past an orchard—I knew it was there, though I could not see it in the fog—then over the wooden bridge which spanned a boggy area that I surmised might be flooded in the spring. Once across this, I was outside the village proper and into the hinterland of Skellig Inishbuffin, an area of open grazing for sheep on the sparse turf that patched over the rock bones of the peninsula, for cutting peat, for fowling. From the wall of the skellig, I had glimpsed solitary huts dotting this rolling land, but it was not the sort of place most people would choose to settle in, given the choice of being closer to the protection of the skellig walls, and anyway the only people on the peninsula were those who belonged to the community. These huts were mostly used for overnight stays, and by the shepherds, hardy men who took the unenviable job of watching over the skellig's flocks while they grazed the summer pasturage. In the fog this early morning, I met none of them on the road, but I could hear the tinkling of the bellwethers all around.

My paces slowed. Surely this was far enough from the village for Bruchan to have stationed himself to meet me. He had said *close* to the village, in fact. I was certainly not close to the village, even allowing for the way the fog seemed to stretch distances. Stopping in the road, I tilted my head to listen.

Almost immediately I heard it: a slither and slip of leather boot on rough stone off to my right, then silence. Not Bruchan, I thought— master would never deliberately scare me with so cheap a trick. My heart began to thud. Should I go on, hoping to make it there on my own if the fellow off in the fog didn't try to kill me first? If I met Bruchan, wouldn't that give us both away?

The latter thought decided me. I turned about, for the stalker's benefit swearing fairly loudly about not being able to see a damn thing in the fog, much less pick damn foxglove leaves, and if Nestor wanted the bloody things, why didn't he come out after them himself? Then I retraced my steps briskly, as though I'd had enough of being an indentured boy under his master's orders. Beneath my cloak, my hand was on my dagger. I strained to hear over my own footsteps, but that was impossible. My back felt exactly like an archery target.

I stopped suddenly. He was behind me and to the right still, off the road, and it took him a moment to realize that I had halted, for he came on a step before he stopped. I swore at my boot thong to give him a reasonable explanation for why I wasn't walking. Very carefully I set the wide basket down in the road; I wanted no encumbrance. As I straightened, a hand clapped over my mouth and an iron grip trapped my dagger hand. I writhed, threw an elbow into his chest, and butted my head back. One brown eye, one blue within a slate gray hood. Angrily I glared over his silencing hand.

Bruchan let go my dagger hand, raised a finger to his lips in a warning to be silent, and released me. He picked up the basket, handed it to me, and made an "over and over" or "more" motion. I caught on and gave a hearty curse and something about the damn things always letting go when you were miles from home and not an extra boot thong in sight. Master nodded vigorously, pointing down the road *away* from the village. He beckoned, walking cat-footed in the left-hand verge of the road. I sighed aloud, stamped my feet as though putting my boot back on after fixing it, and reckoned loudly that I'd be in for a whipping if I didn't get at least a few of the beastly plants for Nestor to see. At Bruchan's nod, I walked down the middle of the road, the flesh crawling beneath my damp robe. The game was dangerous; the stakes too high for losing. I had every faith in Master, but any man may make a mistake, so I kept my hand on my dagger hilt.

It seemed to be Bruchan's plan to lure the stalker on until we reached some place better designed for my master to ambush the ambusher, for we went some distance further on. I noticed at some point that the walls to either side of the road had fallen away and except for the wagon ruts that marked the rough track there was nothing to distinguish it from a sheep trail. When next I thought to look, the wagon ruts were gone. Bruchan must have led me off on one of the branching tracks, and we were now going cross-country to the right of the original road, as nearly as I could ascertain. I could see his shadowy figure just visible a few feet ahead of me, still slightly to my left, so whatever he heard of the follower must have told him that our spy was still to the right of us. But why was Bruchan allowing the fellow to come with us? Surely there were better ways of dealing with one of Jorem's sneaks than to take him on a hike across half of Inishbuffin peninsula! I swallowed an impatient sigh, stumbled on a stone, and cursed resignedly. I fancied Bruchan looked back and smiled, but I could scarcely make out his features in the draping fog.

I saw his hand suddenly rise, though; I saw that clearly and froze in my tracks. From out in the opaque mist right of us came a soft thud, a quick splash, and a horrible, gargling scream cut short. Ice shot through my blood, and my knife was out of my dagger without the thinking about it.

Ahead of me Bruchan had gone rigid at the thud and by the time that awful cry abruptly ended, he was already running toward where the sounds had come from. I was damned if I'd be left alone in that smothering mist, so I ran after him.

I caught my foot again on a tussock of rough grass and pitched full-length onto the spongy turf. When I began to get up, my hands pushed into the mire, and a flicker of panic lighted at the pit of my stomach, but I hauled myself to my feet and lurched after my master. I nearly ran into him. "No, don't look!" he said quickly. " 'Tis too horrible!"

But I was already under his arm and very close to the brink of the bog hole myself. His strong grip hauled me back to safety, which was as well, because at that moment I could not have done it for myself. My eyes took it all in, and my stomach did a slow roll.

The man's head was half under, the rest of him save for one arm already sunken out of sight. His wide eyes stared up through the vault of the sky, his mouth was frozen in that last yell, and it had been the dark brown bog water that he had gargled. There was something clutched in his fist that under the slime may have been a strip of cloth.

Though there was little recognizable in that contorted rictus, I knew him. "Mallory."

Bruchan's hands on my shoulders were trembling. "Aye," he breathed. "Poor lad."

I snorted. "The poor lad was set on murdering us, don't forget."

His voice was flinty enough to make me involuntarily cringe when he answered, "I do not forget, Aengus, but I remember him when he

was as young as thee, and I tell thee he was
not a bad boy then."

There was no answer for that, and I prudently—for once—held my tongue.

Bruchan lifted his head. "There is no more
to do here just now. Do thee go back to the
road—it is thirty-four paces that way—" He
pointed. "And I will cover our tracks. When
the search is made for him, it will not do to
have so many prints in this soft earth. Nay, say
no more word against him, boy, I will not hear
it." His eyes were angry. I had been going to
apologize for my hasty remark, but I couldn't
now. Silently, I left him and began counting off
my paces.

I waited for him on the road, which was exactly where he had said it would be. When Bruchan came out of the bog, his face was grim,
but I knew it was no longer for me when he
brushed some mud from my cloak and his hand
paused for a moment on my head like a benedic-
tion. The fog seemed to break for me, though in
reality it had gotten thicker, if that was possible.
"I was going to say I was sorry," I murmured.

"And so am I. For many things. Come, it is
not much farther, but I beg thee to leave me
silent. I have much to ponder, and not much
solitary time in which to do it. Thee understands, Aengus?" he asked softly.

I nodded.

We went forward on our "venture" with only
the smells of bog, and salt, and wet wool for
company.

Chapter 8

"Hold a moment," Bruchan said. I drew up next to him, and we listened. I heard nothing but the far-off bleating of a sheep and the somewhat closer surge of the sea. I glanced up at my master. He was frowning as he listened, but eventually his brow smoothed and he nodded, though he signaled that we should be quiet from this point on. I nodded, and he went before me.

We were coming to some rise of the ground; the wind was cut a bit, and if I strained my eyes, I could just make out something substantial that rose up ahead of us in a broad swell in the fog. A few steps further on I was surprised to be confronted not with a natural hill, but with a man-made wall that grew out of the turf so gradually and so neatly it seemed to be part of the earth itself. We turned and walked along the base of this, and it grew to a height over our heads by at least four feet. Squinting up in the drizzling mist, I saw that the wall was surmounted by turf. It was a barrow, then. My feet halted of their own accord, and I made the sign of protection against the Hag. Not even for Bruchan would I enter a grave.

He looked over his shoulder inquiringly, having heard me stop, and saw my hand up, fingers crossed in the sign. A flash of irritation came and went in his face, and he shook his head, probably at my ignorance. He walked away from me, following the curving wall into the fog.

The old man had me there; I wasn't going to stand outside a barrow in the fog. I might as well at least go to the entrance with him. Nothing wrong with that. I hurried after him.

The wall took an abrupt corner, and the master of Inishbuffin was waiting for me before what appeared to be a carved threshold, a huge block of stone, squared, and incised with the four spirals that I had hitherto only seen on our brooches. I dropped my protective hand sign, adopted an outward calm that had nothing to do with the butterflies in my gut, and walked to meet him with as much nonchalance as I could summon. "So this is the place of your rituals," I whispered.

He was looking down at me with speculation. " 'Tis that and more," he confirmed in a normal tone. At my quick glance, he added, "There is no one here but ourselves. Thee may speak freely."

"You worship in a barrow?" I had not intended the squeak in my voice.

He smiled. "Thee need fear no evil wights: this be no dead man's chamber."

I began to relax, and he put a hand to the stone, tracing the spirals with his index finger. I could not tell if this was a ritual gesture, or merely appreciation of the craftsmanship, but I said nothing till he had done. "Are we . . . is it permitted for me to go in with you?"

"Would thee prefer to remain out here alone, enemy eyes maybe watching?" he teased.

"Nay, 'tis safe enough for thee to come as far as the anteroom with me. Thee shall remain there, for it is not permitted the uninitiated to go further. I must obtain something here for the Fire ritual to bless the new homes," he explained. "Also," his voice softened, "I feel the need to pray awhile. Maybe in this hallowed place, I may find guidance to set our course."

"Um ... " I licked my lips. "I don't think such places are for the likes of me, master. Maybe I had better stay outside."

He smiled the shining smile I have seen from him once or twice before. "Oh, thee are most welcome here, boy, I assure thee."

He still didn't get it, so I took the bull by the horns and asked him directly, "Look, is there a wolf in there? I've heard that wolves are part of your rituals."

His eyes were steady. "There are no wolves on Inishbuffin, Aengus, neither the beasts nor the human variety. Will thee come in?" He gave me a moment to think about it, then climbed over the threshold stone.

Awkwardly I clambered after and caught up with him just inside the entrance. He smiled at me approvingly, reaching over my head to touch one of the stones. This grated back a finger's length, and a snick—of a lock, perhaps?—echoed to us from deep in the mound. "Thus we protect our sanctuary from enemies," the master said. "A trap is set for the unknowing."

Was he warning me off from returning on my own, assuming that I could somehow find the way? He needn't have worried; the gooseflesh covered me like a case of the pox. "There's no light," I said, my voice falling by instinct into

a whisper as I peered into the rough passageway.

"There is none in the hall itself," he agreed,
"but thee will find thy eyes adjusting. In the
antechamber is a light, and it will guide us on."
So saying, he stooped and entered the passage.

I gulped a swallow of air and followed.

The unmortared blocks of stone were dry to
my trembling touch and the floor smoothed.
Whoever had built this place had taken care to
make it watertight. The passage quickly narrowed at the height of my head, Bruchan's
shoulders, so that we were crowded into a
sideways hunch to make our way at all. The
weight of the stones above, tons of stone, all
the bones of the earth, pressed down upon my
head. Freezing terror shot through me and my
breath would not come. I dropped to my knees,
turning to bolt out the way we had come.

Bruchan touched my shoulder. "Peace, lad,
peace. The place has stood for ages of the
world and seen many pilgrims before now.
Does thee think 'twill choose this moment to
collapse?"

Well, no, probably not, I thought and fought
down the fear. But it was a battle.

He led me on. I did not think to count the
steps, but possibly it was not a long way. I began to see light beyond his silhouetted form.
At last he stepped out into a place where the
roof leaped up off my head, and the stones
drew back, giving me room to breathe. I sucked
a lungful of air and looked about.

We were standing in a chamber shaped like
a barrel sawed in half, with high above me—at
least thirty feet—the capstone where the barrel end would have been. As Bruchan had

promised, there was light here: to the left of
the passageway from which we had just
emerged, a huge chunk of what looked to be
alabaster had been smoothed and hollowed to
hold oil and a wick of moss. This cast a soft
golden glow over the carvings which decorated
most of the rock surfaces. These were shapes
and forms only, no animals or figures that I
could recognize, mostly the spirals or a series
of diamonds. There were four low lintels to entrances of other passages or rooms leading
from this antechamber, two directly ahead and
one to either side at right angles. The lintels
were so low I could not see much beyond them
and it would not be seemly to stoop and peer
in, but there was a single motif above each of
these entrances. Above the one to my left were
chiseled three parallel wavy lines that may
have represented water. To my right the motif
was, I thought, a leaf. Of the two ahead of me,
one showed a circle and rays, obviously the
sun, and the other was engraved with jagged
vertical lines that I did not comprehend.

"The Four," Conor's grandfather had
blurted. They did indeed worship four Powers
here.

Bruchan had watched me. "Thee's disturbed."

My breath was a little short again, and I was
hiding the sign against evil in the fold of my
cloak. "One hears the old stories, b-but I didn't
think people still worshiped this way. Aren't
you afraid of the Fire's wrath, giving such
honor to the Hag, the Ill Wind, and the Fickle
Friend?" (So we named the Powers you Ilyrians call Ritnym of the Earth, Aashis of the
Winds, and Tychanor the Warm.)

"No," he said simply.

I was stunned at this blasphemy, and I know that my mouth fell open.

"Aengus, our Fire is the eldest Power, and thus we revere him as being first and mightiest in all things, but Tydranth has Siblings, Powers in their own right, to whom he entrusted the governance of parts of the earth and of life."

Now, everybody in the Burren knows the Name of the Fire, but it is never—never—spoken aloud. I bit my lips and winced, expecting at any moment the barrel vault to come crashing down on us.

Bruchan seemed unaware of the terrible thing he had done and went on. "The Hag who takes men to her underworld realm also makes the earth to bear fruit and grain for us. The Ill Wind blows not only storms, but also the breeze that warms the land in the spring and the thoughts that run through a man's head, as well as stars and sea creatures. And the Fickle Friend, Tydranth's younger twin, makes the sun to shine and love to blossom between a young man and a young woman, though he is in other ways a chancy friend, for mischief turning brother against brother and playing tricks on people. For their gifts, should we not honor these Powers, hoping to encourage their goodwill toward us of earth?"

I gulped. "You don't think the Fire minds?"

"I think he tries the hearts of men, burning off the dross in the crucible of his Flame, so he may know that what is left is true metal apt for his shaping and tempering. How could the Lord Flame find deserving of his help the man who does not honor the other Powers as they carry out his plans?"

His quiet, confident voice calmed the shivers in me. "I will think on it, master, while you go about your work."

"Do so, lad, and be not afraid to take knowledge where it is offered. Wisdom is not necessarily a hurtful thing. Wait for me here, or go back up to the entrance if thee prefer. Do not venture outside, though."

"Aye, master."

He nodded, bent almost double, and went into the doorway marked with the wavy lines. At once the antechamber seemed—was it my imagination?—much colder and utterly silent. I had never experienced such quiet before. At first it frightened me, so that I snapped my fingers to be sure I had not suddenly been stricken deaf, but gradually I found it calming. In fact, the steady golden light, the perfect carvings, and the sand floor all combined to give me a sense of security. Perhaps it was merely a delayed reaction to the danger and death I had seen out there on the bog, but I began to fancy that this solid chamber was utterly peaceful, a haven.

I could hear nothing from Bruchan, no chanting, no words of prayer, but doubtless the old man would not be so free in his ritual as he would if alone in the temple. My hand freed itself of the sign against evil, and feeling a bit sheepish, I rubbed my nose, settled my back against the wall, and composed myself to wait for my master.

But, you know, it is a very difficult thing to be alone in a secret place, a place of obvious mystery and not a little attraction, without

feeling intense curiosity about what is done in
that place. The low lintels, each with its little
rough square of darkness beneath and carved
motif above, were passive, waiting. True, he
had told me that the uninitiated weren't supposed to go further than the antechamber
where I now stood, but hadn't he also said that
he'd take me with him to the ritual at the turn
of summer into fall? Aye, he had. So there
could be nothing so terrible in it, it was just a
matter of timing. He might punish me with a
dressing-down and some extra chores, but then
again, maybe not: he'd been surprisingly forth-
right about their religion so far. I pursed my
lips, studying the carved motifs. The leaf was
for the Hag, and that way I would not go; wild
horses couldn't have dragged me. And I wasn't
cheeky enough to walk right into Lord Flame's
sanctuary, just in case he really didn't care for
all this attention to his Siblings. Bruchan had
taken Water, the Ill Wind's door. That left the
Fickle Friend to me. I took a breath, crossed
my fingers, and hoped the chancy Power was
feeling amiable today.

I went in.

Immediately I perceived why the passages
appeared so dark; this one, at least, bent
sharply left not more than three crouching
paces past the lintel. I eased myself around the
rough corner, being careful not to brush the
stones (the thought of other traps had belat-
edly occurred to me), and there was the
faintest of lights before me, beckoning me on.
Another few paces and I emerged into a shallow chamber, much smaller than the antechamber, and much darker. There was no torch
or candle here, and I strained my eyes, trying

to see what gave the light. A small vessel that my fingers identified as a kind of flat dish or saucer seemed filled with a powder that barely glimmered. I thought perhaps it was the kind of phosphorescence that you see on fish scales sometimes, and I dipped my finger into it experimentally to see if I could see the outline held up against the darkness.

All at once the light flared and grew before my startled eyes, the powder grains spilling from one side of the divided dish into the oil well on the other, and everything ignited. Instinctively I flinched away from it, and the dish slipped through my shaking fingers to shatter on the stone floor. I inhaled a horrified gasp, tried inanely to gather the shards, and the thought went through my mind that Bruchan would surely kill me for this. Something got into my throat that made me cough. I lifted my cloak to my face and straightened.

I was face-to-face with him, and he had come out of that sweep of colored sand on the wall before me that was no wall at all but a shining curtain that drew aside and let me see what was beyond the golden robe trimmed with sparks of fire. A pretty place, a corie high in the mountains, a meadow with a thousand greens and a hundred yellows and a palace that stepped into the sky. "Come Home." He smiled, the young Power with the eyes that danced and the red cheeks of a boy.

I heard my voice, curiously deeper, a man's voice. "To thy place?"

"And yours," the Fickle Friend whose name was Tychanor said. "She awaits you here."

"Nay, my lord," my man's voice answered.

"Nay, not for me. Thee knows for whom she waits."

"I do," the Power said. "But it is all one. You will see that, my friend. Come Home when you have need. I will await you." He turned his head as if listening, and I saw that the sunlight that drenched the meadow was darker somehow, as though a thundercloud was rolling in. "Make haste, Aengus, make haste."

"What would thee have me do, my lord?"

Tychanor the Immortal looked full on me, and I knew he could see my secret self. "Find the colors and take the Rainbow in your hand, Painter. The struggle begins even as we speak, and it shall not be ended, save one way only."

"I fear." The man's voice had gone, and an adolescent boy's hoarse one, my own, quavered the words.

The Power nodded. "And so do I, if my Brother and his worshipers are not stopped. Go now, my friend." His image flickered, the carved wall showing clearly through him. "And tell Bruchan not to waver. We have not forgotten our promise." He was gone, the golden sunlight was gone, and I was staring streaming eyed at the spiral in the stone that had sucked him back into itself.

Of a sudden I could not breathe. My head reeled and then I was on hands and knees, straining for air, while a thick white foam ran out of my mouth and dripped from my chin. Panicked, I tried to get up, but the stone floor came up and suffocated me.

Damp against my face, cold. Stinging like nettles, like lying in a bed of nettles, I was mad with the burning and tried to roll away but it was too hard so I lay in agony.

Voices somewhere above me, wavering as if they spoke from the bottom of a well. ". . . whoreson hell happened?" A rough voice with a thick accent that made it difficult to understand him.

"The drug took him, and he was unprepared for it." Bruchan's voice. There was something I was supposed to tell him. "He'll recover. I got some of the antipotion into him in time."

"Dangerous stuff ye Wolfhounds play around with. By His Beard, I'm glad we do things in a more civilized fashion back home!"

"An easier fashion, thee means. Well, we keep the old way. It has served us well these many years."

The icy-hot stinging in my hands and feet was easing, and my throat didn't hurt so much. I could draw a breath.

The rough voice observed, "Your lad's coming 'round."

"Aye. Sleep, Aengus," Bruchan soothed. "Thee needs not to wake for some time yet."

At the sound of his voice, I was lulled deeper, cocooned in drowsiness. There was something I was supposed to tell him, though.

Boots shifted near my head, a man resettling himself on the hard ground. We were outside, I realized. Rough Voice said, "Your old ways have served ye well enough till now, friend, but not for much longer if we don't find the way to do it."

Bruchan's voice sharpened. "Thee's had news?"

I heard him spit. "Jorem's got the king to

declare the Wolf Cult to be the only form of religion allowed in the Burren."

"We are the Wolf Cult," Bruchan said quickly.

"Only on the surface, and it's not fooling anybody. Wearing the stamp of the cult gives ye some protection, but my guess is it'll not be for long. He'll try to force ye into declaring yourselves, one way or other." There was silence. Then he added more quietly, "Jorem will be coming after ye now—maybe not tomorrow, but within these next two years, before the prince comes to his majority—with everything he's got, and he's got the whole of the king's army if he wants it. Come, Bruchan: give it up and sail with me and my men when we leave for Jarlshof. We can get ships enough to move your folk and everything—"

"No."

"Bloody hell, man, it's suicide to stay!"

A rustle of clothing, as though Bruchan had stirred impatiently. "And how would thy fine ships carry away this to safety?"

"Ye could shut up the temple, seal it with rocks, there are ways."

"And ways to unseal it! Think thee that Jorem will not find them? And what then, Timbertoe? Ask thyself if thee would want the mysteries here to fall into the hands of that demon, knowing that he would use them to free his master's spirit into the world!"

There was a growled curse. "All right, but ye know if Jorem attacks with the full might of that Wolf Cult of his, he'll—"

"Win, and take the temple anyway?" Bruchan asked grimly. " 'Tis possible. But we are sworn, my friend, and we will not waver."

"Do not waver. . . ." I mumbled.

Startled silence. "Sleep, Aengus," Bruchan bade again.

I struggled to open my eyes and finally did so. My throat was dry, and I croaked, "He said to tell you not to waver."

Master's face was dim. The daylight must be fading behind the fog. "Who said so?"

"Tychanor the Warm, inside the little chamber. He came off the wall and I could see the valley beyond him, all green and yellow and—" A hand gripped my shoulder painfully hard.

"Ow," I complained, and tried to move away, but my limbs were still too sluggish.

A hood and the jut of a black beard were above my face suddenly. He had a large nose and two angry eyes. "Shut yer mouth, ye little beggar's brat, or ye'll feel the point of my dagger!"

Bruchan's hand touched his wrist lightly. "Nay, Timbertoe, the boy means no blasphemy. Look at his eyes. Aengus," he said to me urgently, "tell us what thee saw!"

I licked my lips and told him.

His face was by turns puzzled, horrified, then resolute and calm. "So," he said when I was done and had struggled up on an elbow. "It has come, and we are not ready for it."

"Better get ready in a hurry, skellig master," the rough-voiced stranger advised, pulling a leather flask from his belt pouch and handing it to me. I saw now that he was a dwarf, powerfully built through the chest and shoulders, but with one leg off and wearing a wooden peg leg. His nickname suddenly was grimly humorous. Timbertoe was studying me with a darkly speculative look.

Whatever was in the flask tasted like licorice and burned like poison all the way down my throat. I coughed, grabbed my bruised ribs, and looked to Bruchan, who was sitting back on his heels, troubled and silent. "I think it's about time you tell me what it is that you bought me to do for you."

His eyes lifted to mine, and the blue and the brown were equally dark. "Yes," he said. "I suppose it is."

The dwarven pirates left us alone on the aft deck. Bruchan saw my hostile stares at them after I realized that the woven rug they had wrapped me in was one of our own, marked with the four spirals. "Peace, Aengus," he cautioned. "How else could I have communication with Timbertoe, except to leave messages on the cows they steal? Cathir and his fellow spies must never know that the periodic 'raids' which this dwarf and his men conduct are but a screen for our real business."

I slugged down some hot tea, wincing as it scorched me, and still angry. "The burned houses are a nice touch, then. Very convincing. And Conor's dog."

He sighed and put a finger to his temple. For the first time, he looked truly old to me. "Timbertoe's crew does not know of the ruse. They sail for booty, and only his order restrains them from much worse havoc. Will thee hear me now? We must be finished ere they put us ashore, for there will be much to do afterward."

I clamped down on the anger. "What is this business that you and this pirate are in together?"

He sipped his own tea, avoiding my eyes. " 'Tis mostly a matter of trade."

"What do you trade, then?"

The master of Inishbuffin smoothed an eyebrow with his index finger. "Chalcedons," he answered quietly.

"Chalcedons!"

"Ssh! By the Fire, keep thy voice down and do not look so amazed! Those two over there are eyeing us already." He made a business of drawing the rug more warmly about me. "Aye, chalcedons. The gem is much valued among other folk, dwarfs included, and it happens that there is an ancient mine for them under Inishbuffin."

"Under the skellig itself?" I whispered hoarsely.

He nodded.

I whistled soundlessly. "Master, that must make you the richest man in all the Burren, maybe all the world!"

Bruchan smiled. "It is a well-guarded secret, known only to me and my brother Ruan. Not even my people of the skellig know, though the wealth has been carefully used on their behalf."

I put my teacup down, troubled at the thrill of pure pickpocket delight that had run through me. "Then why have you told me?"

He was silent so long that I glanced up at him and was surprised to find his cheeks suffused with a pale wash of red. "Thee remembers the day thee drew me a t'ing, and the talked turned then to thy parents?"

I nodded, puzzled. "And you told me not to let anyone know my mother's clan or village. To be honest, I thought it was strange, because you didn't seem to care if anyone found out who my father was, and I'd have thought having a drunk for a father would have been a great deal more disgraceful in your skellig folk's eyes than having a mother who wasn't from a highland clan."

He smiled tightly. "She was highland, but went at an early age to live among the Spotted Sheep people. I sent her there for protection. She was my daughter."

We stared at each other. Finally he looked down. "You're my . . . my grandfather?" I managed to say in a strangled voice.

"Aye."

"But why? Why did you leave me all those years with him?" I bludgeoned him with the words, anger boiling up for all the filth and poverty and his drunken fits.

"I did not know until a fortnight before the fair at Bhaile ap Boreen. Your mother was bitter at being sent away, Aengus—as bitter as you are now. She . . . left the family with whom I had placed her and ran away."

"With the handsome young Gill Fisher."

"Aye," he confirmed. "But that is what I did not know. I thought she had been lost in the hills. The river that runs near the place was swollen at that time of the year." His voice had fallen, and I could tell he was reliving that agonizing search. He straightened. "Before the fair, one of my men passed through thy village and saw thee. Thy red hair and blue eyes attracted his attention, and when he saw thy face, he knew. In haste he returned to the skellig to tell me. Having other business at the time which could not be put off even for a reason so near my heart, I—"

"Palomar's ring?" I guessed.

His brows drew down. "Indeed. By the time I could go to thy village, thee and thy father had left for the fair. I followed. Then I saw thee outside the alehouse." The lines in his face deepened. "Thee are very like to her, Aengus." He fumbled for the teacup and drank, though the stuff must have been cold.

How can I explain what it meant to me to be handed at one stroke not so much a new identity as a sense of place? Here at Inishbuffin my forebears had been masters of a peaceful, prosperous community for generations, had worked the soil, raised the flocks and herds, built the byres and walls and weirs. They had seen the sun set over the village as I had, and the fog roll in off the ocean. For the first time in my life, I felt a powerful sense of other presences behind me, a long line of them, probably stretching all the way back to the builders of the temple. I raised my head, and though I tried to keep my voice light, my next words came out with the force of an accusation. "So instead of telling me we were kin, you bought me for an indentured boy."

" 'Twas impossible to reveal our relationship! Even now, there are those who would realize instantly that the gift has been passed if they found out that thee are Breide's son."

"What gift? The painting?"

"Nay." He picked up the cup, then put it down without tasting it, seeming to debate in his own mind how much he should tell me. "At the skellig we have chronicles of the early times—"

"I know. Nestor told me. Five hundred years he said they go back."

"They do, indeed. As thee may imagine, having had some experience of the drug we use to induce the trance, much of the writing concerns visions that have been given to various masters of the community."

"I wasn't supposed to have seen one, then."

The boat rocked sharply as we came around some headland in the fog. Timbertoe bellowed an order in his own language, and the pirate crew jumped to trim the sails. The deck settled once more, and Bruchan answered, "Thee wasn't supposed to have survived. Why does thee look so shocked? I warned thee not to go beyond the antechamber, and told thee there was a trap for the unknowing."

"The drug is the trap?"

"Part of it." He let that set in my mind, and his stern expression softened. "But thee has seen the Fickle Friend; so much cannot be denied; he gave thee words thee could not know otherwise."

I sat forward, bringing our faces closer, Some of the dwarfs were fastening lines too close to us for my comfort. "What was the promise made by the Four to your—our people? The one the Friend said to tell you they have not forgotten?"

The master of Inishbuffin knitted his gnarled hands. "In the chronicles is related the story of Colin Mariner. Thee remembers I told it to thee?"

"A little. I think I was half out most of the time."

"More than half, lad, but doubtless thee heard enough. Well, Colin the Mariner was a living man once, and his tale is not all fancy. He came sailing his ship from the west, a fine ship that needed no sail nor oar to advance upon the sea. Now, he was a king's son with a thirst for adventuring, and his crew was of the same temper, young nobles all who for the sake of seeing new sights and meeting new challenges followed the fearless prince."

I drew up my legs and clasped my arms about my knees, taken into the tale by his storyteller's voice.

"So they went a-roving, and many adventures did they have which thee may learn of another day. For now it is enough to say that one day while Colin was gone from home, his father the king died. The word went out by swift couriers who sought him at all speed, for Colin was his father's eldest son and needed but return home and claim the crown to be declared king.

"There was a younger brother, however, a jealous, scheming sort of man that is bad enough to have in a clan, but much worse to have in a family. As thee can guess, he, too, sent riders seeking for Colin, but not to bid him come home and claim his rightful place. No, they were bent on murder. And they found Colin first.

"On a day much like this one, foggy, with no sight of land to guide him, Colin Mariner found his ship perilously close to a rock reef. Hastily he ordered his boat to come about and they were quickly going back out to open sea when a single fast ship appeared out of the mist and rammed him with an iron ram. The mysterious ship ran through the Mariner's boat, and the last Colin saw of it as he clung to a broken timber was the black keel of it vanishing into the fog. Then he was alone on the sea, all of his friends dead, his ship sent to the bottom, himself sore hurt. He thought he would die.

"But he washed ashore on a rocky beach and was found there by some fisherfolk and taken to their village, and he did not die, though his leg was never straight again. He fell in love with the daughter of the family that had taken him in, and when he thought of returning to his own kingdom and having to fight for his crown with no good friends to aid him, it seemed a long way back to his own land. In short, until the end of his life Colin Mariner lived in the place he had adopted as his own, this Burren. He was first in the favor of King Dilin, at that time the High King of all the Burren, and served him as his friend and counselor. Finally he knew he would soon die and a longing took him to see once more the land of his birth and maybe to die a king, so he took with him two of his three sons and many loyal men, and they sailed west.

"Only twelve of their number ever returned. They brought with them the news of what had happened. Colin had sailed until his lookouts had espied a large river which emptied into the sea. Knowing this for his own river, Colin sailed up it until he reached a riverside stronghold, his own gates. Then he made himself known, and the brother who had claimed the kingship long years before pretended to make him welcome, drawing him into the hall and spreading the board with fine food and drink, the fruits of that bounteous land. He swore fealty to Colin, and the Mariner, believing that such ties were binding and having at any rate the protection that a guest has in any hall, allowed his men to join in the feast, though they were watchful for treachery all the while. At length, on the third day of the feasting, a poison was put into their food, and they ate of it. There, in the hall that should have been his own, Colin Mariner died, cursing the craven brother and all his descendants unto the twentieth generation. Only the twelve men who had been left to guard the ships escaped, and that only because of the quick thinking of the loyal captain, Macguiggan the Bold, who realized from the silence inside the stronghold that something was terribly wrong and slipped the moorings on one ship before they were attacked.

"The survivors came home here to the Burren, and they brought Colin's wife and young son the only thing they had been able to save, the Mariner's signet ring, which he had left in safekeeping with Macguiggan." He paused, and we both stirred. "Ever since, we Burreners, the descendants now of Colin Mariner, have looked to the west, knowing that beyond the mountains, where the large river meets the sea, lies the land which is by right ours."

"Ilyria," I said, nodding. Everybody knew the name of our great enemy.

"Aye, today they name it Ilyria." He sighed. "And today we have a king unsteady in his ways, whom Jorem has been able to influence into thinking that the time is ripe to reclaim our ancient inheritance. There is an old king in Ilyria, Aengus, and a prince they name Beod who has not yet attained his majority; conditions favor a victory if the blow is struck quickly."

"But why don't you support Jorem, then? Don't you want to see us win Ilyria back?"

The wind was freshening, and Bruchan's eyes lifted to follow the streaming wraiths of fog that flew past the rigging. "Oh, I want to unite the Burren and the land of the river as one, yes." His eyes came to rest on me. "But not by war, and not for Jorem and his puppet king. They are not worthy inheritors of Colin Mariner. The present king came to the throne through murder, as the folk in thy village probably tell."

I frowned and glanced to follow a dwarven sailor as he went forward with a sounding line in his hand. We must be coming onto a shoal. My mind must have been slow in recovering from the effects of the drug, for it only then hit me. "By the Fire!" I whipped my head around to face him. "The ring that Palomar died to bring you!"

My grandfather nodded.

"You hold it in guardianship for the true descendant of Colin Mariner, and it's been kept in the shrine all these years! Then it was stolen, and you sent Palomar after it!"

"Palomar went of his own will; indeed, I could not restrain him, so great was the fire of his zeal. In only one other respect have thee guessed wrongly, though." While I tried to puzzle it out, his quiet voice said, "I am not the guardian of the ring, Aengus. It is mine by right of birth."

I stared.

"I would have passed it to my son, but he was slain by our enemies many years ago. So when I die . . . " His eyes were steady. "It will be thine."

Chapter 9

I have no memory of how long we sat there, silence between us, the dwarven pirates going about their business of sailing, and once Timbertoe stumping down the deck toward us, then seeing the look on our faces, turning abruptly about and retreating. I know that Bruchan flipped the dregs of our cold tea over the low rail and poured some hot from the wrapped copper pot. He set the cup near my hand, and nervelessly I sipped. "I've got to read those old books sometime," I said.

The master of Inishbuffin laughed. "When thee does, thee will have no greater shock than thee's just had!"

I muttered something to that, and it was just as well he didn't hear what it was. "I'm curious about one thing. Why—"

"Only one?" he teased.

"One will do for now. Why, if the keepers of the temple have known for all these years that they were the true kings, the rulers of Ilyria, why didn't they go back and press the claim?"

"Nay," Bruchan countered quickly to my first comment. "Nay, kingship does not lie in ruling, Aengus. It is the protection of thy people, and nurturing them and the land, that makes a king. As to why our forebears never have gone back, that is easily answered: there was terrible death in the land of the Burren in the years immediately after Colin's death, a plague of some sort. By the time it had scythed the population, Colin's wife was dead, and his son was an orphan in the fostering of a new king, the nephew of the Mariner's liege lord. When the boy came to manhood, how could he have raised the army necessary to do the thing?"

I considered. "And that's why the skellig was founded, to teach Colin's descendants and followers how to protect the people and care for the land in the hope that one day they would grow strong enough to return to Ilyria?"

"In part. Also, thee must know that Colin was a man who talked with the Powers. He knew them by their names: they were friends, insofar as mortal and immortal may be friendly. And as friends, they shared with him many of their secrets. The skellig and the temple were founded to keep alive that knowledge. Some of it has been lost, but some we still remember. Some of it is bound with his ring, though that part is obscured now, and some is associated with other things belonging to him. We have the ring, but Jorem has the other thing needful to reclaim Colin's heritage in Ilyria." He glanced about. "A vision given to a seer of the temple nearly two hundred years ago prophesied that a boy of the line of Colin should take the rainbow in his hand and open a way for the Powers to come to earth. He would be king maker here in the Burren, and king in Ilyria, uniting the two lands in a friendship which will make them the strongest co-kingdoms in this corner of the earth, prosperous and well able to support their people in peace."

"Ah," I breathed. "A painter." I swallowed. "Am I the one, do you think?"

"I hoped so when I saw thee painting outside the alehouse and knew thee for my grandson. Now, after the Fickle Friend has spoken, I am sure of it. To that end, we must exert all our energies in a twofold effort: to train and protect thee whilst thee becomes a painter, and to recover from Jorem's grasp the other of Colin's precious heirlooms."

"And what would that be?"

"His color pots." My eyes widened. Bruchan nodded. "Yes, Colin was a painter, too." He straightened, casting a look over the rail. Just discernible off the starboard bow was a deep gray smudge that might have been land. The old man stretched, grasped the rail, and hauled himself up. I sprang up to assist him, but only managed to tangle my feet in the rug and stumble to the rail. Bruchan looked down at me. "I do not know what will happen when the Mariner's ring and his color pots are both in the hands of his heir, but I believe the Powers have not misled us all these years. Surely the result will be the one we look for, and we will place a worthy king on the throne of this poor, misused land."

"Who do you have in mind?"

"Nestor."

Another lamp lit. The Dina prince must be the younger brother of our present king in Dun Aghadoe. "But what am I to paint? Who will tell the story?" Then, "Oh!" I realized stupidly and grinned suddenly at my grandfather.

His eyes lit, and he grinned back.

My own smile faded as I thought of something. "I am not the only painter of Colin's line, though. Maybe it's Ruan's to do."

He shook me gently by the nape of the neck. "Thee are not thinking. The prophecy was of a boy. And Ruan is my younger brother; the line of Colin passes from me through my daughter to thee. No, Aengus. It is thee, or none."

On that sobering thought, the small rocky headland swam up out of the fog, and Timbertoe thumped the length of his ship to, as he put it, "dump the scuppers and put the riffraff ashore."

He and Bruchan exchanged a handclasp and a long, silent look. "Mind yer back," the pirate advised, and my grandfather nodded. Timbertoe swung his eyes to me. "And you stay the hell out of places you're not supposed to be, youngster."

"That must include pirate ships."

The seadog's eyes narrowed, and he suddenly spat past my head over the rail, missing me by a scant handsbreadth. I ducked instinctively, and he sniffed. "It must." He pivoted on the wooden leg and stumped away.

The pirate crew were all laughing, and I felt the heat rise in my face. Bruchan urged me over the side into the shallows, and we splashed ashore. By the time we had scrambled up the rocky beach to the line of beach roses, the ship had disappeared into the fog and the lowering darkness. The old man cautioned, "Remember, when we arrive back at the skellig, thee went out to pick foxglove."

"Oh, damn! I lost the bloody basket!"

"Yes, and became lost in the fog thyself. Thee has been wandering all the day. I found thee on one of my walks. Say nothing else, especially when Mallory is found to be missing from supper." He cocked an eye at me. "Can keep so many secrets?"

"I think so. But I keep having the urge to call you Your Majesty, or sire. Grandfather, at least."

He patted my back. "But thee must know me only as Cru and Bruchan and Master. Else thee may slip and alert our enemies."

"Can't you do something about Cathir? Arrange for Timbertoe to take him the next time the pirates raid us, or something?"

"I have considered it. But then Jorem would only send another spy. I think it better to keep the evil that we know and try to feed him false information to relay to his master. Meanwhile, I must take thought upon a plan to keep thee safe. Clearly I have not been as careful as I ought." A bell's ringing carried clearly to us on the wind. "Ah, we are home, and supper is set. Powers forgive us the lie we must begin to live now." He sighed and murmured. "Even Mallory deserves better than to lie out there alone."

I said carefully, "I saw that his neck was broken." There was a question implied.

"Aye," the master acknowledged. He looked down at me. "Pirates, I suppose."

One wooden-legged pirate who must have been protecting your back, anyway, I thought, returning his direct look. "I suppose," I agreed.

His arm rested briefly across my shoulders, and then the first house in the village, new and still smelling sharply of dung, materialized out of the fog, and we walked up through the people, our people, ducking out of their doors and pulling on their hoods against the drizzle to go up to the evening meal.

With all I had to think about, I was not much help to Kevyn as he tried to tease Gwynt about the little brown-haired girl. My tall friend flung one burning look at Kevyn, and that was the end of that. Plainly the subject was not open for discussion except in the most respectful and virtuous terms. Kevyn was having none of that, and turned the talk to their masters and a comparison of their new living accommodations. A couple of the other boys joined in, and the rise and fall of their talk floated around me like the background noise of the sea. I found that I was very thirsty, probably the last dregs of the drug, and I supped my salt-fish stew and drank nearly an entire jug of spring water, cocooned from their boyish enthusiasms by my experiences that day. I was covertly watching Cathir. Surely he would be the first to realize it.

Kevyn suddenly nudged my elbow. "You're the quiet one tonight. What's the matter? Has all that reading given you a walloping headache?"

"He hasn't spent much time reading today. His cloak is a mess and his boots are soaked. Our lad's been out in the muck today, I'm thinking," Gwynt observed shrewdly.

I clanged my spoon into my empty bowl with what I hoped was convincing disgust. "Do you know, my master sent me out in that today to collect some bloody foxglove for him?" There were some exclamations of incensed indignation to support me, and some grins at my discomfiture. "And I couldn't see a damned thing, so of course I got lost and spent the day wandering around, hoping I wouldn't fall off a cliff in the damned fog." I mentally excused myself to Nestor for using him in this way. My poor master. Your brother king, a little voice whispered deep in my mind, but I pushed the thought away.

"You were lucky not to," Kevyn was saying, and it took me a moment to come back and connect this with the last thing I had said.

"Or fall in a bog hole," a boy named Tadh contributed.

I controlled a shudder only by knotting my fists under the table. "Ah, well," I said lightly to turn aside the conversation, "someday I'll be sitting in my neat little apothecary, warming myself over a distilling kettle, while you're up on the ridge pole of a barn," I directed to Kevyn, "and you're shoveling horse shit," I told Gwynt, and ducked his grinning cuff. "If collecting herbs on a rainy day is as bad as this job gets, I'll take it!" They agreed that I had drawn a lucky lot.

Brother Finian cleared his throat behind us. "Would thee boys happen to have seen Brother Mallory?"

The pit of my stomach fell out, not at the mention of the dead man, but at what I thought was the revelation of the third agent of Jorem's Wolf Cult. Oh, no, not you! I moaned inwardly. I liked you!

Gwynt and Kevyn shook their heads, and there were negative murmurs down the length of our table. I let my silence pass for part of it. Finian looked puzzled rather than upset. "Hmm. That's odd. No one's seen him today."

I was glad Gwynt asked, "What did you want him for, Brother?"

"We have sentry duty together tonight down at the lower gate. I wanted to remind him to bring the draughts." He smiled, glanced around, and lowered his voice. "We pass the time playing the game." Whatever he saw in my face, he mistook. "Oh, we would not endanger the skellig! 'Tis a game that does not take our attention from listening for enemies in the night."

You'd not hear them if they were sitting right next to you, half-wit, I thought irritably. Could this fellow be as innocent as he seemed? Bruchan obviously trusted him, but that might be misplaced affection. I would watch myself around Finian. I would watch Bruchan around Finian.

"Well, thank thee anyway, boys. Warmth." The needleworker drifted away, asking after Mallory at this table and that until he reached my grandfather's seat. I saw him lean, and his hand lifted to punctuate his question. Bruchan shook his head and turned to Cathir, who sat next to him. The steward of the skellig frowned, pursed his pudgy lips, and made a business of craning past Finian to sweep the dining hall with a searching gaze. I looked down quickly.

A spoon clanging against an earthenware water pitcher eventually brought the room to silence. Members of the community turned on their benches to give their attention to Cathir, who was standing at his place with a worried look on his face. "Has anyone seen Brother Mallory this day?" he asked of the room in general.

Men shook their heads and glanced to their wives and children, who mainly shrugged or merely raised their eyebrows. One man near the door called, "I saw him this morning, Master Cathir." While he rose at his place, heads turned toward him. "I was on my way up into our back field to fetch our milch cow right before the breakfast gong sounded, and I met Mallory on the path. He said he'd ewes to check on, ready to drop late lambs, out beyond the bridge."

A crackle of tension went through the room as people realized the implications of this. Cathir looked grave and glanced to Bruchan. The master of the skellig slowly rose. "Had he a lantern with him, Dru?" he asked.

The man who had seen Mallory shook his head. "I think not, master. I saw none, and he had no pack on his back."

Bruchan straightened. "Then likely he is benighted out beyond the bridge. Finian, take a cowbell from the barn to the top of the lower wall and station thyself there, letting the bell ring out often, at regular intervals. Perhaps he will hear it and be guided in." He paused and glanced around the room, but didn't let his eyes meet mine. "However, it seems likely that he would have heard the dinner bell if he were close enough to the skellig and able to make his own way. Therefore, we shall err on the side of caution and presume that he is not, for whatever reason, able to make his way home." I saw several of the brothers exchange glances with their wives, and then look to see whether the younger children had understood Bruchan's delicate phrasing.

Kevyn leaned to whisper, "You didn't hear him calling or anything while you were out there?"

A gargling scream rose in my ears once more, and suddenly the salt-fish chowder got as far as the back of my throat. I swallowed hard. "No," I answered shortly.

Bruchan was saying, "The women and children will stay within doors, please—we want no one else lost. Brothers, we will take torches and candle lanterns and form a line, each staying within sight of his companion's light, from the bridge as far as we may go. Let us keep silence when we pass the bridge and listen carefully. Symon, thee has the most powerful voice among us, so thee and I will walk the length of our line, calling him. Nestor, bring thy kit."

My companions were disappointed at being left out of what they viewed as an adventure and asked Padraig if we might go along, but he put them off with the reasoning that being new to the skellig, we knew none of the surrounding territory and might easily leave the road and be lost ourselves. So Gwynt and Kevyn led the others to the lower wall, where they would watch if they could do nothing more, and for show, I went with them.

It was a long, cold vigil in the windy drizzle, and of course, quite pointless, which made it even harder for me to bear. It must have been dismal work for Bruchan. Shortly after the large bell had sounded from the round tower to mark the third hour since dinner, we saw the line of torches and lanterns coming back through the village.

"They're walking awfully slowly," one boy said. "I bet they found his body."

I'll bet you a quarter gold sovereign they didn't, I thought to him.

Bruchan and Symon led them up through the gate, and the boys ran down to meet them,

Sheila Gilluly

halting suddenly when they saw the men's faces and no heavy bundle shrouded in cloaks. I trailed after them and took a place near the end of the group of boys. My grandfather glanced up as he passed, and for a moment our eyes met, but then Symon came between us, and they had gone by.

"Nothing," Gwynt said at my shoulder.

He meant that they had found no trace of Mallory, but I was thinking of Bruchan's eyes.

"No, nothing," I echoed quietly.

It may have been that he was already thinking in that direction, but the incident with Mallory had the effect of strengthening Bruchan's resolve to know who were Jorem's spies—and assassins—within his skellig. Cathir we knew about, but though the watcher on the cliff at Gull's Cove may have been there for a perfectly innocent reason, neither Bruchan nor I thought so. When we made discreet inquiries through Padraig, Symon, and Thyr—the men my grandfather was certain he could trust along with Nestor and Ruan, of course—we could turn up no one who would admit to being on the cliffs that day, and Nestor was certain that it had not been a dwarf, one of Timbertoe's men. I tried drawing the man, as I had once drawn Cathir, but even that was to no avail: no portrait came from my fingertips.

That the need to identify the spy or spies was urgent was brought home to us not long after. We were in the height of the harvest season, and the work was going well enough, though we would have been glad of less wind and rain and a few more dry days, when a boat nosed up the coast of the peninsula, beating against the wind with a crew of rowers. Gwynt and I were out chasing sheep that day—you cannot call it herding when the beasts scramble this way and that—and we stopped to watch the high-prowed vessel pass our vantage offshore of the Caldron.

"It's got a wolf for a figurehead," my companion reported, shading his keen eyes with his hand.

I pursed my lips and drew a breath, thinking of Timbertoe's news that this skellig's form of worship would soon be outlawed. "I hope it isn't Jorem again."

Gwynt dug the end of his crook into the thin turf and looked worried. "I hope he hasn't come to take me and Seamus with him. It isn't a year yet. He's got no right."

I didn't blame him. Even if I had not known so much more than he about the leader of the Wolf Cult, I would not have wanted to serve him. "No, I don't think it's him. Look. There's no flag at the mainmast. Jorem's boat had one, remember? He's such a princox he'd want to declare for the world to see that he was on that ship."

My friend relaxed visibly. "Maybe you're right. Well, let's try to get this lot to the fold before they run themselves off into the Caldron. Aengus, are you all right?"

The raven again, squawking and flapping in my mind's eye. "Yes," I told him, and forced the image away. "I'm fine—it's just a burr I've picked up." There was one in my boot that had been bothering me for some time. I bent and plucked it free, and he went loping away to gather in the strays and head them toward the temporary pen that had been built in the field to hold the flock while the brother in charge did the culling. A moment later I followed more slowly.

That evening as we pitched horseshoes after dinner, Seamus electrified us with the news. "That boat that came in today? Do you know what was on it?" he asked, elaborately casual.

"That emissalery from Dun Aghadoe," Brin replied, holding his horseshoe steady at the level of his eyes and sighting carefully for the stake. "Master Bruchan introduced him to everybody at dinner—Brother Oisin, his name is."

"Emissary," I corrected.

"Whatever. Messenger, it amounts to." Brin swung his arm and landed his shoe about a hand's width from the stake.

Kevyn scratched his ear, allowed it was a good throw, and stepped up with his horseshoe. We all went quiet. This toss was for the win. Our carpenter sighted over his shoe.

"There was a wolf on that ship," Seamus dropped into the silence.

At once the horseshoes were forgotten. "Go on!" more than one boy said. "A wolf?"

The cook's boy nodded, satisfied with the reaction he had gotten. "A real, live, wild wolf, and it nearly got out of its cage in that storm we had the other night."

My skin was prickling. "What the hell's he got a wolf aboard ship for?"

Seamus took a look around, but no masters were near. He dropped his voice confidentially. "It's been delivered from Lord Jorem for a ritual they're supposed to hold here pretty soon, and Master ain't too pleased about it from what Brother Cook says."

No, I thought, he wouldn't be. Jorem was forcing his hand.

Seamus had gone on to say, "It's right down in the cargo bay. Brother Oisin was some pissed off at that, said the Lord Beldis should be out somewhere that everyone could see him, but Master wouldn't allow it. He said the wolf scent would spook every animal on the place, and anyway, Lord Beldis ought to have a little peace and quiet after his sea journey. There wasn't much Oisin could say after that, so they carried the cage from the boat up to the cargo bay and left it there. I'm not fooling!" he protested to our skeptical faces. "If you go in the kitchen, you can hear it howling!"

Well then, of course, there was nothing that would satisfy us but to go to the kitchen to hear the howling of the wolf-god. We trooped in, finding the place empty and scrubbed down for the night. Gwynt took an early apple from the wooden bowl on the chopping block and polished its fine green skin against his tunic while we all listened. Sure enough, if you listened you could hear a faint moaning.

"Oh, that ain't a wolf," Kevyn snorted disgustedly. "Sounds more like somebody with a toothache."

"It *is* a wolf!" Seamus retorted heatedly.

Gwynt put a hand up. "There's one easy way to find out." His look challenged.

"I'm game," Kevyn agreed. "You did say it was in a cage, right?" Seamus gave him an impatient nod.

In the end, everybody elected to go. It was the kind of thing you cannot refuse to do when you are a boy among other boys. So we crept out of the kitchen, along the hall, and to the door of the long stairway to the cargo bay. All in a gaggle of thin legs and wrists sticking out of our robes, we made a knot that moved together through the door at the head of the stair and then, slowly, down it.

The beast must have tired itself with howling, for it seemed to be dozing when we cautiously craned to look over the handrail on the last landing. We peered at it. Gwynt straightened. "Well, hell, I can't see anything from here with only that one torch." He moved off the steps, walking softly toward the cage.

"Be care—" Kevyn started to call to him in a low voice.

A shuddering howl rose to echo off the sides of the rock cavern, and there was a thud of a large body hitting the sides of the stout wooden cage.

Gwynt took one flying leap, clearing some of the shorter boys, and was bounding up the stairs as fast as his legs could take him before the rest could get uprooted from the spot. They ran up those stairs as if all the furies of hell were after them and the door slammed, leaving me alone with the howling wolf. The beast sank on its haunches, muzzle raised to the high door, and then its howling subsided into a few snuffling growls and silence. It swung its head to look at me.

Despite the fear that even the caged animal inspired, I found myself staring into those amber eyes with a far different feeling than that which the raven had inspired in me. This was an intelligent beast, and I didn't think it was a malevolent one. I walked to Ruan's fish barrel, lifted the lid, and found a few mackerel floating belly up. These were probably my painting master's bait for morning, but I didn't think he would mind missing one.

I took it as close to the cage as I dared, watched all the while by those sharp eyes. He growled, a subterranean rumbling that continued even after I had tossed him the fish and gone back up the stairs. But he did not howl.

When I came through the door, Kevyn clutched my tunic. "We thought it got you!"

"How could it get me from the cage?"

"What were you doing down there, then?" Seamus demanded.

"I fed him," I replied, and pushed through them to get to a watering trough. My hands were reeking of fish. I turned back to say maliciously, "You might consider making friends with him yourselves. That way, if they choose you for the victim in their filthy ritual, maybe Wolfie won't tear you apart."

I left them arguing about it and went to find a sand bucket to scrub with.

"What will you do about the wolf ritual?" I asked Bruchan late that night, after the skellig had quieted for sleep. His private study was becoming as familiar to me as the dormitory, and I sat on the footstool while he smoked. "Obviously, you'll have to hold one. Otherwise Jorem's spies will report back to him that you refused."

"Jorem's spies will try to report it." A smoke ring was aimed at the ceiling.

I sat up straighter. "You have a plan."

He cocked an eye at me. "Indeed. I have waited long for an opportunity such as this. As thee says, with such important news in his hands, our spy could not hold it back from his master. Now, what if Cathir were unable to send the message?"

"He'd have to get his ally, or one of his allies, to send it for him."

"Just so. Then we shall discover not only who this ally is, but also how the messages to Jorem are passed, and that is information we can use against them."

"But how are you going to keep Cathir occupied?"

He smiled over the mouthpiece of his pipe. "Watch."

The next day at midmorning the "emissalery" from Dun Aghadoe departed with the tide after an apparently fraternal enough send-off from Bruchan. The community was already well into it's workday, we boys sweating at Symon's calisthenics in the practice yard, and there was no meal until evening, so Bruchan had no opportunity until then to put his plan into effect.

I waited expectantly, barely tasting my supper. When most of the community had pushed back their trenchers and bowls, Bruchan rose in his place. He had no need to clang his spoon against a water jug to gain people's attention. There was an immediate call for quiet from Symon, and the hush quickly spread. The master of Inishbuffin smiled. "Supper was good, wasn't it? Aye, and we thank the cooks for putting it on the table for us. Now, I think thee will all have been aware that a message was brought to me from Lord Jorem concerning our ritual."

The silence penetrated every corner of the room now. Bruchan explained, "Thee's no doubt also heard that we have a wolf in our keeping in the cargo bay, thanks to Dun Aghadoe's generosity. It was noted by our brethren there that we have no wolves naturally occurring on Inishbuffin, so we have been provided with one to use in the ritual at the full moon four nights from now." No one stirred. Bruchan came from behind his table to stand before his people. "I am also to deliver a message to all of thee: it has been declared by our lord the king that from this time forward, only the Wolf Cult is to be let carry on its religious practices freely in the Burren. Any who knowingly break this law may be punished severely."

People looked to one another, shocked. A voice came from the back of the hall. "He's outlawed us, then, master?"

"Not precisely, Timon. This is not so direct a threat, since technically we are still members of the Cult of the Flame. But, yes, that is what it will come to very soon, unless I miss my guess. So we are faced with an ugly choice, my people. Either we may forswear our ancient way of life and the beliefs which go with it, remaining safe, or we may stand firm and suffer the consequences."

Padraig rose at his place, consternation written plainly on his features. "Ye do not thinking of yielding, surely, master?"

"I do not. But I wished to make clear the choices so that others who have families may consider their course. If they wish to leave, we must wish them Warmth of the Fire and bless their decision, understanding the reason for it."

I have never seen any king, before or since, who had his people so securely in hand as Bruchan had his that night. The mood changed in an instant from fear of the future to defiance. "Why should we change our ways?" a man at the next table asked of the group. "Jorem and his Wolves are the ones who have left the true path! Let *them* change!"

"Aye!" shouted a score of voices.

Bruchan held up his hand. "I know thy faith burns bright, but consider the hard road ahead. Thee knows, my brothers, that we cannot hold out against the might of the entire cult forever." The room had hushed once more. He turned his hand, palm upward, and asked simply, "Will thee stay with me?"

Of course they would. Who could leave such a leader? He nodded and smiled gently at their roar, and when the room had quieted to hear what he would say next, he looked around at them. "May the Four bless us, then, and help us in our trial."

Clear across the hall where I sat with the other boys, I could hear the audible intake of breath from many of the people. For the first time, someone had openly acknowledged that they did not follow the Wolf alone. I moved a little to peer past Brin, who was across the table from me, so that I could have an unobstructed view of Cathir's face. He didn't look happy. In fact, he was giving rather too much away for a spy. There was sweat on his forehead, and he blinked rapidly.

Bruchan went on. "I thought I might have thy agreement in this." He shared the affectionate laugh that went around. "No, Inishbuffin will not stoop to the Wolf Cult's foul rituals and call them honoring the Power. We will celebrate the harvest as our forefathers have done for time out of mind, and we will do it at the proper time, not at this full moon."

"Aye, master!" shouted Symon, thumping the table with approval.

Cathir's hand wavered into the air. "I—I don't feel—" He suddenly gasped, lurched to his feet, and collapsed across the table. By the time Ruan, who was also seated at the master's table by right of age, was able to reach him, the stout man had slipped to the floor.

Bruchan turned in surprise, and Nestor darted past him to assist the stricken man. I eeled my way through the press of people to my medicine master's side. He glanced around to find Bruchan. "He's had a shock, I think. We must take him to the infirmary, master." Bruchan nodded and gestured several people to help. I managed to be one of them. This all looked awfully convincing to be part of the old man's plan, but Dina were Dina. If anything was on, I wasn't about to miss it.

We bore the heavy steward quickly to the infirmary, where Nestor indicated which cot to lay him upon. "Everyone but master and my assistant out, please," he ordered firmly, opening his kit and pulling out small labeled jars and boxes. The others filed out, hushed, and closed the door behind them.

Bruchan stepped to pull the shutters to. "How is he?"

Nestor straightened from taking Cathir's pulse. "Steadying." There was disapproval in his face.

Bruchan folded his arms, staring down at Jorem's spy. "It was the only way, Nestor. I am sorry to have had to involve thee, however. I know thee has no liking for using thy knowledge in this fashion."

The healer frowned, digging through his packets. "The only thing that convinces me to do it is thinking what will happen to us if Cathir and his confederate are allowed to continue supplying Jorem with news of our every move."

He found what he was looking for. "Aengus, my wide-eared young friend, mix all of this envelope with exactly one measure of water in a small bowl."

I took the medicine packet. "He won't die, I take it?"

"No, he'll only feel that way for some time," Nestor answered, gesturing me to be about my business. "Oh, don't get any of that on your hands, by the way."

In the apothecary adjacent to the infirmary, I got down the measuring cup and mixed up the medicine, being careful not to splash any on myself. When I carried the bowl back into the ward, Bruchan was standing at the foot of the bed, and Nestor was laying out strips of linen. "The watch is already set, I take it?" the medicine master was saying.

"Done," Bruchan replied with satisfaction. "Though I think our unknown friend will make no move until he has definite news of Cathir to report. When I go out and tell them some minutes from now, he will have a morsel or two to pass along to his master in Dun Aghadoe."

"Here, master," I said to Nestor, and put the bowl down on the floor by the bed.

He nodded, dropped several strips of cloth into the bowl, waited until they were soaked, and then pulled one out gingerly. Bruchan held Cathir's limp right hand up from the blanket, and Nestor began hurriedly wrapping it with the poultice, wincing. "Good!" he gasped. "It's working already!"

"By the Fire, what is it?" I asked, alarmed at his face.

"Powdered nettles," he grunted.

"To stimulate tingling in Cathir's hands," Bruchan explained. "That is often one of the symptoms of a brain seizure, which is what we want the steward to think has happened to him. In addition, Nestor has given him a drug which affects his eyes and balance." He nodded. "It will be very convincing to Brother Spy and his fellow."

A few minutes later, the business was done. To all appearances, Cathir slept, his hands bandaged so that he could do himself no harm if he had another seizure. Nestor washed his throbbing hands, but of course it would take time for the swelling and the pain to subside. He stuck his hands in the pockets of his robe and stoically adjusted his face, nodding to Bruchan that he was ready. I was directed to stay behind to watch the patient. They opened the door and stepped out into the courtyard, lit with torches.

I heard the lie told, and the murmuring reaction of the crowd. Nestor made it clear that Cathir's condition was serious, and that he needed absolute quiet. People got the message and obediently broke up their gathering. Nestor and Bruchan came back in hiding grins. "So," said the master of the skellig. "Now we do a bit of hunting. Come, Aengus. This affects thee directly, and thee should share the pleasure. Good night, Nestor. If thee has need, do not hesitate to call me. I have stationed Finian outside to keep the inquisitive away."

"All will be well here." Nestor smiled. "Good hunting, master."

We left the infirmary, ducking from shadow to shadow in the bobbing torchlight, and made our way to the angle between the round tower and the practice yard. Ruan was waiting for us. He reported, "Everyone is in place, lights, signal bells, so forth. Padraig has the sharpest eyes, so he's up in the tower seeing what he can see. Nothing yet, but then it's early in the game."

Bruchan stroked his beard. "If they fly out their messages by birds—"

"Timon is already at the dovecote. No fear there, the birds wouldn't fly till dawn, anyway."

My grandfather nodded, his eyes narrowed. "I suppose we have it all covered, then."

"Relax," his brother advised, patting his arm. "We've thought as much as we can think, now is time to wait, speaking of which I've got my station and I'd best get to it. Wouldn't want the bugger to leave by one of my boats." He waved hastily and hurried away toward the dining hall. His post must be the cargo bay. I didn't envy him down there with the wolf for company.

"Come, Aengus, let us make the rounds."

Padraig had seen nothing from the round tower, but the night was an excellent one for observation, with a three-quarter moon that gave enough light to see the sheep and cattle moving below us in the fields. My own eyes were confused by the sharp shadows of the rock walls and stony terrain, but Padraig, knowing that view well, felt confident he would pick out anything unusual, such as a man hurrying away from the skellig walls. But of course, he could not look in every direction at once, and that was our chief danger. Bruchan clapped him on the back, and we climbed back down to ground level.

We checked in with Thyr at the postern leading to the cliffside stairs down in the jetty, with Ruan in the cargo bay, with Timon at the dovecote, and with Symon, who was fully armed and ready to race wherever he was needed. For now, he waited in the darkened dining hall, directing the operation in whispers passed on by Niall the horse master, who was our runner for the night.

We waited. The stars wheeled overhead, a chilly wind came up off the ocean. At the turn of the tide, we could hear the surf pounding the cliffs three miles distant. It was a long watch.

But finally we had him. Bruchan and I were checking in for the fourth time with Symon in the refectory when Niall came racing in. "Padraig's seen someone climbing over the outer wall, headed for the Caldron side!"

Symon sprang for the door, and the rest of us were right after him. I thought I was fleet enough, but the weaponsmaster ran like a whippet, soon outdistancing us. He was up the steps and over the inner wall so quickly that he left us panting in his wake. Bruchan drew me to a stop, and Niall halted also. "They do not call him Rabbitfoot for nothing!" The horse master grinned.

"We could not follow him over the wall in any case," Bruchan whispered. "Our spy would surely hear three or four pursuers. Let us go up into the tower and try to see what passes out there."

So they had entrusted it all to Symon. If he could not stop Jorem's agent . . . I didn't like it at all and thumped my fist into my palm in frustration. The master saw it. "Peace, boy. Symon is worth three men, or four. He will not let the spy escape."

"Any man may be cut down by an arrow in the dark," I pointed out as we climbed the ladder into the tower.

"Not Symon." Niall laughed softly. "He would only be angry that someone tried."

Padraig was leaning on the thick sill of the east-facing window. He pointed silently as we came past the bell rope. Out on the burren a speck of darkness was moving across the moonlit spaces, now in light, now in shadow. Our spy. Another dark patch was pursuing, moving smoothly on a line to merge with the other near the cliffs. Symon Rabbitfoot.

We watched the race for some moments. The first figure must not have been very quick, for Symon gained on him rapidly, and I don't think he ever heard the weaponsmaster behind him, because from our vantage the scene was much like watching an owl swoop on an unsuspecting mouse.

"He's got him!" I cried. "Let's—"

Padraig's index finger lifted to silence me.

From out of the burren came a single flash of lantern light, quickly extinguished with shields. "Ah," Bruchan breathed. "Good man, Symon." He straightened. "Brother will bring him to my study. I invite thee all to help me receive our snake-in-the-grass." A swift glance to me: yes, be sure I wanted to meet the rat who had helped Cathir put the adder in my blanket. We had all turned to leave when the master added, "And please help me not to do him bodily harm. I fear my temper is not at all certain at this moment."

I thought that was probably more a warning to me to keep a firm grip on my own anger than it was an actual request on Bruchan's behalf. We wound down the stairs, closed the door, and returned the ladder back to its place in the shed nearby. Then the master led us to his own private room, Padraig lit the candle, and we waited for Symon to return with his night's prey. Bruchan motioned me back toward a corner, and from there I watched the grim emotions in the faces I was just beginning to know. Whoever the spy turned out to be, they knew he had been one of them, had shared their work and their bread, and now had put them and their families in danger of their lives. There were beads of sweat on Thyr's forehead, and Padraig gnawed on a thumbnail. Bruchan and Ruan sat quietly in the two chairs, but both stared into space somewhere near their feet.

The door downstairs grated on the threshold, and there were steps on the stair. Bruchan's head came up, and he and his brother exchanged a glance. Ruan got up and stepped a few feet away among the other men. The symbolism was obvious: this spy would face Bruchan as judge. From the look on the master's face, I didn't think Jorem's man could hope for much clemency.

There was another bit of symbolism in that room, but this was an unconscious one; all of the brothers save Bruchan had folded their arms, put their hands in their pockets, or tucked their hands behind their backs in their broad belts. For men who believed so much in self-discipline, it was some measure of the smoldering anger they felt that they should not trust themselves.

I was under no such discipline. I drew my dagger, bent, and stuffed it under one of the cushions near my foot so that I would not be tempted. When I straightened, I thought I saw the twitch of a smile on my grandfather's lips. A foot scraped the stone landing outside, and the smile froze and died. The door swung open.

A blur of cloak and robe was hurled into the room at the end of Symon's powerful arm to land sprawling at Bruchan's feet. The master of Skellig Inishbuffin leaned to tug the man's hood back. Through the bruising around one eye and the swelling under his jaw, I recognized the cook. He moaned and clamped both hands around his throat, evidently in too much pain to care where he was.

The weaponsmaster shut the door and let the small barrel he was carrying slip to the floor. Bruchan looked from the prisoner to his captor. "Symon?" he asked quietly.

The big man looked defiant and pulled a leather thong strung between two wooden handles from his pocket. "I used a snare on him, master, and I'm not a bit sorry for it, please excuse me."

Bruchan nodded gravely. "I see. The lantern and barrel he had with him?"

"Aye, master. There's a boat lying in the cove below the cliffs he was headed for. I secured him and took a quick peek whilst he was coming to. The lantern was for signaling, I'd guess, and then he'd drop the barrel over for them to pick up. Again this is only a guess, but I think we can be sure that it's the Dun Aghadoe ship."

"No doubt. Bring the barrel here, would thee? Niall, hold this vermin away from me till I want him. Thy dagger, Aengus, please."

I fetched it for him. Quickly he prised the top off, and the smell of salt pork permeated the room, though there was no meat in the barrel. Cook had used an old one, perfect for the job because the wood retained both the salt and the fat, making it waterproof. Master reached in and withdrew a packet bound in oiled leather, then knocked the barrel over with his foot and absently gave it a shove to roll toward

Symon. The weaponsmaster caught it, put the top back on when I tossed it to him, and upended it, resting his foot upon it. "Now," said Bruchan. "Let us see what is the news from Skellig Inishbuffin." He untied the thongs, unfolded the wrapping, and withdrew some crackling sheets. A white eyebrow went up over the steel blue eye. "Parchment, Dermot? Thy friends have expensive tastes."

"I did nothing save what Brother Cathir ordered me to do!" the cook protested.

"Of course thee didn't," Bruchan murmured as he unfolded the papers. I was standing next to him, but of course it did me no good; I could pick out a couple of B's, a double handful of A's, and four or five C's. My grandfather read rapidly; he was done with the first page and scanning the second while I was still counting. "Well, well. Thee'll be pleased to know thee is mentioned, Symon."

"I'm glad I knocked his face in, then. Whose writing?"

Bruchan's eyes flicked up. "It is Cathir's hand. He reports: 'Dear Master, There has been a disturbing development. Mallory is missing, and it is feared that he has been lost in a bog hole. This is perhaps the truth, but I had sent him to trail the old man and the boy, and it seems too much coincidence to suppose that the events are unrelated. So they know about Mallory. How they came to suspect him, I do not know and cannot discover. I believe the rest of us are safe, however.' " A bitten-off exclamation came from Thyr, and I felt my own heart sink.

Bruchan showed nothing and continued, " 'Now to the matter of the wolf. It has survived the sea voyage very well and is presently howl-

ing its lungs out in the cargo bay. The old fool
will not allow it to be displayed to the people,
and I think we may take that as an indication
of his decision regarding the ritual you have all
but ordered him to perform: Bruchan will not
do it. I am sure already of this, as you are, my
lord, and will refrain from sealing this cask only
that I may report definitely his refusal after our
evening meal tonight. Doubtless that is when he
will make the pronouncement to the community, though he will couch it in his usual manip-
ulation of their emotions.' " For the first time a
tremor entered the master's steady voice. He
cleared his throat. " 'Nevertheless, there will be
no dissent, and the fools will have baited their
own trap for you to spring upon them.' "

"Just as we thought," Ruan murmured.

Bruchan nodded without looking up. " 'Now,
regarding the young pickpocket, I have not as
much news as I would wish, Your Grace. He
seems a rascal, and has had several beatings
from Symon to mend his rough manners. He
has been set to 'prentice with Nestor, not Ruan,
though he and the painter met at a secluded
spot the other day when Nestor took him on a
collecting hike. My man could not tell if the
meeting was an innocent one, or by prear-
rangement. By the time he arrived, a picture
was drawn in the sand, but there is no way to
tell whether Ruan may have merely been dem-
onstrating his art for a curious boy. I have
taken the precaution of setting a watch upon
Ruan, the obvious thing to do if, as we think,
he is training a new painter. Even if the boy
they call Aengus is not the one, old Ruan will
be the magnet that draws the object of our
search. Nonetheless, I wish things had not gone

awry with the serpent; I would feel better if we eliminated this possible threat to our plan. Here is my thought, master: perhaps we should try to subvert the boy. With appropriate inducements, we may influence him to act unknowingly as we want him to do. Let me know if this idea has merit, and I will put it into action at once. For now, farewell, and believe me to be ever—Your Faithful Servant.' "

Bruchan tipped the second sheet to the light. "There is a postscript, written in a hurried hand. 'Brother Cathir took ill at dinner. I fear it serious. They will not honor the Wolf ritual. Please tell me what to do. D.' " He regarded the damning letter for some moments while no one moved, then folded the sheets slowly. His gaze fastened on the man crouched against the wall. "Dermot, approach."

The cook looked up out of his good eye, the other already swollen to a slit. He glanced around at the brothers, who were holding themselves well back, their faces as stony as the landscape of Inishbuffin. Slowly he hauled himself to his feet, using the wall for balance, and crossed to kneel before Bruchan. He went too close to the old man, though, and realized it when Symon took a step away from the door. Hurriedly, Dermot backed up and knelt abjectly, head down. He expected to be killed: I could read it in every line of his body, and in truth it was no more than he deserved.

"Thee believes in the Wolf?" Bruchan's voice, surprisingly gentle, asked.

Dermot's eye widened. "Of course!" he blurted.

The old man studied him. "The more fool, thee. Has done this service—" he tapped the papers—"because thee loved the Wolf and believed it to be right?"

The cook was puzzled that the angry accusations he expected had taken so philosophic a turn. Reluctantly he answered quietly, "Aye, master."

Bruchan held up a finger. "Ah, no, Dermot, thee cannot claim both Jorem and me as masters. Choose."

For perhaps four heartbeats there was utter silence in the room. "He holds my sister hostage!" Dermot cried desperately. "I would not have betrayed you else, master!"

Bruchan's face lost some of its strained stiffness. "Does he?" the master murmured. "I am not surprised. And what hold has he over Cathir?"

"Master, I do not know. I think Brother Cathir is of the same mind as His Grace."

"A real Wolfhound, thee means."

Dermot nodded carefully.

"I see. And Mallory?"

"Mallory's brother is esquire to one of the king's knights."

"Ah. Another of the Wolf Cult faithful." The blue eye sharpened to a steel gimlet, the brown a bottomless boghole. "And who besides these are thy fellows in Jorem's service, whether willingly or under threat?"

Dermot swallowed and licked his lips, glancing nervously around at the silently listening men. His head went down again. "Bors. They have his mother."

"One of our fishermen, very convenient for passing messages," Ruan observed.

Bruchan drew a breath and leaned back in his chair. "There were only four of thee, Dermot?"

"Aye, master." He frowned. "At least as far as I know."

"Yes, we must not forget that point. Well, now. On thy feet, man." The cook looked scared. It was coming now, he could tell. Slowly he got up. "Bare thy left shoulder."

Dermot's mouth dropped open. When he seemed frozen, Padraig grabbed one arm and Niall the other, and Symon tore off the cook's cloak, then ripped his tunic open. Exposed in the hollow of his collarbone for all to see was a small tattoo in the shape of a wolf's fang.

Bruchan rose, and Dermot cowered. "Did think I knew not about the tattoo of the cult, Dermot? How long has thy sister been Jorem's hostage, then?"

"Since I was no older than the boy here." His voice firmed, though his good eye reddened. "She bore Jorem a child, master, before he became what he is now. He killed the child and threatened the same to her if she ever revealed it."

My grandfather's brows drew down, and he bent his eyes on Dermot for several moments. The man met his look straightly, but with no defiance. Bruchan reached to the candle's flame and cupped his hand around it, warming his fingers absently. "There is no shame to thy sister, Dermot. She has acted in terror, as thee has done."

The cook let out his held breath, and wetness gleamed in his good eye. Padraig and Niall glanced at each other and pulled their hands from the belts behind them, the training master leaning one shoulder against the wall, and the horseman rocking back on his heels with one hand on his hip and the other tucked in his cloak. I glanced Symon's way and found his smoldering eyes nailed to Dermot's back. My grandfather might be inclined to clemency, but the weaponsmaster surely was not.

"Two paths open before thee, Dermot, and thee will choose one ere thee leave this room tonight," Bruchan told him gravely. "Either thee will renounce thy allegiance to the Wolfhounds, purify thyself in our way, and help us withstand what Jorem intends to unleash upon us, or thee will go to thy allies in that boat tonight and never return to Inishbuffin. Go to Jorem, and thee will certainly die, and thy sister also. Stay, and we may win against all odds, and Jorem shall not know thee has turned to our service. Say which it will be."

"I would rather die at your hands than at Jorem's, the filthy pig. As for my poor sister, I don't even know whether she is still alive. They tell me she is, but . . ." He shrugged painfully.

"Nevertheless, we shall hope for her and do what we can. Now, the boat: how long is it to lay in the cove waiting for thy message?"

"Until the tide goes out."

"About a turn of the glass more," Ruan informed us.

Bruchan nodded briskly. "Then there is no time to waste. Who among us can counterfeit Cathir's hand?"

The brothers took up the spy's letter and studied it briefly. "I think I could manage well enough if we said something to the effect that I had hurt my writing hand—broken a finger, whatever," Padraig volunteered.

"Then thee shall be our correspondent to Jorem from now on." Bruchan turned to Dermot, who had rubbed the tears from his face. "And thee shall be the go-between as usual. Was it always the barrel to a waiting boat?"

"No, master. Sometimes Cathir's reports were sealed in shipments going between here and Dun Aghadoe; sometimes he slipped them to a messenger. Once or twice another brother going on trading business carried them in his baggage without knowing, and Jorem has had him robbed, supposedly set upon by highwaymen."

"Has any communication passed between Cathir and Dun Aghadoe since Jorem's visit?"

"No, master."

A slight smile crossed Bruchan's face. "Very good. All right, Dermot. Thee will wait under Symon's good guardianship outside, please. We will ready another letter for thee to pass. Thee might use the time to prepare for the ritual of purification."

The man bowed and turned for the door. Symon locked eyes with him and slowly stepped aside to follow him out.

Old Ruan might give the impression of being scattered in his wits, but I was learning tonight he was as sharp as a man half his age. "So," he said with satisfaction. "They know nothing of our getting the ring back, and not much more than they had guessed about Aengus, we ought to be able to make some headway, thee thinks, Brother?"

Bruchan drew a deep breath and stretched. "Exactly, thank the Powers. It has not gone all ill tonight. Niall, to Nestor immediately with the news, but take care that Cathir cannot hear thee, even though he seems to sleep. Then to the dovecote and tell Timon it is all over. Padraig, to the tower once more, if thee will: we must know if that boat leaves betimes. Thyr, we will need more wax and a mallet to seal the barrel again." The study emptied rapidly. Bruchan turned to the lovingly polished flat box with the tilted top that lay across his footstool tonight. I had remarked it already, but never having seen one before, I did not recognize a writing case. He opened the top and withdrew a sheet of paper, a quill, and a sealed pot that I thought at first must be a painter's sand pot, but which proved of course to be ink. I was curious about how it was used and drew closer to Padraig as he settled himself at Bruchan's nod in the master's chair and set the desk on his lap. He ruled the paper by creasing it lightly, dipped the pen, and looked up inquiringly, waiting for the master's dictation.

Bruchan clasped his hands behind him and paced the length of the chamber. "We will make our note to His Grace considerably shorter than Cathir's. Say this, Padraig: 'Greetings, my lord. I fear I have ill tidings to report to thee—' No, make that 'ill tidings to report to you. Mallory is lost. The day being an extraordinarily foggy one of the kind this coast is plagued with, Brother apparently stepped in a bog hole. The skellig was turned out to look for him, and of course I have conducted my own search with Dermot's aid, but there is little doubt, my lord, that he was swallowed by the treacherous ground.' "

"You might say something about cursing the Hag for it," Padraig interrupted, busily writing. "It would sound like something a Wolfhound would write."

"I will not profane one of the Four even to play a part," Bruchan answered quietly, still pacing. "Are ready for more?" Padraig nodded. " 'There has been considerable talk of Mallory these past days as a result, but he was a shepherd, so had good reason to be where he was, and I have heard no speculation that it was anything else than looking for lost sheep that sent him out there.'

" 'As to other matters—the wolf survived the voyage very well, my lord. Bruchan refuses to display it to the folk, using the reason that it will upset all the animals on the place if wolf is scented on the people's clothing and on the wind. This is undoubtedly true, though he is probably using it for an excuse not to encourage worship. To my surprise, he has agreed to hold the ritual of the Wolf. We had not looked for this development, my lord. Immediately after the new moon, I will report to thee—to you—whether the ritual actually took place.' "

Ruan and Padraig both nodded. This would give us breathing room to decide what to do next.

" 'Finally, to the boy. He is quite a forward brat, as Your Grace observed.' " Here Bruchan threw me a twinkling glance. The others were smiling broadly in the candlelight. " 'But he seems to have no particular thing to recommend him except for that. Already he has been disciplined for stealing and fighting with the other boys. I cannot think he is worth spending much of our time to watch, my lord, but we shall continue to do so. He has been set to 'prentice, by the way, not with Ruan, but with Nestor the herbalist.' "

Bruchan stopped on the square of the carpet. "Add something about a broken finger, as thee suggested before, and sign it as Cathir did. At least he used no wax seal on the letter itself, so we need not hunt for a signet ring. Then if thee will be good enough to seal up the barrel once more, I think we may send Dermot on his way under Symon's watchful eye. After that, I do not know about thee, Brothers, but I am for bed. This has been ... a wearying night," he added with quiet understatement.

Ruan stirred in his chair. "But at least we may breathe a little easier now that we have stolen a march on Jorem's faction. With the Powers' blessing we may keep them chasing their tails for quite a while, long enough if we're all sharp about"—he glanced at me—"what we're doing."

I gave him a nod, but I was thinking, And how will you steal Colin Mariner's color pots out from under Jorem's very nose with him drawing the noose tighter around Inishbuffin all the time?

Had I known the cost that would be exacted of us, I think I may have had the hardihood to find a bigger barrel, seal myself in, and roll it off the cliffs to the boat which waited below.

Certainly it would have been easier for all concerned, and I cannot see that such a course would have been any more desperate than the charade we entered upon as Dermot lugged the barrel across the moonlit burren that night with Symon's glowering presence dogging his every footstep. But the Powers' ways are often inscrutable, and as we were to find, They were far from done with us yet.

PART TWO

The Painter

Chapter 10

I suppose the miracle was that the breathing room we had engineered lasted so long. For nearly eighteen months, Bruchan fed Jorem a false chronicle of the community at Inishbuffin through the steadily improving forgery of Brother Padraig and the willing help of Dermot the cook. Cathir recovered soon enough from his "stroke," and we were all grimly amused when one of his secret letters confided to Jorem that he lived in constant fear of another attack. How near he was to the mark he could never have guessed, but the only time Nestor ever spoke sharply to me was one day when I cleaned the apothecary and moved the box containing the drug he had used to induce the symptoms in the steward. Bors the fisherman was carefully monitored, and we never had to use it on him.

Sometimes a visitor would arrive from Dun Aghadoe, and on those occasions Cathir would be off on a trading trip for iron, or for a blooded ram or bull to improve our flocks and herds. The visitor would of course be handed the letter Brother Steward had prepared for him and assured by Dermot that all was well with Jorem's little covey of spies. This happened often enough that Cathir complained of it in a letter, to which "Jorem" (Ruan's hand this time) replied that his absence was excellent cover, and he should continue, if possible, to make himself scarce whenever a messenger was sent from court to check up on us so that no connection between himself and Jorem's man could ever be traced. "For," wrote the false Jorem, "if I had intended you to be everywhere at once, I would not have given you helpers for your task." This effectively shut Cathir's mouth and made it much easier for Bruchan to keep him out of the way, and since Cathir's normal duties would entail his being away from the skellig much of the time anyway, no messenger from Dun Aghadoe was the wiser. Of course, Bruchan took the precaution of sending Brother Timon with Cathir every time the steward went on a trip to block any move the portly man might have made to contact Jorem while he was away from the peninsula.

I thought the first few times Bruchan sent Cathir away just before a Dun Aghadoe boat showed up that it was mere coincidence, but gradually I caught on. Obviously the master had his own spy or spies in Jorem's stronghold, but I never asked who they were, and he never volunteered the information. I was too busy at my various lessons to spend more than a few moments a day with my grandfather, and in any case I trusted that he was carefully putting into place the elements which would enable us to put Colin Mariner's ring and his color pots together some day in the not-very-distant future.

So I studied with Nestor and learned to read and write, as well as a good deal of his healing lore, which I found fascinating and managed to absorb fairly easily, much to my own surprise and his. I was far enough advanced by the time Seamus and Gwynt had to leave to begin their service at Dun Aghadoe to make presents to each of small kits of medicines for their own use. I remember that I put into each pouch packets individually tailored to the boy's likely hazards in his new job: a burn lotion for Seamus's work in the royal kitchen, and for Gwynt a pot of liniment strong enough to use on his horses or on the bruises he'd get if they trod on his feet. I spent a long time alone on the cliffs, watching their boat until it vanished in the bank of haze lying off to sea, and afterward felt much worse than I had at leaving my father.

From Ruan I learned to shape and develop the talent that lay in my fingers and in my mind's eye. Indeed, apart from teaching me how to use color and helping me to make my own color pots, the old master spent a great deal more time training my mind than he did disciplining my hands. A painter paints with his spirit, he told me repeatedly; *see* the story, *feel* the line and shadow and movement of it, and eventually you will be able to paint without sands, without charcoal or chalk. "How?" I demanded, but he would only smile his sly smile and bid me work harder. And in all that time I did not figure out how to paint a teardrop to his satisfaction.

Symon, too, helped train my mind, but in a far different way than Ruan's impish teasing. The weaponsmaster taught all the indentured boys the rudiments of self-defense, but my lessons with him secretly continued beyond what my companions learned to include practice with sword and throwing knife, and my un-aided hands. I rebelled only once, when he took me to a small walled field far from prying eyes and ordered me to kill a tethered sheep with a sharp blade only half the length of my forefin-ger. When I angrily refused on the grounds that the poor creature had done nothing to deserve such torture, he grimly reminded me that war was generally nothing but butchery, and how would I kill a man if I could not bear to kill an animal, how would I know the feel of blade hacking muscle or be able to stand the hot blood spraying my face when any hesitation might mean my own death if I had not done it before? When the lesson was over, and I was drenched with the animal's blood and excre-ment, I threw the knife from me and lashed out at Symon in a paroxysm of revulsion and shame. He allowed me to hit him a couple of times, and then we fought in earnest all over that bloody and trampled meadow. Eventually he knocked me flat, but we both bore the marks of it for many days, and I have never in my life been able to touch mutton or lamb since. But I will say now it was a valuable lesson. The brutal ones always are.

I learned to ride from Niall, I learned some needlework and design from Finian, I learned of the Powers from my grandfather; practical matters and ones of the spirit I learned in equal measure during those days. I was even able to go along on a few trading trips with Thyr. The chief attraction of these was the pos-sibility of quenching my burning lust with girls of the kind I had already known at fourteen before Bruchan brought me to the skellig. Certainly I would not stoop to dallying with any of the daughters of the community—it would have seemed like incest—and at that age a young man thinks more often with his loins than with his head, so it was quite remarkable that I managed to keep my mind on my lessons at all. I think Thyr knew what I was about when I disappeared for an hour or two when we tied up at a port town, and possibly he even had me followed at my grandfather's orders, but no one ever spoke to me about it, and I imagined then that I was putting something over on them all. How young!

Taken in sum, when I look back, my time at Skellig Inishbuffin remains the happiest period of my life. But the rent on my innocence was coming due, and the reeve with his sickle waited in the shadows.

Winter with its roaring gales and sleet storms had cracked. I knew the back of it was broken as I sat in a warm patch of sunlight in the apothecary and leaned on my elbows over a perfectly enchanting little tale I had discovered in one of the old scrolls. For three days past, bright sun and blue skies had blessed the peninsula, though the air outside coming right off the ocean was still cold enough to freeze the water troughs even at midday. Indoors, however, it was warm enough not to need the braziers for a few hours each day. A fly had hatched out; I could hear it buzzing amongst the dried herb bunches hanging from the rafters. Its drone, so hated during the summer, made me smile now. I unrolled a bit more of the scroll and shifted my chin to a cupped palm, reading.

The noisy creak of the apothecary door brought me around on my stool. Nestor was gone for the day to attend at a hard birthing in the village, and I thought when I saw Finian in the doorway that my medicine master might have sent a message to bring down something that he needed.

"Aengus! Is Brother Nestor here?" Finian peered around the middle-sized chamber as though he thought the healer might be stashed on a shelf with the powdered poppy. I had gotten to know Finian fairly well and respected his skill at designing tapestries, a skill not so very different from my own, but though I reckoned him a pretty good fellow, he was occasionally dense, and this drove me to distraction. Like Biddie Macroom's son, Fin was one who would have done well in the Cloud Kingdom.

I snorted a laugh. Usually he would color and then join me in a smile at his own folly, but today he was too much in a nervous state to care what I thought of him. I frowned and slid off the stool. "No. What's the matter, Fin? If you're sick, maybe I—"

He interrupted me, a thing I had never known him to do before. "No, it's not me." He went a little pale and carefully shut the door behind him. "Listen, Aengus, there's a person needs thy help, but it will mean danger and maybe punishment for thee. But he's alone, and I couldn't just leave him out there—"

I began slinging together the emergency kit that I was supposed to have repacked for Nestor that morning after making sure the herbs in it were still good. "Slow down, Fin, slow down. Somebody's hurt out in the fields?"

"Out beyond the bridge, yes, and—"

"Let's get some help to carry him in, then."

I whirled for the door and had my hand on the latch when to my shock Finian the gentle pushed me back. "No!" he cried. "No one can know!"

"What do you mean no one—"

"Aengus, it's Gwynt. He's run away from Dun Aghadoe and come home." He had gone stark white now, dark eyes enormous. "He's killed a man."

I knocked the pot of painkilling datura over and righted it again without even realizing. "By the Fire! They'll—"

"Aye," he said simply. "They'll hunt him down and kill him. They've already tried, an arrowhead is still in his shoulder. He wants thee. Will come?"

My frozen knees moved to the shelving to collect the medicines Nestor had prepared against fever, against humors of the blood, against pain. I added linen pads, bandage, and knife, gut thread, and a needle. "Is there anyplace near where we can hide him?"

He nodded jerkily. "One of the huts is not far from where he fell."

"All right, take some of the turf from the basket there. Stuff it in this." I tossed him a sack and ran out into the ward for two blankets from the cots. By the time I got back, Finian had the sack filled and had thought to grab the flint and firedog from the hearth and add a handful of tinder from the kindling basket. I took my own earthenware tea bowl from the table and hesitated over the iron kettle. If Nestor returned and found it missing, I would have to give him an explanation of how so pre-

cious an article had disappeared. I seized the
bucket and handed it to Finian. "Fresh water?" I questioned.

Again, that single nod. "The place is near the
Swan Pool." This was a small pond which the
women of the community counted a sacred
place. They held their own women-only rituals
there in honor of the Hag upon occasion, and
the men of the skellig would not go near it for
that reason. Rare are the ways of women and
their Power. However, the only thing that concerned me at the moment was that Swan Pool
was one of the few sources of fresh, clean water beyond the bridge. It would serve us well
both for bracing tea and to mix the healing
medicines Gwynt would need. I hurriedly
strapped the bag and with Finian close behind
me left the apothecary.

No one questioned us as we went down
through the gates. To their eyes the healer's
assistant was hurrying more supplies to him,
and everyone knew that Finian was often used
as a messenger. As we went through the village
I am sure we were seen, but no one left a seat
near a warm hearth to inquire what business
was sending us to the burren. Fin had the
bucket in plain sight together with his sack, I
had flipped my cloak over to cover the heavy
satchel I carried, and it may have seemed we
were on our way to gather some bark or the
root of a plant that had to be boiled down out
in the field. At any rate, we were not stopped.

Beyond the bridge we left the road and
struck out across the half-frozen heath. Finian
led me on the path which skirted a region of
tumbled rock and then looped Swan Pool. We
cut off at the far end of the small body of wa-

ter. In the distance was the narrow neck of land that connected the peninsula to the mainland, fine sand beaches on both sides and marshland in between. At that point Inishbuffin was no more than a couple of miles wide and flat as a saucer full of water. The road there had been laboriously built up of stones thrown into the bog to form a rough causeway, dams holding back the seawater. I had heard Bruchan say this was one reason the skellig had been left relatively alone from the landward side. Any attacks by pirates came from the sea. Gwynt must have realized that he would be seen if he crossed the bogway during the daylight hours, and so he had made the final stage of his journey at night. Finian, looking for a specific plant to dye some yarn he wanted to use in a project he was planning, had found him early this morning.

I kept up with Finian as we trotted about a half mile beyond the pool, the filled bucket slopping between us. We rounded a low outcropping, and I would have tripped over Gwynt if Fin hadn't caught me. "I left him a little further on, by that patch of blackberry canes. He must have crawled here since."

I was already kneeling by the huddled figure I would scarcely have recognized as my friend. He was mired to his very hair with falling in the bog, and beneath the light reddish beard he had grown in the past half year his lips were bluish with shock. I got his muddy cloak and tunic out of the way, quickly peeled off the wad of sleeve that he had somehow ripped off and stuffed against the wound, and—steeled by my training with both the medicine and weapons-masters—probed at the broken stub of the arrow shaft. Gwynt was so deeply unconscious he never even moaned, but Finian did and turned away. "It's gone proud, of course," I reported. "It must have been some days ago that he was shot. But the arrowhead isn't so far in. If we can get him to the hut, I think I can get it out."

"How will thee know the way to do it? Thee's never treated an arrow wound."

I held a finger against the pulse in my patient's throat and thumbed up an eyelid. His heartbeat was stuttering and his eyes were rolled back, and despite my calm manner I was frightened, so I spoke more sharply than I should have to poor Finian, who had done nothing but speak the truth. "Nestor's explained it to me. Look, if you want to try it, go ahead!"

"I can only work on canvas."

Despite myself I smiled. "That's right. You can do the suturing afterward, then." The Dina didn't see the joke, and looking at his shaken face, I wondered how he had fared when it was his turn to butcher the sheep in Symon's school. "Sorry, Fin. Where's the hut?"

"Beyond the rise." He nodded off to our right in the direction of the sea, which I could hear booming in across the boulders that formed a reef just offshore.

"All right. Help me carry him there, and then we'll come back for the supplies."

"I will bear the lad. Thee take the supplies which will be needful first, and then I shall return while thee begins work." He bent and lifted Gwynt easily, though I would have thought the tall youth would have been too heavy for the slender needlework artist.

I snatched up the medical kit, blankets, and pail and tumbled two bricks of peat out of the sack, then walked quickly after him. The hut, a rude shelter built of unmortared stone with a straw roof upon which the moss grew, was not far off, perhaps a quarter mile. If Gwynt had found his way to it during the night, he would have been able to see the outcropping of stone that marked Swan Pool and quite possibly had started off for the fresh water to assuage the thirst of the fever.

When we reached the hut, Finian did not pause and wait for me, but merely kicked in the flimsy door of woven reed on a willow frame and strode the couple of steps to the left wall to lie Gwynt down upon the old pile of bracken that someone had last summer gathered for bedding. Then, while I stripped off my patient's sodden clothing, Finian quickly set the turves and tinder within the small stone ring that served as a rough hearth and struck several sparks into the pile until the fire caught. "Mind the tinder," he advised, and slipped out the door, pulling it to behind him. I wet one of the cloths from the kit with a bit of the cold water from the pail and washed the area around the wound, reaching over to feed the fire more tinder and more until the peat caught and began to smoke. There was ample opportunity for the smoke to escape and a strong draft to feed it, so the fire was soon throwing enough heat that I could feel it. When the first layer of ash covered a couple of the turves, I kicked three of the stones from the fire ring into the heart of the coals to heat them. This was the price I'd had to pay for leaving the iron kettle back at the apothecary:

now I would have to heat the water in the pail by baking the rocks and dropping them into it. It took time and of course dirtied the water, but there was no help for it. The secret must be kept.

I could not wait for the hot water, though. I had worked enough with Nestor to sense that time was critical, so I used the minutes waiting for Finian to wash a bit more of the grime off, wrap Gwynt as warmly as possible, and ready both my patient and my instruments by dripping brandywine the length of my knife and needle and into the wound. Nestor always did this, though he had admitted honestly that he did not know why this sprinkling seemed to reduce the risk of the incision's going proud. Perhaps the brandy was taken as an offering by the Fickle Friend, whose realm included the fiery liquors and the easing of the heart that they produce, and the Power prevailed upon his sister the Hag not to take the patient to her underworld lair. Well, this wound had already gone proud, as I could plainly see, but if the Power who had spoken to me at the temple would look with favor on a few drops of brandy, I would give Gwynt the chance, by the Fire!

Finian must have run the whole way, because he was back before I expected him with the rest of the turf and, though at first I did not believe my eyes, another bucket of water! "Where on earth . . . ?"

"At the pool," he gasped, and grinned. "It must be a part of the women's ceremonies. I'm sure they would not mind our using it in this great need."

Maybe the Fickle Friend had some influence with his sister after all, I thought, and the idea steadied me. "Build up the fire, would you?" I directed. "Then I'm going to need your help." He joined me beside Gwynt a few moments later. I eyed him. The run had done him good, because he had his color back and his eyes were steady. "While I cut a little here and here to widen the wound, you're going to hold the incision as open as you can, taking care not to press down, but only outward. All right?"

"Aye. Then thee will cut down to the arrowhead?"

"Yes, and work it out without breaking off what remains of the shaft, I hope. Here, rinse your hands with this brandy. There will be pus and blood. Ignore it. Ready?" He nodded firmly. Wishing I'd thought to bring a candle, for the hut was dim even with sunlight finding its way through chinks in the stone, I leaned over Gwynt and began.

I had not thought, that day with the sheep in the meadow, that I might ever be grateful for the experience, but now as I did my first surgery I saw that the training that had been directed toward the moment when I killed a man might also go to saving one. Finian did well enough and somehow we got the damned thing out without breaking either the sharp iron point or the wooden stub of shaft. When it came, I could see down into the wound for an instant before it filled and there were no bone fragments, though the arrowhead had grazed a rib. The brandy bottle nearly slipped from my bloody fingers, but I managed to pour a liberal splash of the liquor into the wound, being sure to soak the area around it also. "All right, let go," I told Fin. As he withdrew his fingers the incision lapped closed, though the place

where the arrow had come out remained somewhat open. At first the wound bled and I
pressed the linen pad to it, asking Finian to
meanwhile fish the hot rocks out of the fire
somehow and get the water heated. By the time
this was done, I had eased the pad off. The
wound showed a gaping deep maroon eye, and
the flow of blood had slowed to a sluggish well-
ing. I regarded it. I didn't like the looks of that
at all and decided that I would not suture it
yet, but let the blood carry the evil humors off
as much as possible before I closed the incision. "Is the water hot?" I asked absently.

"It is," Fin answered.

"Dip some into the bowl, then. Here, strain
it through this cloth." While he fetched the hot
water, I dug through the satchel and found the
packet of dried and shredded willowbark. This
I steeped in the bowl for several minutes, then
added brandy—good inside as well as out—and
motioned to Finian to raise Gwynt's head. We
fed him the brew as you might dose a dog, but
more slowly so that we should not choke him.
His breath caught several times and once he
coughed by reflex, but the medicine went down
and stayed there. I lay my hand against his
heart and waited, for several minutes noting
no change. Between the wound itself, his
struggle to reach Inishbuffin, and the time he
had lain out in the night, Gwynt felt as cold to
my touch as a burren stone and nearly as life-
less. Finian caught my eye, voicing no question
but plainly asking one. "No," I replied shortly.
"He isn't well at all. You might wrap some of
the firestones to put against his feet. Don't let
them touch the bracken, of course—I don't
want him that warm." The weak joke drew a

weak smile from Brother Embroiderer, and he busied himself with the winter stones. I drew the blankets closer around my patient and set more willowbark to steep.

"I have been thinking on a story to explain thy absence from the skellig," Fin volunteered softly. He peered over his shoulder. "Thee will be staying with Gwynt, of course?"

"I can't leave him alone."

"Just so. I would keep vigil with thee, but I would be missed on watch tonight. Let this be the story, then: I shall return home and fetch whatever thee thinks will be needful, food, more fuel, and so on, bringing them back to thee here, on the way letting Padraig and Nestor know that one of the shepherds summoned a healer to attend a ewe that could not drop her lambs."

"A ewe?" I said sarcastically.

His eyebrows went up. "I have known Brother Nestor to answer such a call for help," he replied mildly. I waved him on. "And since Nestor was busy, thee went in his stead this time."

I fingered my chin. "That will do to explain why I'm not at supper tonight, but someone's likely to ask after me at breakfast tomorrow."

"Then I will have seen thee heading off with thy collecting basket," he said promptly. "Meanwhile, I shall come here to watch over Gwynt, and thee shall return to the skellig and let thy presence be known. Then we will trade duties once more."

"You know, for someone who's had so little practice at lying, you're not half bad at it."

He scrambled to his feet, grinning all over his face. "Maybe I have profited by association with thee, Aengus. Now, what else would thee like brought down from the apothecary?"

"I'll need a light, and it would be good to have another couple of bowls. The rug off my bed if you can manage it. More turf. Oh, and another flask of brandy. Nestor keeps it in the hanging cupboard."

"Food also will I bring, and tea. Fare thee well. I will return as soon as I may." He pushed through the door, and I heard his footsteps going away.

I got the winter stones out of the fire and put them wrapped in the blanket at Gwynt's feet, then had a thought and did the same with smaller ones at his hands. I managed to feed him more willowbark-and-brandy tea, carefully nudged the glowing turves closer together to nurse the fire along, and then settled near Gwynt to wait for some change in his condition to tell me whether I had won or lost the gamble.

The next time I took his pulse, I noticed at once both that his skin was warming to the touch and that his heartbeat was steadier. I breathed a sigh of relief that I am sure could have been heard outside the hut, exchanged the cooling stones for hot ones, and fed him a sip or two more of medicine.

The sun slanted in through different gaps in the rocks now; evidently the day was well toward midafternoon. Sunset occurs early at that time of year, and it would be a long and probably cold night. I hoped Finian brought enough turf to see us through it. My idle thoughts turned once more to Gwynt, and I wondered what madness had caused him to commit murder. It had happened at Dun Aghadoe, I knew that much from what Finian had said, and it was unlikely to have been a tavern brawl. No one looses an arrow in the confines of a tavern. So he had been shot by one of the king's archers. I surmised this from an examination of the arrowhead, which, when I washed off the blood, proved to be an iron one. A hunter uses bronze or even, in some of the poorer districts, flint. Iron was expensive, too valuable to chance on a stag. Only a king or a very wealthy noble would squander iron to make arrowpoints. I regarded my friend's face, swathed in the blankets. He looked a singularly unlikely outlaw. I wondered if I should tell Alyce, the daughter of Niall, that her sweetheart was back.

Finian returned when the light had grown rose gold, and the sun stood just a hand span above the rock outcropping that marked Swan Pool. He swung a heavy basket full of turf and other supplies off his back. "How is the boy?"

"Better by a little, I think. Ah, bread and cheese, too. Thanks, Fin."

He picked up the nearly empty pail with its silt of ash from the heating stones. "I'll fetch some water."

I jumped up. "No. Stay with Gwynt, if you will. I'd like a chance to stretch my legs a bit. Get warm by the fire before you have to make the trip back."

"Thy will," he conceded. "I put the story about as we agreed, and no one questioned it, but I heard that Brother Symon has sought thee today."

Yes, he was supposed to start teaching me the poisons and antidotes to them this afternoon, I suddenly remembered. Well, Symon would have to wait. "He's probably after me about edging swords again, or something." We pretended to the eyes of the community that I sometimes drew that punishment for my quick tongue. It was a convenient explanation for the fact that I was often in the armory.

As Finian smiled and crouched to the fire, I swung aside the door and went out into the chill salt wind. The sun was losing its warmth quickly as night came on, and I broke into a trot to get my blood moving. The sky arched above me, blue still in the east, flaring now toward persimmon in the west, where bars of purple cloud marched in ranks up out of the ocean. My heart lifted, and I skimmed down the path, bucket clanking in my hand.

When I reached Swan Pool, there were wind ripples breaking the sky reflection in its black surface, and the breeze blew through the dried reeds like fingers shaking small seedpod rattles. The sound made me uneasy, but I advanced through the tussocks of thick low growth near the edge and bent to dip the pail. I froze suddenly. Set on a rock at the very edge of the water was a Sugan Vanu, or Hag's Plait, a braided knot of straw of the kind that may be seen above every hearth and byre in the country to ward away the evil eye. To find it here at the pool dedicated to Her while she hovered about, hungry for my friend's spirit, was a blow that momentarily took my breath away. I straightened as slowly as if the sugan had been an adder I did not want to provoke into biting me.

"Thy pardon, old one," I murmured to the Power in the pool. "I would not have intruded but that the need is great." And the water you take from the pool may very well deprive her of the prey she seeks, the dark voice warned within my head. She won't like that.

I licked my lips, touched my hand to my breast in token of respect, and gingerly reached to dip the pail.

The rim of the wooden bucket broke the surface and sent wavelets out to further disturb the pool. My eye was drawn by a flash of white in the center, where, uncannily, the water was suddenly calm. A swan floated there, so still it might have been a carved decoy such as fowlers use, but the glistening black eye was alive and watching me. Faintly, very faintly in the wind, I heard a woman's voice say, "Oh, begone, you, and leave the boy alone."

I thought confusedly that a couple of the women from the skellig were spying upon me, and one said this to the other. "I mean no harm, Mothers," I called weakly. "I'm just getting some water."

There was no reply, no tittering from concealment, no sound at all except the wind soughing in the reeds. The swan did not, as I expected, start and fly off. Instead she dipped her long graceful neck to preen a wing feather. The women must have tamed the wild swans, I thought, and despite the fact that the sun had dipped behind the clouds, I felt easier. I pulled the bucket up, made the gesture of respect again, and backed away. I was a good way up the path before I dared turn my back on that pool.

Fin looked up as I entered hastily and firmly shut the woven door. "Thee was gone a time," he remarked. "Look, the stones have brought the other bucket to boiling. I brought tea. Will have some?"

A candle lantern's comforting glow lit the hut, and I cradled a bowl of tea in hands that were chilled with more than the cold air. "When you go back to the skellig, Fin, go by another path. Don't go near the pool." He frowned, and in spite of myself I blurted, "Just don't, please. The Hag's about—I can feel it."

His hands grew still; he had been chafing them over the fire. The needlework artist's eyes widened in the lamplight. "Does thee fear Her, Aengus?"

I swallowed some tea. "A man would be a fool not to."

Finian looked into the coals. "I do not. No, truly, though you think me a fool for it—and for other things, too." My face grew hot at this accurate observation, and I buried it in the tea bowl. He continued. "The Hag's true name is Ritnym, did thee know? As chatelaine of Earth, she has many secrets, and some of them she will share."

"Aye, with the women."

"Not only with them, though I believe they will always know her better than we men. But even to us, Ritnym reveals herself in bud and flower, flower and fruit."

"And pool," I murmured.

"What say thee?"

"Nothing. So you think she doesn't prey on people's spirits?"

He cocked his head. "It is not a preying, I think, but more a gathering to her of guests she wishes to conduct to her home."

I snorted uncomfortably. "Amounts to the same thing."

"Nay. It is the reception that awaits the people she takes that makes the difference. Thee believes Ritnym's Realm to be a place of terror, of darkness. I think it is not so. Surely a Power who can give us flowers here above the earth would not choose to live without them herself below the earth. Dost think?"

He was the oddest fellow. But the image of gardens in some cavern under the earth was not unappealing. Maybe fruit trees, too, and there would have to be water and sun somehow ... I shook myself and finished my tea. "It's a pretty fancy, Brother," I said quietly, looking across the peat fire at the serene face that I had once thought vacant. "I wish for thee, when it comes thy time, it may be so."

He smiled and reached to pat my arm awkwardly. "Thee's closer to Her than thee knows, Aengus."

At once the beautiful image evaporated and scalding fear ran down my back. "That's a hell of a thing to say!" I snapped, and glanced involuntarily toward Gwynt's still form.

Finian, surprised, followed my look. "I did not mean—"

"Look, you'd better be getting back to the skellig, don't you think?"

He looked hurt, but nodded and rose. "I shall make the offering for Gwynt," he said in a small voice. "Fare thee well until the dawn. I will be here as soon after as I can. Warmth of the Fire."

"Warmth," I answered without looking up.

The door closed behind him. I kicked a piece of turf into the heart of the fire, kicked it again when it didn't land where I wanted it to, and then had to spend some minutes tending the smoking peats until they burned cleanly once more. Finally I cut a piece of cheese off the

wedge he had brought, added a chunk of the
farl of oat bread, and had my solitary supper
while the breeze rustled the thatchlike reeds
by a black pool.

I did not know when the fever had begun to
soar.

I had checked him once, fed him willowbark
tea, and gone back to sit by the fire. Then I must
have dozed, because the next thing I knew his
rasping breathing filled the hut, and he stirred
restlessly under the blankets. I got to him just
as he threw the covers off. "No, Gwynt, no," I
murmured, drawing them back over him.

His chest heaved and, alarmed, I felt for the
heartbeat. It thudded beneath my palm, a
blacksmith gone mad with hammer and tongs,
and I hastily covered him up again. I had expected fever, but I had not been prepared for
it to burn him alive while I watched.

He moaned something in the stumbling nonsense that one hears from a person in the midst
of a nightmare, repeated it, and just as I
reached to soothe him and hold his head, tore
out a scream that ripped at the night and
raised my hair like a cat's stroked backward.

The cold spot of reason centered in my sniv-
eling brain told me that I had to get Nestor. I
had been afraid of killing Gwynt by revealing
his secret when all along I should have been
afraid of killing him by my proud ignorance. I
a healer! The idea was idiotic! Quickly I began
removing the bowls and buckets from near the
feverish boy so that he could not hurt himself
on them if he flailed.

I had my hand on the door when I looked
back a last time to be sure there was nothing I

had forgotten. In the dim candlelight he flung out one hand, then slept again, exhausted. Damn it, why hadn't Finian stayed? I thought angrily. Then one of us could have run to the skellig while the other minded Gwynt. I couldn't stay and I couldn't go. Either way, he could die.

Well, if he did, I resolved, he wouldn't be alone when it happened at least. But I would not wait to meet death here in this hut with a friend who had trusted me to save him, not while I had the use of two good legs. So I did the only thing, bundling him well in the blankets and adding my cloak over all to cover his head and keep him warm, then I left the fire and the candle burning, got Gwynt on my back somehow, and kicked my way through the door as though it were the Hag's gateway.

At first it was fair going. I told myself if Finian could carry him, so could I, but I soon discovered the frail-looking needleworker must be stronger than he seemed. My breath came in gasps that nearly matched Gwynt's, and my back felt as though a hot iron had been laid against the muscles. I bit my lips on the groan that wanted to escape into the freezing night air and plodded grimly on.

The shortest route was the path by Swan Pool and I was damned if the Hag herself was going to come between me and Nestor's healing hands, so I followed the rocky way, stubbing my toes often, but it didn't matter anyway because they were already numb. I could see the outcropping looming ahead and made for it like an ox that can only see to the end of the field without realizing he must turn around and tread it all again. The ignorance is all that makes the dumb beast go on, and it was probably the same with me.

The pool lay black against the ragged tussocks, starlight illuminating its surface faintly. I had my hands locked across my chest, trapping one of Gwynt's twitching wrists and a foot that wanted to kick my head off, and I could not make the gesture of respect and out of defiance would not make the one against evil (as if I could trick Her into thinking I was not afraid!), so I merely nodded civilly as you would to any goodwife of the town and bore left past the place where, I knew, the Sugan Vanu perched on its rock.

From the pool suddenly there was a heavy flap of wings, and she flew by me so low I could have put out a hand and touched the sleek, outthrust neck. I fell to my knees, bruising them painfully, but almost immediately heaved back onto my feet and began to run, though with my heavy burden it was really more of a fast walk that wanted to be a trot but couldn't.

The swan circled the pool, rising higher into the starlit sky, and now the wind passing over her wing feathers set up a soft music, unearthly beautiful and piercingly sweet. I stopped in my tracks and followed the white form's flight across the moor, marveling, and the swan circled once more, this time passing again low over my head, straight up the path that I must follow. I could have sworn her slim neck was turned back to see if I would come along. Settling Gwynt on my shoulders as if he had been a lamb wandered from the fold, I listened to the music and walked on, and my back did not hurt and my feet didn't stumble, and where I was it was warm.

Chapter 11

They found us not far from the bridge in a frosted patch of grass, on a line between the road and the hut that blazed like a beacon three miles distant. The wind blowing in through the open door must have sent sparks from the turf coals up to catch the straw roof. Fin, on his lonely night watch from the walls, had seen the conflagration and run to my grandfather with a gasped story and an urgent demand for help. My needleworker friend was, I am told, off down the road and through the gates so fast that Bruchan had no opportunity to refuse him permission to open them, even if he had wanted to do so.

I was only overcome with the cold and exhaustion, and those were easy enough to treat: Nestor ordered me put to bed with hot stones and enough brandy poured down my throat to bring me around in short order, blissfully warm and rather delightfully drunk. I poked a hand out from under the blanket to wave jauntily at my grandfather and gave him a loose grin. " 'S warm."

His brows drew down. " 'Twill get warmer, I promise thee." He reached for the stool, put it firmly by my cot in the ward, and I thought, Oh, boy, thee's going to catch holy old hell now,

Aengus. Bruchan grasped his knees with both hands. It may have been my drunken imagination, but I thought I saw his right hand twitching, hungry for the feel of a stout razor strop. "Why did thee not tell me at once?" he asked sternly.

I licked the remains of the brandywine off my lips, pushed against the pillow to sit up, weaving a bit, and got my eyes focused on his stony countenance. "Because we—I had to keep Gwynt's secret."

He nodded. "I know already of Finian's involvement, so thee need not say 'I,' and he has told me about Gwynt, though I could have predicted the matter when I saw the wound. I asked—"

I shouldn't have interrupted, but the question came pressing out my lips: "Is Gwynt alive?"

"Dost think I would take time to have talk with a drink-befuddled, impudent wretch if the boy were dead or dying? Nay, thee need not look so light, young master painter, thy friend is far from well. Nestor tends him. As to thee—" He bent that fierce eye on me again. "I asked why thee felt I could not be trusted to welcome a sick boy out of the winter's cold?"

He really was angry. Hurt, too, I perceived even through the brandy vapors. I swallowed and looked down at my hands on the edge of the blanket. "Stupidity, master."

Bruchan was silent for a long moment, then sighed suddenly. "If so, thee's not the only one, boy." He patted my arm and, when I looked up, shook his head in rueful apology.

An apology entirely undeserved. I had been stupid, risking a boy's life, and I had been doubly stupid not to inform the master of the skellig that he and all the community were in terrible danger. "Jorem's got to know Gwynt would return here."

My grandfather straightened. "Aye. The storm will break over us soon, Aengus. Jorem has long sought an excuse to be rid of this thorn in his side, as thee knows. He will seize upon the opportunity now." His eyes had slid past me to the unshuttered window, where a cloudy dawn barely grayed the sky. The weather must have turned toward rain or sleet, blown in by last night's wind. Bruchan regarded the patch of gray light for several moments without speaking.

I did not interrupt his thoughts, feeling that I had already given him trouble enough, but with him watched the light grow and heard the first hard rattle of sleet against the portico paving.

"Well," he murmured at last. "It could not be held off much longer in any event, I suppose." He looked down at me and smiled a little. "Nestor said thee might be hungry when thee woke, and then would want to sleep again."

I was hungry as soon as he mentioned it.

"Finian is outside, and Dermot has put a pot of broth on in the kitchen. Could thee eat?"

"A horse," I assured him.

"Much too valuable an animal to squander," he assured me, and rose to cross to the door. He pulled it a few inches open, spoke briefly, and Finian passed the window. Guiltily, he did not look in to see how his co-conspirator was getting on.

When Bruchan shut the door and stood leaning on one hand against the rough-plastered window frame, resuming his dark meditation of the morning, I said quietly, "I saw the swan last night."

He turned to me so quickly you'd have thought he burned himself on the windowsill and wanted to get away from it. "Thee *what*?"

So I told him about the Sugan Vanu, the woman's voice whispering, and the swan with the music in her wings who had guided my way.

His eyes, those uncanny eyes, first narrowed, then closed as he listened. Finally when I was done there was a faint smile showing through his silver-and-black beard. "Was it an old woman's voice thee heard?" he murmured without opening his eyes.

"It sounded like no crone to me, sir. A soft voice, younger, I would say, but not a girl's."

"Ah. Is it so?" he asked softly, but without seeming to expect an answer. He nodded to himself then looked at me. "I thank thee for the comfort thee has brought to me this morning."

I frowned. "The Swan is beautiful, but should we reckon her appearance a blessing? I mean . . . she's still the Hag." The harbinger of death, I meant.

Bruchan absently touched the four-spiral brooch in his cloak. "Death will come when it will come, Aengus. 'Tis no wit to try to avoid what is unavoidable. But the Power's manifesting herself to us is a comfort, indeed; in fact, I may tell thee it was one of the prophesied signs to be looked for when Colin's ring awoke."

"One of them? What are the other signs?"

"One thee knows already, the one we believe concerns thee directly—"

"The boy with the rainbow in his hand?"

"Even so," he confirmed. "So two signs have we had. The third has not yet appeared, but I will not tell it to thee, for knowing it, thee might try to bring it about, and that will avail us nothing. But if the two have been given, surely we may expect the third." He flashed a smile that was soon quenched at some other thought. The master turned and walked toward the window, hands clasped behind him. With his back to me, he asked, "Has Symon yet taught thee the maneuver called the Hag's Embrace?"

"No. We've done some odd ones, but never one called by that name. How does it go?"

Still standing before the window, he bent his head. "Thee shall learn it soon enough." The sleet was beginning to blow in, and he closed the shutters against it. A moment later there came a knock at the door, and he let Finian through with a bowl, some bread, and a pitcher of steaming broth. My grandfather surveyed the breakfast and looked across at me. "Eat now, thee needs to build up thy strength. I shall go to see Gwynt. Nestor has him guarded in his own chamber until we may meet with all the people to explain what has happened." He nodded to Finian, who avoided his eye like a puppy who has messed on the floor, and paused with his hand on the latch. His finger lifted to point at me sternly. "And no more brandy!"

Bruchan left me laughing and went about the heavy business of receiving a murderer into his skellig.

* * *

I slept well into the afternoon, as Nestor had predicted. The ward was empty but for me when I awoke, and I lay for some minutes cocooned in my warm blankets and listened to the rain. Then I grew worried about Gwynt and with a sigh got up and dressed. I discovered some painful bruises and my back was stiff, but altogether I felt well enough, especially considering my friend's plight. There was one thing I had to do before I went to see him, however.

I limped to the hearth and searched through the basket of turf and kindling, which was much depleted by Finian's foraging of the day before, but did not find what I wanted, so I dragged the stool to the window where the eave of the thatched roof dropped to meet the stone wall and stood upon it to tear down a few wisps. They would probably be too brittle and dry, but would have to do. A few minutes later I had plaited a miniature Sugan Vanu, which I attached to my cloak pin as an amulet. It might be a woman's symbol, but I owed something to the Lady of the Swan for Gwynt's sake, so I would wear it and sniggers be damned. Anyone who laughed at me would get his mouth shut in a hurry.

Feeling much better, I went along to Nestor's room.

At my light tap on the door, my medicine master admitted me. "Ah, the surgeon," he whispered, and though he did not smile, I got the impression his irritation was mild compared to what Bruchan had showed me earlier.

"Have I killed him?" I asked, not at all joking, for what I could see of Gwynt's face was not reassuring. He was scarlet with fever, and

the hair which fell over his forehead was
curled with sweat. I stole to the bedside like a
thief returned to the scene of his burglary.

"You are not looking carefully. Come, phy-
sician, you've learned your lessons better than
this, I hope."

Yes, that was a very definite edge of raspy
humor I'd heard in his voice. I realized what
had made him sarcastic, though, and set my
hand to Gwynt's forehead. "When did the fever
break?"

"At midday," Nestor replied with satisfaction. "The infection is pouring out of him with
the sweat. If I can keep him from parching,
you might just have saved your first difficult
case." Our eyes met, and the slow smile was
genuine.

"I should have sent for you the instant I saw
that the wound had already gone proud."

"Yes, you should have," he agreed briskly.
"Though I'm not sure I could have done much
more for him than you did without a hot iron
to cauterize it. The cutting was a good enough
job, given the tools Finian told me you had to
do it with. You might consider taking a scalpel
next time you answer an emergency call." He
held up a thin bladed knife that I had never
seen before. At the face I made, he laid it carefully back down on the worktable. "All considered, thanks to the Powers, things have not
gone badly." His eye was on the sugan in my
cloak pin.

I sat down on the stool drawn close to the
bed. "Did he wake at all?"

"Not yet."

Regarding my friend, I shook my head.
"Whatever happened at Dun Aghadoe, it must

have scared him out of his wits. He mumbled something when the fever hit last night, and then let out a scream that would have frozen your b— well, it turned my blood to ice, I can tell you."

The healer had folded his arms on his chest. "That isn't unusual for a person in his condition. The raging humors work on the brain, and the most horrible fancies can take hold. I know a man who killed his wife and two small children with an ax in the midst of one such episode because he thought they were fanged monsters come to drink his blood."

I shivered, and the healer immediately poured me tea and put the bowl into my hand. I thanked him with a nod, sipped, and looked up at him. 'So, what happens now, Nestor? With Jorem, I mean."

He leaned on the edge of the table and studied his boots for a moment. "He'll bring an army against us, I should think, though he'll probably demand that your grandfather—oh, yes, I am in his confidence." He smiled. "We princes have had much to say to each other, you know."

Of course they would have. I motioned him to continue.

"Jorem will demand that your grandfather release this poor lad to the royal justice of an assizes, a king's court, to hear the case. There will be no champion to speak for the accused, of course, as he is not a noble, and I doubt they'd stand for hearing any argument in Gwynt's defense, anyway."

"Bruchan won't turn Gwynt over to them, will he?"

Nestor unfolded his arms and stuck his

hands in his pockets. "I don't know, Aengus. I would think it might depend on whom the boy killed, and why. Remember: the law is all against Gwynt. He is an indentured servant. If he struck any blow that was not in self-defense, his life is forfeit."

I looked away, my stupid eyes burning. "But Bruchan wouldn't . . . I mean, he can't! Not after . . ."

"After Aengus the Painter saved him from death?"

That stung to the quick, and I rounded on him angrily. "No! I was going to say, not after Gwynt tried so damned hard to get home, dragging himself every inch of the way, because he thought it was the one place he'd be safe! You can't betray that kind of need to an animal like Jorem!"

We stared at each other. Nestor asked quietly, "But can you sacrifice the lives of all these men, women, and children to save one boy, however good a boy he is?"

"You have to, if he's *your* good boy. Gwynt is one of us."

A slow smile spread across the chiseled features. "You are Bruchan's grandson for certain. I had the same discussion with him not two hours ago."

I leaped from the stool. "And what was his decision?"

"That we won't give Gwynt up."

"Not even if Jorem himself sits with an army outside the lower wall and demands it?"

The healer rubbed his nose. "You'd be amazed at the descriptive language your grandfather can employ when he is discussing someone he loves so little as His Grace. I be-

lieve his comment ran something to the effect
that Jorem could—well, I have known it to
happen, but it is painful for both man and
beast, I understand."

I laughed with relief and held up my tea bowl
to toast the master of Skellig Inishbuffin, a man
with a fine command of language.

For the next couple of hours, Nestor and I
played at tiles, and I won. I do not say that I
won fairly, but I won. Time spent watching my
father at alehouses had not been entirely
wasted, and my medicine master should have
known better than to turn his back on a former
pickpocket. So Nestor regularly changed the
compresses on Gwynt's forehead and lost. I
think he didn't mind a bit, but he was rather
puzzled.

The footsteps of the lamplighter had just
gone past Nestor's door when Gwynt sighed
and croaked, "Water?"

Tiles clattered to the floor as my sleeve
brushed them. Nestor was there before me,
bending to put one hand against his patient's
brow and the other against the beat under his
jawline. "In a moment," he murmured quietly.
I was already fetching cool water. "How do you
feel, Gwynt?"

The flaxen-haired boy winced. "All right, I
suppose, master. Hot, though."

"Yes, I know. You've a fever. Here, sip." He
held the bowl I handed him to Gwynt's lips.

My friend swallowed thirstily, then licked his
lips and sank back into the pillow, eyes closed
as if even that small effort had taken all his
reserve. After a moment, his eyes swam open
again. "I made it to the skellig, then?"

"Yes." There would be time for the details

later, and all Gwynt really needed to know for the moment was that he was safe from pursuit.

"I didn't think I could, it hurt so bad."

"I can imagine," Nestor agreed in a soothing voice. He glanced at me, and I stepped around him to the bedside.

"Hullo, horsemaster," I said, restraining the more exuberant greeting I wanted to give him.

"Fat Lip!" he breathed, and smiled, glassy-eyed. Nestor went to the table to fetch the decoction he had prepared for when Gwynt woke.

I knelt on one knee so that he wouldn't have to squint up at me. "I'll go tell Alyce you're awake if you think you're up to handling a woman's pretty hysterics." Nestor cocked an eye at me, but said nothing.

Gwynt did not smile, as I expected. Instead his face grew strained. "No. Does everyone know I'm here, then?"

Now Nestor came over with the bowl, nudging me out of the way. "No," he answered firmly. "Only Finian and Aengus, myself, and the master have any idea. We were not seen carrying you in last night. Relax, Gwynt: your secret is safe for the moment. Drink this, please, as much of it as you can."

A moment later the sick boy grimaced and raised a weak hand to push the bowl away, and Nestor set it aside. Gwynt swallowed the taste several times, then looked up at the healer. "Am I going to make it?"

Nestor laughed the way doctors do when you ask a silly question that is burningly important. "Quite likely, if the taste of the medicine doesn't kill you."

Gwynt regarded him expressionlessly for a moment. "Then I've got to talk to the master."

Nestor met my eyes, and a moment later I was running through the portico toward my grandfather's study, heedless of the cold rain sluicing off the thatch.

I burst through the door, tore up the winding stair, and met Bruchan peering down in the candlelight at his small landing. "Gwynt's awake, and he wants to talk to you," I panted.

"Ah," was all he said and motioned me to lead the way.

Bruchan paused outside the door of the healer's chamber to shake off some of the wet, then went in with me at his heels. He walked directly to the bed and took one of Gwynt's hot hands in both his own cool ones. "I'm glad thee's home, boy," he said simply.

Tears of weakness spilled down Gwynt's face to trickle toward the pillow through his sparse beard. "Oh, master, I've did a terrible thing."

Bruchan drew off his hood with one hand, keeping the other still where the sick boy clutched it, and pitched the wet thing toward the table. He sat down upon the stool. "Would thee rather Aengus and Nestor left us now?" he asked quietly.

"N-no. They can hear. Everybody will know soon, anyway."

"All right. Tell the hard thing now, gently, and get it off thy heart. What happened, Gwynt?"

My friend motioned for the water bowl again, and after a glance at Nestor, I gave him two or three swallows. He sniffed and sighed. "That Dun Aghadoe's a bad place, master. There be weird folk there."

"Aye," Bruchan agreed. We waited.

"My new duties started well enough, though

I didn't much care for the way them nobles used their horses. They ride them too hard in all kinds of weather, hunting, you know. But I figured it wasn't my place to say nothing, so I just did like Master Niall had taught me, and the head groom told me I was going to work out fine." He sighed again and frowned. "I had some fights with the other stableboys, of course, you have to expect that." He cocked an eye at Bruchan suddenly. "They aren't trained as well as Master Symon trained us."

Bruchan and he shared a smile. The master drew an edge of the blanket further up on Gwynt's chest.

The boy collected his hazy thoughts for a moment. "Anyway, it was all right. Not like being here, but all right. After a while, they even raised me to second stableboy," he reported proudly. "I saw Seamus sometimes, and he'd been given responsibility, too."

"Very good," Bruchan murmured. "Thee's both good lads."

A stricken look crossed Gwynt's face, and he looked suddenly ten years older than we were. "Not anymore, master. Not anymore." He swallowed and went on in a lower voice. "They'd found out I could do shoeing, so I was assigned to do several of the horses' winter shoes. I did it carefully, just the way Master Niall does, I swear!"

Bruchan squeezed his hand. "One of the nobles took a serious fall because his horse had split a hoof, and they blamed thy shoeing, I take it."

Gwynt stared. "How did you know?"

Nestor and my grandfather exchanged

glances. "As thee said, Gwynt, Dun Aghadoe is a bad place. The man who fell—who was he?"

"I'd seen him often, master." My friend's face twisted. "Several times he'd said a good word to me about how I'd taken care of his horse. Brandon Mac Maille was his name."

"Brandon!" Nestor gasped, shock plainly written on his face.

Bruchan seized his arm warningly, and the healer turned away from us to lean on the table. "Well, well," the master of the skellig breathed. "Mac Maille."

Gwynt's eyes welled again. "I didn't mean for him to be killed!"

Immediately Bruchan recalled himself and patted the boy's arm. "Nor did thee kill him, Gwynt. At best it was an accident of the sort that will happen; at worst, as I believe, it was treachery, but not any of thine."

I spoke up, alarmed at Nestor's reaction. "Who was this Brandon Mac Maille, master?"

"A friend, Aengus, who was more honest than was wise in a place like a king's court."

"He spoke against Jorem's influence," I guessed.

His eyes flashed and touched mine. "Even so."

I glanced to Gwynt, wondering if it mattered whether he understood the next thing. "Then you've lost your support at court," I said to Bruchan.

"Hush," Nestor warned, straightening though he did not immediately turn around again.

"Not all of it," my grandfather said at the same time. He stroked his beard worriedly. "It does make things more difficult, however." His

eyes raised to Gwynt, staring cloudily unfo-
cused at us, the fever weakening him. "So thee
were seized as Mac Maille's murderer, lad?
How did thee manage to escape, then?"

Gwynt fumbled for the water bowl, and I
jumped to hold it for him. He drank, coughed
as the water found the wrong way down, and
Nestor was immediately there to raise his
shoulders and hold the sutures firmly so they
wouldn't tear through his skin. Looking over
the healer's shoulder, I was astonished to see
a smear of wet along his cheek. Whoever Mac
Maille was, Nestor had known him well.

The boy lay back in the pillow, painfully trying not to cough again. Nestor looked across
him to Bruchan. "He should rest."

"Well do I know it," the master replied.
"Only a moment more, by thy leave, Brother.
Now, lad, how is it thee was able to reach us
here?"

"They shut me up in the dungeon," Gwynt
related hoarsely. "Horrible. There are people
down there, master, who have been there for
years! Years with no sun and fighting the rats
just to keep them from gnawing your fingers
off!"

"Peace, peace. I know it is an evil memory.
Pass it over now, and go on," Bruchan's soft
voice counseled.

Gwynt caught his breath and cleared his
throat. "Well, I was in chains, of course, and I
expected to be hauled out anytime and sent to
the gallows, but they never came for me, and I
wasn't flogged, either. I had nothing to eat,
though: I couldn't reach the pan the guard set
down every day, and none of the poor wretches
down there would spare a second thought for

me, they were too hungry themselves." He drew a breath.

Bruchan used the pause to ask, "How long were thee in the dungeon?"

"Only three days, I think."

"And did they put thee down there as soon as Mac Maille's death was discovered?"

Gwynt nodded wearily.

"And thee's been how long on the road? A week, perhaps?"

"Not so long," the boy said. "I hid away on a boat and landed about a day down the coast here. I think it was only three days since Dun Aghadoe."

"Barely a week altogether," Nestor murmured. He and Bruchan met each other's eyes.

The master of the skellig prodded, "Go on, boy. I know thee's weary, and this will soon be over. How did thee get out?"

"They came for me in the night. They kept shoving the torch close to my face, so I couldn't see much, but I think there were three of them, though two never spoke. They took me from the dungeon, and I figured this was it, so I might as well make a break for it. But they had hold of my chains, so there wasn't much I could do until we were outside.

"They marched me across the courtyard—there's a courtyard outside the door going down to the dungeon—"

"I know," Bruchan murmured. "Go on."

"Across the courtyard to the stable, and the odd thing was that one of them held my chains up off the paving stones so they wouldn't make any noise. I couldn't understand why we were in the stable, either, but there wasn't any time to worry about it, because before I knew it one of them was kneeling down to unlock my fetters, and another unlocked the ones at my wrists, and the third who held the torch took a cloak from a peg in one of the stalls and threw it to me. 'Put it on, it's cold,' he said.

"By that time I was shaking. It's bad enough to face death, but then to make it crueler by unlocking you and giving you a cloak to stay warm was too much. I spit on the soldier. He grabbed a fistful of my tunic and pulled me up to him. 'I'm trying to save your life, idiot!' he said. 'Now, shut up and listen! You'll crawl in here.' He shoved me toward a wagon standing nearby and pulled up a false floor in it. 'Tomorrow morning early it will leave here and drive down to the port. When you hear the sounds of the winches and water, choose your time carefully and take a peek. If it's clear, get yourself out. You'll be drawn up right in front of a ship with the figurehead of a ram. Go aboard—no one will question you if you're wearing this cloak. Go belowdeck, down with the cargo. Stay there, and she'll put out to sea with the tide. You're going to Master Bruchan, I presume?' I gave him a nod, for it seemed he knew it already. 'Excellent,' he said. 'This boat will land you a day's journey to the southeast. You should be able to make your way from there. Just follow the coast path.'"

Gwynt winced, and his hand went to the wound. "Everything was just as he said, except that as I was getting into the wagon, one of the night watch walked by and saw me. He shot me, but before he could raise an alarm, the three of them had knocked him out. They broke off the shaft and stuffed my sleeve against the blood. I think they argued, but in the end they put me in the wagon, anyway." He had run out of strength and closed his eyes.

"What did this soldier look like, the one who spoke to you?"

"Light-haired, like me. Tall, as old as Finian, maybe. Eyes the color of Fat Lip's. He had a scar that twisted his lip."

Nestor started, and Bruchan's arm shot out to seize Gwynt's limp hand. The master held the strain in his voice down, but I could still hear it clearly. "Did he give thee aught for me, Gwynt?"

The sick boy opened his dull eyes. "How did you know, master? Yes. A pin or something. It's in my cloak, in the hem. Oh, and he said to tell you it's in the star chamber, whatever that—"

His hoarse voice was lost in Nestor's gasp.

"Did I say something wrong?" my friend asked confusedly.

If Bruchan had smiled any wider, he would have split his face at the ears. "Nay," he said warmly. "Nay, Gwynt. Thee's said the first right thing I've heard in many a year. Rest now. Sleep, and Nestor will make thee well again." Gwynt nodded, turned his head on the pillow, and was instantly asleep, his face sheened in sweat. Bruchan rose, and Nestor straightened from leaning over the bed. The master held out a hand to him, and the healer grasped it. "A high price, Brother, but it is done," Bruchan said quietly.

"Aye, master. Warmth of the Fire."

"Come, Aengus. We will let these two brothers rest," my grandfather said, "for both of them have need of it." Nestor smiled painfully, and I followed Bruchan out.

As soon as we were outside and the door closed, I demanded, "What's happened? Who was the soldier and—"

He sniffed deep of the chill night air. The rain had slowed to drizzle. "I feel a walk coming on. Will come?" he asked, throwing his cloak over his shoulder jauntily.

I stared at him. "You're mightily pleased about something."

"Aye," he admitted at once, tugging at his beard.

His secret smile was infuriating. I stuck my fists on my hips. "Look, if you're going to be a bloody mute about it—"

"That pin Gwynt brought."

"Yes, what about it?"

He tilted his head up, eyes closed, and let the light rain sprinkle his face. "It is the third sign. The time foretold has come." He turned to look at me. "Isn't it a beautiful night?"

I wasn't sure about that.

Chapter 12

There was no time to squander in sleep that night. Bruchan did, indeed, walk with me for a little—down to the second wall and back—but then he had the alarm bell rung, and the people ran from their houses to the dining hall, pipes smoking or a bit of stitchery unnoticed in their hands. It was the quiet hour after dinner, and some of the little ones had been grabbed out of their loft beds and wrapped hastily in a blanket. They knuckled their eyes and stared at everyone out of rosy cheeks. There was no fire visible, and no one had seen any pirates, but the brazen call of the bell had sent ice through people's veins, and they quickly slid onto the benches or lined the walls to hear what the master had to say.

Bruchan, uncharacteristically, spoke to no one while the hall filled. He stood at his place at the table that was already set up for the morrow's breakfast and idly pushed a pewter spoon this way and that, his head bent. People looked at him and knew it could only be one thing. The hall was silent but for a child's querulous cry and a mother's quieting murmur.

"I am sorry to have broken the peace of thy hours this night," the master began, "but something has happened that thee should know. Knowing it, we may be prepared. So then, this is the matter: thee remembers one of our young indentured lads name of Gwynt, tall with flaxen hair, prenticed with Niall?" There were nods around the hall, puzzled looks. "Then thee remembers also that Gwynt was one of those picked by Lord Jorem to go to court, and that those boys left us for Dun Aghadoe early last fall. Well . . ." He pushed the spoon up on the table. "Gwynt has come home."

From the table immediately to Bruchan's right there was a scrape of bench against the stone floor, and when I glanced that way, I saw Alyce, her face flaming red above the end of shawl she had involuntarily clamped to her mouth. Her eyes were shining, but the look in them died with Bruchan's next words.

"He stands accused of murdering a man and escaped from the king's dungeons, sore hurt from an arrow wound." The buzz of many voices rose at that. Alyce went white and buried her face in her hands. Bruchan glanced at her and waited them out, then held up one hand. In the quiet, he said, "Thee should know, brothers and sisters, that the boy did not, in fact, commit the murder, though murder was indeed done. I have no doubt that thee can guess by whom 'twas planned." Then he told them about Mac Maille and the horse with the split hoof, the help Gwynt had in making his escape, and the desperate journey up the coast and across the burren. "By Swan Pool he was found and is presently under the excellent care of Brother Nestor and his assistant." Not quite true, since the assistant was sitting on a bench two tables away, but it won me some warm looks. "Brother tells me the boy will recover and strengthen again." Someone clapped, and the master nodded. "Yes, thank the Power."

Not the Wolf, I thought. Not him. It was the Swan who saved Gwynt. She's the Power to be thanked. I touched the sugan in my cloak pin.

People were stirring. Bruchan let them come to it on their own. Far down the hall Padraig had stood as he had come in, his little son asleep on his shoulder. Not to wake the boy, the training master walked a little between the tables to call in a low voice, "Master?"

"I hear thee, Padraig. What is it?" At Bruchan's carrying voice, people hushed and turned to hear.

"Jorem will come against us now," Padraig said flatly. "It's the excuse he's been waiting for. How long do we have to get ready for him?"

The hall was utterly silent.

"It will take even the Wolfhounds time to gather their troops and supplies to march on us. I think we may have a fortnight before the main body of the army arrives, but I should not be surprised if a small attack force arrived before then to bar us inside the skellig gates." There was no despair in his voice and no anger, merely reason, and this had a calming effect.

Padraig nodded as if the stunning news were no more than he had expected and absently patted his boy's back.

Ruan spoke from his place at Bruchan's right. "Time enough, Brothers, to put into effect our plans, *the* plan, I should say, the parents here will know what I am talking about.

And time enough to secure ourselves. They will not find us unprepared, thanks to the forethought of the master." He gave Bruchan a nod and smile of support.

Bruchan returned it. "As Brother Fish Trap says—" He waited out the little laugh that ran around the room. "We all know our duties. We have rehearsed for this day many times, and insofar as care may be taken, we are ready. I will tell thee a thing to strengthen thee: we do not fight alone."

Timon called, "The Powers . . . ?"

Bruchan nodded. "The signs are given," he reported quietly.

Relief swept through the room like spring air through a sickroom. Heads came up; shoulders straightened.

The master rubbed his hands together briskly. "And now to work—in thy own homes tonight, and at dawn the bell shall ring to send us all to our appointed tasks. Let us go now." Folk began to scrape back the benches and stand talking to neighbors for a few moments before they went home. Bruchan caught Symon's eye and beckoned him. The big man asked another of the brothers to take the two children he carried and waved his wife away, apparently telling her that he would be right along and to get the children home. Then the weaponsmaster came up to Bruchan, and the two of them walked to me. "I would have thee teach Aengus about the Hag's Embrace tonight, Brother, before thee goes home. There is much to be done still, and little enough time for it."

Symon looked startled at first, but then his face subtly hardened. "Aye, master. I hear."

"Thank thee." Bruchan turned to me. "When thee's done with this lesson, I would talk with thee in my study."

I touched my hand to my breast and followed Symon out into the night with the definite feeling that whatever this Hag's Embrace maneuver was, I wasn't going to like it.

For privacy, we went to the armory. It was deserted and cold, the racks of burnished swords and spears casting deep shadows in the light of the single candle Symon lit. He motioned me to sit on one of the stools, and I did, drawing my cloak around me and keeping my hood up against the damp chill. "I gather you don't much like teaching me this trick," I said to break the silence.

He gave me a sharp look. " 'Tis no trick, Aengus, and no, I do not like teaching it to a youngster. But if master thinks you need to know it, I'll do it.

"It's dangerous, then."

"Aye. Very much so, which is why of the more than three-score brothers in this skellig, only four of us know it: Nestor, Master, Brother Ruan, and myself." He rolled a bit of warm candle wax between his thumb and forefinger aimlessly. "I have not taught it even to Padraig, who, as you may know, has been like a brother to me—a real one—since the two of us came here together as indentured boys nigh thirty years ago." He stared into the candle for a moment, then flattened the little ball abruptly against the table. "Well, I shall teach it to him now, you may believe." His eyes came up to mine. "But first, you." The weaponsmaster set his thumbs in his belt. "I asked you once before to trust me."

"Yes, and I nearly knocked your head off with that dummy sword."

We both smiled reflexively, our smiles fading in a moment. Symon nodded. "Will you trust me again?"

For answer, I set my hands on my knees, looked up at him, and prepared to let him put me under.

"Aye, that's part of it, but only part, and not the dangerous thing." He walked to the rack of spears, lifted one end of it easily though the thing must have weighed as much as a yearling calf, and swung it aside, meanwhile saying over his shoulder, "I suppose it should properly be Nestor to show you this, but he's occupied with Gwynt. 'Twas Brother Herbalist who discovered it." He pushed on one of the stones in the wall, and I heard a lock snapping open. The stone moved back some three or four inches, just as the one at the temple had done, and Symon reached into the hollow beneath it. He withdrew a smallish amber bottle, and by that alone I knew that the fluid in it was precious. As I have said before, we of the Burren do not make glass. It must be purchased from the filthydwarfs, and at great cost.

"A drug?" I questioned, my eyes on the bottle.

"You're quick. Aye, a drug that Nestor stumbled on. It nearly killed him." He set the bottle on the table with the label toward me and pointed to it to emphasize his point. I recognized the medicine master's fine handwriting: *Th' Hagges Embrace*. Above it was drawn a small Sugan Vanu, the apothecary's symbol for a poison. I swallowed and looked up at Symon.

"Right," he said. "Now you see why so few know about it."

"If you're in a situation in which suicide is all that's left to you, I should think you'd want to go by your own dagger," I said grimly.

"But suppose you had been captured and stripped of your weapons, or because of wounds could not use your dagger. What then?"

I lifted my chin. "Then you'd wait for death honorably from your enemy's sword."

He snorted, kicked the other stool close to me, and sat down. "You have a warped sense of war, boy. I thought we took care of that down at the sheep pen."

My lips tightened. "You taught me how to kill, not how to die, Symon."

"I taught you that war is butchery, little brother. Remember it, and let's have no more talk of merciful deaths at the hands of an enemy." He picked up the amber bottle and regarded it. "Particularly when the enemy is Jorem or any of his Wolfhounds." Under his heavy black brows, his eyes moved to my face. "And even more so if His bastard Grace has any inkling you're the blood of Colin Mariner. Do you see now why your grandfather wants to give you the protection of this last bit of our lore?"

I ignored his question for the moment and asked irritatedly, "Does everyone in this whole damned skellig know the relationship between Bruchan and me?"

A genuine smile eased his square face. "A body wouldn't guess from your temper, that's for certain. No, your secret's known only to a few. Of course master had to give me some rea-

son why you were to get all the special training, didn't he?"

"And why you were to be one of my body-
guards." That stopped him. He hadn't thought
I'd figured it out, and until that moment, I
hadn't. "All those hours I was assigned to 'lessons' with you, and I never realized it was to
keep me out of harm's way as much as to teach
me weapons craft. You, Nestor, and Ruan.
Well, well."

He scratched one heavy brow. "All right, if
you want to know the truth: yes." He pointed
a blunt finger at me. "But don't think it was
any privilege for me."

I grinned. "Nor any pleasure, certainly."

Symon tugged at his ear. "Never that." He
seemed to be swallowing a smile, but then he
realized the amber bottle was still cradled in
his other hand and sobered. "Well, boy, if you
ever learned anything from me, learn this." His
voice slipped into the tone he adopted when
instructing a class of indentured boys. "This,
as you can plainly see, is called the Hag's Embrace. Take too much of it, and you'll die, simple as that. It's not a bad going, Nestor tells
me: fairly painless as these things are reckoned; there's a convulsion that stops your
breath, and then you don't know any more
about it, you understand?" I nodded. We had
many such poisons, and Nestor had taught me
about them. Sometimes there was an antidote
to them to be learned; sometimes the poison
itself, if given in minute dosages, could actually be beneficial to a patient.

Symon continued, "However, this Hag's Embrace has an interesting property that Nestor
stumbled on, as I said. If you take it in just the

right quantity, there's a convulsion that stops your breath, your limbs go stiff, skin cold, lips gray, no heartbeat. You appear by all accounts to be dead." He shook the bottle gently. "But you're not."

"How long does the effect last?"

"About twelve hours."

"Long enough for your enemy to conclude he's killed you and leave you on the battle-field." I eyed the brown bottle. "Of course, he might spear you for good measure."

The weaponsmaster cocked an eyebrow. "Then you don't wake up," he said reasonably. He nodded at the look I gave him. "It's a dire ploy, all right. A last resort."

I cast back my hood and nervously ran a hand through my hair. "Even your friends, if they happened to find you, might think you were dead. You could be in your grave without anyone's realizing!"

"How do you think Nestor discovered it? Aye, if you think you're startled, you ought to have seen me when I was on vigil beside his bier, and he suddenly drew a breath and sat up." He thumped his chest a couple of times. "My heart nearly failed me, it did." He straightened on the stool and sniffed. "So we know the drug works. None of us has ever had to use it, but we've kept the knowledge of it all the same as a handy, if dangerous, thing to know. There's another thing Nestor's found out: if you've a trigger word planted in your mind, someone who knows it can call you out of the drug sooner, and the aftereffects don't last so long."

I nodded. "And you're going to plant the word now?"

"Aye. Just as a precaution, as your grandfather, the healer, Ruan, and I have all done. Are you willing?"

"Of course. Plant away."

He pulled the little bob from his pocket. "Relax, then, and listen."

I don't even know what he said. I remember hearing nothing, but I suppose I was still so tired from the night before that I went willingly enough into the sleep.

"Three," I heard faintly, and suddenly the armory with its flickering candlelight was around me again. I drew a breath. "Is it done?"

"Aye. You make a beautiful chicken, by the way."

"Thanks. What's the word? I should know it, don't you think, in case I have to bring one of you out of the drug?"

"Ilyria."

A word that would hardly pass the lips of any Burrener unless he was of Skellig Inishbuffin, where the dream was kept alive. I nodded. "And now, how much of the drug do you use?"

"As much as will fit on the head of a pin. Take this up to master. He'll show you." He handed the amber bottle over to me. "And don't drop it, by the Four!"

I put it in my pocket, patted it with elaborate care, and swung open the door.

"Aengus?"

I turned.

The big man rose slowly to his feet. "Take care of yourself."

I thought it was just the image of Jorem's army getting closer and closer that was starting to work on the man with five children and another on the way. "We'll all take care of each other, Master Sy."

"Aye, boy, we will."

I drew the door closed behind me, shook off the chill feeling, and strode briskly toward my grandfather's study.

"And the soldiers who freed Gwynt were Mac Maille's sons?" I guessed.

He puffed at the urn pipe. "Two sons and daughter, I think, though of course I cannot be sure. The one who spoke, at any rate, was Owen. Gwynt's description of him fits exactly." Bruchan set the mouthpiece aside and took from the candle table a long pin with a hinged ring at the end of it.

"That's an old-fashioned cloak pin, by the look of it."

"It is," he confirmed, handing it to me.

I examined the bronze length of it, and then opened and closed the ring, looking closely at the small stones which were inset in the scrolled metal. "Surely these aren't real rubies around the ring."

"Oh, yes. They are. What else does thee see?"

"Well, the upper end of the pin is unusual. I've never seen one flattened this way, like a square nail, and whoever did the engraving must have had a steady hand to get it so fine, some light and some heavier."

Bruchan smiled and motioned for the pin. When I handed it to him, he tipped the candle to let a bit of wax drip on the table. Then he pressed the end of the pin into it. I craned to see over his hand. Imprinted on the wax was a flowing network of lines which might have seemed random, except that clear in the midst of them was a single spiral. "By the Four!" I exclaimed.

My grandfather chuckled. "A very effective signet, wouldn't thee say?"

"Was it Mac Maille's?"

"Yes. And his father's father's before him, on back to Macguiggan, the faithful friend of Colin Mariner."

I stared. "And Macguiggan's family still counts itself bound to ours after five hundred years, so much so that a man will risk death to defy our enemies?"

"It is not so simple as that. Brandon Mac Maille—the name of the family was changed nearly two hundred years ago to protect them—was a great and powerful lord in his own right. He knows . . . he knew Jorem coveted his holdings. And also, Brandon and his family keep the old way, as we do here at Inishbuffin. There are some folk around who do, Aengus, though most of them prudently hide it under the current fashion of belonging to the Wolf Cult. We have allies in unexpected places."

"You must, if they reach even to the king's court!"

He regarded the rug. "I fear it has cost the family Mac Maille dearly. Brandon, of course, and now probably Owen and the others. I cannot imagine that Jorem has not discovered their deception by now." He shook his head. "We will hope they have not died in vain." He reached to clip the mouthpiece to the pipe and became all business. "Symon gave you the bottle?"

I drew it from my pocket and handed it to him. He uncorked the amber flask and carefully dipped the pin into the drug, letting the excess drip off the sharpened point, and then set it aside on the candle holder to dry.

"Master, where are the color pots?" I asked quietly. "If all the signs are given, and Jorem's on his way here, then we haven't much time for doing whatever painting it is that's to make our return to Ilyria possible."

He sat back in his chair and eyed me. "They are in Dun Aghadoe."

"Is one of your allies going to steal them and send them to us? If so, it'll have to be before Jorem's fleet—"

"Jorem's fleet is no matter, as long as it does not arrive by the second turn of the tide tomorrow, because thee will be safely away before then."

"*Away?* You're sending me *away*? *Now?*" I was on my feet, staring. "But I—"

"But thee's an indentured boy still, remember, and if thy master chooses to send thee to safety, thee'll go."

"That's not—"

"True? Of course 'tis true. What thee expected? Well, we cannot always hope to have things as we expect."

I was still staring, but I was beginning to be angry. "You can't think I'd go now and leave you in danger. That's faithless."

"That is wisdom. Thee's the Painter, Aengus. Thee must be kept safe to do the job. It has been a constant worry to me to have thee here these past months, but for the training thee needed, there was no other choice. Now that training is complete, and the enemy approaches. If thee loves me, grandson, thee'll go and ease my mind."

"But what about you?" I retorted hotly. "Why don't you ease *my* mind and come with me?" He smiled indulgently, and in the face of that understanding look I couldn't curse his immovable will, as I wanted to do. I sighed bitterly. "No, I suppose that would never do for the master of Inishbuffin."

"No," he agreed.

"So I fly before Jorem. Where am I going?"

"A boat will pick thee up at Gull's Cove. A pirate boat."

I said carefully, "Timbertoe and I don't get on very well together."

"Then thee must learn tact, eh?" His eyes twinkled, but only for a moment. "He is one of the allies of whom I spoke. And also, perhaps more importantly, he has been well paid to provide sanctuary for our children."

"Children! Thanks!"

"I did not refer to thee, young hothead, though well I might. No, I mean the children of the skellig. We will get them away to safety, and the women with them, those who will leave. I think most of the young mothers will go."

My mind was somewhat lightened at that. Somebody would be safe, anyway. "We all go to the dwarfs' island, what do they call it—Jarlshof?"

"No, that would make the connection between the skellig and the dwarfs too obvious to the spies Jorem no doubt has in every port. Instead, Timbertoe will take thee by the first boat to his own home on Inishkerry, a smaller island in the dwarfs' domain, and the women and children will follow as soon as may be." Bruchan regarded me. "Thee will stand in my place for them on Inishkerry while the community is sundered this way. Care for them well."

"I could never stand in your place for anybody." I looked away. "The color pots will be brought to me there?"

"Yes. As soon as Jorem leaves the gates of Dun Aghadoe, our confederate will send them to thee by swift courier."

I nodded. "But you'll be here. Who will be my storyteller?"

"Ruan. He will be on the boat with the women and children." He laughed at my expression. "Thy grand-uncle has many talents, lad; he is not a painter only."

No, indeed. Ruan was also fisherman, sailor, forger, bodyguard, and, I was beginning to realize, co-architect of much of this plan. Now he would be storyteller as well. I felt better. Brother Ru was a good man to have around in a tight place, I'd bet. I thought about that, and about the painting I was to make while Bruchan wove the Macguiggan pin through my cloak, concealing it in the hem.

"Have care when thee gathers it around thee to sit," he cautioned.

"Just my luck, I'll stab myself in the ass with it," I muttered.

My grandfather threw his head back and laughed. But it was a forced laugh, and we both heard it. He drew a breath suddenly, smoothed the cloak, and motioned me to put it back on. I did, fastening my brooch with its Four Spiral insignia and carefully inserting the miniature sugan back in the clasp. He twisted the chalcedon ring from his finger and handed it to me. It fitted my finger exactly. When it was done, I stood there, and he sat, and neither of us could say it. The candle flickered, and the pipe smoked forgotten.

I reached for his hand at the same time he rose to take me by the shoulders. We fumbled a double handclasp. "Fare thee well, boy. I pray the Powers to guide thee."

"I pray them to get us all back together again soon. Warmth of the Fire, Grandfather."

"Warmth, Aengus." He touched the sugan lightly, clapped me on the shoulder, and then pushed me gently toward the door.

As I went out, the candlelight cast his shadow up the wall and across the blackberry mountains above the wide river.

It was the last time I ever saw him.

I had little enough to pack, really only an extra tunic with my secondary amulets, a few packets and pouches of common medicines, and my own color pots, though I had no doubt these would look poorly measured against Colin Mariner's gilded ones (I was sure they would be gilded). In the morning at breakfast I would add a farl of bread and a handful of dried berries, if I could get them from the kitchen. I didn't quite trust Timbertoe to feed me and wasn't sure I wanted to try whatever dwarvish pirates ate, anyway. Better to have my own supplies.

Every time I moved I was conscious of the new ring on my finger and the point of the pin secreted in my cloak. Both made me uneasy. There wasn't much I could do about the pin, but I decided that openly wearing a chalcedon ring aboard a ship full of pirates wasn't the brightest thing I could do, so I cut a length of leather thong from the braided strap on my walking stick, tied the ring securely in the loop, and slipped it on over my head. I put the cord inside the neck of my tunic and touched the ring through the rough wool. It felt much more secure.

I knew it would be prudent to try to sleep, but I could not bring myself to lie down until I had seen at least Nestor and Gwynt, and Padraig if I found him in the skellig, though likely he was down in the village at his own home. In any case it would have been difficult to sleep amid the noise of purposeful activity that hummed over the nighttime community. Through the crack in my shutters I could see the kitchen brightly lit up, and from the courtyard outside came the to-and-fro tramping of many feet as some of the brothers brought supplies up to the round tower. Very probably Nestor would be busy even now with decocting, mixing, or grinding the healing herbs that would certainly be needed in the weeks ahead. He would need an extra pair of hands.

I left my pack strapped and waiting and walked through the portico toward the apothecary workroom. "Aengus!" a voice called behind me. When I turned, Brother Timon beckoned. "Have ye time to give me a hand, lad?"

"I have, though I should get to the apothecary before long."

"This won't take but a few minutes." I followed him to the barn and up the stairs to the dovecote. There a sleepy cooing greeted us as he ducked under the low lintel. "I must take four of them up to the wall above the jetty and put them in the little hutch there so they'll get

off at first light." He caught one of the pigeons softly and handed her to me, then added
another. "Ye look surprised. Didn't ye know?"

"No. I had no idea master used such messen-
gers. Where are these bound for?"

He closed the dovecote, and we carefully ne-
gotiated the ladder down. "Inishkerry." He
glanced over his shoulder. "You know?"

"To summon Timbertoe."

"That's it. It's an easy flight for these little
beauties, and quick. He'll have the message before his breakfast eggs are boiled."

"How long a sail is it?"

We strode through the courtyard past the
tower. The ladder was down, and a lantern
shone from the door above, with one of the men
silhouetted against it lifting in a small barrel.
Timon replied, "Oh, four hours, I should
guess—less with a good, stiff wind."

"I didn't know we were such close neighbors."

He chuckled and cautiously raised one
thumb to scratch his chin. "Aye. Makes a body
feel comfortable, doesn't it?" he said with grim
good humor.

Actually, it did, if the dwarf was as good an
ally as my grandfather believed. I said as
much, and Timon glanced at me. I added quietly, "It's good to have a refuge for the women
and children."

He looked away toward the tower. "I suppose."

There was something there. I had thought
him to be a bachelor, but I wondered now if he
might be a widower instead. It was no time for
such private confidences, however, and I did
not mention women or children again as we

went through the refectory, past the store-rooms, and across the small yard to the steps. There was a hutch at the top, a woven-basket affair. While I gently held the carrier pigeons upside down, Timon drew the thin message strips from his pocket and inserted one in each bird's tiny leg pannier. We set them inside the basket, dropped the little door open, and left our lifelines to the pirate captain cooing drowsily in the dark.

Tim bade me a busy and distracted good night by the tower, and I walked on down to Nestor's workroom. I found him, as I had expected, with his sleeves rolled up and elbow-deep in a bowl of some questionable-smelling concoction. I wrinkled my nose, and he explained, "Rancid butter and aloe. Sovereign for burns, but it stinks, I'll grant you. Gwynt's awake, if you'd like a word with him."

"Thanks. I'll be back to help you."

He nodded absently, and I went two rooms along the portico to the healer's own chamber where my friend was dozing, propped up on the pillows. His color was better and his eyes clearer when he heard me come in and opened them. "There's a flap on, I take it," he said. He waved a hand at the shuttered window. "I heard the bell, and now it sounds like everybody in the skellig's awake."

"Nearly everyone. I think there might be one or two babies still asleep." I hooked the stool close to the bed and sat down. "How do you feel?"

"Better," he said firmly. "I'll be ready."

I wasn't sure how much he knew. "For what?"

He spat an exasperated curse and turned his face away.

"They've got a boat coming to take the women and children to safety," I told him.

That brought his eyes back to me in a hurry. "Really?"

I nodded solemnly. "Apparently they've been planning for something like this all along. I suspect it's why they trained even us indentured boys to arms." It was on the tip of my tongue to tell him I was being sent away, but I couldn't.

"Oh." His brow knotted. "Oh," he said again, softly as though to himself.

"Listen, Gwynt, it isn't your fault, you know. You haven't put anyone in any danger they weren't already expecting." I held his eye. "It would be foolish to think of sacrificing yourself in battle, especially with Alyce safely away."

I had guessed correctly; his face was suddenly washed with red. He pulled the blankets higher on his shoulder. "I just thought . . . "

"Don't think," I advised. "It's not your strong suit." That wrested a crooked smile from him, and I stood up to leave.

"See you on the wall, Fat Lip," he said. "I'll be next to Brother Sy."

I fought to keep my voice steady. "I'll be where I'm ordered. Warmth, Gwynt." I turned at the door. "Give Alyce a kiss for me. Give her more if you feel up to it." I slammed the door hastily and heard the soft thump of the pillow bouncing off it, followed by his weak laugh. Smiling to myself in the darkness, I touched the door in farewell and went back to help Nestor mix up his burn ointment.

* * *

Next morning I finagled a loaf from Dermot on the explanation that Nestor was sending me out to the cliffs to collect seaweed as a wound dressing. Some people will believe anything a healer—or his assistant—says, and I got not only the bread but he added a bit of cheese as well, casting an eye out at the cold fog swirling about the high wall and advising me to be careful on the rocks.

I did not see Padraig on my way down through the skellig, but Finian was busily checking the ropes and winches that controlled the heavy iron-studded gates. His eyes widened at the sight of the collecting basket on my back, in which I'd secreted my pack, and then a most knowing look came across his face. He smiled, touched his hand to his breast, and bent again to his work. I slipped through the gates, bore to my right, and quickly passed the few houses to pick up the cliff path that led to Gull's Cove.

It is true that fog carries sound; for quite a while as I walked I could hear clearly the whirring of Symon's whetstone in the armory, the clang of a heavy hammer on metal, possibly Niall working at the forge, the disturbed bleating of the sheep as the cattle were driven inside the lower wall to be penned with them, the creak of the windlass as water was drawn from the underground spring to fill the reserve cisterns. With the fog came, too, the sharp smell of peat smoke and cooking smells. The women were emptying their larders and preparing provisions to accompany themselves and their children on the dwarven ships which would be here no later than early evening.

My own ship was due about midday, but it would be difficult to tell the nooning, since the sun was nowhere visible. I would, at any event, be ready on the beach for Timbertoe when he arrived. I fingered the ring on its thong and picked up the hem of my tunic to hold the needle away from me while I scrambled amongst the rocks to the edge of the cliff above the cove. I eased my way over the drop, landed safely, and made my cautious way down the ladders, which were a little slick with the cold and wet. I congratulated myself that I hadn't had to make the descent the day before, when the ladders would have been rimed with ice from the sleet storm. Finally I worked my way down through the last jumble of boulders, hopped onto the sand, and cast an eye up to where I knew the surrounding cliffs loomed, but I couldn't even see them as darker substance behind the wall of fog.

I left my pack in the relative shelter of the boulders and walked along the water to work the muscles in my calves that had pulled a little with the tension of coming down the cliff. I could hear the surge, at this hour more a quiet hissing over the strand than the booming thunder it would be at high tide, and see about twenty feet out over the choppy wavelets. Experimentally I looked toward the back wall of the cove, and the visibility dropped to less than ten feet. I didn't envy the men Nestor had told me were sent during the night to dig out the dams at the landward end of the peninsula in order to flood the seawater through the canal between the two sandy beaches. By now they should be done with the task, and it was some security knowing that an army would be held

there until they managed to throw down
bridges to cross or get enough ships to ferry
them around the obstacle. By that time, Bruchan would have the skellig as defensible as
possible.

I paced up and down the beach, kicking at
old remnants of seaweed and some scallop
shells. I considered having lunch, but that was
silly, since it could scarcely be more than a
couple of hours after breakfast. I dropped
down moodily on a rock near my pack and
picked some driftwood to bits while I stared
out to where the sea lay behind its lambswool
blanket.

The pack and the fog gave me the idea, and
in this weather there was absolutely no chance
anyone would see. I got out my color pots, took
them down to the damp strip where the tide
would soon rush in to erase the picture, and
began to paint for Skellig Inishbuffin. There
was no storyteller, but there was no audience,
either, so good form hardly mattered.

The subject was a natural one, given the circumstances. I laid down greens in broad
strokes at first to sketch in the valley with its
gentle hills, so different from the fierce ridges
of stone familiar to me. Then blues for the
river, a curving wash of blue that seemed to
roll toward the sea which I knew without
knowing would be beyond the left-hand border
of my painting. Now the mountains beyond the
river, violet and lovely, their tops wreathed in
cloud. Finally, and purely for myself, I leaned
and let the graceful white neck and proud back
trail from my fingers. The Swan, beautiful as I
had seen her, floated on Willowsrill the Fair. I

straightened, brushing the powdered colors from my hands.

A rasp of steel brought my startled eyes up from the painting.

"Ah, so the pickpocket is the painter. I thought so." Jorem's pointed teeth showed within the chain-mail hood as he smiled over the leveled sword. Dim in the fog behind him was a troop of Wolfhounds, mail-clad, fully armed, their eyes glittering past their nose guards. Behind me was the sea. I had a dagger at my belt and perhaps five feet in which to use it.

I drew back a foot, hands palm out in front of me as a token that I would give them no trouble, and when the first man came for me, I exploded, my hands flying in the slicing drives that Symon had taught me. I dropped the first Hound at my feet, whirled to the second, and got past his guard with a stiff kick that folded him up like an earwig that's been stepped on. I was seized from behind and tried to throw him, but he hampered my arm enough that I was unable to get my knife in my hand. Suddenly Jorem's face was before me, lips drawn back in a snarl of rage, and he clubbed the haft of his sword down across the side of my head. I felt as well as heard the snap as my jaw went, and then the scuffled sand was under me, the colors running before my rolling eyes. The last thing I heard was the clanging of the alarm bell from the round tower.

Chapter 13

I crawled up out of a black mere where sounds echoed, and a man's jaw stretched wide, gulping bog water. My head was crushed in a vise of pain.

For some time I could not summon the strength to open my eyes, my consciousness shrinking from the touch of reality. Gradually through the pounding in my ears other sounds began to be sensible: the shrill squealing of a pig that went on and on and on; a thump and rasp, something being dragged past me; the roar of a foundry and snapping of twigs as though all the trees in a forest were . . . Smoke, thick enough to lie in my mouth with the blood. Burning. I woke up, and my eyes swam open.

The fog, the damned fog that had hidden them, had melted again into light drizzle that did nothing to quench the fires, but left everything visible under a leaden sky. The Wolfhounds were pillaging the houses far enough from the lower wall to be out of bowshot of our men. They had piled all the household goods in the middle of the street and the bonfire was blazing high, the smoke of it joining the hungry flames that had already reduced one house to embers and were spreading to others.

I was sitting propped against the stone wall that lined one side of the street, trussed like a fowl for the spit, my wrists secured to my ankles by thick ropes. My whole head was a flaming agony centered below my left eye. The rough stone under my cheek pressed, but I kept my head turned to it, both because the stone was cold enough to have some numbing effect and because it was the only way I could watch what Jorem's men were doing. I did manage to glance down and saw what I had expected: the leather sheath at my waist was empty, and the thong had been taken from around my neck. So my dagger and Colin Mariner's ring were gone. I could not feel the hidden needle against my leg, but the Wolfhounds might well have missed it.

As I have said, despite the light mist the fires were spreading, not quickly enough, however, to suit Jorem or his men. While I watched, two of them stepped to the edge of the safe range, notched arrows wrapped with pitch-soaked rags, touched them to the streaming torch a third man carried, and sent the fire arrows whizzing the length of the street to catch in the roofs of two houses near the wall. One merely smoldered in the wet straw thatching, but the other flared up, and soon there was a row of cottages burning along the lower wall of the skellig. I saw Bruchan's men wrapping what I presumed to be wet rags around their mouths and noses against the dense smoke, but there was little enough they could do, and their anger must have been at least as hot as the flames.

And fear, too, there would be that up on the walls. Not so much for themselves—they were, after all, trained fighting men in a pitched battle they had been expecting—but rather fear for their families, for of course the women and children were still in the skellig. There had been no chance for escape.

I closed my eyes as there came from behind one of the houses an end to the pig's screaming. I hoped it was a pig.

A boot, finest-quality leather, though a little splashed with mire, prodded me. I twisted my head off the wall, though it took all my strength, and stared up at Jorem. He laughed at that look. "Now, now, we mustn't take things personally, thief. This is only to set the stage, as it were. Your master knows that as well as I. A village leveled, some few wounded in the initial surprise, domestic animals slaughtered within sight of those watching and then left carelessly to rot. It is the way these things are done. The real battle has not yet started." He slapped leather gauntlets against his thigh, looking through the smoke toward the walls. I wondered who was wounded, and how seriously. Padraig had been down in the village, I thought. I wondered also whether the dwarfs would land if they spied the pall of smoke.

Jorem returned his attention to me. "We have some moments yet before the time is ripe, I think. Now, what I'd like to know is why you were down in that cove with a pack and your color pots in fog so thick there was nothing to be gained by making a picture." He squatted, balancing easily before me, and asked conversationally, "You'll tell me that, eh?"

Our eyes were on a level, though one of mine was nearly shut with swelling. I kept my head up. I'd tell him something, but I'd make him work for it.

"Ah, the cat's made off with your tongue. I see." Very deliberately he reached to press a place on my cheek, though I craned my neck back until the stones were gouging into my scalp trying to get away from him.

"Running away!" I gasped out of a slit of mouth on the other side of my head while dark flecks danced in front of my eyes. "Running away. They . . . knew you . . . were coming."

"I should hope they did. Obviously I would pursue the king's justice most vigorously in this instance." I nodded dizzily. He smiled slyly. "So you were running away. But in the midst of this activity, barely a mile from the skellig, you stopped to paint. Now what am I to make of that?"

Two of the black-cloaked Wolfhounds tugged a stumbling ram down the street past us, a rope biting deep into the thick fleece, and the animal's eyes already glazing. A little way beyond us, one of them suddenly thrust his dagger in under the rope, and blood sprayed in a fan. His companion leaped out of the way of it, swearing, and the butcher laughed and pushed the dying ram into the bonfire, where it staggered and fell, still kicking even as the fire caught its fleece. I looked back at Jorem. "Brave men thee has, to make war on sheep."

"What can happen to a sheep can happen to you. I ask again, why were you painting?"

I lifted one shoulder in a shrug. "Why not? I wouldn't be missed for a long time in the confusion, and nobody could see me."

He snorted impatiently. "So you just happen

to paint a picture of—well, you tell me: what
was that scene?"

I tried to think what he was trying to find
out. "There's a pretty tapestry . . . up there. In
the refectory." Bad move, I realized at once.
Jorem had been in our refectory. Not for
nearly two years, though. Maybe he'd think it
was new.

His dark eyes narrowed. "And you stole this,
I suppose you'll tell me." He pulled my ring
from his belt pouch and held it up before my
eyes. The chalcedon caught what little light
there was in its pearled surface, white and
sleek, like a swan's head.

I nodded painfully. "What thief could pass it
up?" Too late I realized the matter-of-fact
agreement would sound like sarcasm. Jorem,
after all, had stolen it off me. I was already
trying to duck away from the blow, but it still
caught me with enough strength to thud my
head off the stone wall. If not for the ropes, I
would certainly have toppled over to the road.
As it was, my ears sang, and I could only see
Jorem's face in a far-off circle of dim light
which closed and closed until, thankfully, he
was gone.

I was not out long. The bonfire was still roaring when I lifted my head and focused on it,
but the houses were mostly crumpled haystacks of smoldering wet straw, their roofs
having caved in and drawn the wattle-and-daub
walls down with them. The light was darker,
too. At first I thought this was my eyes, but
then realized through the haze of pain that it
had indeed grown darker; nightfall, the early
night of barely spring, was already falling. So

the dwarfs would not land to help us. My heart soured.

I turned my head to the tramp of booted feet just as two of them reached to haul me up and hold me there while the ropes were rearranged. I did not bother trying to fight. It would have been pointless, and I had to conserve my strength. With my hands bound behind me and ankles encircled by a double loop that allowed only a small stride, I was hustled up the street to where Jorem waited with his men around him. He smiled at me, and they dragged me with them when they went to talk to my grandfather.

Just out of range we stopped. Jorem took hold of my bonds and yanked me before him. A torchbearer held the blazing light up so that those on the walls could see my face. I have no doubt it looked hideous enough, but they would have recognized me anyway by my clothes. I could see no one; the pitch-smelling flames were between me and them.

"Hail, Your Eminence!" Jorem called loudly. "I wish you—" He paused and swept a hand to indicate the smoldering ruins around us. "Warmth of the Fire."

His men guffawed, hooting raucous obscenities to the shadowy figures standing motionless on the wall.

I swore to myself that if I ever got the chance, I'd shove those pointed teeth of his right down his bastard throat.

From Skellig Inishbuffin there came back only silence, until even the Wolfhounds shuffled uneasily and spat off to the side in the growing darkness. Jorem's crafty smile went out like a snuffed candle, and his expression set in stone. "As you will, Bruchan. You know the matter. I want the murderer you harbor. As you can plainly see, I have your painter." (Not "grandson," I noted and felt a cautious relief.) The Wolfhound continued, "I propose a trade: one little vermin for the other. Come, I ask you: is it worth the destruction that will inevitably befall you if you refuse?"

Again that silence. I felt Jorem stir angrily behind me, and the tether shook. My grandfather's voice, that storyteller's carrying voice, rose above the snapping of the cooling timbers in the fires behind us. "But then it may equally be asked whether 'tis worth risking destruction to trust the word of a common marauder. Thee has urged no proof that thy quarry is within these walls, yet thee has put to the torch my people's homes, wounded those who only fought to protect their own, and now thee's made a hostage of a 'prentice boy. Thee usurps the law to thy own ends, Thy Grace. Get thee gone from here, thy Hounds at thy heel, while thee still has legs to bear thee."

Jorem laughed harshly. "Very good, Your Eminence. You do not disappoint. I had an idea you might say something of the sort, so I will let you in on a little secret: my army's ships follow this advance guard closely. By this time tomorrow, we will have scoured this mucking peninsula from one end to the other. Everything you love, everything you have worked a lifetime to build up will be gone. That includes the old temple—yes, I knew about that filthy place—and, oh, incidentally, the boy here, and the ring he's carrying. You do remember the ring, don't you? I believe it belonged at one point to your family. I'm surprised you'd send this little wretch ahead with it to await you at your Four Spiral shrine. That is where he was going, isn't it? And there you'd try to paint the picture foretold. Well, my friend, you'd not be able to do it without these, would you?" He flicked a hand. I heard beside me a clink as one of his men set down a sack, and the torch-bearer lowered the light to illuminate the cov-ered earthenware bowl, sealed with red wax, which tumbled out. Pressed into the ocher clay was the Four Spiral design. The color pots of Colin Mariner were no further from me than a toddler's step, and I could not touch them.

I raised my eyes to the wall, but in the dark-ness I could not see him.

Our confederate had failed, probably losing his life in the vain effort to get the color pots to the Painter. Now Jorem had brought them here and gloatingly displayed them for my grandfather to see and despair. Jorem had the ring, he had the pots, he had the painter. All he lacked was the storyteller, and he would get him soon enough. I knew in a moment's insight that Bruchan would never give up Gwynt, and that the Wolfhound had known it, had counted upon it, because the master of the skellig would give himself up instead. He would not expect Jorem to honor his pledge not to harm the folk of the community, but he would take the desperate gamble that between us, he and I might somehow paint the picture that would bring about the reign of the Powers on earth. Even if both of us died in the venture, we might be able to take Jorem and his Hounds with us, for surely their wickedness would not be tol-erated in that new age.

Don't, I begged the silently watching figure,

trying to reach him with my thoughts. The Four don't need us as badly as that. They are the Immortals, after all; let them find some other way, use some other tiles in their Game. If we are to die, we die, but I'll be damned if I'll paint at the point of this bastard's sword.

Bruchan's voice came down, floating a little on the wind that had risen with the dark. "Thee meddles in things thee does not understand, Jorem. Again I warn thee: get gone. The Powers know thee well and will repay thy injuries to us a hundredfold."

Jorem's men muttered angrily. He chopped a hand down, and they ceased at once. "Your blasphemy shall be your undoing, old man! The Wolf will have your entrails at the ritual we hold tomorrow night!"

"Thy Wolf!" Bruchan cried in scorn. "Thy Wolf's but a tale to scare those poor confused people who follow thee out of fear of thy spies and thy knives in the darkness! Thee knows nothing of Lord Flame, else thee would fear his wrath for this lie thee has wrought in his name!"

A sword slithered out of its sheath behind me, and I very nearly tried to whirl to attack, but before I could move, the length of cold steel was laid across my shoulder, its edge barely touching my neck. Jorem's voice grated, "Your life is forfeit, old man. But I give you the night to think about the penalty for your followers. If you would avert it, lay down your arms and open your skellig's gates by the third hour after dawn. That is all. There will be no more parleying." He yanked me to my knees, and I was hauled away like an ill-trained dog in the sight of the whole skellig.

But despite the painful scrapes and bruises I acquired from the stony path, I learned one interesting thing: Macguiggan's pin was still in my hem. If any of Jorem's men had been sharp enough, they might have marked how I took care to swing my tunic away from me on that side, but they were too busy cursing my grandfather and kicking dead hens out of the way to notice. Jorem himself stalked ahead of us, having thrust the end of my rope into the hands of his lieutenant, so in the bobbing torchlight I was virtually invisible except as a weight at the end of the tether. When the last few men in the group halted for a few moments while one of them chased the last live goose around a smoking house, I seized the opportunity. There was a bit of ember, still warm, under my palm. I used it as chalk in the darkness, hoping it was leaving a mark, to scrawl a single spiral as large as I could on a flat rock that lay like a paving stone in the middle of the road. In the morning, they should be able to see it from the wall, and maybe Bruchan would understand Macguiggan's sign to mean that we still had one weapon left to us.

A hazy plan was forming in my mind.

They had left standing one house near the bridge to use as their camp, the obvious thing to do in weather like this, particularly if you did not expect the military exercise to take long. There was an attached lean-to shed, rough-thatched and with the barest woven walls, where the turf and some few farming implements were kept. Two of the Wolfhounds dragged me there and hurled me to the floor. One looped my lead around a stout rafter, pulling on it first to check that it was adequate,

hauled on the end of it like raising a pulley,
and when he had me dangling from my wrists
with my feet barely touching the floor, tied off
the end of the rope across the shed on one of
the corner posts. He used sailor's knots, I
noted. Good. He'd be a superstitious man, then.
I had drawn a breath to begin when he came
back over to me, glared, and spat in my face.
"That's for being one of them stinking, miscre-
ated lice up there." He ripped the brooch pin
from my cloak, the good wool giving way at the
savagery of it, and hurled it across the shed.
The sugan fluttered to the floor at his feet. He
scraped it toward him with his toe until he had
backed out of range of my feet and bent to pick
it up. A grunt came from him, and he turned
to his comrade. "Look at this, Hugh. Even the
men wear women's signs up there."

Before it could go further, I said conversationally, "You'd wear one, too, to protect you
against the Hag if you knew anything about
that old man up there. Did they tell you in the
barracks at Dun Aghadoe that he's a powerful
mage?"

The second soldier laughed, and after a moment the one who had tied me, the sailor,
joined him, but his eyes shifted to me uncomfortably. "If he's such a damned powerful
mage, what's he doing cooped up behind his
skellig walls, then?" the second soldier
mocked, hands on hips. "What, will he turn us
all into chickens come morning light and throw
out a pan of grain for us to peck at while your
filthy lot chop our heads off with a butcher
knife?"

Not a bad idea, I thought. I'll bet Symon
could do it. Aloud I said, "I didn't say he was

some cheap street magician. I said he was a mage. There's a difference, soldier. A magician does tricks. A mage doesn't need them. He just curses you instead, and the curse sticks."

The second soldier guffawed and turned for the door, slapping his gauntleted hands together to warm them and looking forward to the fire they had lit inside the house. But the sailor was making the sign behind his back; I knew it, though he kept the hand out of sight. "You know this for a fact?" he demanded.

"Oh, by the Fire himself, Niall!" his companion snorted from beyond the door. "Come along!"

The sailor held up a hand to him, keeping his eyes on me. I stared back, thinking how unlike our steady Niall he was. Out of the side of my throbbing mouth I told him, quietly, "Look, maybe you've got more wits than yon asshole. I'm telling you, the old man has power. Why do you think even the pirates don't ravage this place?" He was thinking furiously; it was true that as far as they had seen this afternoon, the skellig had looked singularly unmarked by any raids, though it stood right on the coast, and of course he would know nothing of the business relations between Timbertoe and Bruchan. "And of course you know that Cathir, your master's spy inside the skellig, was struck down by a mysterious attack that left him senseless for a day and weak for many more." Yes, I thought there might have been some rumor of that in the barracks at Dun Aghadoe. I nodded as well as I could. "The old man cursed him for mucking up some shipment of supplies. I heard it myself, and not an hour later there was Cathir, collapsing into the chowder at supper. You figure it out. I've given you what warning I can. You seem a decent enough fellow, a fisherman like my folk. Take my advice: wear a sugan tonight, because sometime in the dark hours the curse will begin to strike home, I promise you."

If I say so myself, I did it well. Perhaps I had something of my grandfather's gift for telling a story, maybe it just went with being an accomplished thief, but the man believed me. I saw it in his lurching step as he hurried away out the door. Their footsteps went around the side of the shed and faded, and I could hear him saying, "No, but really, the kid says so." I began to smile, but the sudden increase in pain made my eyes water, so I contented myself with pushing up on my toes to give my wrists what ease I could while I blinked and looked about.

They had prudently removed the hoe and hayrake, pitchfork and mattock, all of which were made of wood and therefore useless to my purpose. I slowly swung on my rope, scanning the shed. Neither of the soldiers had touched any of the turf. The sailor wouldn't have known anyway, and apparently the other man wasn't raised on a farm or he would have remembered that a countryman often leaves his precious iron scythe inserted in a stack of dry peat to protect the blade from moisture. I was looking now for the telltale stub of a wooden handle.

They had taken the torch with them, of course, and I waited several minutes for my night vision to sharpen, letting my mind grow quiet, trying to block the pain from my broken jaw with some of the meditations Symon had taught me. I would need all the strength and every bit of training my masters had instilled in me. Even if I had been whole, it would have been a formidable task, but with my jaw sagging like a one-hinged door, I only hoped I could hang on to what remained of my senses long enough to do the thing. I opened my eyes, scanned the mound of turf, and spotted what might have been a scythe handle.

I breathed a prayer to the Swan, raised myself up, and cautiously swung one leg out from the hip until my foot grounded on the top of the turf, and I could wedge it into the bricks. With that leg braced it was an easy enough matter to lever the rest of my body up until I had both feet on the mound and could stand, or more accurately lean dangerously, using the rope that tethered my hands to the rafter as a brace. For moments it felt so wonderful to have relieved the awful strain on my shoulders that I just hung there, my hands now below the level of my head.

When I had caught my breath, I shinned the rope toward me on the rafter until I was standing straight on the mound and could work on loosening my bonds. At this time, I judged that perhaps two hours had passed. The air was growing colder and through the open door of the shed I could see that the fog had risen again. There had been a rich smell of cooking meat not long ago, so I guessed that they had eaten their supper—probably a roasted joint from one of our poor beasts—and would be idly tossing dice or maybe playing at tiles now. Jorem would have posted sentries out there in the darkness, but that should be no problem; likely they would be backlit against the heaps of glowing embers from the burnt-out village, and they would be facing away from the house, guarding against attack from the skellig side. One of the knots gave a little.

I worked steadily at the rope, keeping an ear cocked in the unlikely event that one of the guards took it into his head to check on me. I got one of the knots undone. I went on working. No doubt the scythe would have been simpler, but for the idea I had in mind I could not cut the rope just yet.

It cost me a torn thumbnail and took possibly another hour and a half to two hours, but I was finally free. I left the rope hanging over the rafter, hopped down from the turf stack, and flexed my hands to work the cramping out of them while I leaned cautiously from the door. The fog was coming in billows across the walled field behind the house, one moment thick, the next broken into streaming wraiths, as it was blown by the wind off the water. I located one of the guards standing out by the road, his pike at precisely the right angle over his shoulder. He would be the most alert one, being within sight of his master in the house. I ducked back into the security of the shed.

The scythe I stuck through my belt, though I did not intend to use it unless I had to. My brooch was somewhere in here, but I did not take the time to search for it by touch. The sugan, though, I would not leave. I felt around on the floor until I found it and, having no better place, tucked it in my belt as well. The pin of Macguiggan was still in my hem, and I touched its bronze length through the wool to reassure myself that this wild plan had some chance of working. "Lady Swan," I whispered, "if you're still around, I pray thee help me now." I waited until a thick cloud rolled through the yard and slipped out of the shed.

I crept to the back corner of the house, away from the road, and crouched to listen. From within I could hear, not the click of tiles that I was expecting, but rather the chant and counterchant of ritual prayer. The hair rose on my nape, but then I reminded myself that Jorem would no doubt be a stern taskmaster. Very likely there would be no amusements for these men, after all, and after evening prayer they would turn in for the night. Better and better. I went back to my shed, gathered my cloak around me, and waited. Presently I heard clipped strides going across the yard, the exchange of sign and countersign, and slower steps coming toward the house. The watch had changed. I listened intently, prepared for the next several minutes to spring for the doorway, but the old sentry was too glad to get into the warmth to check on me, and the new one stayed at his post out by the road. Now the troop would bed down. I gave it, as nearly as I could tell, nearly an hour more, and then next time I went out to listen at the eave of the house, I could hear snores.

I could have escaped there and then through the back fields, through the orchards behind the village, and come up to the skellig wall at some point likely to be only cursorily watched by the guards Jorem would have posted. Probably I could even have gotten in if the man on the wall recognized me in time not to give an involuntary shout. Very possibly I should have done just that.

But to gain the temporary safety of the skellig was actually pointless, for with Jorem's army not far off—and I believed the Wolfhound on that score, at least—we would be corked in a bottle, and of course bottles can be smashed. There was a limit to how long Bruchan and the others could hold out against overwhelming numbers. The end might take days, but it would surely come.

The only strategy which made any sense was to try a flanking attack on the attackers before the rest of the filthy Hounds arrived on the scene. And I had planted the seed of fear in that sailor's mind. Though he would have said nothing of it in his master's hearing, I had no doubt he had whispered it to one or more of the men with him, and that was all to my advantage.

The first thing was the most difficult. I had to find Jorem inside the house. While I had been waiting for them all to fall asleep, I had been mulling it over. If it had been any other military commander, I would have thought immediately that he would choose to sleep nearest the hearth. One of the privileges of rank was to be warm on a night like this. But the Wolfhound was the sort who would pride himself on being strict, both with his men and with himself. He would fast, he would subject himself to chastisements of the flesh. He was celibate, wasn't he? And that kind of man would make it a point to seek the coldest sleeping spot, farthest from the hearth, and probably disdaining even the comfort of a blanket, rolling himself only in his black cloak. I worked Macguiggan's pin from the hem of my tunic, threaded it through the throat of my cloak, and drew a deep breath to steady my nerves. Then

I used the thick fog to work my way around the house until I could just make out the sentry at the road. He was motionless, sitting on the wall, not standing. Possibly he was even asleep. I waited until the fog blocked out his dark figure and slithered in through the door that they had battered in when they'd sacked the village.

I crouched just inside. All around me were the snores and the heavy breathing of sleeping men. My palms were sweating, my head throbbed, my heart was beating loudly enough that I was sure somebody would hear it. The turf fire had been banked for the night, but even its little light after the darkness outside gave me enough to see the mounded figures lying with their heads toward the wall and their feet toward the center of the one-room hut, naked swords by their sides, ready to snatch up. Most of the men were to my right, on the hearth end of the house. I looked left, and a wrist came snaking out of the darkness to grab me by the throat.

Of course, I should have realized it: in front of a broken-down door would be the coldest place in the house. I had time for only that one thought before his hand, groping for my throat, struck my jaw a glancing blow and then found its purchase on my windpipe. The moan of agony was cut off with my breath, and the darkened house was already swinging around me as his other hand came up to join the one that was choking me. My own hand whipped forward with the pin held needle end first.

If there was an explosion of breath from him when the needle hit, I didn't hear it, being too occupied with prising his one stiffened hand from my neck, but surely in every other way what Symon had warned me to expect was true. Even knowing what I did, I thought the Wolfhound was dead.

My head pained very badly, and I had to fight to remain conscious. Jorem had taken off his belt before lying down for the night. I reached over his unmoving figure and opened the pouch, extracting my ring and carefully replacing the belt exactly as I had found it. The sack containing the color pots was near his head. With a glance around at the other sleeping men, I hastily spread my cloak on the floor and began removing the pots of Colin Mariner into it, replacing them in the sack with the bricks of turf stacked near the door. This was necessary. The first man who had lifted that empty sack would have known immediately that some human agency was responsible for his master's "death," and I wanted to give them no cause to suspect it.

Finally I had them all bundled in my cloak. I moved toward the door, and a sleeper near the hearth stirred. I threw myself prone beside Jorem and watched through slitted eyelids while the man lifted his head, looked around briefly, scratched his nose, and rolled to his other side. I lay waiting for him to snore again, and when he did, I arose and crouched at the door to look out at the sentry. He was standing now, facing away. Quickly I went out and around the house.

At a safe distance, I set the sackful of pots against the bole of an apple tree and sat down with my head between my knees until the sickness passed. Elation seized me: I had Colin's ring and color pots, and I was free! I fished the

miniature sugan from my belt, touched my lips
to it, and then went about the rest of the night's
activity with the echo of the Swan's music in
my head.

I did it to the last sentry, and he dropped in
a heap as the others had done. Then I worked
my way to the wall, taking care not to be seen.
I recognized the lean profile up there. "Niall!"
I called in a harsh whisper made weaker by the
fact that I could not open my mouth much. He
did not hear. "Niall!" I called again, and this
time I allowed a little sound to carry. "Don't
shoot—it's me!" I added frantically as his bow
swung to cover the sound at the base of the
wall.

"Aengus?" he whispered.

"Of course. Drop me a ladder or something,
will you? I have to come in."

The bow did not move. "What's Gwynt's
nickname for you?" He wasn't sure I was
alone.

"Fat Lip, and I've earned it again, I'm afraid.
Don't worry: I've taken care of all the guards
but two. The only one you have to worry about
is the man directly out from the front gate."
We were on the side of the skellig facing on
the cliff path.

He took a great chance, though I heard him
call something quiet to the man on duty next
to him. There would be a sword ready to cut
off my head as I came up the ladder that came
rumbling over the side, I knew. The precaution
was all right with me, and I went up the ladder
with the sack of pots nestled in the hollow of
my back. With Niall drawing up the ladder behind me, I swung the sack to the grassy plat-

form and caught a surprised Padraig in a fierce one-armed hug. "Easy, boy, easy," he whispered gruffly. "Watch my ribs." But he clapped me on the back and then held me off to look at my swollen face. "You look like a cow trod on your face."

"Feels like it," I mumbled out of the side of my mouth. "Listen, where's the—"

"How did you get away from them?" Niall interrupted in a whisper.

I glanced at Padraig. "The Hag's Embrace." His eyes widened, so Symon had indeed taught him the secret, but Niall was plainly mystified. I waved away his question and demanded, "Where's the master?"

Padraig answered, "Up in his study, sleeping, I hope, though I doubt it."

I bent and handed him the sack. "Take this to him, not now, first light will be soon enough, I think. And this." I twisted the chalcedon ring from my finger and put it in the training master's hand. "Now, here's what I've worked out: I used the Hag's Embrace on Jorem, tell master, about midnight, so we have till noon or thereabouts. You understand?"

"Aye. Go on."

"And what was left I used on all the sentries but the one at the front gate and the one at the house near the bridge where they've made their camp. In the morning when they discover it, those men will swear that no one went in or out of the skellig or the house. I've told them that master's a mage and—"

"A what?" Niall asked.

"A mage, and he's put a curse on them. When they wake up in the morning and find what they find, they'll have to believe it's true."

Padraig's face relaxed into a slow grin. "You're a master liar, boy."

"Thanks. Now with a little luck, they'll get out of here and put as much distance between themselves and this skellig as they can, leaving their dead behind to travel faster. You go out when they leave, collect Jorem and bring him inside here, and when his army lands tomorrow, we'll show them their general with a noose around his neck, ready to be kicked off this wall if they don't withdraw."

"It's good," Niall said, nodding.

"It is that," Padraig said admiringly.

"But in the meantime, tell my gr—tell Master I'll wait for him at the temple to do the thing we have to do."

"You're going straight there tonight?" Padraig asked. "Why not wait up here with us until yon Hounds leave?"

I shook my head. "No, that won't do it. I have to be down there, exactly as they left me, or they'll never believe the curse story."

Padraig frowned. "Nay, Aengus—"

I held up a hand. "There isn't time. Dawn can't be far off. Come on, put the ladder down again."

Niall looked at Padraig, and Padraig looked at me, thinking. Then he moved to help me drop the ladder. As I put a leg over the rough battlement, he stayed me with a touch. "Here," he said. He fumbled a long thin shape that I recognized in the darkness as a needle from his sleeve. Our eyes met. "You may find use for this." I thanked him with a nod and went down the ladder.

By the time they drew it up behind me, I was already cutting across the burren to circle the

smoking village once more. I made it safely
back to the house by the bridge, noted with
satisfaction that the sentry by the wall was
nodding over his pike, and whisked into my
cozy shed.

I put the scythe back in the turf stack, its
handle closer to my reach than it had been
originally, scuffed some straw and peat dust
over my boots to hide the wet, and wove Padraig's needle more securely in the collar of my
cloak. Macguiggan's pin went back into my
hem, since I had no other safe place for it. I
tied a double loop in the end of the rope that
dangled over me and tried slipping it on and
off my wrists several times until I was sure it
would look convincing but let me get my hands
freed quickly.

Then I settled on my turf seat to wait.

Chapter 14

I suppose the first man to rise was the soldier who had drawn the breakfast cooking detail. I heard him come out, relieve himself against the side of the house, and walk across the yard, a bucket clanking quietly at every step. There was a murmur as he exchanged some word with the sentry, then a low laugh, and the cook headed for the town well. I slipped my hands through the rope bracelets and stood expectantly.

He was back much too soon to have drawn water, hurrying now. His booted footsteps approached the sentry. I heard a name—Lleu or possibly Hugh—and then both of them went down the street to investigate.

They came for the yard at a run, and I think one of them vaulted the low stone wall at the road. The door creaked loudly.

Now it would come.

A yell broke the dawn quiet, a man's inarticulate cry of shock and fear, and it was quickly followed by a hoarse voice shouting, "My lord? My lord!"

A great deal of commotion now, carrying across the eaves to me. Voices demanded to know what had happened, one was yelling, "Treachery!" over and over at the top of his

lungs, and somebody came out the door to the
yard to cup his hands and bellow, "Denys! Malcolm!"

I was pretty certain Denys and Malcolm
would not be answering his summons. In the
dim shed I sniffed and leaned the unhurt cheek
against my upstretched arm. By the Fire, they
were slow.

A voice rose above the others. "—mage, I told
you!" he cried hoarsely. "—cursed us!"

Angry, frightened oaths, only some of which
were to the Wolf, I noticed. Another voice:
"Shut up with that, Niall! It's an assassin has
done this, not some sodding witch man. Probably that damn kid."

Finally. There were running steps, many of
them, rounding the corner of the house. I
stretched onto my toes just in time and was
motionless, hanging from my rope, staring at
them out of one good eye, when the first of
them burst in through the opening, daggers in
hand. They were plainly shocked to find me
there, their knife hands falling to their sides.
The one who had led the way in, a man with a
bushy black beard and small eyes, demanded
roughly, "Did you hear anything or see anything in the night, boy?"

I let my head fall as though holding it up
were too great a strain after a whole night of
hanging. "No," I mumbled. "Nothing. There
weren't even any rats."

"That's true," the man who had been on sentry duty confirmed quickly. "Not a thing was
stirring, Donal. I could see the door the whole
time, and I swear by the Wolf that nobody went
in or out."

"You can't see a curse," I said quietly to the floor.

That chilled them to the marrow. No one said anything.

In the yard outside more running steps pounded across the yard, veering for the shed here when he saw them all gathered outside it. "It's true, Donal! I've been around to every one of our positions, and except for Rhys—he's coming along behind me—all our men are dead without a wound on them!"

A storm of near-hysterical voices was quieted when the last man came through the yard and up to the door to look in. Donal glanced at him briefly. "Did you see anything in the night?"

"Nothing," Rhys replied quietly. "Nobody came out of the skellig." His eyes and Donal's met.

The black-bearded man ordered, "All right. We'll pull back to the beach and wait for the boats." He snapped a shout at those who instantly turned and were running for the road. "Stand! Do you want those scum up in the skellig to see us running like rabbits! We'll withdraw in ranks, and we'll take Lord Jorem's body with us."

I lifted my head. "I wouldn't. The curse will follow you if you're carrying his corpse."

"Shut up about a poxy curse!" he roared, and his fist, carrying all the stunned anger of the hour, slammed into my midsection. "Of course we'll take him with us—we Wolfhounds don't leave our fallen for the crows!"

I was too far gone to care and hung sagging from the rope while they spilled out of the shed. I heard them moments later tramp in

measured cadence out of the yard and across
the bridge. I slipped my wrists out of the rope
and fell to the floor, bile trickling between my
lips as I lay in the peat clods.

Sometime later I came to myself staring toward the rough oblong of fog that was the door
to the shed. There was something I was supposed to—

Oh. I rolled to my knees and after a moment
was able to pull myself up by using the stack
of peat. I could not straighten, but my legs still
worked. I wiped a hand carefully across my
mouth, stuck the scythe in my belt, and lurched
for the doorway. The cold, wet touch of the fog
against my face helped clear my head somewhat. I braced a hand on the stone wall
bordering the road and set off for the temple.

The only thing that sustained me on the journey across the bridge, out onto the bog road
where once I had watched a dead man sink in
the pool, and along the side-branching path
that I had long since learned was the way to
the ancient shrine, was the thought that my
grandfather would be meeting me there with
the ring and the colors and soon this whole or-
deal would be over. I concentrated on staying
upright and on not losing the path and wondered how accurate Nestor's estimate of a
twelve-hour coma was.

No swan went over my head with music in
her wings, but in my partial consciousness I
thought it might be that I had missed her in
the fog.

The truth was, she had missed me, but I did
not know that until later.

* * *

I reached the temple and let myself slide down until I was sitting with my back propped against the stones just inside the entrance. Here I was reasonably out of the weather and, if the fog should happen to part for an instant, out of view. I drew my legs up under my cloak, rested my head back against the stones, and settled myself to wait. Doubtless it would take Bruchan a little time after the men from the skellig discovered the retreat of Jorem's force to make their guarded way down into the village, and more time after that to realize that in one important respect the plan had gone awry, that the Wolfhounds had taken Jorem's body with them. So I would rest and try to gather my strength until the master arrived.

I did not mean to sleep, and it was probably more of a faint, but I awoke with the sense that hours had passed, though I had no way of knowing for sure that this was so. The fog still lay over the burren like a cold blanket, and no sun or even a sense of it was visible. Gradually I realized what had unconsciously given me the feeling time had passed; I could hear the roll of surf from the shallow beach nearby. So the tide had turned. It was at least midday, maybe later.

Bruchan had not come.

Sick fear propelled me to my feet, heedless of the stiff aches in every muscle. I went to the entrance and bent my head, eyes closed, listening intently. Far off and faint, but carrying in that foggy air, I could hear a drum. Then, much nearer, a man's groan.

The scythe was in my hand. I crept outside, advancing in the direction from which I thought the sound had come. Within seconds the mist enveloped me. The groan came again, and this time at the end of it I could hear the sigh that any doctor recognizes at once. Whoever he was, the man was wounded in the lung. My grandfather was lying out there on the turf and stones, dying. I ran toward him.

I stumbled over a rock sticking up out of the grass and pitched down into a little hollow where the fog, surprisingly enough, cleared, the blanket sitting above it at the level of the higher land. There was a huddle of blue cloak lying half in the small seep of water that had collected, and the water was dyed red. I pulled myself up and went to him in a crouching run, knowing already that it was not Bruchan.

When I reached to turn him gently over, Finian groaned again. I could see why. I pulled his cloak over the terrible spear wound. His open eyes focused. " 'nguss." One limp hand flopped in the direction of the satchel he'd dropped. "There . . . "

I forestalled the words he was struggling to gasp out. "All right, Fin. They're the color pots. I know."

"R-ring . . . finger."

It wasn't on the hand I held. When it seemed he would struggle to free the other one trapped under his body, I pulled it out for him. The hand was covered with blood, the chalcedon mired in it. I intended to remove it from his finger minutes afterward when he was gone, but he groped toward me with the hand, and I had to do it then to ease him. "Easy now," I told him. "I've got it all safely." If I could have spared him by using Padraig's needle, I would have, but Fin would have woken hours later only to pass within minutes, maybe seconds.

So I left the needle in the neck of my cloak. He would be in the Hag's Embrace soon enough.

Probably I should have spared him, but I had to know. "Where's Bruchan?"

Finian's eyes fluttered. "Sskellig . . . army . . ."

"Jorem's army attacked the skellig, and Master is bottled up in there with the rest of the men?"

A nod, no more than a slight contraction of the neck muscles. Although it was dire news, my heart rose in spite of me.

He sighed, a long exhalation, and one eye slipped closed. I dug at my belt and extracted the small sugan. "Here, Fin. Think of the flowers you'll see, all kinds of them." I pressed the straw braid into his hand. "Foxglove and gentian, harebells, iris," I named them off desperately, as though the catalog might hold him. "And roses." But I need not have bothered. My needle-working friend was gone. I closed his stiffening fist around the sugan, arranged his cloak like a blanket, and swished the ring in the maroon water till I could bear to put it on. "Warmth of the Fire, Fin," I told him, grabbed the satchel, and stumbled my way up out of the hollow.

Between the fog and the water in my eyes, I could distinguish nothing. I stopped, brushed my sleeve across my face, and peered. Nothing. The rocks and turf I could see near at hand were the same as a hundred thousand others on the peninsula. If my footprints had left any trail, I could not see it.

I licked my lips and tried to gather my thoughts, fighting down the panic. The sea, I could still hear the surf. It had been on my left at the entrance to the shrine; I would keep it on my right now. If it were true that lost people walk in a circle, then surely on some arc of that circle I would find the mound that hid the temple, even if I did not walk straight up to the entrance. The only frightening thing, I told myself, was that all the while I was stumbling around out here, the people of Inishbuffin were fighting for their lives. I set off at a fast trot, though my head began to ring almost immediately.

A small snag of withered thistle loomed up, and I checked. Had I passed it on the way out? I didn't remember it. The sea sound had shifted a little, and I straightened my heading, striding off into the wall of mist once more.

Some minutes later I realized that the roar of the surf had shifted again, though I'd thought I was walking as straight a line as possible. It came to me that I must have missed the mound and actually curved a little around the cove. I swore, turned until the surf was on my left, and ran back, bent to the ground until I could see something that may have been the marks of my boots across the spongy turf. The land suddenly dropped, and at the edge of the hollow a toehold was gouged in the mud. I drew up, panting out of one side of my mouth. I would not go down into that depression again.

The satchel of color pots clanked heavily as I straightened and buffed the ring of Colin Mariner against my cloak nervously. There was nothing for it but to begin again. Carefully I put the surf to my right, resisting the impulse to run, and walked slowly away from the sea. In my previous effort I had concentrated so much on the sound to guide me that I must have unknowingly walked toward it, missing the temple on the right. This time I would cast left and hope to the Powers I was better in my reckoning.

When I had walked a couple of minutes, I thought of something I might try. Putting my fingers to my lips, I tried to whistle, but my jaw was so swollen I couldn't get my mouth open enough to do it. I bent, searched in the turf at my feet until I found two stones, and stood, poised to listen. I clicked the rocks together. It seemed to me that the sound deadened almost at once. I walked a little further on and clicked them again. This time there was no doubt of it: something ahead of me was absorbing the sound.

Within another thirty paces I found the wall of the mound rising up before me. I followed it around to the entrance and ducked inside, grateful for the solidity of hewn stone surrounding me. For a moment I leaned my forehead against it, then reached for the trigger stone that would nullify the traps.

As my fingers touched the stone I heard in the distance outside the shuddering howl of a wolf.

My blood turned to ice, and I whirled to look, though I could have seen nothing even if the beast had been within a few feet.

Steady now, my reason advised. There may not be a beast, after all; it may be some kind of hunting horn the Wolfhounds use to scare their victims. It would be like them to stoop to such tactics. But then again, it may be a real wolf used as a tracker, in which case there isn't much time at all. My hand went to my empty belt sheath and then searched for the scythe. I looked down. I must have left it lying out there by Fin.

I punched the trigger stone, crouched, and bolted down the passageway, dragging the satchel after me. It seemed farther than I remembered from my last visit at the midwinter

festival in honor of the Fickle Friend's returning sunlight. Also, more ominously, there was
no dim light up ahead.

Finally the passage widened. I felt cautiously to either side of the doorway where I
stood to verify that I was in the antechamber.
I should have thought of this: the lamps had
burned out, for no one had been able to leave
the skellig in almost two days to replenish the
oil in the ritual vessels. Despair threatened to
overwhelm me, and then anger flared. "How
do you expect me to do this by myself?" I raged
at the presences I imagined listening from
their individual chambers.

There was no faintest draft of air, no sound,
no sight. I thought of Bruchan and tried to puzzle out what he would do, but instead it was
Ruan's voice I heard in my memory. What was
it he had said to me once? Something about
painting without colors? The picture is in the
mind, Aengus, in the mind, Aengus. . . .

So. I unstrapped the satchel, searched out
the pots by touch, and scraped off their wax
seals with a fingernail. The floor here was sand,
and I knelt to it, arranging the pots by my side
as though this were the floor of a telling hall.
"What story would thee hear, Immortals?" I
asked them quietly. No answer came—I had
expected none—so I simply took up the first
pot and began.

The image of the ruddy young Power who
had come off the wall in the adjoining chamber
filled my mind, and the meadow behind him
with its thousand greens and hundred yellows. I
drew the line of his head, cocked as if listening,
swiftly sketching in the golden robe he wore, with

its sparks of fire twinkling in the border. "Does thee like thy portrait, my lord?" I asked.

He laughed a little. " 'Tis very like. And the Sun Palace, Aengus, do not forget that," his voice, the voice I had heard once before, whispered in my mind. I drew it, ruby windows flaming with the sunset, stepped levels rising one above the other at the edge of the world. Then the green-and-yellow valley with a curious mill in the center, wide sails of gossamer gold creaking slowly around in the warm sun, distilling the precious oil with which he fueled his Lamp. "Ah, excellent," the Power breathed with satisfaction. "I can smell the Kindle logs already."

"My lord?" I asked, puzzled.

"Never mind, Painter. Pass on, pass on. Haste, boy, the darkness is coming!"

His voice in my mind faded and for a time I was alone in the dark, sprinkling a few more grains of color, a few more specks of light. Then the music of her wings filled the nighttime of my mind. "You mourn your friend," she whispered, a young woman's voice. "Paint for him in death as you never could do in life."

I saw her standing on a small island in the midst of a pond with water lilies about her slim feet. I had been wrong perhaps about her being so young; her hair was white as a swan's feather and bound back from her brow by a crown of leaves. But her face was as young as my own. I limned the graceful form in her robe of springtime green and girdle of sugan straw plaits. The wise brown eyes twinkled at me, and her lips moved to say, "And the flowers, Aengus. It would please Brother Finian." And so the purple swords of iris, the clustered cherry blossoms, and the nodding narcissus flowed from my hand, together with a mighty tree that drew my sands up and leafed them out in a canopy of red leaves and sprinkles of white berries. "Wonderful!" the Lady exclaimed, and I smiled with my sore mouth. "But you have forgotten the time, my friend!" I drew in the sundial with its bronze hour marker casting a shadow across all that dew-fresh garden. "Haste!" she urged, and the music of her wings receded.

I floated alone in the dark, the air of the cave buoying me, warm and salt healing against my wounds. A tinkle of crystal chimes came across the water, across the air, like a far-off memory of love, perhaps. "Well, Painter," a new voice said quietly, his sound a soft whisper of breeze. "And what would thee paint for me?" I caught the line of his gray hair streaming in the wind, and his eyes were deep wells of thought, cowled in a robe of cloud through which I could see the dance of porpoises in his heart. Over his shoulder, down at the surface of the glinting sea, was another island, and I glided toward it on a stream of midnight blue sand, careful not to go too near the falls that cascaded at World's End. The Wind's tower rose above me, purest crystal jumping up to form turrets and battlements where the butterflies were the only inhabitants, and the Power blew his Realm into being through a window that led onto . . . "No, no," he told me. "Not yet. Thee's done thy painting here." The crystal tinkling faded, and a star shot across the night sky, leaving its trail of silver. I watched it until it faded.

A wolf howled beside me on the hilltop. "I don't want to," I whispered. "I don't want to paint for You."

"It is all or none, Painter," said a dark voice, my own dark voice that had come to me too often when I was tired or frightened.

"I know," I told him wearily, and indeed it came clear to me then: I could not open a Door for the Three without opening it to Him, also. Jorem's hysterical worship had already wedged it ajar, so the Dark One would find a way through it in time. And if there were no Three to protect us on this side . . . ?

The sand outlined the stretched jaw, the fangs snarling. "So little?" the voice whispered. "So little for Lord Fire?" My hand moved again, coloring the black robe, the shrewd eyes, the red lips. He smiled. "Better, Painter. And now?"

"Now," I echoed in a whisper, and a jagged streak of lightning shot across the vault, leaving my eyes with dark flecks that grew to molds on bog water that filled a gaping dead mouth. I threw down color, and a conflagration spread, burning on the mountaintops, burning in men's veins, in war and fever. "Well done!" he breathed. "You know me well, I see. This painting suits at every point. And now?" he prompted again.

"Now?" I asked.

"Now," said Tychanor the Warm.

"It is now," Ritnym of the Earth agreed.

"Now!" Aashis of the Winds urged.

My hand rose, drawing me to my feet. From the passage behind me came the howl of the wolf, echoing from the stone. Fear shot through me and I clenched my hand on the ring that had come five hundred years to my stewardship. "Now!" I shouted, and the chalcedon flared suddenly in the darkness of the ancient temple, casting a prismed rainbow light on the painting at my feet.

My eyes flinched at the brightness, smarting, the tears making the colored sands begin to run and coalesce. A dark shape struck me back against the wall, and I gasped at the burns that seared my flesh. The Dark One flowed past me through the walls of the passageway, his laugh echoing in my ears. Then his Twin, Tychanor was after him, golden robe flying in his wake, and the Swan seemed to fly above his head and lead him on the path that he must go. Last the Wind, roaring in fury now, swept my sands into a streak as he spun after.

But the Three would not catch the One, I knew. His Wild Fire was loosed into the world. I wearily dropped my hands, the rainbow ring glowing softly on my finger.

The wolf struck me from behind, but missed its grip on my neck, fangs clicking emptily beside my ear. The momentum of its rush sprawled us both across the floor. I rolled to the right, desperate to escape, and bolted through the entrance to Ritnym's shrine. My hand found the ritual knife on its slab, and the other hand hurled the basin of powdered drug in the beast's face as it pointed it slavering muzzle through the low arch.

The shrine exploded with the beast's howls of agony as the drug seared its eyes. It careened away. I held the knife in front of me and crawled out. The wolf heard me and raked a claw that caught me across the back as I was stooping for the passageway to the entrance, but then it bounced off the stone wall as it tried to follow, and raced around the antechamber, pawing frantically at its eyes.

I ran down the narrow tunnel toward the growing light of the everyday world with the chalcedon dimming and the knife shaking in my hand. At any moment I expected the maddened wolf to find the opening and come charging after me. I would not even be able to turn and fight it before its fangs ripped my neck open.

The oblong of the entrance was right before me. I groped for the trigger stone and pulled it back out, setting the traps. But I was too late. The wolf was already in the tunnel.

I sprang out of the temple, running for all I was worth. I looked back, caught my foot in the turf, and went down, trying to get the knife reversed in my grip to strike back at it, but the wolf leaped me in one jump and raced toward the seawater it needed to put out the fire in its blind eyes. I could not believe I was unhurt, and still tried to free my knife for use in case the thing came back.

A boot stamped down on my wrist, numbing my hand. He leaned quickly and took my dagger, spinning it away in the fog that had broken up into wisps while I had been in the shrine. "Tell me you haven't done it," Jorem grated.

I stared up at him wordlessly.

He saw the ring on my hand. "No!" he shouted, raising the sword. "I was supposed to have told the story! You were supposed to have painted *my* story!"

I watched the sword, stark against the leaden sky. "I painted the story the Powers told me. Yes, the Fire was there. Perhaps he told me the story he would have told you, Your Grace. The painting is still on the floor, of course." I met his eyes. "Why don't you go in and see for yourself what the Fire really looks like? Study the painting, and afterward, who is to know that you didn't tell me the story?"

The sword tip wavered. He looked off toward the temple. I lay still and saw the decision come to him. His gaze swung back to me. "We have taken the skellig, pickpocket. My army occupies this peninsula. There is no place for you to run." He rammed the sword back in its sheath. "So don't try."

The Wolfhound turned on his heel and went across the turf into the entrance of the ancient temple. I lay back against the wet ground, listening for it.

A hiss of vapor came out of the opening, dulling my senses even here. I rolled to an elbow, gingerly holding a hand over my nose and mouth. A deep rumble shook the earth, building in strength until, even though I had expected it, I was frightened and got to my knees, peering toward the low doorway. Then with a crash, the passageway caved in. I shielded my eyes from the bits of dust and stone blown out in a thick cloud and stood. "Did see the Wolf, Thy Grace?" I intended it to be a mocking shout, but it came out of me like the mumbling nonsense of an idiot.

I cradled my broken jaw in my hand and set off on the path for the skellig that Jorem said his troops had taken. I looked for the Swan, but she was nowhere in the light mist, and I looked for the Wind and Fire, but they were not there, and so I knew it even before I saw the smoke rising from the broken ruins on the distant hill.

Jorem's men might control the peninsula, but they apparently would not stay so near the scene of their crime, preferring to withdraw back to the beach where they had landed. As I walked across the bridge at the end of the village, I was alone. No dog came to cavort and bark at my heels, no cat eyed me from its perch on a window ledge, and there were certainly no voices of people inviting me to sup with them. I walked past the remains of yesterday's bonfire in the street and continued on toward the gates of the skellig.

Here, as approached the wall, I began to find the bodies.

They were crumpled where they had fallen, transfixed with spear or arrow, or their bodies hacked by swords that had cut through chainmail tunics to find the life beneath. Both Jorem's men and ours sprawled in ungainly death. I crawled over them, looking for the faces I knew best, one thought and one only driving me on.

I found Niall where he had fallen from the wall, with a bill hook still in his hand and an arrow through his eye. I passed on. They must have withdrawn from one wall to the next as the attack pressed, for Padraig was not here.

I climbed the hill past the slaughtered cattle and sheep, some of them still twitching feebly, and passed through the second gate, or where the second gate had been. Jorem's troops must have used a ram to batter it down. The first body I saw was Conor's, though his head was half turned around from his body and smashed in; the second was Padraig. I dropped down beside him and set my hand to the spear shaft, as though I could possibly draw it out and bring him back. I wondered whether at the end he had regretted giving me his needle.

After a time, I made it to the third gate. The bodies were piled three deep here where the defense had been most desperate. I never found Timon, or perhaps I did not recognize him, but Prince Nestor was there, and Symon. No, they had not had time to use the Hag's Embrace, or had chosen not to do so. Both had been hideously butchered. I pulled Sy's good right hand back to him from the spot it had been thrown a few feet away and left them.

I looked for Gwynt, who had told me that he would be by Symon's side, but he was not anywhere in that mess that I could see. I squeezed through the wooden gate hanging off its hinges and propped open by bodies and headed for my grandfather's study.

A glossy trail of blood was on the stairs, but I could not tell if it had been made going up or coming down. I wound up the stone steps, closed my eyes briefly, and then stepped into his study.

His chair was overturned on the floor, the tapestry hanging from the wall in strips where they had shredded it with their daggers. The pipe's urn was dented in and the mouthpiece cut away. The dregs of a last half-drunk cup of tea were in his bowl, which had not been touched. Maybe they'd thought it was poison. A scroll had been burned where he had dropped it. Bruchan was not here.

I went back downstairs and picked my way through the jumbled mounds of simple furniture, tools, and stores that the Wolfhounds had disdained to take for booty and left strewn all over the courtyard. I went to the refectory, but he was not there. I went to the back stairway, the one coming up from the jetty, and there I found Ruan.

My painting master had given a good accounting of himself. Six of the enemy had fallen to his sword, but in the end sheer weight of greater numbers had been his undoing. He had fallen or been pushed from the high landing, and I could tell from the way he lay that I had no need to check whether he had used the drug. Even if he had, he was dead now. I touched my hand to my breast in farewell and continued my search.

When I came out of the kitchen, I found Dermot and near him the pan lid he may have tried to use as a shield. Further on, in the angle of the round tower and the wall, I found Gwynt and Alyce. Even in death they were holding hands, and there was a single wound in the throat of each, with the knife in his free hand. I did not blame them. I went around the tower and left them to their peace.

I knew now where the master was to be found. The ladder had been drawn up, but I took a table from the pile, drew it up to the tower, and propped a bench on top of it, and a crate on top of that until I could reach the door. But when I put my hand to the ring pull, it was still so hot that I snatched my hand away. Puzzled, I tried it again, this time bracing myself on the stone sill. The rock itself was warm to my touch. I looked up. I had thought the thick pall of smoke was merely hanging in the window openings up there, but now I saw that it was curling slowly from within them. My nerveless hand slipped from the stone, and I thrust myself backward, falling from my makeshift platform to thud to the courtyard paving. The breath was knocked from my lungs, but I needed no breath now, anyway. I

scurried around the tower until I found them:
on opposite sides, two of the heavy stones had
been shifted slightly, just the width of a hand.
On one of them the pitch still ran.

The Wolfhounds had emptied barrels of pitch
into those openings, dropped in lighted wicks,
and the flames had gone roaring up the round
tower like a chimney, incinerating the women
and children huddled inside, and my grandfather, who had dropped back at the last,
mortally wounded, to try to protect them.

I do not know how long I lay in the courtyard, dry-eyed and hollow, but finally I got up,
went down through the gates once more, and
struck off across the burren toward the Caldron. That was where the raven waited for me;
that was where I would willingly go to meet it.

I reached the edge of the cliff above the
whirlpool and stood looking down into it, remembering that day of sun and boys splashing
and the bird that had hurtled past my ear,
screaming for my blood. I took Padraig's needle from my cloak.

A stone rolled off to my right. I turned my
head to the sound and saw disinterestedly a
man with a sword in his hand and a troop at
his back throw up his hand and yell something.

I did not stay to listen. I jabbed the needle in
my hand and toppled over the edge.

It took me a long, long time to wake, for I
was dreaming of painting a teardrop. Even
when I had come to my senses, I wasn't posi-
tive I was alive. I could feel nothing, see nothing.
But after a time I could hear, a little.

Lapping, a slap of water against wood somewhere. A rustle of clothing nearby and the gurgle as liquid was poured. It sounded nice, and I listened to it, thinking of crystal tinkling in a dream I'd had. "He's awake," a voice said quietly above me.

No, I'm not, I wanted to reply.

"Are ye sure?" a second voice questioned in a thick accent I'd heard before.

"Oh, yes."

One of them shifted, his leather belt creaking. "Boy? What the hell's his name?" he asked himself, and then, "Aengus?"

"He hears you, but probably can't reply," the first voice, a healer, said. He got that right: I wouldn't talk to that old pirate if my life depended on it.

"Perhaps the crushing of his head against the rocks has left him witless," a third voice said. A young man, I'd judge, and not too many wits himself if he couldn't tell a comatose patient when he saw one.

"Perhaps, my lord Beod," the healer agreed in a murmur.

A rustle of linen, and a cool hand caressed my forehead, though I could only feel one side of it. A woman's voice, sweet and low. "Oh, I do hope not. Surely the Powers will not have it so."

I heard Swan's wings in her voice. It was like wrestling a t'ing, but I got one eye open. Green eyes, as green as the summer sea, peaches in her cheeks, hair black and shiny as a seal's. Surely Ritnym's daughter. Her lips parted a little at my look. "I'm Aengus," I mumbled through the bandages. "And I'm not dead."

Merriment lit in the depths of those green eyes. "How do you do?" she said softly. "I'm Rose. And I'm not, either."

About the Author

Sheila Gilluly was born in Rhode Island and attended high school and college in Arizona, graduating from the University of Arizona with a BA in English in 1973. Since then, she has earned an MA in Religious Studies from Maryknoll School of Theology, lived in Taiwan briefly, taught for a couple of years in Guam, and now teaches English and Creative Writing at a rural district high school in Maine. Ms. Gilluly is an avid gardener. Since midcoast Maine has only two seasons (winter and July Fourth), she has a lot of time left over from gardening to devote to her writing.